Laurell K. Hamilton is the bestselling author of the acclaimed Anita Blake: Vampire Hunter novels. She lives near St. Louis with her husband, her daughter, two pug and two part-pug dogs and an ever-fluctuating number of fish.

Find out more about Laurell K. Hamilton and other Orbit authors by registering for the free monthly newsletter at www.orbitbooks.co.uk

BLOODY BONES

AN ANITA BLAKE, VAMPIRE HUNTER NOVEL

LAURELL K. HAMILTON

www.orbitbooks.co.uk

ORBIT

First published in Great Britain by Orbit 2000
Reprinted 2002, 2003 (twice), 2005, 2006

A CIP catalogue record for this book
is available from the British Library.

ISBN-13: 978-1-84149-050-2
ISBN-10: 1-84149-050-4

Printed and bound in Great Britain by
Mackays of Chatham plc

Orbit
An imprint of
Time Warner Book Group UK
Brettenham House
Lancaster Place
London WC2E 7EN

ACKNOWLEDGMENTS

As always to my husband, Gary, more precious to me now than ever. To my editor, Ginjer Buchanan, whose input changed Serephina for the better. Paty Cockrum, who you can blame for the bathtub scene. Marella Sands, who was right about our reaction to Stirling. Mark Sumner for emergency reading, and questions. Who else can I call at midnight and know I won't wake them? Deborah Millitello as always for emergency phone calls and hand-holding. Rett MacPherson, who heard parts of this book over the phone. To Tom Drennan and N. L. Drew, new talent in the group. Alternate Historians forever. Jean-Claude, truce at last. Sergeant St. Clair, Public Information and Education Officer for the Missouri State Highway Patrol, who answered my last-minute questions. Brynda Mitchell, thanks for the penguin. Thanks to everyone who has written to us.

1

IT WAS ST. Patrick's Day, and the only green I was wearing was a button that read, "Pinch me and you're dead meat." I'd started work last night with a green blouse on, but I'd gotten blood all over it from a beheaded chicken. Larry Kirkland, zombie-raiser in training, had dropped the decapitated bird. It did the little headless chicken dance and sprayed both of us with blood. I finally caught the damn thing, but the blouse was ruined.

I had to run home and change. The only thing not ruined was the charcoal grey suit jacket that had been in the car. I put it back on over a black blouse, black skirt, dark hose, and black pumps. Bert, my boss, didn't like us wearing black to work, but if I had to be at the office at seven o'clock without any sleep at all, he would just have to live with it.

I huddled over my coffee mug, drinking it as black as I could swallow it. It wasn't helping much. I stared at a series of 8-by-10 glossy blowups spread across my desktop. The first picture was of a hill that had been scraped open, probably by a bulldozer. A skeletal hand reached out of the raw earth. The next photo showed that someone had tried to carefully scrape away the dirt, showing the splintered coffin and bones to one side of the coffin. A new body. The bulldozer had been brought in again. It had plowed up the red earth and found a boneyard. Bones studded the earth like scattered flowers.

One skull spread its unhinged jaws in a silent scream. A scraggle of pale hair still clung to the skull. The dark, stained cloth wrapped around the corpse was the remnants of a dress. I spotted at least three femurs next to the upper half of a skull. Unless the corpse had had three legs, we were looking at a real mess.

The pictures were well done in a gruesome sort of way. The color made it easier to differentiate the corpses, but the high gloss was a little much. It looked like morgue photos done by a fashion photographer. There was probably an art gallery in New York that would hang the damn things and serve cheese and wine while people walked around saying, "Powerful, don't you think? Very powerful."

They were powerful, and sad.

There was nothing but the photos. No explanation. Bert had said to come to his office after I'd looked at them. He'd explain everything. Yeah, I believed that. The Easter Bunny is a friend of mine, too.

I gathered the pictures up, slipped them into the envelope, picked my coffee mug up in the other hand, and went for the door.

There was no one at the desk. Craig had gone home. Mary, our daytime secretary, didn't get in until eight. There was a two-hour space of time when the office was un-manned. That Bert had called me into the office when we were the only ones there bothered me a lot. Why the se-crecy?

Bert's office door was open. He sat behind his desk, drinking coffee, shuffling some papers around. He glanced up, smiled, and motioned me closer. The smile bothered me. Bert was never pleasant unless he wanted something.

His thousand-dollar suit framed a white-on-white shirt and tie. His grey eyes sparkled with good cheer. His eyes are the color of dirty window glass, so sparkling is a real effort. His snow-blond hair had been freshly buzzed. The crewcut was so short I could see scalp.

"Have a seat, Anita."

I tossed the envelope on his desk and sat down. "What are you up to, Bert?"

His smile widened. He usually didn't waste the smile on anybody but clients. He certainly didn't waste it on me. "You looked at the pictures?"

"Yeah, what of it?"

"Could you raise them from the dead?"

I frowned at him and sipped my coffee. "How old are they?"

"You couldn't tell from the pictures?"

"In person I could tell you, but not just from pictures. Answer the question."

"Around two hundred years."

I just stared at him. "Most animators couldn't raise a zombie that old without a human sacrifice."

"But you can," he said.

"Yeah. I didn't see any headstones in the pictures. Do we have any names?"

"Why?"

I shook my head. He'd been the boss for five years, started the company when it was just him and Manny, and he didn't know shit about raising the dead. "How can you hang around a bunch of zombie-raisers for this many years and know so little about what we do?"

The smile slipped a little, the glow beginning to fade from his eyes. "Why do you need names?"

"You use names to call the zombie from the grave."

"Without a name you can't raise them?"

"Theoretically, no," I said.

"But you can do it," he said. I didn't like how sure he was.

"Yeah, I can do it. John can probably do it, too."

He shook his head. "They don't want John."

I finished the last of my coffee. "Who's they?"

"Beadle, Beadle, Stirling, and Lowenstein."

"A law firm," I said.

He nodded.

"No more games, Bert. Just tell me what the hell's going on."

"Beadle, Beadle, Stirling, and Lowenstein have some clients building a very plush resort in the mountains near Branson. A very exclusive resort. A place where the wealthy country stars that don't own a house in the area can go to get away from the crowds. Millions of dollars are at stake."

"What's the old cemetery have to do with it?"

"The land they're building on was in dispute between two

families. The courts decided the Kellys owned the land, and they were paid a great deal of money. The Bouvier family claimed it was their land and there was a family plot on it to prove it. No one could find the cemetery."

Ah. "They found it," I said.

"They found an old cemetery, but not necessarily the Bouvier family plot."

"So they want to raise the dead and ask who they are?"

"Exactly."

I shrugged. "I can raise a couple of the corpses in the coffins. Ask who they are. What happens if their last name is Bouvier?"

"They have to buy the land a second time. They think some of the corpses are Bouviers. That's why they want all the bodies raised."

I raised my eyebrows. "You're joking."

He shook his head, looking pleased. "Can you do it?"

"I don't know. Give me the pictures again." I set my coffee mug on his desk and took the pictures back. "Bert, they've screwed this six ways to Sunday. It's a mass grave, thanks to the bulldozers. The bones are all mixed together. I've only read about one case of anyone raising a zombie from a mass grave. But they were calling a specific person. They had a name." I shook my head. "Without a name it may not be possible."

"Would you be willing to try?"

I spread the pictures over the desk, staring at them. The top half of a skull had turned upside down like a bowl. Two finger bones attached by something dry and desiccated that must once had been human tissue lay next to it. Bones, bones everywhere but not a name to speak.

Could I do it? I honestly didn't know. Did I want to try? Yeah. I did.

"I'd be willing to try."

"Wonderful."

"Raising them a few every night is going to take weeks, even if I can do it. With John's help it would be quicker."

"It will cost them millions to delay that long," Bert said.

"There's no other way to do it."

"You raised the Davidsons' entire family plot, including Great-Grandpa. You weren't even supposed to raise him. You can raise more than one at a time."

I shook my head. "That was an accident. I was showing off. They wanted to raise three family members. I thought I could save them money by doing it in one shot."

"You raised ten family members, Anita. They only asked for three."

"So?"

"So can you raise the entire cemetery in one night?"

"You're crazy," I said.

"Can you do it?"

I opened my mouth to say no, and closed it. I had raised an entire cemetery once. Not all of them had been two centuries old, but some of them had been older, nearly three hundred. And I raised them all. Of course, I had two human sacrifices to ride for power. It was a long story how I ended up with two people dying inside a circle of power. Self-defense, but the magic didn't care. Death is death.

Could I do it? "I really don't know, Bert."

"That's not a no," he said. He had an eager, anticipatory look on his face.

"They must have offered you a bundle of money," I said.

He smiled. "We're bidding on the project."

"We're what?"

"They sent this package to us, the Resurrection Company in California and the Essential Spark in New Orleans."

"They prefer Élan Vital to the English translation," I said. Frankly, it sounded more like a beauty salon than an animating firm, but nobody had asked me. "So what? The lowest bid gets it?"

"That was their plan," Bert said.

He looked entirely too satisfied with himself. "What?" I asked.

"Let me play it back to you," he said. "There are what, three animators in the entire country that could raise a zombie that old without a human sacrifice? You and John are two of them. I'm including Phillipa Freestone of Resurrection in this."

"Probably," I said.

He nodded. "Okay. Could Phillipa raise without a name?"

"I don't have any way of knowing that. John could. Maybe she could."

"Could either she or John raise from the mass bones, not the ones in the coffin?"

That stopped me. "I don't know."

"Would either of them stand a chance of raising the entire graveyard?" He was staring at me very steadily.

"You're enjoying this too much," I said.

"Just answer the question, Anita."

"I know John couldn't do it. I don't think Phillipa is as good as John, so no, they couldn't do it."

"I'm going to up the bid," Bert said.

I laughed. "Up the bid?"

"Nobody else can do it. Nobody but you. They tried treating this like any other construction problem. But there aren't going to be any other bids, now are there?"

"Probably not," I said.

"Then I'm going to take them to the cleaners," he said with a smile.

I shook my head. "You greedy son of a bitch."

"You get a share of the fee, you know."

"I know." We looked at each other. "What if I try and can't raise them all in one night?"

"You'll still be able to raise them all eventually, won't you?"

"Probably." I stood, picking up my coffee mug. "But I wouldn't spend the check until after I've done it. I'm going to go get some sleep."

"They want the bid this morning. If they accept our terms, they'll fly you up in a private helicopter."

"Helicopter—you know I hate to fly."

"For this much money you'll fly."

"Great."

"Be ready to go at a moment's notice."

"Don't push it, Bert." I hesitated at the door. "Let me take Larry with me."

"Why? If John can't do it, then Larry certainly can't."

I shrugged. "Maybe not, but there are ways to combine power during a raising. If I can't do it alone, maybe I can get a boost from our trainee."

He looked thoughtful. "Why not take John? Combined, you could do it."

"Only if he'd give his power willingly to me. You think he'd do that?"

Bert shook his head.

"You going to tell him that the client didn't want him? That you offered him to the client and they asked for me by name?"

"No," Bert said.

"That's why you're doing it like this; no witnesses."

"Time is of the essence, Anita."

"Sure, Bert, but you didn't want to face Mr. John Burke with yet another client that wants me over him."

Bert looked down at his blunt-fingered hands clasped on the desktop. He looked up, grey eyes serious. "John is almost as good as you are, Anita. I don't want to lose him."

"You think he'll walk if one more client asks for me?"

"His pride's hurt," Bert said.

"And there's so much of it to hurt," I said.

Bert smiled. "You needling him doesn't help."

I shrugged. It sounded petty to say he'd started it, but he had. We'd tried dating, and John couldn't handle me being a female version of him. No; he couldn't handle me being a better version of him.

"Try to behave yourself, Anita. Larry's not up to speed yet; we need John."

"I always behave myself, Bert."

He sighed. "If you didn't make me so much money, I wouldn't put up with your shit."

"Ditto," I said.

That about summed up our relationship. Commerce at its best. We didn't like each other, but we could do business together. Free enterprise at work.

2

AT NOON BERT called and said we had it. "Be at the office packed and ready to go at two o'clock. Mr. Lionel Bayard will fly up with you and Larry."

"Who's Lionel Bayard?"

"A junior partner in the firm of Beadle, Beadle, Stirling, and Lowenstein. He likes the sound of his own voice. Don't give him a rough time about it."

"Who, me?"

"Anita, don't tease the help. He may be wearing a three-thousand-dollar suit, but he's still the help."

"I'll save it up for one of the partners. Surely Beadle, Beadle, Stirling, or Lowenstein will appear in person sometime this weekend."

"Don't tease the bosses either," he said.

"Anything you say." My voice was utterly mild.

"You'll do whatever you want no matter what I say, won't you?"

"Gee, Bert, who says you can't teach an old dog new tricks?"

"Just be here at two o'clock. I called Larry. He'll be here."

"I'll be there, Bert. I've got one stop to make, so if I'm a few minutes late, don't worry."

"Don't be late."

"Be there as soon as I can." I hung up before he could argue with me.

I had to shower, change, and go to Seckman Junior High School. Richard Zeeman taught science there. We had a date set up for tomorrow. At one point Richard had asked me to marry him. That was sort of on hold, but I did owe him more than a message on his answering machine, saying sorry, honey, can't make the date. I'm going to be out of town. A message would have been easier for me, but cowardly.

I packed one suitcase. It was enough for four days and

then some. If you pack extra underwear and clothes that mix and match, you can live for a week out of a small suitcase.

I did add a few extras. The Firestar 9mm and its inner pants holster. Enough extra ammo to sink a battleship and two knives plus wrist sheaths. I'd had four knives. All hand-crafted for little ol' *moi*. Two of them had been lost beyond recovery. I was having them replaced, but hand forging takes time, especially when you insist on the highest silver content possible in the steel. Two knives, two guns should be enough for one weekend business trip. I'd wear the Browning Hi-Power.

Packing wasn't a problem. What to wear today was the problem. They'd want me to raise them tonight if I could. Hell, the helicopter might fly directly to the construction site. Which meant I'd be walking over raw dirt, bones, shattered coffins. It didn't sound like high-heel territory. Yet, if a junior partner was wearing a three-thousand-dollar suit, the people who'd just hired me would expect me to look the part. I could either dress professionally or in feathers and blood. I'd actually had one client who was disappointed that I didn't show up nude smeared with blood. There could have been more than one reason for his disappointment. I don't think I've ever had a client that would have objected to some kind of ceremonial getup, but jeans and jogging shoes didn't seem to inspire confidence. Don't ask me why.

I could pack my coverall and put it over whatever I wore. Yeah, I liked that. Veronica Sims—Ronnie, my very best friend—had talked me into buying a fashionably short navy skirt. It was short enough that I was a little embarrassed, but the skirt fit inside the coverall. The skirt didn't wrinkle or bunch up after I'd worn the outfit to vampire stakings or murder scenes. Take the coverall off, and I was set to go to the office or out for the evening. I was so pleased, I went out and bought two more in different colors.

One was crimson, the other purple. I hadn't been able to find one in black yet. At least not one that wasn't so short that I refused to wear it. Admittedly, the short skirts made me look taller. They even made me look leggy. When you're five-foot-three, that's saying something. But the purple didn't match much that I owned, so crimson it was.

I'd found a short-sleeved blouse that was the exact same shade of red. Red with violet undertones, a cold, hard color that looked great with my pale skin, black hair, and dark brown eyes. The shoulder holster and 9mm Browning Hi-Power looked very dramatic against it. A black belt cinched tight at the waist held down the loops on the holster. A black jacket with rolled-back sleeves went over everything to hide the gun. I twirled in front of the mirror in my bedroom. The skirt wasn't much longer than the jacket, but you couldn't see the gun. At least not easily. Unless you're willing to have things tailor-made, it's hard to hide a gun, especially in woman's dress-up clothes.

I put on just enough makeup so the red didn't overwhelm me. I was also going to be saying good-bye to Richard for several days. A little makeup couldn't hurt. When I say makeup, I mean eye shadow, blush, lipstick, and that's it. Outside of a television interview that Bert talked me into, I don't wear base.

Except for the hose and black high heels, which I would've had to wear no matter what skirt I wore, the outfit was comfortable. As long as I remembered not to bend directly at the waist, I was safe.

The only jewelry I wore was the silver cross tucked into the blouse, and the watch on my wrist. My dress watch had broken and I just had never gotten around to getting it fixed. The present watch was a man's black diving watch that looked out of place on my small wrist. But hey, it glowed in the dark if you pressed a button. It showed me the date, what day it was, and could time a run. I hadn't found a woman's watch that could do all that.

I didn't have to cancel running with Ronnie tomorrow morning. She was out of town on a case. A private detective's work is never done.

I loaded the suitcase into my Jeep and was on the way to Richard's school by one o'clock. I was going to be late to the office. Oh, well. They'd wait for me or they wouldn't. It wouldn't break my heart to miss the helicopter ride. I hated planes, but a helicopter . . . scared the shit out of me.

I hadn't been afraid of flying until I was on a plane that plunged several thousand feet in seconds. The stewardess ended up plastered against the ceiling, covered in coffee. People screamed and prayed. The elderly woman beside me recited the Lord's Prayer in German. She'd been so scared, tears had come down her face. I offered her my hand, and she gripped it. I knew I was going to die and there was nothing I could do to prevent it. But we would die holding on to human hands. Die covered in human tears, and human prayers. Then the plane straightened out and suddenly we were safe. I haven't trusted air transportation since.

Normally in St. Louis there is no real spring. There's winter, two days of mild weather, and summer heat. This year spring had come early and stayed. The air was soft against your skin. The wind smelled of green growing things, and winter seemed to have been a bad dream. Redbuds bent from the trees on either side of the road. Tiny purple blossoms like a delicate lavender mist here and there through the naked trees. There were no leaves yet, but there was a hint of green. Like someone had taken a giant paintbrush and tinted everything. Look directly at them and the trees were bare and black, but look sideways, not at a particular tree but at all the trees, and there was a touch of green.

270 South is about as pleasant as a highway can be; it gets you where you're going fairly fast, and it's over quickly. I exited at Tesson Ferry Road. The road is thick with strip malls, a hospital, and fast-food restaurants, and when you leave the commerce behind you hit new housing developments so thick they nearly touch. There are still stands of woods and open spaces, but they won't last.

The turn to Old 21 is at the crest of a hill just past the Meramec River. It is mostly houses with a few gas stations, the area water district office, and a large gas field to the right. Where the hills march out and out.

At the first stoplight I turned left past a little shopping area. The road is a curving narrow thing that snakes between houses and woods. There were glimpses of daffodils in the yards. The road dips down into a valley, and at the bottom of a steep hill is a stop sign. The road climbs quickly to the crest of a hill, to a T, turn left and you're almost there.

The one-story school sits on the floor of a wide, flat valley surrounded by hills. Having been raised in Indiana farm country, I'd have called them mountains once. The elementary school sits separate, but close enough to share a playground. If you got recess in junior high. When I was too little to go to junior high, it seemed you did get recess. By the time I got there, you didn't. The way of the world.

I parked as close to the building as I could. This was my second visit to Richard's school, and my first during the actual school day. We'd come once to get some papers he'd forgotten. No students then. I entered the main entrance and ran into a crowd. It must have been between classes when they moved the warm bodies from one room to another.

I was instantly aware that I was about the same height as or shorter than everyone I saw. There was something claustrophobic about being jostled by the book-carrying, backpack-wearing crowd. There had to be a circle of Hell where you were eternally fourteen, eternally in junior high. One of the lower circles.

I flowed with the crowd towards Richard's room. I admit I took comfort in the fact that I was better dressed than most of the girls. Petty as hell, but I had been chunky in junior high. There isn't a lot of difference between chunky and fat when it comes to teasing. I'd had my growth spurt and never been fat again. That's right; I'd been even tinier once. Shortest kid in school for years and years.

I stood to one side of the doorway, letting the students come and go. Richard was showing something in a textbook to a young girl. She was blonde, wearing a flannel shirt over a black dress that was three sizes too big for her. She was wearing what looked like black combat boots with heavy white socks rolled over the tops of them. The outfit was very now. The look of adoration on her face was not. She was shiny and eager just because Mr. Zeeman was giving her some one-on-one help.

I had to admit that Richard was worth a crush or two. His

thick brown hair was tied back in a ponytail that gave the illusion that his hair was very short and close to his head. He has high, full cheekbones and a strong jaw, with a dimple that softens his face and makes him look almost too perfect. His eyes are a solid chocolate brown with those thick lashes that so many men have and women want. The bright yellow shirt made his permanently tanned skin seem even darker. His tie was a dark, rich green that matched the dress slacks he wore. His jacket was draped across the back of his desk chair. The muscles in his upper arms worked against the cloth of his shirt as he held the book.

The class was mostly seated, the hallway nearly silent. He closed the book and handed it to the girl. She smiled and scrambled for the door, late to her next class. Her eyes flicked over me as she passed, wondering what I was doing there.

She wasn't the only one. Several of the seated students were glancing my way. I stepped into the room.

Richard smiled. It warmed me down to my toes. The smile saved him from being too handsome. It wasn't that it wasn't a great smile. He could have done toothpaste commercials. But the smile was a little boy's smile, open and welcoming. There was no guile to Richard, no deep, dark plan. He was the world's biggest Boy Scout. The smile showed that.

I wanted to go to him, have him wrap his arms around me. I had a horrible urge to grab his tie and lead him out of the room. I wanted to touch his chest underneath the yellow shirt. The urge was so strong, I put my hands in the pockets of my jacket. Mustn't shock the students. Richard affects me like that sometimes. Okay, most of the time when he's not furry, or licking blood off his fingers. He's a werewolf. Did I mention that? No one at the school knows. If they did, he'd be out of a job. People don't like lycanthropes teaching their precious kiddies. It's illegal to discriminate against someone for a disease, but everyone does it. Why should the educational system be different?

He touched my cheek, just his fingertips. I turned my face into his hand, brushing lips against his fingers. So much for being cool in front of the kiddies. There were a few oohs and nervous laughs.

"I'll be right back, guys." More oohs, louder laughter, one "Way to go, Mr. Zeeman." Richard motioned me out the door and I went, hands still in my pockets. Normally, I'd have said I wasn't going to embarrass myself in front of a bunch of eighth-graders, but lately I wasn't entirely trustworthy.

Richard led me a little ways from his classroom into the deserted hallway. He leaned up against the wall of lockers and looked down at me. The little-boy smile was gone. The look in his dark eyes made me shiver. I ran my hand down his tie, smoothing it against his chest.

"Am I allowed to kiss you, or would that scandalize the kiddies?" I didn't look up at him as I asked. I didn't want him to see the raw need in my eyes. It was embarrassing enough that I knew he sensed it. You can't hide lust from a werewolf. They can smell it.

"I'll risk it." His voice was soft, low, with a warm edge that made my stomach clench.

I felt him bend over me. I raised my face to his. His lips were so soft. I leaned against his body, palms flat against his chest. I could feel his nipples harden under my skin. My hands slid to his waist, smoothing along the cloth of his shirt. I wanted to pull his shirt out of his pants and run my hands over bare skin. I stepped back from him feeling just a little breathless.

It was my idea that we wouldn't have sex before marriage. My idea. But damn, it was hard. The more we dated, the harder it got.

"Jesus, Richard." I shook my head. "It gets harder, doesn't it?"

Richard's smile didn't look innocent or Boy Scoutish in the least. "Yes, it does."

Heat rushed up my face. "I didn't mean that."

"I know what you meant." His voice was gentle, taking the sting out of the teasing.

My face was still hot with embarrassment, but my voice

was steady. Point for me. "I've got to go out of town on business."

"Zombie, vampire, or police?"

"Zombie."

"Good."

I looked up at him. "Why good?"

"I worry more when you go away on police business, or vampire stakings. You know that."

I nodded. "Yeah, I know that." We stood there in the hallway, staring at each other. If things had been different, we'd be engaged, maybe planning a wedding. All this sexual tension would have been coming to some kind of conclusion. As it was . . .

"I'm going to be late as it is. I've got to go."

"Are you going to tell Jean-Claude bye in person?" His face was neutral when he asked, but his eyes weren't.

"It's daylight. He's in his coffin."

"Ah," Richard said.

"I didn't have a date planned with him this weekend, so I don't owe him an explanation. Is that what you wanted to hear?"

"Close enough," he said. He took a step away from the lockers, bringing our bodies very close together. He bent to kiss me good-bye. Giggles erupted down the hall.

We turned to see most of his class huddled in the doorway gazing at us. Great.

Richard smiled. He raised his voice enough so they'd hear him. "Back inside, you monsters."

There were catcalls, and one small brunette girl gave me a very dirty look. I think there must have been a lot of girls that had a crush on Mr. Zeeman.

"The natives are restless. I've got to get back."

I nodded. "I'm hoping to be back by Monday."

"We'll go hiking next weekend, then."

"I put Jean-Claude off this weekend. I can't not see him two weeks in a row."

Richard's face clouded up with the beginnings of anger. "Hike during the day, see the vampire at night. Only fair."

"I don't like this any better than you do," I said.

"I wish I believed that."

"Richard."

He gave a long sigh. The anger sort of leaked out of him. I never understood how he did that. He could be furious one minute and calm the next. Both emotions seemed genuine. Once I was angry, I was angry. Maybe it's a character flaw?

"I'm sorry, Anita. It's not like you're dating him behind my back."

"I would never do anything behind your back; you know that."

He nodded. "I know that." He glanced back at his classroom. "I've got to go before they set the room on fire." He walked down the hallway without looking back.

I almost called after him, but I let him go. The mood was sort of spoiled. Nothing like knowing your girlfriend is dating someone else to take the wind out of your sails. I wouldn't have put up with it if it was the other way around. A double standard that, but one we could all three live with. If living was the term for Jean-Claude.

Oh, hell, my personal life was too confusing for words. I walked off down the hall, having to pass by his open classroom door. My high heels made loud, rackety echoes. I didn't try to catch a last glimpse of him. It would make me feel worse about leaving.

It hadn't been my idea to date the Master of the City. Jean-Claude had given me two choices; either he could kill Richard, or I could date both of them. It had seemed a good idea at the time. Five weeks later I wasn't so sure.

It had been my morals that had kept Richard and me from consummating our relationship. Consummating, nice euphemism. But Jean-Claude had made it clear that if I did something with Richard, I had to do it with him too. Jean-Claude was trying to woo me. If Richard could touch me but he couldn't, it wasn't fair. He had a point, I guess. But the thought of having to have sex with the vampire was more likely to keep me chaste than any high ideals.

I couldn't date both of them indefinitely. The sexual tension alone was killing me. I could move. Richard might even let me do that. He wouldn't like it, but if I wanted free of him, he'd let me go. Jean-Claude, on the other hand . . . He'd never let me go. The question was, did I want him to let me go? Answer: hell, yes. The real trick was how to break free without anybody dying.

Yeah, that was the $64,000 question. Trouble was, I didn't have an answer. We were going to need one sooner or later. And later was getting closer all the time.

3

I HUDDLED AGAINST the side of the helicopter, one hand in a death grip on the strap that was bolted to the wall. I wanted to use both hands to hold on, as if by holding very tightly to the stupid strap it would save me when the helicopter plummeted to earth. I used one hand because two hands looked cowardly. I was wearing a headset, sort of like ear protection for the shooting range, but with a microphone so you could talk above the teeth-rattling noise. I hadn't realized that most of a helicopter was clear, like being suspended in a great buzzing, vibrating bubble. I kept my eyes closed as much as possible.

"Are you all right, Ms. Blake?" Lionel Bayard asked.

The voice startled me. "Yeah, I'm fine."

"You don't look well."

"I don't like to fly," I said.

He gave a weak smile. I don't think I was inspiring confidence in Lionel Bayard, lawyer and flunkie of Beadle, Beadle, Stirling, and Lowenstein. Lionel Bayard was a small, neat man with a tiny blond mustache that looked like it was as much facial hair as he would ever get. His triangular jaw was as smooth as my own. Maybe the mustache was glued on. His brown suit with a thin yellow tweed fit his body like a well-tailored glove. His thin tie was brown-and-yellow striped with a gold tie tack. The tie tack was monogrammed. His slender leather briefcase was monogrammed as well. Everything matched, down to his gold-tasseled loafers.

Larry twisted in his seat. He was sitting beside the pilot. "You're really afraid of flying?" I could see his lips move, but all the sound came out of my headset; without them we'd never have been able to talk over the noise. He sounded amused.

"Yes, Larry, I'm really afraid of flying." I hoped sarcasm traveled the headsets as clearly as amusement did.

Larry laughed. Evidently, sarcasm traveled. Larry looked freshly scrubbed. He was dressed in his other blue suit, his white shirt—which was one of three he owned—and his second-best tie. His best tie had blood all over it. He was still in college, working weekends for us until he graduated. His short hair was the color of a surprised carrot. He was freckled and about my height, short, with pale blue eyes. He looked like a grown-up Opie.

Bayard was working hard at not frowning at me. The effort showed enough that he shouldn't have bothered. "Are you sure you're up to this assignment?"

I met his brown eyes. "You better hope I am, Mr. Bayard, because I'm all you got."

"I am aware of your specialized skills, Ms. Blake. I spent the last twelve hours contacting every animating firm in the United States. Phillipa Freestone of the Resurrection Company told me she couldn't do what we wanted, that the only person in the country who might be able to do it was Anita Blake. Élan Vital in New Orleans told us the same thing. They mentioned John Burke but weren't confident that he could do all we wanted. We must have all the dead raised or it's useless to us."

"Did my boss explain to you that I am not a hundred percent sure that I can do it?"

Bayard blinked at me. "Mr. Vaughn seemed very confident that you could do what we asked."

"Bert can be as confident as he wants. He doesn't have to raise this mess."

"I realize the earthmoving equipment has complicated your task, Ms. Blake, but we did not do it deliberately."

I let that go. I'd seen the pictures. They'd tried to cover it up. If the construction crew hadn't been local with some Bouvier sympathizers, they'd have plowed up the boneyard, poured some concrete, and voilà, no evidence.

"Whatever. I'll do what I can with what you've left me."

"Would it have been that much easier if you had been brought in before the graves were disturbed?"

"Yeah."

He sighed. It vibrated through the headphones. "Then my apologies."

I shrugged. "Unless you did it personally, you're not the one who owes me an apology."

He shifted a little in his seat. "I did not order the digging. Mr. Stirling is on site."

"*The* Mr. Stirling?" I asked.

Bayard didn't seem to get the humor. "Yes, that Mr. Stirling." Or maybe he really expected me to know the name.

"You always have a senior partner looking over your shoulder?"

He used one finger to adjust his gold-framed glasses. It looked like an old gesture from a time before new glasses and designer suits. "With this much money at stake, Mr. Stirling thought he should be in the area in case there were more problems."

"More problems?" I asked.

He blinked at me rapidly, like a well groomed rabbit. "The Bouvier matter."

He was lying. "What else is going wrong with your little project?"

"Whatever do you mean, Ms. Blake?" His manicured fingers smoothed down his tie.

"You've had more problems than just the Bouviers." I made it a statement.

"Any problems we may or may not be having, Ms. Blake, are not your concern. We hired you to raise the dead and establish the identity of said deceased persons. Beyond that, you have no duties here."

"Have you ever raised a zombie, Mr. Bayard?"

He blinked again. "Of course not." He sounded offended.

"Then how do you know the other problems won't affect my job?"

Small frown lines formed between his eyebrows. He was a lawyer and was earning a good living, but thinking seemed to be hard for him. Made you wonder where he'd graduated from.

"I don't see how our little difficulties could affect your job."

"You've just admitted you don't know anything about my job," I said. "How do you know what will affect it and what won't?" Alright, I was fishing. Bayard was probably right. The other problems probably wouldn't affect me, but you never know. I don't like being kept in the dark. And I don't like being lied to, not even by omission.

"I think Mr. Stirling would have to make the call about whether you are enlightened or not."

"Not senior enough to make the decision," I said.

"No," Bayard said, "I am not."

Geez, some people you can't even needle. I glanced at Larry. He shrugged. "Looks like we're going to land."

I glanced out at the rapidly growing land. We were in the middle of the Ozark Mountains, hovering over a blasted scar of reddish naked earth. The construction site, I presume.

The ground swelled up to meet us. I closed my eyes and swallowed hard. The ride was almost over. I would not throw up this close to the ground. The ride was almost over. Almost over. Almost over. There was a bump that made me gasp.

"We've landed," Larry said. "You can open your eyes now."

I did. "You are enjoying the hell out of this, aren't you?"

He grinned. "I don't get to see you out of your element often."

The helicopter was surrounded by a fog of reddish dirt. The blades began to slow with a thick *whump, whump* sound. As the blades stopped, the dirt settled down and we could see where we were.

We were in a small, flat area between a cluster of mountains. It looked like it had once been a narrow valley, but bulldozers had widened it, flattened it, made it a landing pad. The earth was so red it looked like a river of rust. The mountain in front of the helicopter was one red mound. Heavy equipment and cars were clustered to the far side of the valley. Men were clustered around the equipment, shielding their eyes from the dust.

When the blades came to a sliding stop, Bayard unbuckled his seat belt. I did, too. We lifted off the headsets and Bayard opened his door. I opened mine and found that the ground was farther away than you'd think. I had to expose a long line of thigh to touch the ground.

The construction workers were appreciative. Whistles, catcalls, and one offer to check under my skirt. No, those weren't the exact words used.

A tall man in a white hard hat strode towards us. He was wearing a pair of tan coveralls, but his dirt-covered shoes were Gucci and his tan was health-club perfect. A man and a woman followed at his back.

The man looked like the real foreman. He was dressed in jeans and a work shirt with the sleeves rolled over muscular forearms. Not from racquetball or a little tennis, but from plain hard work.

The woman wore the traditional skirt suit complete with little blousy tie at her throat. The suit was expensive, but was an unfortunate shade of puce that did nothing for the woman's auburn hair but did match the blush that she'd smeared on her cheeks. I checked her neckline, and yes, she did have a pale line just above her collar where the base had not been blended in. She looked like she'd been made up at clown school.

She didn't look that young. You'd think someone somewhere would have clued her into how bad she looked. Of course, I wasn't going to tell her either. Who was I to criticize?

Stirling had the palest grey eyes I'd ever seen. The irises were only a few shades darker than the whites of his eyes. He stood there with his entourage behind him. He looked me up and down. He didn't seem to like what he saw. His strange eyes flicked to Larry in his cheap, wrinkled suit. Mr. Stirling frowned.

Bayard came around, smoothing his jacket into place. "Mr. Stirling, this is Anita Blake. Ms. Blake, this is Raymond Stirling."

He just stood there, looking at me like he was disappointed. The woman had a clipboard notebook, pen poised. Had to be his secretary. She looked worried, as if it was very important that Mr. Raymond Stirling like us.

I was beginning not to care if he liked us or not. What I wanted to say was, "You got a problem?" What I said was, "Is there a problem, Mr. Stirling?" Bert would have been pleased.

"You're not what I expected, Ms. Blake."

"How so?"

"Pretty, for one thing." It wasn't a compliment.

"And?"

He motioned at my outfit. "You're not dressed appropriately for the job."

"Your secretary's wearing heels."

"Ms. Harrison's attire is not your concern."

"And my attire is none of yours."

"Fair enough, but you're going to have a hell of time getting up that mountain in those shoes."

"I've got a coverall and Nikes in my suitcase."

"I don't think I like your attitude, Ms. Blake."

"I know I don't like yours," I said.

The foreman behind him was having trouble not smiling. His eyes were getting shiny with the effort. Ms. Harrison looked a little scared. Bayard had moved to one side, closer to Stirling. Making clear whose side he was on. Coward.

Larry moved closer to me.

"Do you want this job, Ms. Blake?"

"Not enough to take grief about it, no."

Ms. Harrison looked like she'd swallowed a bug. A big, nasty, squirming bug. I think I'd missed my cue to fall down and worship at her boss's feet.

The foreman coughed behind his hand. Stirling glanced at

him, then back to me. "Are you always this arrogant?" he asked.

I sighed "I prefer the word 'confident' to 'arrogant,' but I'll tell you what. I'll tone it down if you will."

"I am so sorry, Mr. Stirling," Bayard said. "I apologize. I had no idea . . ."

"Shut up, Lionel," Stirling said.

Lionel shut up.

Stirling was looking at me with his strange pale eyes. He nodded. "Agreed, Ms. Blake." He smiled. "I'll tone it down."

"Great," I said.

"All right, Ms. Blake, let's go up to the top and see if you're really as good as you think you are."

"I can look at the graveyard, but until full dark I can't do anything else."

He frowned and glanced at Bayard. "Lionel." That one word had a lot of heat in it. Anger looking for a target. He'd stop picking on me, but Lionel was fair game.

"I did fax you a memo, sir, as soon as I realized that Ms. Blake would be unable to help us until after dark."

Good man. When in doubt, cover your ass with paper.

Stirling glared at him. Bayard looked apologetic but he stood his ground, safe behind his memo.

"I called Beau and had him bring everybody down here on the understanding we could get some work done today." His gaze was very steady on Bayard. Lionel wilted just a little; evidently one memo was not protection enough.

"Mr. Stirling, even if I can raise the graveyard in one night, and that's a big if, what if the dead are all Bouviers? What if it is their family plot? My understanding is that construction will stop until you rebuy the land."

"They don't want to sell," Beau said.

Stirling glared at him. The foreman just smiled softly.

"Are you saying that the entire project is off if this is the Bouvier family plot?" I asked Bayard. "Why, Lionel, you didn't tell me that."

"There was no need for you to know," Bayard said.

"Why wouldn't they want to sell the land for a million dollars?" Larry asked. It was a good question.

Stirling looked at him like he'd just appeared out of thin air. Evidently, the flunkies weren't supposed to talk. "Magnus and Dorcas Bouvier have only a restaurant, called Bloody Bones. It is nothing. I have no idea why they wouldn't want to be millionaires."

"Bloody Bones? What kind of name is that for a restaurant?" Larry asked.

I shrugged. "It doesn't exactly say bon appetit." I looked at Stirling. He looked angry but that was all. I would have bet a million dollars that he knew exactly why the Bouviers didn't want to sell. But it didn't show on his face. His cards were close to his chest and unreadable.

I turned to Bayard. There was an unhealthy flush to his cheeks, and he avoided my gaze. I'd play poker with Bayard any day. But not in front of his boss.

"Fine. I'll change into something more bulky and we'll go take a look." The pilot handed out my suitcase. The coverall and shoes were on top.

Larry came up to me. "Gee, I wished I'd thought of the coverall. This suit's not going to survive the trip."

I pulled out two pairs of coveralls. "Be prepared," I said. He grinned. "Thanks."

I shrugged. "One good thing about being nearly the same size." I slipped off the black jacket, which left the gun in plain sight.

"Ms. Blake," Stirling said. "Why are you armed?"

I sighed. I was tired of Raymond. I hadn't even gone up the hill and I didn't want to go. The last thing I wanted to do was stand here and debate whether I needed a gun. The red blouse was short-sleeved. Visual aids are always better than lectures.

I walked over to him with my arms bent outward, exposing the inside of both forearms. There's a rather neat knife scar on my right arm, nothing too dramatic. My left arm is a mess. It had only been a little over a month since a shapeshifting leopard had opened my arm. A nice doctor had stitched it back together, but there is only so much you can do with claw marks. The cross-shaped burn scar that some inventive vampire servants had put on me was now a little crooked because of the claws. The mound of scar tissue at the bend of my arm where a vampire had bitten through the flesh and gnawed the bone dribbled white scars like water.

"Jesus," Beau said.

Stirling looked a touch pale but he held up well, like he'd seen worse. Bayard looked green. Ms. Harrison paled so that the makeup floated on her suddenly pale skin like impressionist water lilies.

"I don't go anywhere unarmed, Mr. Stirling. Live with it, because I have to."

He nodded, eyes very serious. "Fine, Ms. Blake. Is your assistant armed as well?"

"No," I said.

He nodded again. "Fine. Change, and when you're ready we'll go up."

Larry was zipping up his coverall when I walked back. "I could have been armed, you know," he said.

"You brought your gun?" I asked.

He nodded.

"Unloaded in your suitcase?"

"Just like you told me."

"Good." I let it go. Larry wanted to be a vampire executioner as well as an animator, which meant he needed to know how to use a gun. A gun with silver-plated bullets that could slow a vampire down. We'd work up to shotguns, which could take out a head and heart from a relatively safe distance. Beat the hell out of staking.

I'd gotten him a carry permit on the condition he didn't carry it concealed until I thought he was a good enough shot not to blow a hole in himself or me. I'd gotten him the permit mainly so we could carry it around in the car and go to the range in any spare moments.

The coverall went over the skirt like magic. I took off the heels and put the Nikes on. I left the coverall unzipped enough that I could go for the gun if needed, and I was set to go.

"Are you going up with us, Mr. Stirling?"

"Yes," he said.

"Then lead the way," I said.

He walked past me, glancing at the coveralls. Or maybe visualizing the gun under it. Beau started to follow but Stirling said, "No, I'll take her up alone."

Silence among the three flunkies. I'd expected Ms. Harrison to stay behind in her high-heeled pumps, but I'd been sure the two men would come along. So, from the looks on their faces, had they.

"Wait a minute. You said 'her.' You want Larry to wait down here, too?"

"Yes."

I shook my head. "He's in training. You can't learn if you don't see it done."

"Will you be doing anything that he needs to see today?"

I thought about that for a minute. "I guess not."

"I do get to come up after dark?" Larry asked.

"You'll get to see the down and dirty, Larry. Don't worry."

"Of course," Stirling said. "I have no problem with your associate doing his job."

"Why can't he come along now?" I asked.

"At the price we're paying, humor me, Ms. Blake."

He was being strangely polite, so I nodded. "Okay."

"Mr. Stirling," Bayard said, "are you sure you should go up alone?"

"Why ever not, Lionel?"

Bayard opened his mouth, closed it, then said, "No reason, Mr. Stirling."

Beau shrugged. "I'll tell the men to go home for the day." He started to turn away, then stopped. "Do you want the crew back tomorrow?"

Stirling looked at me. "Ms. Blake?"

I shook my head. "I don't know yet."

"What's your best guess?" he asked.

I looked over at the waiting men. "Do they get paid whether they show up or not?"

"Only if they show up," Stirling said.

"Then no work tomorrow. I can't guarantee they'll have anything to do."

Stirling nodded. "You heard her, Beau."

Beau looked at me, then back to Stirling. He had a strange look on his face, half amused, half something I couldn't read. "Anything you say, Mr. Stirling, Ms. Blake." He turned and strode off over the raw ground, waving at the men as he moved. The men began to leave long before he got to them.

"What do you want us to do, Mr. Stirling?" Bayard asked.

"Wait for us."

"The helicopter, too? It has to leave before dark."

"Will we be down before dark, Ms. Blake?"

"Sure. I'm just going to take a quick look around. I'll need to get back in here after dark, though."

"I'll give you a car and driver for your stay."

"Thanks."

"Shall we, Ms. Blake?" He motioned me forward. Something had changed in the way he was treating me. I couldn't put my finger on it, but I didn't like it.

"After you, Mr. Stirling."

He nodded and took the lead, striding over the red earth in his thousand-dollar shoes.

Larry and I exchanged glances. "I won't be long, Larry."

"Us flunkies aren't going anywhere," he said.

I smiled. He smiled. I shrugged. Why did Stirling want it to be just the two of us? I watched the senior partner's broad back as he marched across the torn earth. I followed him. I'd find out what the secrecy was all about when we got to the top. I was betting I wouldn't like what I'd hear. Just me and the big cheese on top of the mountain with the dead. What could be better?

4

THE VIEW FROM the top of the mountain was worth the hike. Trees stretched out and out to the horizon. We stood in a circle of forest that showed no hand of man as far as the eye could see. That first blush of green was more pronounced here. But the thing you noticed most was the lavender color of redbuds through the dark trees. Redbuds are such delicate things that if they came out in the height of summer they'd get lost in all the leaves and flowers, but here with nothing but naked trees the redbuds were eye-catching. A few dogwoods had started to bloom, adding their white to the lavender. Spring in the Ozarks, ah.

"The view is magnificent," I said.

"Yes," Stirling said, "it is, isn't it?"

My black Nikes were covered in rust-colored dirt. The raw, wounded earth filled the mountaintop. This hilltop had probably been just as pretty as the rest once. There was an arm bone sticking out of the dirt next to my feet. The lower arm, judging from the length. The bones were slender and still connected by a dry remnant of tissue.

Once I'd seen one bone, my eyes found more to look at. It was like one of those magic-eye pictures where you stare and stare and suddenly see what's there. I saw them all, studding the ground like hands reaching up through a river of rust.

There were a few splintered coffins, their broken halves spilling out into the air, but mostly it was just bones. I knelt and put my hands palm down on the ruined earth. I tried to get some sense of the dead. There was something faint and far-off like a whiff of perfume, but it was no good. In the bright spring sunlight I couldn't work my . . . magic. Raising the dead isn't evil, but it does require darkness. I don't know why.

I stood up, brushing my hands against the coverall, trying to clean the red dust away. Stirling was standing at the edge of the naked dirt staring off into space. There was a distance to his gaze that said he wasn't admiring the trees.

He spoke without looking at me. "I can't bully you, can I, Ms. Blake?"

"Nope," I said.

He turned to me with a smile, but it left his eyes empty, haunted. "I invested everything I had into this project. Not just my money, but clients' money. Do you understand what I am saying, Ms. Blake?"

"If the bodies up here are Bouviers, you're screwed."

"How eloquently you put it."

"Why are we up here alone, Mr. Stirling? Why all the skullduggery?"

He took a deep breath of the gentle air and said, "I want you to say they aren't Bouvier ancestors even if they are." He looked at me when he said it. Watched my face.

I smiled and shook my head. "I won't lie for you."

"Can't you make the zombies lie?"

"The dead are very honest, Mr. Stirling. They don't lie."

He took a step towards me, face very sincere. "My entire future is riding on you, Ms. Blake."

"No, Mr Stirling, your future rides on the dead at your feet. Whatever comes out of their mouths will decide it."

He nodded. "I suppose that is fair."

"Fair or not, it's the truth."

He nodded again. Some light had gone out of his face, like someone had turned down the power. The lines in his face were suddenly clearer. He aged ten years in a few seconds. When he met my gaze, his dramatic eyes were woeful.

"I'll give you a piece of the profits, Ms. Blake. You could be a billionaire in a few years."

"You know bribing won't work."

"I knew it wouldn't work just a few minutes after we met, but I had to try."

"You really do believe this is the Bouvier family plot, don't you?" I asked.

He took a deep breath and walked away from me to gaze off at the trees. He wasn't going to answer my question, but he didn't have to. He wouldn't be so desperate if he didn't believe he was screwed.

"Why won't the Bouviers sell?"

He glanced back at me. "I don't know."

"Look, Stirling, there are just the two of us up here, nobody to impress, no witnesses. You know why they won't sell. Just tell me."

"I don't know, Ms. Blake," he said.

"You're a control freak, Mr. Stirling. You've overseen every detail of this deal. You have personally seen that every 'i' was dotted, every 't' crossed. This is your baby. You know everything about the Bouviers and their problem. Just tell me."

He just looked at me. His pale eyes were opaque, empty as a window with no one home. He knew, but he wasn't going to tell me. Why?

"What *do* you know about the Bouviers?"

"The locals think they're witches. They do a little fortune-telling, a few harmless spells." There was something about the way he said it, too casual, too offhand. Made me want to meet the Bouviers in person.

"They any good at magic?" I asked.

"How am I supposed to know?"

I shrugged. "Just curious. Is there a reason why it had to be this mountain?"

"Look at it." He spread his arms wide. "It's perfect. It is perfect."

"It is a great view," I said. "But wouldn't the view be equally good over on that mountaintop? Why did you have to have this one? Why did you have to have the Bouviers' mountain?"

His shoulders slumped; then he straightened and glared at me. "I wanted this land, and I got it."

"You got it. Trick is, Raymond, can you keep it?"

"If you are not going to help me, then don't taunt me. And don't call me Raymond."

I opened my mouth to say something else and my beeper went off. I fished under the coverall for it, and checked the number. "Shit," I said.

"What's wrong?"

"I'm being paged by the police. I've got to get to a phone."

He frowned at me. "Why would the police be calling you?"

So much for being a household name. "I'm the legal vampire executioner for a three-state area. I'm attached to the Regional Preternatural Investigation Team."

He was looking very steadily at me. "You surprise me, Ms. Blake. Not many people do that."

"I need to find a phone."

"I have a portable with a battery pack at the bottom of this damned hill."

"Great. I'm ready to head down if you are."

He did one last turn, taking in that breath-stealing billion-dollar view. "Yes, I'm ready to go down."

It was an interesting choice of words, a Freudian slip you might say. Stirling had wanted this land for some perverse reason. Maybe because he was told he couldn't have it. Some people are like that. The more you say no, the more they want you. It reminded me of a certain master vampire I knew.

Tonight I'd walk the land, visit with the dead. It would probably be tomorrow night before I actually tried to raise them. If the police matter was pressing enough, it might be longer. I hoped it wasn't pressing. Pressing usually meant dead bodies. When the monsters are involved, it's never just one dead body. One way or another, the dead multiply.

5

WE GOT BACK to the valley. The construction crew was gone except for Beau the foreman. Ms. Harrison and Bayard stood next to the helicopter, as if huddling against the wilderness. Larry and the pilot stood to one side, smoking, sharing that comradery of all people who are determined to blacken their lungs.

Stirling walked towards them all, his stride firm and confident once more. He'd left his doubts on top of the mountain, or so it seemed. He was the impervious senior partner once more. Illusion is all.

"Bayard, get the phone. Ms. Blake needs to use it."

Bayard gave a startled little jump, like he'd been caught doing something he shouldn't have. Ms. Harrison looked a little flushed. Was there romance in the air? And was that not allowed? No fraternizing among the flunkies.

Bayard ran off across the dirt towards the last car. He fetched what looked like a small, black leather backpack with a handle. He pulled a phone out and handed it to me. It looked like an antennaed walkie-talkie.

Larry walked over smelling of smoke. "What's up?"

"I got beeped."

"Bert?"

I shook my head. "Police." I walked a little ways from our group. Larry was polite enough to stay with them, though he didn't have to. I dialed Dolph's number. Detective Sergeant Rudolf Storr was head of the Regional Preternatural Investigation Team.

He answered on the second ring. "Anita?"

"Yeah, Dolph, it's me. What's up?"

"Three dead bodies."

"Three? Shit," I said.

"Yeah," he said.

"I can't be there soon, Dolph."

"Yes, you can," he said.

There was something in his voice. "What's that supposed to mean?"

"The victims are right near you."

"Near Branson?"

"Twenty-five minutes east of Branson," he said.

"I'm already forty miles from Branson in the middle of freaking nowhere."

"The middle of nowhere is where this one is," Dolph said.

"Are you guys flying up?" I asked.

"No, we got a vampire victim in town."

"Jesus, are the other three vamp victims?"

"I don't think so," he said.

"What do you mean, you don't think so?" I asked.

"Missouri State Highway Patrol has this one. Sergeant Freemont is the investigator in charge. She doesn't think it was a vampire because the bodies are cut up. Pieces of the bodies are missing. I had to do a lot of tap dancing to get that much information out of her. Sergeant Freemont seems convinced that RPIT is going to come in and steal all the glory. She was particularly worried about our headline-stealing pet zombie queen."

"It's the pet part that I mind the most," I said. "But she sounds charming."

"I'll bet she's even more charming in person," Dolph said.

"And I get to meet her?"

"Given the choice between a large chunk of the squad coming down later and just you right now, she chose you. I think she sees you alone, without us to back you up, as the lesser evil."

"Nice to be the lesser evil for a change," I said.

"You might get upgraded," Dolph said. "She doesn't know you too well yet."

"Thanks for the vote of confidence. Let me test my understanding here. None of you are coming up to the scene?"

"Not right away. You know we're shorthanded until Zerbrowski gets back on duty."

"What does the Missouri State Highway Patrol think about a civilian helping them in a murder investigation?"

"I made it clear that you are a valuable member of my squad."

"Thanks for the compliment, but I still don't have a badge to flash."

"You may if that new federal law goes into effect," Dolph said.

"Don't remind me."

"Don't you want to be a federal marshal?" His voice was very mild. Nah, amused.

"I agreed they should license us, but giving us what amounts to federal marshal status is ridiculous."

"You could handle it."

"But who else? John Burke with the power of the law behind him? Give me a break."

"It won't get passed, Anita. The pro-vampire lobby is too strong."

"From your lips to God's ear. Unless they revoke the need for court orders of execution, it won't make killing them any easier, and they won't do that. I've already gone out of state to execute vamps. I don't need no stinking badge."

Dolph laughed. "If you run into trouble, give a yell."

"I really don't like this, Dolph. I'm out here investigating a murder without any official status."

"See, you do need a badge." I heard him sigh over the phone. "Look, Anita, I wouldn't leave you solo if we didn't have problems of our own. I've got a body on the ground here. When I can, I'll send somebody. Hell, I'd like you to come take a look at our corpse. You're our resident monster expert."

"Give me some details and I'll try to play Kreskin."

"Male, early twenties, rigor hasn't set in."

"Where's the body?"

"His apartment."

"How'd you get there so soon?"

"Neighbor heard a fight, called 911. They called us."

"Give me his name."

"Fredrick Michael Summers, Freddy Summers."

"He got any old vampire bites on his body? Healed bites?"

"Yeah, quite a few. Looks like a damn pincushion. How'd you know?"

"What's the first rule of a homicide?" I said. "You check the nearest and dearest. If he had a vamp lover, there'd be healed bite marks. The more of them, the longer the relationship has gone on. No vamp can bite a victim three times within a month without running the risk of killing them and raising them as a vamp. You can have different vamps bite somebody, but that would make Freddy a vampire junkie.

Ask the neighbors if there were a lot of different guys or girls going in and out at night."

"It never occurred to me that a vampire could be someone's nearest and dearest," Dolph said.

"Legally, they're people. Means they get to have sweethearts, too."

"I'll check the bite radiuses," Dolph said, "If they match one vamp, a lover; different ones, and our boy was doing groups."

"Hope for a lover," I said. "If it's all one vamp, he might even rise from the dead."

"Most vamps know enough to slit the throat or take the head," he said.

"Doesn't sound well planned. Crime of passion, maybe."

"Maybe. Freemont is holding the bodies for you. Eagerly awaiting your expertise."

"I bet."

"Don't bust Freemont's balls on this, Anita."

"I won't start anything, Dolph."

"Be polite," he said.

"Always," I said in my mildest voice.

He sighed. "Try to remember that the staties may never have seen bodies with pieces missing."

It was my turn to sigh. "I'll be good, scout's honor. Do you have directions?" I got a small notebook with a pen stuck in its spiral top out of a pocket of the coverall. I'd started carrying notebooks just for such occasions.

He gave me what Freemont had given him. "If you see anything fishy at the crime scene, keep the scene intact and I'll try to send some people down. Otherwise, look over the victim, give the staties your opinion, and let them do their job."

"You really think Freemont would let me close up her shop and force her to wait for RPIT?"

Silence for a second; then, "Do the best you can, Anita. Call if we can do anything from this end."

"Yeah, sure."

"I'd rather have you on a murder than a lot of the cops I know," Dolph said.

That was a very big compliment coming from Dolph. He is the world's ultimate policeman. "Thanks, Dolph."

I was talking to empty air. Dolph had hung up. He was always doing that. I hit the button, turning the phone off, and just stood there for a minute.

I didn't like being out here in unfamiliar territory with unfamiliar police, and partially eaten victims. Hanging around with the Spook Squad legitimized me. I'd even pulled that "I'm with the squad" at crime scenes. I had a little ID badge that clipped to my clothes. It wasn't a police badge, but it did look official. But pretending on home turf, where I knew I could run to Dolph if I got in trouble for it, was one thing; out here with no backup was another story.

The police have absolutely no sense of humor about civilians meddling in their homicide cases. Can't really blame them. I wasn't really a civilian, but I had no official status. No clout. Maybe the new law would be a good thing.

I shook my head. Theoretically, I'd be able to go into any police station in the country and demand help, or involve myself uninvited in any case. Theoretically. In the real world, the cops would hate it. I'd be as welcome as a wet dog on a cold night. Not federal, not local, and there weren't enough licensed vamp executioners in the country to fill a dozen slots. I could only name eight of us; two of those were retired.

Most of them specialized in vampires. I was one of the few who would look at other types of kills. There was talk of the new law being expanded to include all preternatural kills. Most of the vampire executioners would be out of their depth. It was an informal apprenticeship. I had a college degree in preternatural biology, but that wasn't common. Most of the rogue lycanthropes, occasional trolls run amok, and other more solid beasties were taken out by bounty hunters. But the new law wouldn't give special powers to bounty hunters. Vampire executioners, most of them, worked very strictly within the confines of the law. Or maybe we just had better press.

I'd been screaming about vamps being monsters for years. But until a senator's daughter got herself attacked just a few weeks ago, nobody did shit. Now suddenly it's a cause celebre. The legitimate vampire community delivered the supposed attacker in a sack to the senator's home. They left his head and torso intact, which meant even without arms and legs he wouldn't die. He confessed to the attack. He'd been the new dead and just got carried away on a date, like any other twenty-one-year-old red-blooded male. Yeah, right.

The local hitter, Gerald Mallory, had done the execution. He's based out of Washington, D.C. He has to be in his sixties now. He still uses a stake and hammer. Can you believe it?

There had been some talk that cutting off their arms and legs would allow us to keep vamps in jail. This was vetoed mainly on the grounds of cruel and unusual punishment. It also wouldn't have worked, not for the really old vampires. It isn't just their bodies that are dangerous.

Besides, I didn't believe in torture. If cutting someone's arms and legs off and putting them in a little box for all eternity isn't torture, I don't know what is.

I walked back to the group. I handed the phone to Bayard. "I hope it isn't bad news," he said.

"Not personally," I said.

He looked puzzled. Not an uncommon occurrence for Lionel

I talked directly to Stirling. "I've got to go to a crime scene near here. Is there someplace to rent a car?"

He shook his head. "I said you'd have a car and driver while you were here. I meant it."

"Thanks. I'm not so sure about the driver, though. This is a crime scene they won't want civilians hanging around."

"A car, then; no driver. Lionel, see that Ms. Blake gets anything she wants."

"Yes, sir."

"I'll meet you back here at full dark, Ms. Blake."

"I'll be here at dusk if I can, Mr. Stirling, but the police matter takes precedence."

He frowned at me. "You are working for me, Ms. Blake."

"Yes, but I'm also a licensed vampire executioner. Cooperation with the local police takes precedence."

"So it's a vampire kill?"

"I am not free to share police information with anyone," I said. But I cursed myself. By bringing up the word "vampire," I'd started a rumor that would grow with the telling. Damn.

"I can't leave the investigation early just to come look at your mountain. I'll be here when I can. I'll definitely look the dead over before daylight, so you won't really lose any time."

He didn't like it, but he let it go. "Fine, Ms. Blake. I will wait here for you even if it takes all night. I'm curious about what you do. I've never seen a zombie raised before."

"I won't raise the dead tonight, Mr. Stirling. We've been over that."

"Of course." He just looked at me. For some reason it was hard to meet his pale eyes. I made myself meet his gaze and didn't look away, but it was an effort. It was like he was willing me to do something, trying to compel me with his eyes like a vampire. But a vampire, even a little one, he was not.

He blinked and walked away without saying another word. Ms. Harrison toddled after him in her high heels on the uneven ground. Beau nodded at me and followed. I guess they'd all come in the same car. Or maybe Beau was Stirling's driver. What a joyous job that must be.

"We'll fly you to the hotel where we booked your rooms. You can unpack, and I'll have a car brought around for you," Bayard said.

"No unpacking, just a car. Murder scenes age fast," I said.

He nodded. "As you like. If you'll get back into the helicopter, we'll be off."

It wasn't until I was taking off the coveralls and repacking both of them that I realized I could have gone with Mr. Stirling. I could have driven out of here, instead of flying. Shit.

6

BAYARD HAD GOTTEN us a black Jeep with black-tinted windows and more bells and whistles than I could even guess at. I'd been worried they'd saddle me with a Cadillac or something equally ridiculous. Bayard had given me the keys with the comment, "Some of these roads are not even paved. I thought you might need something more substantial than just a car."

I resisted the urge to pat him on the head and say "Good flunkie." Hell, he'd made a great choice. Maybe he'd make full partner someday after all.

The trees made long, thin shadows across the road. In the valleys between mountains, the sunlight had softened to a late-afternoon haze. We might make it back to the graveyard by full dark.

Yes, we. Larry sat beside me in his wrinkled blue suit. The cops wouldn't mind his cheap suit. My outfit, on the other hand, might raise a few eyebrows. There aren't many female cops out in the boonies. And fewer who wear short red skirts. I was beginning to really regret my choice of clothes. Insecure: who, me?

Larry's face was shiny with excitement. His eyes sparkled like a kid's on Christmas Day. He was drumming his fingers on the armrest. Nervous tension.

"How you doing?"

"I've never been to a murder scene before," he said.

"There's always a first time."

"Thanks for letting me come along."

"Just remember the rules."

He laughed. "Don't touch anything. Don't walk through the blood. Don't speak unless spoken to." He frowned. "Why the last? I understand all the others, but why can't I talk?"

"I'm a member of the Regional Preternatural Investigation Team. You're not. If you go around saying golly gee whiz a dead body, they may catch on."

"I won't embarrass you." He sounded insulted; then a thought occurred to him. "Are we impersonating police officers?"

"No. Keep repeating I'm a member of the Spook Squad, I'm a member of the Spook Squad, I'm a member of the Spook Squad."

"But I'm not," he said.

"That's why I don't want you talking."

"Oh," he said. He settled back into his seat, a little of the shine dimming around the edges. "I've never actually seen a freshly dead body before."

"You raise the dead for a living, Larry. You see corpses all the time."

"It's not the same thing, Anita." He sounded grumpy.

I glanced at him. He had slumped down as far into the seat as the seat belt would allow, arms crossed over his chest. We were at the crest of a hill. A band of sunlight fell like an explosion over his orange hair. His blue eyes looked translucent for a moment as we passed from light into shadow. He looked all scrunched and sulky.

"Have you ever seen a dead person outside of a funeral or a freshly raised zombie?"

He was quiet for a minute. I concentrated on driving, letting the silence fill the Jeep. It was a comfortable silence, at least for me.

"No," he said at last. He sounded like a little boy who had been told he couldn't go outside and play.

"I'm not always good around fresh bodies either," I said.

He looked at me sort of sideways. "What do you mean?"

It was my turn to scrunch into the seat. I fought the urge and sat up straighter. "I threw up on a murder victim once." Even saying it very fast, it was still embarrassing.

Larry scooted up in his seat, grinning. "You're just telling me that to make me feel better."

"Would I tell a story like that about myself if it wasn't true?" I asked.

"You really threw up on a body at a crime scene?"

"You don't have to sound so happy about it," I said.

He giggled. I swear he giggled. "I don't think I'll throw up on the body."

I shrugged. "Three bodies, with parts missing. Don't make promises you can't keep."

He swallowed loud enough for me to hear it. "What do they mean, parts missing?"

"We'll find out," I said. "This isn't part of your job description, Larry. I get paid for helping the cops; you don't."

"Will it be awful?" His voice was low, uncertain.

Chopped-up bodies. Was he kidding? "I don't know until we get there."

"But what do you think?" He was staring at me very earnestly.

I glanced back at the road, then at Larry. He looked very solemn, like a relative who'd asked the doctor for the truth. If he would be brave, I could be truthful. "Yeah, it'll be awful."

7

IT WAS AWFUL. Larry had managed to stagger from the crime scene before he threw up. The only comfort I could offer him was that he wasn't the only one. Some of the cops were looking a little green around the edges, too. I hadn't thrown up yet, but I was keeping it as an option for later.

The bodies lay in a small hollow near the base of a hill. The ground was nearly knee-deep with leaves. Nobody rakes in the woods. The drought had dried the leaves to a fine, biting crunch underfoot. The hollow was ringed by naked trees and bushes with branches like thin brown whips. When the leaves came out, the hollow would be hidden on all sides.

The body nearest to me was a blond man with hair cut so short it looked like an old-fashioned butch. Blood pooled around the eyeballs, flowing from them down the face.

There was something wrong with the face, besides the eyes, but I couldn't quite figure out what. I knelt in the dry leaves, glad that the leg of the coverall was protecting my hose from the leaves and the blood. Blood had pooled to either side of the boy's face, soaking into the leaves. The blood had dried to a tacky maroon substance. It looked like the teenager's eyes had been crying dark tears.

I touched the tip of my gloved fingers to the blond's chin. It moved in a boneless, wiggling movement that chins were not meant to do.

I swallowed hard and tried to take shallow breaths. I was glad it was still spring. If the bodies had been sitting this long in full summer heat, they'd have been ripe in more ways than one. Cool weather was a blessing.

I put my hands in the leaves and bent from the waist in an awkward sort of push-up motion. I was trying to see under his chin without moving the body again. There, nearly lost in the blood on the neck, was a puncture mark. A puncture mark wider than my outspread hand. I'd seen knife wounds and claw marks that could make a similar wound, but it was too big for a knife and too clean for a claw. Besides, what the hell had a claw that big? It looked like a massive blade had been shoved under the blond's chin, close enough to the front of his face to slice the eyes up from inside the head. That's why the eyes were bleeding, but still looked intact. The sword had nearly pulled the blond's face off his skull.

I ran my gloved fingers over the blond's short hair and found what I was looking for. The tip of the sword, if that's what it was, had come out the top of his head. Then the blade had been withdrawn and the blond had dropped to the leaves. Dead, I hoped, but dying I was sure of.

His legs were missing just below the hip joint. There was almost no blood where the legs had been bisected. They'd been cut off after he'd died. Small blessing, that. He'd died relatively quickly, and had not been tortured. There were worse ways to die.

I knelt by the stubs of his legs. The left bone had been cut clean with one blow. The right bone had splintered, as if the sword struck from the left side, cut the left cleanly, but only got a piece of the right leg. A second blow had been needed to sever the right leg.

Why take the legs? A trophy? Maybe. Serial killers took trophies, clothing, personal items, a body part. Maybe a trophy?

The other two boys were shorter, neither of them over five feet. Younger maybe, maybe not. They were both small and dark-haired, slender. Probably the kind of boys who looked pretty rather than handsome but, frankly, it was hard to tell.

One lay on his back almost opposite from the blond. One brown eye stared up at the sky, glassy and immobile, somehow unreal like the eyes of a taxidermy animal. The rest of his face was sliced in two huge gaping furrows, as if the tip of the sword had been used coming and going like a backhand slap. The third slice had taken out his neck. It was a very clean wound; they all were. The damn sword, or whatever it was, was incredibly sharp. But it was more than a good blade. No human could have been fast enough to take them all without a struggle. But most beasties that will kill a human being won't pick up a weapon to do it.

A lot of things will claw us apart, or eat us alive, but the list of preternatural beings that will cut us up with weapons is pretty small. A troll may tear up a tree and whap you to death, but it won't use a blade. Not only had this thing used a sword, not a common weapon, but it had some skill.

The blows to the face hadn't killed the boy. Why didn't the other two run? If the blond was killed first, why didn't this one run? Nothing was fast enough that it could take out three teenage boys with a sword before any of them could run. These were not quick blows. Whoever, or whatever, had done this had taken some time with each kill. But they all acted as if they'd been hit by surprise.

The boy had fallen onto his back in the leaves, hands clutching at his throat. The leaves had been scuffed away where his feet had kicked them. I took a shallow breath. I didn't want to probe the wounds, but I was beginning to have a nasty idea.

I knelt and traced the neck wound with my fingertips. The edges of the skin were so smooth. But it was still human flesh, human skin, blood dried to a thick stickiness. I swallowed hard and closed my eyes and let my fingers search for what I thought I'd find. The edge of the wound had two lips, starting about midway. I opened my eyes and traced the double wound with my fingers. My eyes still couldn't see it. There was too much blood. Once the wound was clean, you'd see it, but not here, not like this. The neck had been sliced twice, deeply. One cut was enough to kill. Why twice? Because they were hiding something on the neck.

Fang marks, maybe? Being killed by a vampire would explain why he hadn't tried to crawl away. He'd just lain in the leaves and kicked until he died.

I stared at the last teenager. He was crumpled on his right side. Blood had pooled under him. He was so cut up that at first my eyes didn't want to make sense of what I was seeing. I wanted to look away before my brain caught up to my eyes, but I didn't.

Where the face should have been was just a ripped, gapping hole. The creature had done the same thing to this one as to the blond, but it had been more thorough. The front of the skull had been ripped away. I glanced around, searching the leaves for the piece of bone and flesh, but didn't see it. I had to look back then, at the body. I knew what I was looking at now. I liked it better when I didn't.

The back of the skull was full of blood and gore, like a gruesome cup, but the brain was gone. The blade had sliced him open across the chest and stomach. His intestines spilled out in a thick, rubbery mass. What I thought was his stomach had spilled out from the wound like a balloon half-inflated. The left leg had been chopped off at the hip joint. The ragged cloth of his jeans clung to the hole like the petals of an unopened flower. The left arm had been ripped out just below the elbow. The bone of the humerus was dark with dried blood, sticking up at an odd angle as if the entire arm had been broken at the shoulder and no longer moved. More violent. Had this one struggled a little?

My eyes flicked back to his face. I didn't want to look again, but I hadn't really examined it. There was something horribly personal about disfiguring a person's face. If it had been humanly possible to do all this, I'd have said check their nearest and dearest. As a general rule, only people who love you will cut up your face. It implies passion that you can't get from strangers. One exception is serial killers. They're working through a pathology in which the victims can represent someone else. Someone that the killer has a personal passion for. When cutting up the faces of strangers they'd be symbolically cutting up, say, a hated father figure.

The fine bones of the boy's sinus cavities had been cracked open. The maxillary was gone, making the face look incomplete. Part of the mandible was still there, but it had been cracked apart back to the rear molars. Some trick of blood flow had left two teeth white and clean. One of the teeth had a filling in it. I stared at that ruined face. I'd been doing pretty good at thinking of it as so much meat, just dead meat. But dead meat didn't get cavities, didn't go to dentists. It was suddenly a teenager, or maybe even younger. I was only judging on height and the apparent age of the other two. Maybe this one with no face was a child, a tall child. A little boy.

The spring afternoon wavered around me. I took a deep breath to steady myself, and it was a mistake. I got a big whiff of bowels and stale death. I scrambled for the side of the hollow. Never throw up on the murder victims. Pisses off the cops.

I fell to my knees at the top of the small rise where all the cops were gathered. I hadn't exactly fallen so much as thrown myself down. I took deep, cleansing breaths of the cool air. It helped. A small breeze was blowing up here, thinning out the smell of death. It helped more.

Cops of all shapes and sizes were huddled at the top of the rise. Nobody was spending more time than they had to down among the dead. There were ambulances waiting on the distant road, but everybody else had had their piece of the bodies. They had been videotaped and trooped through with the crime scene technicians. Everybody had done their job, except me.

"Are you going to be sick, Ms. Blake?" The voice was that of Sergeant Freemont, Division of Drug and Crime

Control, DD/CC—affectionately known as D2C2. Her tone was gentle but disapproving. I understood the tone. We were the only two women at the crime scene, which meant we were playing with the big boys. You had to be tougher than the men, stronger, better, or they held it against you. Or they treated you like a girl. I was betting Sergeant Freemont hadn't gotten sick. She wouldn't have allowed it.

I took another cleansing breath and let it out. I looked up at her. From my knees she looked every inch of her five-foot-eight. Her hair was straight, dark, cut just below her chin. The ends were curled under to frame her face. Her pants were a bright sunny yellow, jacket black, blouse a softer yellow. I had a good view of her polished black loafers. There was a gold wedding band on her left hand, but no engagement ring. Deep smile lines put her on the far side of forty, but she wasn't smiling now.

I swallowed once more, trying not to taste that smell on the back of my tongue. I got to my feet. "No, Sergeant Freemont, I'm not going to be sick." I was glad that it was true. I just hoped she didn't make me go back down into the hollow. I'd toss my cookies if I had to look at the bodies again.

"What did that?" She asked. I didn't turn and look where she pointed. I knew what was down there.

I shrugged. "I don't know."

Her brown eyes were neutral and unreadable, good cop eyes. She frowned. "What do you mean, you don't know? You're supposed to be the monster expert."

I let the "supposed to be" go. She hadn't called me a zombie queen to my face; in fact she'd been very polite, correct, but there was no warmth to it. She wasn't impressed, and in her quiet way, with a look or the slightest inflection, she let me know. I was going to have to pull a very big corpse out of my hat to impress Sergeant Freemont, DD/CC. So far I wasn't even close.

Larry walked up to us. His face was the color of yellow-green tissue paper. It clashed with his red hair. His eyes were red-rimmed where his eyes had teared while he threw up. If it's violent enough, sometimes you cry while you vomit.

I didn't ask Larry if he was okay; the answer was too obvious. But he was on his feet, ambulatory. If he didn't faint, he'd be fine.

"What do you want from me, Sergeant?" I asked. I'd been more than patient. For me, I'd been downright conciliatory. Dolph would be proud. Bert would have been amazed.

She crossed her arms over her stomach. "I let Sergeant Storr talk me into letting you see the crime scene. He said you were the best. According to the newspapers, you just do a little magic and figure it all out. Or maybe you can just raise the dead and ask them who killed them."

I took a deep breath and let it out. I didn't use magic to solve crimes, as a general rule; I used knowledge, but saying so would be defending myself. I didn't need to prove anything to Freemont. "Don't believe everything you read in the papers, Sergeant Freemont. As for raising the dead, it won't work with these three."

"Are you telling me you can't raise zombies, either?" She shook her head. "If you can't help us then go home, Ms Blake."

I glanced at Larry. He gave a small shrug. He still looked shaky. I don't think he had the energy yet to tell me to behave myself. Or maybe he was as tired of Freemont as I was.

"I could raise them as zombies, Sergeant, but you have to have a mouth and a working throat to talk with."

"They could write it down," Freemont said.

It was a good suggestion. It made me think better of her. If she was a good cop, I could put up with a little hostility. As long as I never had to see another set of bodies like the ones below, I could put up with a lot of hostility.

"Maybe, but the dead often lose higher brain function faster after a traumatic death. They might not be able to write, but even if they could, they might not know what killed them."

"But they saw it," Larry said. His voice sounded hoarse, and he coughed gently behind his hand to clear it.

"None of them tried to run away, Larry. Why?"

"Why are you asking him?" Freemont said.

"He's in training," I said.

"Training? You brought a trainee in on my murder case?"

I stared up at her. "I don't tell you how to do your job. Don't tell me how to do mine."

"You haven't done a damn thing yet. Except for your assistant throwing up in the bushes."

An unhealthy flush crept up Larry's neck. Embarrassed when he was almost too nauseated to stand.

"Larry wasn't the only one upchucking in the weeds, just the only one without a badge." I shook my head. "We don't need this shit." I brushed past Freemont. "Come on, Larry."

Larry followed, obedient to the last.

"I don't want any of this leaked to the press, Ms. Blake. If the media gets hold of it, I'll know where it came from." She wasn't yelling, but her voice carried.

I turned. I wasn't yelling either, but everyone could hear me. "You have an unknown preternatural creature that uses a sword, and is faster than a vampire."

Something flickered across her face, like maybe I'd finally done something interesting. "How do you know it's faster than a vampire?"

"None of the boys tried to get away. All of them died where they stood. Either it's faster, or it has some amazing mind control."

"It's not a lycanthrope, then?"

"Even a lycanthrope isn't that fast, and they don't have the ability to cloud men's minds. If a lycanthrope came in there with a sword, the boys would have screamed and run. There would have at least been signs of a struggle."

Freemont just stood there looking. It was a very serious look, like she was weighing and measuring me. She still wasn't happy with me, but she was listening.

"I can help you, Sergeant Freemont. I can help you figure out what did this, maybe, before it does it again."

Her quiet, confident mask crumbled around the edge for a second. If I hadn't been staring at her neutral brown eyes, I'd have missed it.

"Shit," I said, loud. I walked back over to her and lowered my voice. "That's it, isn't it? These aren't the first killings."

She glanced down at the ground, then met my eyes, jaw

sort of thrust forward. Her eyes weren't neutral now; they were just a little bit scared. Not for herself, but for what she'd done, or not done.

"The State Highway Patrol can handle a homicide." Her voice was the gentlest I'd heard it.

"How many?" I asked.

"Two before. A couple of teenagers, boy and a girl. Probably necking in the woods." Her voice was soft, almost tired.

"What's the M.E. say?"

"You're right," she said. "It was a blade, probably a sword. The monsters don't use weapons, Ms. Blake. I thought it was the girl's ex-boyfriend. He's got a collection of Civil War memorabilia, including swords. It seemed pretty cut-and-dried."

I nodded. "Sounds logical."

"None of his swords matched the blows, but I thought he'd ditched the murder weapon. I didn't think . . ." She looked away from me, hands shoved so hard into her pants pockets I thought they'd split the cloth. "The first scene wasn't like this. They were killed with the first blow; it pinned them through the chest into the ground. A human being could have done that." She looked back at me as if wanting me to agree with her. I did.

"Were their bodies cut up beyond the death wound?"

She nodded. "Disfigured faces, her left hand missing. The one that had worn the ex-boyfriend's ring."

"Were their throats cut?"

She frowned, thinking, then nodded. "Hers was. Not much blood either, like it'd been done after she died."

My turn to nod. "Great."

"Great?" Larry asked.

"I think you've got a vampire on your hands, Sergeant Freemont."

They both frowned at me. "Look at the body parts that are missing. The legs of the one boy were cut off after he died. The femoral artery is in the thigh near the groin. I've seen vamps take blood from that in preference to the neck. Cut off the legs, and no fang marks."

"What about the other two?" Freemont asked.

"Maybe the smallest boy was bitten. His neck was sliced twice for no reason. Maybe it was just a little extra violence like the disfigurement of the face. I don't know. But a vamp can take blood from the wrist, the bend of the arm. All parts that are missing."

"One of their brains is missing," Freemont said.

Larry swayed gently beside me. He wiped a hand over his suddenly sweating face.

"You going to be alright?" I asked.

He nodded, not trusting his voice. Brave Larry.

"What better way to throw us off the track than to take something a vamp wouldn't be interested in?" I said.

"Okay, say it makes some sense. Why this way? This is . . ." She spread her hands wide, staring down at the carnage. She was the only one of the three of us still looking at it. "This is nuts. If it was human, I'd say we had a serial killer on our hands."

"We may have," I said softly.

Freemont stared at me. "What the hell do you mean?"

"A vampire was a person once. Just being dead doesn't cure you of any problems you had as a live human being. If you have a violent pathology before death, that won't change just because you're dead."

Freemont looked at me like I was the one who was crazy. I think it was the word "dead" that was bothering her. Once her suspects were dead, they weren't suspects anymore. I tried again. "Say Johnny is a serial killer. He becomes a vampire. Why should being a vampire make him suddenly less violent? Why not more violent?"

"Oh, my God," Larry said.

Freemont took a deep breath in through her nose and let it out slow. "Okay, maybe you're right. I'm not saying you are. I've seen pictures of vampire victims and they don't look like this, but if you are, what do you need from me?"

"The pictures from the first crime scene. And a look at where it happened."

"I'll send the file to your hotel," she said.

"Where was the couple killed?"

"Just a few hundred yards from here."

"Let's go take a look."

"I'll have one of the troopers take you over," she said.

"This is a damn small geographic area. I assume you searched it."

"With a fine-tooth comb. But frankly, Ms. Blake, I wasn't sure what we were looking for. The leaves and the dry weather make it almost impossible to find tracks."

"Yeah," I said. "Tracks would help." I glanced back the way I'd come. The leaves were disturbed coming up the hill. "If it is a vampire . . ."

Freemont cut me off. "What do you mean, if?"

I met her suddenly accusing eyes. "Look, Sergeant, if it is a vampire it has more mind control than I've ever seen. I've never met a vampire, even a master vampire, that could hold three humans in thrall while he killed them. Until I saw this, I'd have said it couldn't be done."

"What else could it be?" Larry asked.

I shrugged. "I think it's a vamp, but if I said I was a hundred percent sure, I'd be lying. I try not to lie to the police. There may be no tracks up the hill even if the ground was soft, because the vampire could have flown in."

"Like a bat?" Freemont asked.

"No, they don't change shape into a bat, but they can . . ." I searched for a word and there wasn't one. "They can levitate, sort of fly. I've seen it. I can't explain it, but I've seen it."

"A serial killer vampire." She shook her head, the lines near her mouth deepening. "The Feds are going to be all over this."

"No joke," I said. "Did you find the missing body parts?"

"No, I thought maybe it had eaten them."

"If it ate that much, why not more? If it ate, why no teeth marks? If it ate, why not some scattered body parts, like crumbs?"

She clenched her hands into fists. "You've made your point. It was a vampire. Even a dumb cop knows they don't eat flesh." She turned her brown eyes to me, and there was a lot of anger in them. Not at me, exactly, but I might make a good target. I stared back at her, not flinching. She looked away first. Maybe I wouldn't make a good target.

"I don't like having a civilian contractor in on a homicide investigation, but you spotted things down there that I missed. You're either very good, or you know something that you aren't telling me."

I could have just said I'm good at my job, but I didn't. Didn't want the police thinking I was holding out information when I wasn't. "I've got one advantage over a normal homicide detective, I expect it to be a monster. No one ever calls me in if it's just a stabbing, or a hit-and-run. I don't spend a lot of time trying to come up with nice, normal explanations. It means I get to ignore a lot of theories."

She nodded. "Alright, if you help me catch this thing, I don't care what you do for a living."

"Glad to hear it," I said.

"But no reporters, no media. I am in charge here. This is my investigation. I decide when we go public. Is that clear?"

"Sure."

She stared at me like she didn't believe me. "I mean it about the media, Ms. Blake."

"I don't have a problem with no media, Sergeant Freemont. I prefer it that way."

"For a person who doesn't want the media around, you get a lot of attention."

I shrugged. "I'm involved in only sensational cases, detective. Cases that make good press, good sound bites. I slay vampires, for God's sake; it makes great headlines."

"As long as we understand each other, Ms. Blake."

"No media; it's not a hard concept," I said.

She nodded. "I'll have someone walk you over to the first crime scene. I'll see you get the file at your hotel." She started to turn away.

"Sergeant Freemont?"

She turned back, but it was not a friendly look. "What is it now, Ms. Blake? You've done your job."

"You can't treat this like a human serial killer."

"I'm in charge of this investigation, Ms. Blake. I can do what I damn well please."

I stared up at her, met her hostile eyes. I wasn't feeling too friendly myself. "I am not trying to steal your thunder here. But vampires aren't just people with fangs. If the vamp could catch their minds and hold them while he slaughtered each of them in turn, he could capture your mind, anyone's mind. A vampire that talented could make you think black was white. Do you understand me?"

"It's daylight, Ms. Blake; if it's a vampire then we find it and stake it."

"You'll need a court order of execution."

"We'll get one."

"When you get it, I'll come back and finish the job."

"I think we can handle it."

"You ever stake a vampire?" I asked.

She just looked at me. "No, but I've shot a man. It can't be that much harder."

"It's not harder in the way you mean," I said. "But it's a hell of a lot more dangerous."

She shook her head. "Until the Feds get here, I'm in charge, and not you or anyone else is taking over. Is that clear, Ms. Blake?"

I nodded. "Crystal, Sergeant Freemont." I stared at the cross-shaped pin in the lapel of her suit jacket. Most plainclothesmen had a cross-shaped tie tack. Standard police issue across the country. "You do have silver ammo, right?"

"I'll take care of my men, Ms. Blake."

I raised my hands slightly. So much for girl talk. "Fine, we're leaving. You've got my beeper number. Use it if you need it, Detective Freemont."

"I won't need it."

I took a deep breath and swallowed a lot of words. Picking a fight with the cop in charge of a murder investigation was not the way to get invited back to play. I walked past her without saying good-bye. If I opened my mouth, I wasn't sure what would come out. Nothing pleasant, and nothing useful.

8

PEOPLE WHO DON'T camp much think darkness falls from the sky. It doesn't. Darkness slides from the trees and fills them first, then spreads outward to the open places. It was so dark under the trees that I wished for a flashlight. When we stumbled to the road, and our waiting Jeep, it was only dusk.

Larry looked up at the coming night, and said, "We can get back and walk the graveyard for Stirling."

"First let's eat," I said.

He looked at me. "You wanting to stop for food, that's a first. I usually have to beg for drive-up."

"I forgot to eat lunch," I said.

He grinned. "That I believe." The smile faded slowly from his face. "The first time you offer me food voluntarily, and I don't think I can eat." He stared at me. There was enough light left for me to see him search my face. "Could you really eat after what we just saw?"

I looked at him. I didn't know what to say. Not so long ago, the answer would have been no. "Well, I wouldn't want to face a plate of spaghetti, or steak tartare, but yeah, I could eat."

He shook his head. "What the heck is steak tartare?"

"Raw beef, pretty much," I said.

He swallowed hard, looking just a little paler than he had a second ago. "How can you even think of stuff like that so soon after . . ." He let the words trail off. We'd both seen it; no words were needed.

I shrugged. "I've been going to murder scenes for nearly three years, Larry. You learn to survive. Which means you learn to eat after seeing cut-up bodies." I didn't add that I'd seen worse. I'd seen human bodies reduced to a roomful of blood and gobbets of unrecognizable flesh. Not enough left to fill a gallon-size baggie. I hadn't gone out for Big Macs after that one.

"Are you up to at least trying to eat?"

He was looking at me sort of suspiciously. "Where did you have in mind?"

I untied the Nikes and stepped carefully on the gravel road. Didn't want to snag the hose. I unzipped the coverall and stepped out of it. Larry did the same, but he tried to keep his shoes on. He managed to work his feet through, but it required some hopping on one leg.

I folded my coverall carefully so the blood wouldn't touch the Jeep's immaculate interior. I tossed the Nikes into the back floorboard and got the high heels out.

Larry was trying to brush wrinkles from his suit pants, but some things only a dry cleaner could fix.

"How would you like to go to Bloody Bones?" I asked.

He looked up at me, hands still patting at the wrinkles. He frowned. "Where?"

"It's the restaurant that Magnus Bouvier owns. Stirling mentioned it."

"Did he tell us where it was?" Larry said.

"No, but I asked one of the local cops for restaurants, and Bloody Bones isn't that far from here."

Larry squinted suspiciously at me. "Why do you want to go there?"

"I want to talk to Magnus Bouvier."

"Why?" he asked.

It was a good question. I wasn't sure I had a good answer. I shrugged and climbed into the Jeep. Larry had no choice but to join me, unless he didn't want to continue the conversation. When we were all settled in the Jeep, I still didn't have a really good answer.

"I don't like Stirling. I don't trust him."

"I got the impression you didn't like him," Larry said, his voice very dry. "But why not trust him?"

"Do you trust him?" I asked.

Larry frowned and thought about it. He shook his head. "Not as far as I could throw him."

"See?" I said.

"I guess so, but you think talking to Bouvier will help?"

"I hope so. I don't like raising the dead for people I don't trust. Especially something this big."

"Okay, so we go eat dinner at Bouvier's restaurant and talk to him; then what?"

"If we don't learn anything new, we go see Stirling and walk the graveyard for him."

Larry was looking at me like he wasn't sure he trusted me. "What are you up to?"

"Don't you want to know why Stirling had to have that mountain? Why the Bouviers' mountain and not someone else's?"

Larry looked at me. "You've been hanging around the police too long. You don't trust anybody."

"The cops didn't teach me that, Larry; it's natural talent." I put the Jeep in gear and off we went.

The trees made long, thin shadows. In the valleys between mountains, the shadows formed pools of coming night. We should have driven straight to the graveyard. Just walking the cemetery wouldn't hurt anything. But if I couldn't go vampire hunting, I could question Magnus Bouvier. That part of my job nobody could chase me out of.

I didn't really want to go vampire hunting. It was almost dark. Hunting vamps after dark was a good way to get killed. Especially one that could control minds like this one could. A vampire can cloud your mind and even hurt you, if its control is good enough, and you won't mind. But once its concentration is off you, onto someone else, and that person starts screaming, you'll wake up. You'll run. But the boys hadn't run. They hadn't woken up. They'd just died.

If this thing wasn't stopped, other people would die. I could almost guarantee it. Freemont should have let me stay. They needed a vampire expert with them on this one. They needed me. Okay, they really needed police with expertise in monsters, but they didn't have that. It had only been three years since Addison v. Clark made vampires legally alive. Three years ago Washington had made the blood-suckers living citizens with rights. Nobody had thought what that meant for the police. Before the law changed, preternatural crime was handled by bounty hunters, vampire hunters. Those private citizens with enough experience to keep them alive. Most of us had some sort of preternatural power that helped give us an edge against the monsters. Most cops didn't.

Ordinarily human beings didn't fare well against the monsters. There have always been a few of us who had a talent for taking out the beasties. We've done a good job, but suddenly the cops are expected to take over. No extra training, no extra manpower, nothing. Hell, most police departments wouldn't even spring for the silver ammunition.

It had taken this long for Washington, D.C., to realize they might have been hasty. That maybe, just maybe, the monsters were really monsters and the police needed some extra training. It would take years to train the cops, so they were going to short-circuit the process, just make cops out of all the vampire hunters and monster slayers. For myself, personally, it might work. I would've loved to have a badge to shove in Freemont's face. She couldn't have chased me off then, not if it was federal. But for most vampire hunters, it was going to be a mess. You needed more than preternatural expertise to work a homicide case. You sure as hell needed more than vampire expertise to carry a badge.

There were no easy answers. But out there in the coming darkness were a bunch of police hunting a vampire that could do things I never thought they could do. If I had a badge, I could be with them. I wasn't an automatic safety zone, but I knew a damn sight more than a state cop who had "seen" pictures of vampire victims. Freemont had never seen the real thing. Here was hoping she survived her first encounter.

9

BLOODY BONES BAR and grill lay up a red gravel road. Someone had butchered the trees back to either side, so the Jeep climbed upward towards a black blanket of sky, sprinkled with a million stars. The shine of stars was the only light in sight.

"It is really dark out here," Larry said.

"No streetlights," I said.

"Shouldn't we see the lights from the restaurant by now?"

"I don't know." I was staring at the broken trees. The trunks gleamed white and ragged. It had been done recently, as if someone had gone mad with an axe, or maybe a sword, or something big had ripped off the trunks.

I slowed down, scanning the darkness. Was I wrong? Was it trolls? Was there a Greater Ozark Mountain Troll left in these mountains? One that would use a sword? I was a big believer in a first time for everything.

I brought the Jeep almost to a stop.

"What's wrong?" Larry asked.

I hit the emergency flashers. The road was narrow, barely two cars wide, but it was going uphill. Anybody coming down wouldn't see the Jeep right away. The lights helped, but if someone was speeding . . . Hell, I was going to do it; why quibble? I put the Jeep in park and got out.

"Where are you going?"

"I'm wondering if a troll ripped the trees apart."

Larry started to get out on his side. I stopped him. "Slide over on my side if you want to get out."

"Why?"

"You're not armed." I got the Browning out. It was a solid, comforting weight, but truthfully, against something the size of one of the great mountain trolls, it wasn't too useful. Maybe with exploding bullets, but short of that a 9mm wasn't the gun for hunting something the size of a small elephant.

Larry closed his door and slid across. "You really think there's a troll out here?"

I stared off into the darkness. Nothing moved. "I don't know." I moved to a dry gully that cut the edge of the road. I stepped very carefully into it. The heels sank in the dry, sandy soil. I grabbed a handful of weeds with my left hand and levered myself up the slope. I had to grab one of the butchered trunks to keep from sliding backwards in the loose leaves and pine needles.

My hand came up against thick sap. I fought the urge to jerk away, forcing myself to keep hold of the sticky bark.

Larry scrambled up the bank, slick-soled dress shoes sliding in the dry leaves. I didn't have a free hand to offer him. He caught himself in a sort of half push-up, and used the weeds to move up beside me. "Damn dress shoes."

"At least you're not in heels," I said.

"And don't think I'm not grateful," he said. "I'd break my neck."

Nothing moved in the dark, dark night except us. There was the sound of spring peepers close by, musical, but nothing bigger. I let out a breath I hadn't realized I was holding. I pulled myself up to more solid footing and looked at the trees.

"What are we looking for?" Larry asked.

"An axe makes a wide, smooth stroke. If a troll snapped the trunks, they'll be ragged and full of jagged points of wood."

"Looks smooth to me," he said. He ran his fingertips over the naked wood. "But it doesn't look like an axe."

The wood was too smooth. An axe will come in at an angle. This was almost flat, like each tree had been felled with a single stroke, two at most. Some of the trees had been nearly a foot in diameter. No human could do that, even with an axe.

"Who could have done this?"

I searched the darkness, fighting an urge to aim the gun into the dark, but I kept it skyward. Safety first. "A vampire with a sword, maybe."

He stared off into the darkness. "You mean the one that killed the guys? Why would the vampire chop down a bunch of trees after he killed them?"

It was a good question. A great question. But like with so many questions today, I didn't have a good answer. "I don't know. Let's get back to the car."

We scrambled back the way we'd come. Neither of us fell down this time. A record.

When we were at the car I put the gun away. I probably hadn't needed it at all, but then again . . . something cut down those trees.

I used the aloe and lanolin baby wipes that I kept in the car to wipe off blood, to wipe the sap from my hand. The wipes worked nearly as well on tree blood as it did on human.

We drove on, searching for lights. We had to be close to Bloody Bones, unless the directions were way off. Here's hoping they weren't.

"Is that a torch?" Larry asked.

I stared into the darkness. There was a flicker of fire, too high off the ground to be a campfire. Two torches on long poles illuminated a wide gravel turnaround to the left of the road. The trees had been pushed back here, too, but years ago. It was an old, established clearing. The trees formed a backdrop for a one-story building. A wooden sign hung from the eaves. It was hard to read by torchlight, but it might have read "Bloody Bones."

Dark wooden shingles covered the roof and climbed down the walls, so that the entire building looked like a natural growth that had sprung from the red clay soil. About twenty cars and trucks were parked haphazardly on the dark gravel.

The sign swung in the wind, the torchlight reflecting off the deeply carved words. "Bloody Bones" was carved in smooth, curving letters.

I walked carefully over the gravel in my high heels. Larry's dress shoes worked better on gravel than mine did. "Bloody Bones is a strange name for a bar and grill."

"Maybe they serve ribs," I said.

He made a face at me. "I could not face barbecue anything right now."

"It wouldn't be my first choice either."

The door swung inward directly into the bar. The door swung shut and we were plunged into a fire-shot twilight. Most bars are gloomy places to drink and hide. A place of refuge from the noisy shiny world outside. But as refuges went, this was a good one. There was a bar along one side of the room, and a dozen small tables scattered on the dark polished wood floor. There was a small stage to the left and a jukebox near the back wall where a small hallway probably led to bathrooms and the kitchen beyond.

Every surface was dark wood and polished 'til it shone. Candles with chimney glass over them shone from the walls. A chandelier with more chimney glass and candles hung from the low, dark wood ceiling. The wood was the darkest of mirrors, glowing in the light rather than reflecting it.

The beams that supported the ceiling were carved with fruiting vines and stray leaves that looked like oaks. Every face was turned towards us like a bad western. A lot of the faces were male; the eyes slid over me, saw Larry, and most went back to their drinks. A few stayed hopeful, but I ignored them. It was too early in the night for anybody to be drunk enough to give me grief. Besides, we were armed.

The women were grouped three deep at the bar. They were dressed for a Friday night, if you planned to spend Friday night on a street corner propositioning strangers. They stared at Larry like they wondered if he'd be good to eat. Me, they seemed to hate on sight. If I knew any of them, I'd have said they were jealous, but I'm not the kind of woman to elicit jealousy on sight. Not tall enough, not blonde enough, not Nordic enough, not exotic enough. I'm pretty, but I'm not beautiful. The women looked at me like they saw something I didn't. It made me glance behind me to see if someone had come in behind us, even though I knew no one had.

"What going on?" Larry whispered.

That was another thing. It was quiet. I'd never been in a bar on a Friday night that you could whisper in and be heard.

"I don't know," I said softly.

The women at the bar parted like someone had asked, giving us a clear view of the bar. There was a man behind the bar. I thought what beautiful hair *she* had when I first saw him. The hair fell to his waist like thick, chestnut-colored water. The candle flames gleamed in his hair the same way they shone in the polished wood of the bar.

He raised startling blue-green eyes, like deep sea water, to us. He was dark and lovely rather than handsome, androgynous as a cat. He was exotic as hell and I suddenly understood why the bar was three deep in women.

He sat an amber-filled glass down on a tiny napkin and said, "You're up, Earl." His voice was surprisingly low, like he'd sing deep bass.

A man got up from the tables, Earl probably. He was a large, lumbering man, formed of soft squares like a gentler version of Boris Karloff's monster. Not a cover boy. He reached for his drink, and his arm brushed the back of one of the women. The woman turned, angry. I expected her to tell him to go to hell, but the bartender touched her arm. She was suddenly very still, as if listening to voices I couldn't hear.

The air wavered. I was suddenly very aware that Earl smelled of soap and water. His hair was still damp from the shower. I could lick the water from his skin, feel those big hands on my body.

I shook my head and stepped back into Larry. He caught my arm. "What's wrong?"

I stared at him, clutching his arm, my fingers digging through the cloth of his suit, until I could feel his arm solid under my hand. I turned back to the bar.

Earl and the woman had gone to sit at a table. She was kissing the palm of his calloused hand.

"Jesus," I said.

"What's wrong, Anita?" Larry asked.

I took a deep breath and stood away from him. "I'm okay; it was just unexpected."

"What was?"

"Magic." I stepped up to the bar.

Those amazing eyes stared back at me, but there was no power to them. It wasn't like dealing with a vampire. I could gaze into those beautiful eyes forever, and they would still just be eyes. Sort of.

I placed my hands on the gleaming wood of the bar. More vines and leaves curved around the edge of the heavy wood. I ran my fingers over the deep set carvings. Hand-carved, all of it.

His fingertips caressed the wood like it was skin. It was a proprietal touch, the way some men touch their girlfriends when they're into ownership. I was betting that he'd carved every inch of it.

A brunette in a dress two sizes smaller than it should have been touched his arm. "Magnus, you don't need a stranger."

Magnus Bouvier turned to the brunette. He trailed those caressing fingertips down her arm. She shivered. He raised her hand gently from his arm, pressing his lips to the back of her hand. "Pick anyone you want, darlin', You are too beautiful to be denied tonight."

She wasn't beautiful. Her eyes were small and muddy brown, her chin too sharp, nose too large for a thin face. I was staring right at her from not a foot away, and her face smoothed. Her eyes were suddenly large and sparkling, her thin lips full and moist. It was like seeing her through one of those soft filters they used during the sixties, except more.

I glanced at Larry. He looked like he'd been hit by a truck. A slim, lovely truck. I stared out over the bar, and every other male in the place except Earl was staring at the woman in exactly the same way, as if she'd just appeared before them like Cinderella transformed by her fairy godmother. Not a bad analogy.

I turned back to Magnus Bouvier. He was not staring at the woman. He was staring at me.

I leaned into the bar, meeting his gaze. He smiled slightly. I said, "Love charms are illegal."

The smile widened. "You're much too pretty to be the police." He reached out to touch my arm.

"Touch me and I'll have you arrested for using undue preternatural influence."

"It's a misdemeanor," he said.

"Not if you're not human, it isn't," I said.

He blinked at me. I didn't know him well enough to be sure, but I think I surprised him, like I should have believed he was human. Yeah, right.

"Let's talk at a table," he said.

"Fine with me."

"Dorrie, can you take over for a few minutes?"

A woman came behind the bar. She had the same thick chestnut hair, but it was tied back from her face in a severe ponytail, high and tight on her head. The long, shining tail of hair swung as she moved, like it was alive. Her face, free of hair and makeup, was triangular, exotic, catlike. Her eyes were the same startling seawater green as Magnus's.

The men nearest the bar watched her out of the corners of their eyes, as if afraid to look directly at her. Larry stared at her open-mouthed.

"I'll watch the bar, but that's all," she said. She turned those eyes to Larry and said, "What are you staring at?" Her voice was harsh, thick with scorn.

Larry blinked, closed his mouth, and stuttered. "N-nothing."

She glared at him like she knew he was lying. I got an inkling why the men weren't staring at her.

"Dorcas, be nice to the customers."

She glared at Magnus; he smiled, but he backed down. Magnus stepped out from behind the bar. He was wearing a soft blue dress shirt untucked over jeans so faded they were almost white. The shirt hit him at nearly mid-thigh; he'd had to roll the sleeves over his forearms. Black and silver cowboy boots completed the outfit. Everything but the boots looked borrowed. He should have looked sloppy, too casual among everyone else duded up for a Friday night, but he didn't. His utter confidence made the outfit seem perfect. A woman at one of the tables grabbed the hem of his shirt as he moved passed. He pulled it out of her hands with a playful smile.

Magnus led us to a table near the empty stage. He stood, letting me choose my seat; very gentlemanly of him. I sat with my back to the wall so I could see both doors and the room. It was sort of cowboyish, but magic rode the air. Illegal magic.

Larry sat to my right. He'd watched me and scooted his chair a little back from the table so he could see the room too. It was almost frightening how seriously Larry watched what I did. It would keep him alive, but it was like being followed around by a three-year-old with a carry permit. Kind of intimidating.

Magnus smiled at us both, indulgently, like we were doing something cute or amusing. I wasn't in the mood to be amusing.

"Love charms are illegal," I said.

"You said that already," Magnus said. He flashed me a smile that I think was meant to be charming and harmless. It wasn't. There wasn't anything he could do to make himself less than exotic. He sure as hell wasn't harmless.

I stared at him until the smile wilted around the edges, and he swallowed. He spread his long-fingered hands on the tabletop, staring at them. When he looked up, the smile was gone. He looked solemn, a little nervous even. Good.

"It's not a charm," he said.

"The hell it isn't," I said.

"It isn't. A spell, but nothing as mundane as a charm."

"You're splitting hairs," I said.

Larry was staring at us intently. "Was that stuff at the bar a love charm?"

"What stuff at the bar?" Magnus's face was incredibly mild, as if he thought Larry would believe him.

Larry looked at me. "Is he kidding? The woman went from a three to a twenty-three. It had to be magic."

Magnus turned his attention to Larry for the first time, excluding me— and I felt excluded. It was like a ray of sunshine had moved away from me, and I was just a little colder, a little more in the dark.

I shook my head. "Cut the glamor crap."

Magnus turned back to me, and for a minute I felt that warmth. "Stop it."

"What?"

I stood up. "Fine; let's see how funny you think you are in jail."

Magnus encircled my wrist with his hand. His skin should have been work-roughened, but it wasn't. His skin was unnaturally soft, like living velvet. Of course, that could have been illusionary, too.

I tried to pull my hand away, but his grip tightened. I kept pulling, and he kept tightening with that certainty of some-one who knew that I couldn't get away. He was wrong. It wasn't just a matter of strength, it was a matter of leverage.

I turned my wrist towards his fingers in a quick turning motion, jerking at the same time. His fingers slid over my skin trying to dig in, but it was over. My wrist felt rubbed raw where his finger had scraped along the skin. It wasn't bleeding, but it hurt anyway. It would have felt better if I rubbed it, but I wouldn't give him the satisfaction. I was, after all, a tough-as-nails vampire slayer. Besides, it would have ruined some of the effect, and I liked the surprise on Magnus's face.

"Most women don't pull away once I've touched them."

"You use magic on me one more time, and I'll feed you to the cops."

He stared up at me, a thoughtful look on his face. He nod-ded. "You win. No more magic on you or your friend."

"Or anyone else," I said. I sat back down carefully, putting a little more distance between me and him. I angled the chair just a little to one side so the grab for my gun would be smoother. I didn't think I'd have to shoot him, but my wrist was aching where he'd squeezed. I had arm wres-tled with vampires and shapeshifters. I knew preternatural strength when I felt it. He had it. He could have squeezed until my bones popped out of my skin, but he hadn't squeezed fast enough. He hadn't really wanted to hurt me. His mistake.

"Oh, my customers wouldn't like the magic going away," he said.

"You can't manipulate them like this. It is illegal, and I will turn you in for it."

"But everyone knows that Friday night is lovers' night at Bloody Bones," Magnus said.

"What's lovers' night?" Larry asked.

Magnus smiled, already regaining some of his easy charm, but that flicker of warmth was gone. He was being true to his word, as far as I could tell. Even vampires couldn't work mind control on me without my knowing it. That Magnus could made me nervous.

"I make everyone beautiful or handsome, or sexy, tonight. For a few hours you can be the lover of your own dreams, and someone else's. Though I wouldn't spend the night. The glamor doesn't last that long."

"What are you?" Larry asked.

"What looks like *Homo sapiens*, can breed with *Homo sapiens*, but isn't *Homo sapiens*?" I asked.

Larry's eyes widened. "*Homo arcanus.* He's a fairie?"

"Please keep your voice down," Magnus said. He glanced around at the near tables. No one was playing much attention to us. They were too busy gazing into each other's magically enhanced eyes.

"You can't be passing for human," I said.

"The Bouviers have told the future and made love charms for centuries around here."

"You said it wasn't a love charm," I said.

"They think it is, but you know what it is."

"Glamor," I said.

"What's glamor?" Larry asked.

"It's fairie magic. It's what allows them to cloud our minds, make things seem better or worse than they are."

Magnus nodded, smiling, as if pleased that I knew so much. "Exactly; it's really a minor magic compared to some."

I shook my head. "I've read about glamor, and it doesn't work this well unless you're high court, *Daoine Sidhe*. The seelie court of fairyland doesn't interbreed with mortals often. At least not commoners. The unseelie court, on the other hand, does."

He stared at me with his beautiful eyes, looking, even without glamor, so gorgeous you wanted to touch him. Wanted to see if his hair was as luxuriant as it looked. He was like a really fine sculpture; you wanted to run your hands over it and feel the lines.

Magnus smiled gently. "The unseelie court is evil, cruel. What I do here is not evil. For one night these people can come here and be their own fantasies. They think it's love charms, and I let them. We all keep the secret of this small illegal act. The local police know. They even come down once in a while and join in."

"But it's not love charms."

"No, it's natural talent on my part. Using my own home-grown magic isn't illegal if everyone knows I'm doing it."

"So you pretend it's love charms, and everyone looks the other way because they're having a good time, but it's really fairie glamor, which isn't illegal with permission of the participants."

"Exactly," he said.

"Which makes it all legal."

He nodded. "Now if I was descended from the dark side of fairie, would I do anything to bring pleasure to so many?"

"If it suited your needs, yeah."

"Isn't there a ban on unseelie court moving to this country?" Larry asked.

"Yeah," I said.

"Not if my family moved here before the ban went into effect. The Bouviers have been here for nearly three hundred years."

"Not possible," I said. "Nobody but the Indians have been here that long."

"Llyn Bouvier was a French fur trapper. He was the first European to set foot on this land. He married into the local tribe, Christianized them."

"Bully for him. So how come you didn't want to sell to Raymond Stirling?"

He blinked at me. "It would disappoint me greatly to find out you are working for him."

"Sorry to disappoint you," I said.

"What are you?"

He hadn't asked who, he'd asked what. It was a very different question. It sort of stopped me for a second.

"I'm Anita Blake; this is Larry Kirkland. We're animators."

"I take it you don't draw cartoons," he said.

It made me smile. "No. We raise the dead; 'animate' from the Latin, to give life."

"Is that all you do?" He was staring at me very intently,

like there was something written on the inside of my skull and he was trying to read it.

It was an uncomfortable level of scrutiny, but I've been stared at by the best. I met his eyes and answered. "I'm a licensed vampire executioner."

He shook his head gently. "I didn't ask what you did for a living. I asked what you were."

I frowned. "Maybe I don't understand the question."

"Perhaps you don't, but your friend asked what I was. You said I was a fairie. I ask you what you are, and you describe your job. It would be like me saying I'm a bartender."

"I don't know how to answer you, then," I said.

He was still staring at me. "Yes, you do. I can see a word in your eyes. One word."

When he said it, a word did come to mind. "Necromancer. I'm a necromancer."

Magnus nodded. "Does Mr. Stirling know what you are?"

"I doubt he'd understand even if I told him."

"Do you really have the ability to control all types of undead?" Magnus asked.

"Can you really make a hundred shoes in a single night?" I asked.

Magnus smiled. "Wrong kind of fairie."

"Yeah," I said.

"If you're working for Stirling, why are you here? I hope you didn't come here to try to persuade me to sell. I'd hate to have to say no to such a lovely woman."

"Can the compliments, Magnus. It won't get you anywhere."

"What would get me somewhere?"

I sighed. "I've got too many men on my plate now."

"That's the God's honest truth," Larry muttered.

I frowned at him.

"I'm not asking you out on a date. I'm asking you into my bed."

I frowned at Magnus. No, glared was a better word. "Not in this lifetime."

"Sex between supernatural beings is always amazing, Anita."

"I'm not a supernatural being."

"Now who's splitting hairs?"

I didn't know what to say to that, so I said nothing. I rarely get in trouble with silence.

Magnus smiled. "I've made you uncomfortable. I am sorry, but I'd never have forgiven myself if I hadn't asked. It's been a long time since I was with anyone who wasn't straight human. Let me buy you both drinks, to make up for my rudeness."

I shook my head. "Menus would be fine. We haven't eaten yet."

"The meals will be on the house."

"No," I said.

"Why not?"

"Because I don't particularly like you, and I don't take favors from people I don't like."

He sat back in his chair, a strange, almost startled expression on his face. "You are direct."

"You have no idea," Larry said.

I resisted the urge to kick Larry under the table and said, "Can we have some menus?"

He raised a hand and called, "Two menus, Dorrie."

Dorrie brought them over. "I'm part owner of this place, not your waitress, Magnus. Hurry it up."

"Don't forget that appointment I've got tonight, Dorrie." His voice was mild. She wasn't fooled.

"You aren't leaving me alone with these people. I will not . . ." She glanced at us. "I don't approve of lovers' night. You know that."

"I'll take care of everybody before I leave. You won't have to sully your morals."

She glared at all of us in turn. "You're leaving with them?"

"No," he said.

She turned on her heel and stalked back to the bar. The men who weren't paired off watched her swaying back, carefully, not staring until she couldn't see them.

"Your sister doesn't approve of abusing glamor?" I asked.

"Dorrie doesn't approve of a lot of things."

"She has morals."

"Implying I don't," he said.

I shrugged. "You said it, not me."

"She always this judgmental?" he asked Larry.

Larry nodded. "Usually."

"Let's just order our food," I said.

Larry smiled, but he looked down at the menu.

It was a laminated piece of paper printed on both sides. I ordered a cheeseburger, well done, house fries, and a large Coke. I hadn't had caffeine in several hours; I was running low.

Larry was frowning at the menu. "I don't think I could eat a hamburger right now."

"They've got salads," I said.

Magnus laid his fingertips against the back of Larry's hand. "Something swims up behind your eyes. Something . . . awful just behind your eyes."

Larry stared at him. "I don't know what you mean."

I grabbed Magnus's wrist and pulled him away from Larry. He turned his eyes to me, but there was more than just their color to make them hard to stare at. The pupil of his eyes had spiraled down like the eye of a bird. Human eyes just didn't do that.

I was suddenly very aware that I was still holding his wrist. I drew my hand away. "Stop reading us, Magnus."

"You wore gloves, or I'd be able to tell what you'd touched," he said.

"It's an ongoing police investigation. Anything you discern by psychic means must be held confidential, or you're liable just as if you stole information out of our files."

"Do you always do that?" he asked.

"What?"

"Quote the law when you're nervous."

"Sometimes," I said.

"I saw blood, that's all. My gifts are rather limited in the area of far-seeing. You should shake Dorrie's hand. Far-seeing is her strong suit."

"Thanks, but no thanks," Larry said.

He smiled. "You are not police, or you wouldn't have

threatened me with the police, but you were with them earlier. Why?"

"I thought all you saw was blood," I said.

He had the grace to look embarrassed; nice to know he could be embarrassed. "A little bit more, perhaps."

"Touch clairvoyance isn't a traditional fey power."

"Our many-times-great-grandmother was the daughter of a shaman, so the story goes."

"Getting magic from both sides of the family tree," I said. "Dirty pool."

"Clairvoyance isn't magic," Larry said.

"A really good clairvoyant will make you think it is," I said. I stared at Magnus. The last clairvoyant who had touched me and seen blood had been horrified. He hadn't wanted to touch me again. He hadn't wanted me anywhere near him. Magnus didn't look horrified, and he'd offered to have sex with me. Different strokes for different folks.

"I'll take your order through to the kitchen myself, if you'll just decide what you want," he said.

Larry stared at the menu. "A salad, I guess. No dressing." He thought about it some more. "No tomatoes."

Magnus started to stand.

"Why won't you sell to Stirling?" I asked.

Magnus cocked his head to one side, smiling. "The land has been in our family for centuries. It's our land."

I looked at him and couldn't read his face. It could have been the absolute truth, or a bold-faced lie.

"So the only reason you don't want to be a millionaire is because of what . . . family tradition?"

The smile deepened. He leaned closer, long hair spilling forward. He whispered, and it was quiet enough that he needed to whisper. "Money is not everything, Anita. Though Stirling seems to think it is."

His face was very close, just barely far enough away for me not to complain. I could smell his aftershave, faint as if you'd have to get very near his skin to smell it, but it would be worth the effort.

"What do you want, Magnus, if it's not money?" I stared at him from too close. His long hair trailed over my hand.

"I told you what I wanted."

Even without the glamor he was trying to sweet-talk me, distract me. "What happened to the trees out by your road?" I didn't distract that easily

He blinked long lashes. Something slid behind his eyes. "I happened."

"You cut down those trees?" Larry asked.

Magnus turned to him, and I was glad not to be staring at him from inches away. "Sadly, yes."

"Why?" I asked.

He straightened up, suddenly businesslike. "I got drunk and went on a little rampage." He shrugged. "Embarrassing, isn't it?"

"That's one word for it," I said.

"I'll go get your food. One naked salad coming up."

"You remember what I'm getting?" I asked.

"Meat burned to death; I remember."

"You sound like a vegetarian."

"Oh, no," he said. "I eat all sorts of things."

He walked away through the crowd before I could decide if I'd been insulted or not. Just as well. For the life of me, I couldn't think of a good comeback line.

10

DORCAS BROUGHT OUR food without a word. She seemed angry—maybe not at us, but with us. Or with everything. I sympathized. Magnus went behind the bar, spreading his own special brand of magic to his customers once more. He glanced our way and smiled but didn't come back to finish our talk. Of course; we'd been finished. I was all out of questions.

I took a bite of my cheeseburger. It was almost crispy around the edges, not a smidgen of pink in the center. Perfect.

"What's wrong?" Larry asked. He was nibbling at a lettuce leaf.

I swallowed. "Why should something be wrong?"

"You're frowning," he said.

"Magnus didn't come back to the table."

"So? He answered all our questions."

"Maybe we just don't know the right questions to ask."

"You suspect him of something now?" Larry shook his head. "You have been hanging around with cops too long, Anita. You think everyone's up to something."

"They usually are." I took another bite of burger.

Larry squinched his eyes tight.

"What's wrong with you?" I asked.

"There's juice coming out of your burger. How can you eat that after what we just saw?"

"I guess this means you don't want me to put ketchup on my fries."

He looked at me with something near physical pain on his face. "How can you make jokes?"

My beeper went off. Had they found the vampire? I hit the button, and Dolph's number flashed at me. Now what?

"It's Dolph. Eat hearty. I'll phone from the Jeep and be back."

Larry stood up with me. He put a tip on the table and left his salad nearly untouched. "I'm done."

"Well, I'm not. Have Magnus pack my meal to go." I left him staring forlornly down at my half-eaten burger.

"You're not going to eat it in the car, are you?"

"Just have it packed up." I went for the Jeep and its fancy phone.

Dolph answered on the third ring. "Anita?"

"Yeah, Dolph, it's me. What's up?"

"Vampire victim out near you."

"Shit, another one."

"What do you mean another one?"

That stopped me. "Freemont didn't call you after I talked to her?"

"Yeah, she said good things about you."

"That surprises me; she wasn't too friendly."

"How not friendly?"

"She wouldn't let me hunt vampires with her."

"Tell me," Dolph said.

I told him.

Dolph was quiet for a very long time after I finished.

"You still there, Dolph?"

"I'm here. I wish I wasn't."

"What's going on, Dolph? Why would Freemont call and tell you what a good job I'm doing, but not ask for the squad's help on something this big?"

"I bet she hasn't called the Feds either," Dolph said.

"What's going on, Dolph?"

"I think Detective Freemont is pulling a Lone Ranger on us."

"The federal boys are going to want a piece of this. The first vampire serial killer in recorded history. Freemont can't keep it to herself."

"I know," Dolph said.

"What are we going to do?"

"The body on the ground this time sounds like a straight-forward vampire kill. It's classic, bite marks, no other damage to the body. Could it be a different vamp?"

"Could be," I said.

"You sound doubtful."

"Two rogue vamps in this small a geographical area, this far from a city, doesn't seem likely."

"The body wasn't cut up."

"There is that," I said.

"How sure are you that the first killer is a vamp? Is there anything else it could be?"

I opened my mouth to say no, and closed it. Anybody who could cut down all those trees in one drunken brawl could certainly cut up people. Magnus had his glamor. I wasn't sure it was capable of doing what I'd seen in the clearing, but . . .

"Anita?"

"I might have an alternative."

"What?"

"Who," I said. I hated giving Magnus up to the cops. He'd

kept his secret so long, but . . . what if the question I should ask was, had he killed five people? I'd felt the strength in his hands. I remembered the clean trunks of the trees, cut by just one blow, two at most. I flashed on the murder scene. The blood, the naked bone. I couldn't rule Magnus out, and I couldn't afford to be wrong.

I gave him up to Dolph. "Can you keep the part about him being fairie out of it for a while?"

"Why?"

"Because if he didn't do it, then his life is ruined."

"A lot of people have fey blood in them, Anita."

"Tell that to the college student last year whose fiance beat her to death when he found out he was about to marry a fairie. He protested in court that he hadn't meant to kill her. The fey were supposed to be hard to kill, weren't they?"

"Not everyone is like that, Anita."

"Not everyone, but enough."

"I'll try, Anita, but I can't promise."

"Fair enough," I said. "Where's the new victim?"

"Monkey's Eyebrow," he said.

"What?"

"That's the name of the town."

"Jesus. Monkey's Eyebrow, Missouri. Let me guess. It's a small town."

"Big enough to have a sheriff and a murder."

"Sorry. Do you have directions?" I fished my small, spiral-bound notebook out of the pocket of the black jacket.

He gave me directions. "Sheriff St. John is holding the body for you. He called us first. Since Freemont wants to go it alone, we'll let her."

"You're not going to tell her?"

"No."

"I don't suppose Monkey's Eyebrow has a crime scene unit, Dolph. If we don't have Freemont come in with her people, we're going to need somebody. Can you guys come down yet?"

"We're still working our own murder. But since Sheriff St. John called us in for his murder, we'll be in the area as soon as we can get there. Not tonight, but tomorrow."

"Freemont's supposed to send over crime-scene photos from the first couple that was killed. I bet if I asked she might send over photos from the second scene, too. Show-and-tell tomorrow when you get here "

"Freemont may be suspicious about you asking for more pictures," Dolph said.

"I'll tell her I want them for comparison. She may be trying to hog the case for herself, but she wants it solved. She just wants to solve it herself."

"She's a glory hound," Dolph said.

"Looks that way."

"I don't know if I'll be able to keep Freemont out of the second case or not, but I'll try to give you some lead time, so you can look around without her breathing down your neck."

"Much appreciated."

"She said you had your assistant with you at the crime scene. Had to be Larry Kirkland, right?"

"Right."

"What are you doing bringing him to crime scenes?"

"He'll have a degree in preternatural biology this spring. He's an animator and a vampire slayer. I can't be everywhere, Dolph. If I think he can handle it, I thought it might be nice to have two monster experts."

"It might. Freemont said Larry lost his lunch all over the crime scene."

"He didn't throw up on the crime scene, just near it."

There was a moment of silence. "Better than throwing up on the body."

"I'm never going to live that down, am I?"

"No," Dolph said, "you aren't."

"Great. Larry and I will get out there as soon as we can. It's about a thirty-minute drive, maybe more."

"I'll tell Sheriff St. John you're on your way." He hung up.

I hung up. Dolph was training me never to say good-bye over the phone.

11

LARRY SLUMPED IN the seat as far as the seat belt would let him. His hands were clenched tight in his lap. He stared out into the dark like he was seeing something besides the passing scenery. Images of butchered teenagers dancing in his head, I bet. They weren't dancing in mine. Not yet. I might see them in my dreams, but not awake, not yet.

"How bad will this one be?" he asked. His voice sounded quiet, strained.

"I don't know. It's a vampire victim. Could be neat, just a couple of puncture wounds; could be carnage."

"Carnage like the three boys?"

"Dolph said no, said it's classic, just bite marks."

"So it won't be messy?" His voice was squeezed down to a near whisper.

"Won't know until we get there," I said.

"You couldn't just comfort me?" His voice sounded so small, so uncertain that I almost offered to turn the Jeep around. He didn't have to see another murder scene. It was my job, but it wasn't his job, not yet.

"You don't ever have to see another murder scene, Larry."

He turned his head and looked at me. "What do you mean?"

"You've had your quota of blood and guts for one day. I can turn around and drop you back at the hotel."

"If I don't come tonight, what happens next time?"

"If you aren't cut out for this kind of work, you aren't cut out for it. No shame in that."

"What about next time?" he asked.

"There won't be a next time."

"You aren't getting rid of me that easy," he said.

I hoped the darkness hid the smile on my face. I kept it small.

"Tell me about vampires, Anita. I thought a vampire couldn't drink enough blood in one night to kill somebody."

"Pretty to think so," I said.

"They told us in college that a vampire couldn't drain a human being with one bite. Are you saying that's not true?"

"They can't drink a human dry with one bite, in one night, but they can drain one with one bite."

He frowned at me. "What's that supposed to mean?"

"They can pierce the flesh and drain the blood without drinking it."

"How?" he asked.

"Just put the fangs in, start the blood flow, and let the blood fall down your body onto the ground."

"But that's not taking blood for food, that's just murder," Larry said.

"And your point is?" I said.

"Hey, isn't that our turnoff?"

I caught a glimpse of the road sign. "Damn." I slowed down, but couldn't see over the crest of the hill. I didn't dare U-turn until I was sure there were no cars coming the other way. It was another half mile before we came to a gravel road. There was a row of mailboxes beside the road.

Trees grew so close to the road that even winter-bare they covered the one-lane road in shadows. There was no place to turn around. Hell, if a second car had come, one of us would have had to back up.

The road rose up and up, as if it were going to go straight into the sky. At the crest of the hill I could see nothing in front of the car. I had to simply trust that there was more road in front of us, rather than some endless precipice.

"Jesus, this is steep," Larry said.

I eased the Jeep forward and the tires touched road. My shoulders loosened just a little. There was a house just up ahead. The porch light was on, like they were expecting company. The bare light bulb was not kind. The house was unpainted wood with a rusting tin roof. Its raised porch sagged under the weight of the front seat of a car that was sitting by the screen door. I turned around in the dirt in front of the house that passed for a front yard. It looked like we weren't the first car to do it. There were deep wheel ruts in the powder-dry dirt from years of cars turning in and out.

By the time we got down to the end of the road, the darkness was pure as velvet. I hit the Jeep's high beams, but it was like driving in a tunnel. The world existed only in the light; everything else was blackness.

"I'd give a lot for a few streetlights right now," Larry said.

"Me, too. Help me spot our road. I don't want to drive past it twice."

He leaned forward in his seat, straining against the shoulder belt. "There." He pointed as he spoke. I slowed and turned carefully onto the road. The headlights filled the tunnel of trees. This road was just bare red earth. The dirt rose in a mist around the Jeep. For once I was glad of the drought. Mud would have been a real bitch on a dirt road.

The road was wide enough that if you had nerves of steel, or were driving someone else's car, you could drive two cars abreast. A stream cut across the road, with a ditch at least fifteen feet deep. The bridge was nothing but planks laid across some beams. No rails, no nothing. As the Jeep crept over the bridge, the planks rattled and moved. They weren't nailed in. God.

Larry was staring at the drop, his face pressed against the tinted glass. "This bridge isn't much wider than the car."

"Thanks for telling me, Larry. I'd have never noticed on my own."

"Sorry."

Past the bridge, the road was still wide enough for two cars. I guess if two cars met at the bridge they took turns. There was probably some traffic law to cover it. First car on the left gets to go first, maybe.

At the crest of the hill, lights showed in the distance. Police lights strobed the darkness like muticolored lightning. They were farther away than they looked. We had two more hills to go up and down before the lights reflected off the bare trees, making them look black and unreal. The road spilled into a wide clearing. A lawn spread up from the road, surrounding a large white house. It was a real house with siding and shutters and a wraparound porch. It was two-storied and edged with neatly trimmed shrubs. The driveway was white gravel, which meant someone had shipped it in. Narcissus edged the driveway in two thick stripes.

A uniformed policeman stopped us in the foot of the sloping drive. He was tall, big through the shoulders, and had dark hair. He shined a flashlight into the car. "I'm sorry, miss, but you can't go up there right now."

I flashed my ID at him and said, "I'm Anita Blake. I'm with the Regional Preternatural Investigation Team. I was told Sheriff St. John is expecting me."

He leaned into the open window and flashed his light at Larry. "Who's this?"

"Larry Kirkland. He's with me."

He stared at Larry for a few seconds. Larry smiled, doing his best to look harmless. He's almost as good at it as I am.

I had a good view of the cop's gun as he leaned into the window. It was a Colt .45. Big gun, but he had the hands for it. I caught a whiff of his aftershave; Brut. He'd leaned too far into the window to look at Larry. If I'd had a gun hidden in my lap, I could have fed it to him. He was big, and I bet sheer size saw him through a lot, but it was careless. Guns don't care how big you are.

He nodded and pulled out the car. "Go on up to the house. Sheriff's expecting you." He didn't sound particularly happy about that.

"You got a problem?" I asked.

He gave a smile, but it was sour. He shook his head. "It's our case. I don't think we need any help; that includes you."

"You got a name?" I asked.

"Coltrain. Deputy Zack Coltrain."

"Well, Deputy Coltrain, we'll see you up at the house."

"I guess you will, Miss Blake."

He thought I was a cop and deliberately didn't call me "officer" or "detective." I let it go. If I really had a professional title I'd have demanded it, but getting into an argument because he wouldn't call me "detective" when I wasn't one seemed counterproductive.

I drove up and parked between the police cars. I clipped my ID to my lapel. We walked up the pale curve of sidewalk, and no one stopped us. We stood outside the door in a silence that was almost eerie. I'd been to a lot of murder scenes. One thing they weren't was silent. There was no static crackle of police radios, no men milling around. Murder scenes were always thick with people: plainclothes detectives, uniforms, crime scene techs, people taking photographs, video, the ambulance waiting to take the body away. We stood on the freshly swept porch in the cool spring night with the only sounds the calls of frogs. The high-pitched, peeping sound played oddly with the swirling police lights.

"Are we waiting for something?" Larry asked.

"No," I said. I rang the glowing doorbell. The sound gave a rich *bong* deep within the house. A small dog barked furiously, somewhere deep in the house. The door opened. A woman stood framed in the light from the hall, placing most of her in shadow. The police lights strobed across her face, painting in neon Crayloa flashes. She was about my height with dark hair that was either naturally curly or had a really good perm. But she'd done more with it than I did, and it framed her face neatly. Mine always looked sort of unruly. She was wearing a button-down shirt with long sleeves untucked over jeans. She looked about seventeen, but I wasn't fooled. I looked young for my age, too. Heck, so did Larry. It can't just be being short, can it?

"You aren't the state police," she said. She seemed very sure of that.

"I'm with the Regional Preternatural Investigation Team," I said. "Anita Blake. This is my colleague Larry Kirkland."

Larry smiled and nodded.

The woman moved back out of the door, and the light from the hallway fell full on her face. It added five years to her age, but they were a good five years. It took me a minute to realize she was wearing very understated makeup. "Please come in, Miss Blake. My husband, David is waiting with the body." She shook her head. "It's awful."

She peered out into the colored darkness before she closed the door. "David told him to turn off those lights. We don't want everyone for miles to know what's happened."

"What's your name?" I asked.

She blushed slightly. "I'm sorry; I'm not usually this scattered. I'm Beth St. John. My husband is the sheriff. I've been sitting with the parents." She made a small motion towards a set of double doors to the left of the main entrance.

The dog was still barking behind those doors like a small furry machine gun. A man's voice said, "Quiet Raven." The barking stopped.

We were standing in an entryway that had a ceiling that soared up to the roof, as if the architect had cut a piece out of the room above us to create the sweeping space. A crystal chandelier sparkled light down on us. The light cut a rectangle out of the darkened room to our right. There was a glimpse of a cherrywood dining room set so polished it gleamed.

The hallway cut straight back to a distant door that probably led to the kitchen. Stairs ran along the wall with the double doors. The bannister and door edges were white, the carpet was pale blue, the wallpaper white with tiny blue flowers and tinier leaves. It was open and airy, bright and welcoming, and utterly quiet. If we could have found a piece of uncarpeted floor, we would have dropped a pin and listened to it bounce.

Beth St. John led us up the blue-and-white stairway. In the center of the hallway on the right-hand side was a series of family portraits. They began with a smiling couple; smiling couple and smiling baby; smiling couple and one smiling baby, one crying baby. I walked down the hallway, watching the years pass by. The babies became children, a girl and a boy. A miniature black poodle appeared in the pictures. The girl was the oldest, but only by about a year. The parents grew older, but didn't seem to mind. The parents and the girl smiled; sometimes the boy did, sometimes he didn't. The boy smiled more on the other wall where, the camera had caught him tanned with a fish, or with hair slicked back from just coming out of the pool. The girl smiled everywhere you looked. I wondered which of them was dead.

There was a window at the end of the hallway. The white drapes framed it; no one had bothered to draw them. The window looked like a black mirror. The darkness pressed against the glass like it had weight.

Beth St. John knocked on the last door to the right, next

to that pressing darkness. "David, the detectives are here." I let that slide. The sin of omission is a many-splendored thing.

I heard movement in the room, but she stepped back before the door could open. Beth St. John backed up into the middle of the hallway so there would be no chance of her seeing inside the room. Her eyes flicked from one picture to another, catching glimpses of smiling faces. She put a slender hand to her chest, as if she was having trouble breathing.

"I'm going to go make coffee. Do you want some?" Her voice was strained around the edges.

"Sure," I said.

"Sounds good," Larry said.

She gave a weak smile and marched down the hallway. She did not run, which got her a lot of brownie points in my book. I was betting it was Beth St. John's first murder scene.

The door opened. David St. John was wearing a pale blue uniform that matched the one his deputy wore, but there the resemblance ended. He was about five-foot-ten, thin without being skinny, like a marathon runner. His hair was a paler, browner version of Larry's red. You noticed his glasses before you noticed his eyes, but the eyes were worth noticing. A perfect pale green like a cat's. Except for the eyes it was a very ordinary face, but it was one of those faces you wouldn't grow tired of.

He offered me his hand. I took it. He barely touched my hand, as if afraid to squeeze. A lot of men did that, but at least he offered to shake hands; most don't bother.

"I'm Sheriff St. John. You must be Anita Blake. Sergeant Storr told me you'd be coming." He glanced at Larry. "Who's this?"

"Larry Kirkland."

St. John's eyes narrowed. He stepped fully into the hallway, closing the door behind him. "Sergeant Storr didn't mention anyone else. Can I see some ID?"

I unclipped my badge ID. He looked at it and shook his head. "You're not a detective."

"No, I'm not." I was mentally cursing Dolph. I'd known it wouldn't work.

"How about him?" He jerked his chin at Larry.

"All I have on me is a driver's license," Larry said.

"Who are you?" the sheriff asked.

"I am Anita Blake. I am part of the Spook Squad. I just don't happen to have a badge. Larry is a trainee." I fished my new vampire executioner's license out of my jacket pocket. It looked like a glorified driver's license, but it was the best I had.

He peered at the license. "You're a vampire hunter? It's a little early for you to be called in. I don't know who did it yet."

"I'm attached to Sergeant Storr's squad. I come in at the start of a case instead of the end. It tends to keep the body count down that way."

He handed back the license. "I didn't think Brewster's law had gone into effect."

Brewster was the senator whose daughter got eaten. "It hasn't. I've been working with the police for a long time."

"How long?"

"Nearly three years."

He smiled. "Longer than I've been sheriff." He nodded, almost as if he'd answered a question for himself. "Sergeant Storr said if anybody could help me solve this, it was you. If the head of RPIT has that much confidence in you, I'm not going to refuse the help. We've never had a vampire kill out here, ever."

"Vampires tend to stay near cities," I said. "They can hide their victims better that way."

"Well, no one tried to hide this one." He pushed the door open and made a little arm gesture, ushering us in.

The wallpaper was all pink roses, big old-fashioned cabbage roses. There was an honest-to-God vanity, with a raised mirror and everything, that looked like it might be an antique, but everything else was white wicker and pink lace. It looked like the room for a much younger girl.

The girl lay on the narrow bed. The bedspread matched the wallpaper. The sheets twisted up underneath her body were jellybean pink. Her head lay on the edge of the pillows, as if it had slipped to one side after she was laid on them.

The pink curtains fanned against the open window. A cool breeze crawled through the room, ruffling her thick black hair. It had been curled and styled with hair gel. There was a small red stain under her face and neck where the sheets had soaked up some blood. I was betting there was a bite mark on that side of the neck. She wore makeup not nearly as well applied as Beth St. John's, but the attempt had been made. The lipstick was badly smeared. One arm hung off into space, the hand half-cupped as if reaching for something. The nails were shiny with fresh red nail polish. Her long legs were spread-eagled on the bed. There were two fang marks high on her inner thigh—not fresh, though. Her toenails were painted to match her fingers.

She was still almost wearing the black teddy she'd started the night in. The straps had been pushed down her shoulders, exposing small, well-formed breasts. The crotch had been ripped out, or was one of the ones that snapped open, because the bottom was pushed up nearly to her waist until the teddy was little more than a belt. With her legs spread wide, she was completely exposed.

That, more than anything, pissed me off. He could have at least covered her up, not left her like some whore. It was arrogant and cruel.

Larry was standing across the room at the other window. It was open too, spilling cool air into the room.

"Have you touched anything?"

St. John shook his head.

"Have you taken any photos?"

"No."

I took a deep breath, reminding myself that I was a guest here and had no official status. I could not afford to piss him off. "What have you done?"

"Called you, and the state cops."

I nodded. "How long ago did you find the body?"

He checked his watch. "An hour ago. How did you get here so fast?"

"I wasn't ten miles away," I said.

"Lucky for me," he said.

I looked at the girl's body. "Yeah."

Larry was hugging the windowsill, gripping it with his hands. "Larry, why don't you run down to the Jeep and get some gloves out of my bag?"

"Gloves?"

"I've got a box of surgical gloves in with my animating stuff. Bring the box."

He swallowed hard and nodded. Every freckle stood out on his face like ink spots. He moved very quickly to the door and shut it behind him. I had two sets of gloves in my jacket pocket, but Larry needed air.

"This his first murder?"

"Second," I said. "How old is the girl?"

"Seventeen," he said.

"Then it's murder even if she consented."

"Consented? What are you talking about?" There was the very first hint of anger in his voice.

"What do you think happened here, Sheriff?"

"A vampire climbed in her window while she was getting ready for bed and killed her."

"Where's all the blood?"

"There's more blood under her neck. You can't see the mark, but that's where he drained her."

"That's not enough blood to kill her."

"He drank the rest." He sounded a little outraged.

I shook my head. "No single vampire can consume the entire blood supply of an adult human in one sitting."

"Then there was more than one," he said.

"You mean the bites on her thighs?"

"Yeah, yeah." He paced the pink shag carpet in quick, nervous strides.

"Those marks are at least a couple of days old," I said.

"So he hypnotized her twice before, but this time he killed her."

"It's awfully early for a teenager to be going to bed."

"Her mother said she wasn't feeling well."

That I believed. Even if you want it to happen, that much blood loss can take the sparkle out of your step.

"She fixed her hair and makeup before she went to bed," I said.

"So?"

"Did you know this girl?"

"Yes, hell yes. This is a small town, Miss Blake. We all know each other. She was a good kid, never in any trouble. You never found her parked with a boy, or out drinking. She was a good girl."

"I believe she was a good girl, Sheriff St. John. Being murdered doesn't make you a bad person."

He nodded, but his eyes were sort of wild, too much white showing. I wanted to ask how many murders he'd seen, but didn't. Whether this was his first or his twenty-first, he was sheriff.

"What do you think happened here, Sheriff?" I'd asked the question once, but I was willing to try it again.

"A vampire raped and killed Ellie Quinlan, that's what happened here." He said it almost defiantly, like he didn't believe it either."

"This wasn't rape, Sheriff. Ellie Quinlan invited her killer into this room."

He paced to the far window and stood like Larry had, staring out into the darkness. He wrapped his arms around himself like he was hugging himself. "How am I going to tell her parents, her kid brother, that she let some . . . thing make love to her? That she'd been letting it feed off her? How can I tell them that?"

"Well, in three nights, two counting tonight, Ellie can rise from the dead and tell them herself."

He turned back to me, his face pale with shock. He shook his head slowly. "They want her staked."

"What?"

"They want her staked. They don't want her to rise as a vampire."

I stared down at the still-warm body. I shook my head. "She'll rise in two more nights."

"The family doesn't want it."

"If she was a vampire, it would be murder to stake her just because her family doesn't want her to be one."

"But she's not a vampire yet," St. John said. "She's a corpse."

"The coroner will have to certify death before she can be staked. That can take a little time."

He shook his head. "I know Doc Campbell; he'll speed it along for us."

I stood there, staring down at the girl. "She didn't plan to die, Sheriff. This isn't a suicide. She's planning on coming back."

"You can't know that."

I stared at him. "I do know that, and so do you. If we stake her before she can rise from the dead, it's murder."

"Not according to the law."

"I am not going to take out the head and heart of a seventeen-year-old girl just because her parents don't like the lifestyle she's chosen."

"She's dead, Miss Blake."

"It's Ms. Blake, and I know she's dead. I know what she'll become. Probably better than you do."

"Then you understand why they want it done."

I looked at him. I did understand. There was a time when I could have done it and felt good about it. Felt like I was helping the family, freeing her soul. Now, I just wasn't sure anymore.

"Let her parents think about it for twenty-four hours. Trust me on this. They're horrified right now, and grief-stricken; are they really in a position to decide what happens to her?"

"They're her parents."

"Yeah, and two days from now would they rather have her on her feet, talking to them, or dead in a box?"

"She'll be a monster," he said.

"Maybe, probably, but I think we should hold off for just a little while until they've had some time. I think the immediate problem is the blood-sucker that did this."

"I agree, we find him and kill him."

"We can't kill him without a court order of execution," I said.

"I know the local judge. I can get you a court order."

"I bet you can."

"What's the matter with you? Don't you want to kill him?"

I looked at the girl. If he'd really wanted her to rise as a vampire, he'd have taken the body with him. He'd have hidden her until she rose to keep her safe from people like me. If he cared for her. "Yeah, I'll kill him for you."

"Alright, what can we do?"

"Well, first, the killing took place just after dark, so his daytime resting place had to be very near here. Are there any old houses, caves, some place where you could hide a coffin?"

"There's an old homestead about a mile from here, and I know there's a cave down along the stream. I used to go there when I was little. We all did."

"Here's the deal, Sheriff. If we go out into the dark after him now, he'll probably kill some of us. But if we don't try it tonight, he'll move his coffin. We might not find him again."

"We'll look for him tonight. Now."

"How long have you and your wife been married?" I asked.

"Five years; why?"

"You love her?"

"Yes, we were high school sweethearts. What kind of question is that?"

"If you go out after the vampire, you may never see her again. If you've never hunted one out there at night in its own territory, you don't know what we're up against, and nothing I can tell you will prepare you for it. But think about never seeing Beth again. Never holding her hand. Never hearing her voice. We can go out in the morning. The vampire may not move its coffin tonight, or it might move from the cave to the homestead, or vice versa. We might catch it tomorrow without risking anybody's life."

"Do you think it won't move tonight?"

I took a deep breath and wanted to lie. God knows I wanted to lie. "No, I think it'll leave the immediate area tonight. That's probably why he came just after full dark. It gives him all night to run."

"Then we go after him."

I nodded. "Okay, but we have to have some ground rules here. I'm in charge. I've done this before and I'm still alive; that makes me an expert. If you do everything I say, maybe, just maybe, we can all live until morning."

"Except for the vampire," St. John said.

"Yeah, sure." It had been a long time since I had gone up against a vampire at night in the open. My vampire kit was at home in my closet. It was illegal to carry it with me without a specific court order of execution. I had the cross I was wearing, the two handguns, the two knives, and that was it. No holy water, no extra crosses, no shotgun. Hell, no stake and mallet.

"Do you have silver bullets?"

"I can get some."

"Do it, and find me a shotgun and silver ammo for that too. Is there a Catholic or Episcopalian church around here?"

"Of course," he said.

"We need some holy water and holy wafer, the host."

"I know you can throw the holy water on the vampire, but I didn't know you could throw the host."

I had to smile. "They aren't like little holy grenades. I want the host to give to the Quinlans so they can put one at every windowsill, every doorsill."

"You think it'll come for them?"

"No, but the girl invited it in, only she can revoke the invitation, and she's dead. Until we get the bastard, better safe than sorry."

He hesitated, then nodded. "I'll go to the church. I'll see what I can do." He went for the door.

"And, Sheriff?"

He stopped and turned to me.

"I want that court order in my hands before we leave. I'm not going to be up on murder charges."

He nodded, sort of nervously, head bobbing like one of those dogs you see in the backs of cars. "You'll have it, Ms. Blake." He left, closing the door behind him.

I was left alone with the dead girl. She lay there pale and

unmoving, growing colder, deader. If her parents had their way, it would be permanent. And it would be my job to make it happen. There were schoolbooks scattered beside the bed, as if she had been studying in bed before he came. I pushed one of the book covers closed with my toe, careful not to rearrange it. Calculus. She'd been studying calculus before she put on her makeup and black teddy. Shit.

12

WHILE WE WAITED for the court order, I talked to the family. Not my favorite thing to do, but necessary. This hadn't been a random attack, which meant they probably knew the vampire, or had known him before he died.

The living room continued the pastel theme, blue predominating. Beth St. John had made coffee. She'd shanghaied Larry into carrying up a tray. I guess she didn't want to see the body again. Couldn't say I blamed her. I'd seen bloodier murder scenes, a lot bloodier, but each death has its own peculiar poignancy. There was something very piteous about Ellie Quinlan stretched across her pink candy sheets, and I hadn't known her. Beth St. John had. Made it hard.

The family sat huddled on the white sofa. The man was broad, not fat, but square like a linebacker. He had short black hair that was going nicely grey at the sideburns. Very distinguished. His complexion was ruddy, not tanned, but colorful just the same. He was dressed in a white dress shirt unbuttoned at the neck, but sleeves still sporting their cufflinks. His face was very tight, immobile like a mask, as if underneath something entirely different was going on. He looked calm, composed, but the effort thrummed along his skin. Anger glittered in his dark eyes.

His arm was around his wife's shoulders. She leaned into him crying softly, eyes closed as if that would make it better. Her eye makeup had smeared in long, multicolored steaks like an oil slick down her cheeks. She had thick black hair done in some short, complicated style that looked too stiff to touch. She wore a long-sleeved, button-down blouse with a delicate flower pattern on it, pink predominating. Her slacks were a matching pink. Her feet were bare except for dark hose. A delicate gold cross and wedding rings were her only jewelry.

The boy was only about my height and slender as a willow. He hadn't hit his growth spurt yet, and it made him look younger than he was. His face had that soft, perfect skin that said he'd never had a pimple and shaving was a distant dream. If the girl was seventeen, he had to be at least fifteen, maybe sixteen. He could have passed for twelve. A perfect victim, except for his eyes and the way he held himself. Even in the midst of grief with the lines of tears drying on his face, he looked sure of himself, self-possessed. His eyes held a quick intelligence and a rage that would hold the bullies at bay.

His hair was the perfect black of his father's, but it was baby fine, probably the natural texture of Mrs. Quinlan's before she styled it to death.

A little black poodle was in his lap. It had barked like a machine gun, rat-a-tat-tat, yip-yip-yip until he'd picked it up and held it. A soft growl tickled out of its curly jaws.

"Hush, Raven," the boy said. He petted the dog as he said it, thus rewarding the growling. The dog growled again; he petted it again. I decided to ignore it. If the poodle got loose, I figured I could take it. I was armed.

"Mr. and Mrs. Quinlan, my name's Anita Blake. I need to ask you a few questions."

"Have you staked the body yet?" the man asked.

"No, Mr. Quinlan, the sheriff and I agreed to wait twenty-four hours."

"Her immortal soul is in jeopardy. We want it done now."

"If you still want it done tomorrow night, I'll do it."

"We want it done now." He was holding his wife very tight, fingers digging into her shoulder.

She opened her eyes and blinked at him. "Jeffrey, please, you're hurting me."

He swallowed hard and loosened his grip. "I'm sorry, Sally. I'm sorry." The apology seemed to take some of the anger out of him. The lines in his face softened. He shook his head. "We must save her soul. Her life is gone, but her soul remains. We must save that at least."

There had been a time when I believed that, too. Down to my toes I thought all vampires were evil. Now, I wasn't so sure. I knew too many of them who didn't seem that bad. I knew evil when I felt it, and that wasn't what they were. I didn't know what they were, but were they damned? According to the Catholic Church, yes, they were, and so was the girl upstairs. But then, according to the Church, so was I. I'd become Episcopalian when the church declared all animators excommunicates.

"Are you Catholic, Mr. Quinlan?"

"Yes; what difference does that make?"

"I was raised Catholic. So I understand your beliefs."

"They are not beliefs, Miss . . . What is your name?"

"Blake, Anita Blake."

"They are not beliefs, Miss Blake. They are facts. Ellie's immortal soul is in danger of eternal damnation. We must help her."

"Do you understand what you're asking me to do?" I asked.

"To save her."

I shook my head. Mrs. Quinlan was looking at me. Her eyes were very intent. I was betting I could cause a little family disagreement.

"I will put a stake through her heart and chop off her head." I left the fact out that most of my executions were done with a shotgun now, at close range. It was messy and you needed a closed coffin, but it was a lot easier on me and a quicker death for the vampire.

Mrs. Quinlan started to cry again, huddling against her husband. She buried her face against him, smearing makeup on his clean white shirt.

"Are you trying to upset my wife?"

"No, sir, but I want you all to realize that two nights from now Ellie will rise as a vampire. She'll walk and talk. Eventually, she'll be able to be around you. If I stake her, all she'll be is dead."

"She is already dead. We want you to do your job," he said.

Mrs. Quinlan wouldn't look at me. Either she believed as strongly as her hubby, or she wouldn't fight him. Not even for her daughter's continued existence.

I let it go. I could stall for twenty-four hours. I doubted that Mr. Quinlan was going to change his mind. I had hopes for Mrs. Quinlan.

"Does the poodle always bark at strangers?"

They all three blinked at me like rabbits caught in headlights. The change of subject was too abrupt for their grief.

"What has that got to do with anything?" he asked.

"There is a murderous vampire out there somewhere. I'm going to catch him, but I need your help. So please just answer my questions as best you can."

"What does the dog have to do with it?"

I sighed and sipped my coffee. He had just found his daughter dead, murdered, raped, I'm sure he'd told himself. The horror of it cut him some slack, but he was beginning to use it up.

"The poodle barked its head off when I came to the door. Does it bark every time a stranger comes to the house?"

The boy saw what I was getting at. "Yeah, Raven always barks at strangers."

I ignored his parents and talked to the most reasonable person in the room. "What's your name?"

"Jeff," he said. God, Jeffrey Junior, of course.

"How many times would I have to come to the house before Raven stopped barking at me?"

He thought about that, rolling his lower lip under, really thinking about it.

Mrs. Quinlan sat up, a little apart from her husband. "Raven always barks when someone comes to the door. Even if she knows you."

"Did she bark tonight?"

The parents frowned at me. Jeff said, "Yeah. She barked like crazy until Ellie let her in her room just after dark. Ellie let her in, then a few minutes later Raven came back down-stairs."

"How'd you find the body?"

"Raven started barking again and wouldn't stop. Ellie didn't let her in. Ellie always lets her in. I mean, I'm not al-lowed in her room, but Raven gets to go in even when Ellie wants her privacy." He made that last word sound like he usually said it with a lot of eye-rolling.

"I knocked at the door and she didn't answer. Raven was scratching at the door. It was locked. She locked her door a lot, but she wouldn't answer." A tear escaped from his wide eyes. "I went and got Dad."

"You unlocked the door, Mr. Quinlan?"

He nodded. "Yes, and she was just lying there. I couldn't bear to touch her. She's unclean now. I . . ." He was choking on tears, trying so hard not to cry that his face was turning purple.

Jeff came and put his arm around his dad, leaning against his mother, the poodle still gripped in his other arm. The dog whined softly, licked the makeup from Mrs. Quinlan's face. The woman looked up and gave a choked laugh, petting the curly fur.

I wanted to leave. I wanted to let them huddle together and grieve. Hell, the death was so fresh, they hadn't gotten to grieving yet. They were still in shock. But I couldn't leave. Sheriff St. John would be back with the warrant, and I needed as much information as I could get before we braved the darkness.

Larry was sitting in the corner in a pale blue chair. He was being so quiet you'd almost forget he was there. But his eyes were eager, noticing everything, filing it all away. When I first realized he damn near memorized everything I said and did, it was intimidating. Now I counted on it.

Beth St. John came into the room with a tray of sand-wiches, coffee, and soft drinks. I didn't remember anybody asking for them, but I think Beth was needing something to do besides sit here and watch the Quinlans cry. Me, too.

She set the tray on the coffee table between the couch and the love seat. The Quinlans ignored it. I took a fresh mug of coffee. Grilling grieving families always goes down better with caffeine.

The group huddle broke up. The poodle was transferred to the wife's arms, and the two men sat on either side of her. Jeffrey and Jeff looked at me with identical eyes. It was almost eerie. Genetics at work.

"The vampire had to be in the room with Ellie when she let the dog in at full dark," I said.

"My daughter would not have let in her murderer."

"If she was eighteen, Mr. Quinlan, it wouldn't be murder."

"Being made a vampire against your will is still murder, Miss Blake."

I was getting tired of everyone calling me "Miss," but the grieving father could do it a few more times. "I believe your daughter knew the vampire. I believe she let him in willingly."

"You are crazy. Beth, go get the sheriff. I want this woman out of my house."

Beth stood up uncertainly. "David's gone to get some things, Jeffrey. I . . . Deputy Coltrain's upstairs with the body, but . . ."

"Then get him down here."

Beth looked at me, then back to him. She gripped her small hands together, almost wringing them. "Jeffrey, she's a licensed vampire hunter. She's done this a lot. Listen to her."

He stood up. "My daughter was raped and murdered by some soulless, blood-sucking animal, and I want this woman out of my house, now." If he hadn't been crying at the same time, I'd have been pissed.

Beth looked at me. She was willing to stand up to him if I needed her to. Mucho points for her. "Has anyone you know vanished or died recently?" I asked.

Quinlan squinted at me. He looked confused. The change of subject again was just too abrupt. I was hoping I could distract him from throwing me out long enough to learn something.

"What?"

"Has anyone you know gone missing or died recently?"
He shook his head. "No."

"Andy's missing," Jeff said.

Quinlan shook his head again. "That boy is no concern of ours."

"Who's Andy?" I asked.

"Ellie's boyfriend."

"He is not her boyfriend," Quinlan said.

I caught Jeff's gaze. The look said it all. Andy had been a boyfriend, and dear old dad hadn't liked him one little bit.

"Why didn't you like Andy, Mr. Quinlan?"

"He was a criminal."

I raised my eyebrows. "In what way?"

"He was arrested for drug abuse."

"He smoked some pot," Jeff said.

I was beginning to wish I could just go off and talk with Jeff. He seemed to know what was going on and wasn't trying to hide it. Trick was how to manage it.

"He was a corrupting influence on my daughter, and I put a stop to it."

"And he's missing?" I asked.

"Yes," Jeff said.

"I will answer Miss Blake's questions, Jeff. I am the man of the house."

Jesus, man of the house. Hadn't heard that in a while. "I'd like to see the rest of the house in case the vampire entered somewhere other than her room. If Jeff could show me the doors, I'd appreciate it."

"I can show you around, Miss Blake," Quinlan said.

"I'm sure your wife needs you right now, Mr. Quinlan. Jeff can show me around, but only you can comfort your wife."

Mrs. Quinlan looked up at him, then at me, as if she wasn't sure she wanted to be comforted, but I knew the image would appeal to him.

He nodded. "Perhaps you're right." He touched his wife's shoulder. "Sally needs me right now."

Sally cooperated with fresh crying, using the poodle as a sort of impromptu handkerchief. The poodle squirmed and whined. Quinlan sat down and took his wife in his arms. The dog squirmed free and trotted over to Jeff.

I stood. Larry stood. I moved toward the door and looked back at the boy. Jeff stood and the poodle trotted at his side. I opened the doors and ushered us all outside. Raven the poodle eyed me suspiciously, but she came along.

I caught a last glimpse of Beth St. John gazing at the door as if she wanted to go with us, but she sat down beside the unwanted sandwiches and the cooling coffee. She sat like a good soldier. She would not abandon her post.

I closed the door, feeling cowardly. I was glad it wasn't my job to hold the Quinlans' hands. Facing the vampire even in the dark didn't seem so bad by comparison. Of course, I was still safe inside the house. Out there in the dark with the vampire, I might feel different.

13

WE STOOD OUT in the entryway. The air felt cooler out here, easier to breathe. Had to be my imagination. The poodle was sniffing at my foot. She gave a low growl and Jeff picked her up, tucking her under one arm, in a familiar gesture like he'd done it a hundred times before.

"You don't really want to see the doors, do you?" He asked.

"No," I said.

"Dad's all right. He's just . . ." He shrugged. "He's just right, and everyone else is wrong. He doesn't mean anything by it."

"I know. He's scared right now, too. That makes everyone bitchy."

Jeff grinned. I wasn't sure if it was the "scared" comment or the word "bitchy." Probably didn't hear many people saying either about his dad.

"How serious were Andy and your sister?"

He glanced at the closed doors and lowered his voice just a little. "Dad'll say not very, but they were serious. Real serious." He glanced at the door again.

"We can go somewhere else to talk," I said. "Your choice of rooms."

He looked at me. "You're really a vampire hunter?" If the circumstances had been different, he would have been enjoying himself. It's hard not to think it's cool to put stakes through people's chests.

"Yeah, and we raise zombies, too."

"Both of you?" He sounded surprised.

"I'm a full-fledged animator," Larry said.

Jeff shook his head. "We can talk in my room." He led the way up the stairs. We followed.

If I'd been a cop, questioning a juvenile without a guardian or lawyer present would have been illegal, but I wasn't a cop. And he wasn't a suspect. Just gathering information, folks. Just grilling a sixteen-year-old boy about his sister's sex life. Murder investigations are never pleasant, and some of that unpleasantness has nothing to do with the corpse.

Jeff hesitated at the head of the stairs, peering down the hallway. Deputy Coltrain was standing outside Ellie's room, back stiff, hands behind his back, alert for intruders. The door was open. Too hard to stand in the room with the body, I guess. He saw Jeff and closed the door, still standing in front of it. Nice of Coltrain to make sure Jeff didn't see the body. But standing outside the closed door was not the best idea. A vampire, if it was old enough, could have come in the room behind him and opened the door before he could have drawn his gun. The undead make no noise.

I debated on whether to tell him that. I let it go. If the vamp had meant to take out more people, it could have. He could have taken out the entire family. Instead, when the dog barked he panicked and ran. This was not an ancient bloodsucker. This was someone who was new at the job. I was betting on the boyfriend, Andy, but I'd keep an open mind. Andy might have just driven to California to find fame and fortune, but I doubted it.

Jeff opened the door near the head of the stairs and went in. His room was smaller than his sister's. Being firstborn does have its advantages. The wallpaper was tan with cowboys and Indians on it. The bed had a matching spread. It was the room of a much younger person, just like his sister's. The walls were bare, no pinups, no sports figures. There was a desk stacked high with books. A small pile of clothes lay near the closet door. Raven the poodle sniffed the clothes. Jeff shooed her away and kicked the clothes into the closet and closed the door.

"Sit down anywhere you can." He pulled the desk chair out a little, then stood near the window, not sure what to do. I doubted he had many adults up to his room for a talk. Parents didn't count. Though frankly I couldn't imagine either of the Quinlans coming in for a quiet chat.

I took the chair. I figured Jeff would feel more comfortable lounging on his bed with Larry than with me. Besides, I wasn't used to wearing skirts this short yet, and every once in a while I forgot. The chair seemed safer.

Larry sat down on the bed with his back pressed against the wall. Jeff sat down next to him, propping some of the pillows into the corner for a back rest. Raven jumped up on the bed, circled his lap twice, and lay down. Cozy.

"How hot an item were Andy and your sister?" No prelims; off with the clothes.

He glanced at both of us. Larry gave him an encouraging smile. He shifted more securely against his mound of pillows and said, "Pretty hot. I mean, they hung all over each other at school."

"Embarrassing," I said.

"Yeah. I mean, she was my sister. She's only a year older than me, and there's this guy pawing her." He shook his head. He rubbed the poodle's ears, hands moving down her small curly body. He pet her like it was habit, a comfort measure.

"Did you like Andy?"

He shrugged. "He was older and sort of cool, but no, I thought Ellie could have done better."

"How so?"

"He did smoke pot and didn't have any plans for college. Andy wasn't going anywhere. It was like the fact that he loved my sister was everything. Like they'd live on love or something stupid like that."

I agreed that that was stupid. "When your dad put a stop to it, did it stop?"

He grinned at me. "No. They just started sneaking around. I think if anything, telling Ellie she couldn't see him made it worse."

"It usually does," I said. "When did Andy disappear?"

"About two weeks ago. His car went missing, too, so everybody thought he'd run off, but he wouldn't have left Ellie behind. He was sort of creepy, but he wouldn't have left her."

"Was Ellie upset at being left behind?"

He frowned, hugging the dog against his chest. Raven licked his chin with her small pink tongue. "That was the weird part. I mean, I know she had to pretend not to care in front of Mom and Dad, but even at school or out with our friends she didn't seem to care. I was kinda glad. I mean, Andy was a loser, but it was like she didn't believe he was gone or knew something the rest of us didn't. I thought he'd just gone off to find like an out-of-town job and was going to send for her."

"Maybe he did," I said.

The frown deepened between his smooth, unblemished brows. "What do you mean?"

"I think Andy may be the vampire that did your sister."

A look of disgust crumbled his face even further. "I don't believe that. Andy loved Ellie; he wouldn't kill her."

"If he's a vampire, Jeff, he wouldn't think turning her into the undead is killing her. He'd probably think of it as bringing her over."

Jeff shook his head. Raven wiggled out of his grasp as if he was squeezing too hard. She hopped off his lap and lay down on the covers. "Andy wouldn't hurt Ellie. Doesn't it hurt to die?"

"Probably," I said.

"The bushes underneath her end window are all crushed," Larry said.

I looked at him. "Say again."

He smiled, pleased with himself. "I took a look around outside. That's what took me so long when you sent me out for gloves that you didn't need. The bushes under the end window to the girl's room are all smashed like something heavy fell on them."

I had a moment to visualize Larry out in the dark all alone, unarmed except for his cross. The thought made my skin cold. I opened my mouth to yell at him and closed it. Never dress anyone down in public unless it's an object lesson. I said, "Any tracks?" I gave myself a dozen brownie points for not yelling.

"Do I look like Tonto? Besides, the ground is just grass and it's been so dry lately. I don't think there'd be any tracks." He frowned at me. "Can you track vampires?"

"Not normally, but if this one is as new as I think he is, then maybe." I nodded. "Yeah." I stood up. "I've got to go ask the deputy something. Thank you for your help, Jeff." I offered him my hand to shake. He took it. His handshake was a little uncertain, as if he wasn't used to it.

I went for the door and Larry followed.

"You will find him and kill him, even if it's Andy?" Jeff asked.

I turned back and looked at him. His dark eyes were still intelligent, still full of purpose, but there was also a little boy needing reassurance.

"Yeah, we'll find him."

"And kill him?"

"And kill him," I said.

"Good," he said. "Good."

I wasn't sure if "good" was the word I would have chosen, but it wasn't my sister lying dead in the other room.

"You got a cross?" I asked.

He frowned, but said, "Yeah."

"You wearing it?"

He shook his head.

"Get it and wear it until we catch him. Okay?"

"You think he'll come back?" Fear glittered at the edge of his eyes.

"No, but you never know, Jeff. Just humor me."

He got up and went to his bureau. There was a line of glittering chain on one corner of the mirror. When he picked it up, a tiny gold cross dangled from it. I watched him put it on. The dog watched it all with anxious eyes.

I smiled. "We'll see you later."

He nodded, fingering the cross, scared now underneath the shock. We left him in the tender care of Raven.

"You really think the vamp will come back to the house?" Larry asked.

"No," I said, "but just in case your little visit out into the dark gives him ideas, I want Jeff to at least have a cross on."

"Heh," he said. "I found a clue."

Deputy Coltrain was watching us, but we were running out of privacy. I kept my voice down and hoped that was enough. "Yeah, and you went out, alone, unarmed, in the dark with a vampire that had already killed once on the loose."

"You said it was a really new vampire."

"Not before you went out after the gloves."

"Maybe I figured out that it was a new one all on my own," he said. He was looking stubborn, like far from taking my warning to heart, he just might do it again."

"New vampires can still kill you, Larry."

"With a cross on?"

He had a point. Very few of the new dead could get past the pain of a cross, or play enough head games to get you to take it off voluntarily.

"Fine, Larry, but where's the vampire that made him? That one may be a couple of centuries old, and it's out in the dark, too."

He went a little pale around the edges. "I never thought of that."

"I did."

He gave a shrug and had the grace to look embarrassed. "That's why you're the boss."

"That's right," I said.

"All right, all right. I promise to be good."

"Great; now let's go ask Deputy Coltrain if he knows any-one who could track our vampire."

"Can you really track a vampire like that?"

"I don't know, but with one less than two weeks old, one that falls out a window and into some shrubs, you might be able to. They at least might be able to narrow down where we should look first."

He was grinning very broadly at me.

"Yeah, knowing it fell out the window is useful informa-tion. It might not have occurred to me to check for tracks outside the window."

If he grinned any wider, he was going to pull something.

"And if a vampire old enough to get past your cross had eaten your face, I'd have never known about the shrubs."

"Ah, Anita. I done good."

I shook my head. For all that Larry had seen of vampires, it wasn't enough. He still didn't fully appreciate what they were. He didn't have any scars yet. If he stayed in the busi-ness long enough to get his license, that would change.

God help him.

14

THE WIND WAS cool and smelled of rain. I turned my face to the soft touch of it. The air smelled of green growing things. It smelled clean and new. I stood on the grass look-ing upward. Ellie Quinlan's window shone like a soft yellow beacon. Ellie had opened the windows, but her father had turned on the lights. She had met her vampire lover in dark-ness. The better not to see him for the walking corpse he was.

I had the coverall back on, unzipped halfway so I could get to the Browning. I'd only brought an inner pants holster for the Firestar, so I shoved it into a pocket of the coveralls.

Not handy for a quick draw, but better than not having it. An inner pants holster just doesn't work well with a skirt on.

Larry had his very own gun in a shoulder rig. He stood beside me shrugging his shoulders, trying to get the straps more comfortable. It isn't really uncomfortable if it's a good fit, but it isn't really comfortable either. It's sort of like a bra. They fit and they are necessary, but they are never completely comfortable.

He was wearing the extra coverall unzipped and flapping nearly to his hips. A flashlight flicked over us, glinting on Larry's cross. The light swept over me, glaring in my eyes. "Now that you've ruined my night vision, get that damn thing out of my eyes."

Deep masculine laughter came from behind the brilliant beam of light. Two state cops had arrived just in time to join us on the hunt. Oh, joy.

"Wallace," a man's voice said, "do what the lady says." The voice was deep and vaguely threatening. A voice to say, "lean on the hood of the car and spread 'em." And you'd do it or else.

Officer Granger walked up to us, his flashlight pointed at the ground. He wasn't as tall as Wallace, and a gut was beginning to creep over his belt, but he moved through the dark like he knew what he was doing. Like maybe he'd hunted in the dark before. Maybe not vampires but something. Maybe men.

Wallace walked over to us, flashlight swimming around us like an oversized firefly. It wasn't in my eyes, but it was still not helping my night vision.

"Turn off the flashlight . . . please," I said.

Wallace took a step closer, looming over me. He was tall, built like a football player, with long legs. A running back, maybe. He and Deputy Coltrain could arm wrestle later. Right now I just wanted him to back the fuck off me.

"Turn it off, Wallace," Granger said. He'd already clicked off his own.

"I won't be able to see a damn thing," he protested.

"Afraid of the dark?" I asked, smiling up at him.

Larry laughed. It was the wrong thing to do.

Wallace turned on him. "You think that's funny?" He stepped up to Larry until they were almost touching, using his size to intimidate. But Larry's like me; he's been small all his life. He'd been bullied by the best. He stood his ground.

"Are you?" Larry asked.

"Am I what?" Wallace asked.

"Afraid of the dark?"

Animating wasn't the only thing Larry was learning from me. Unfortunately for Larry, he was a boy. I could get away with being a pain in the ass and most people wouldn't take a swing at me. Larry wasn't so lucky.

Wallace balled his hands into Larry's coverall and lifted him to tiptoes. His flashlight fell to the grass, rolling around spotlighting our ankles.

Officer Granger stepped up close to them but didn't touch Wallace. Even in the dark you could see the tension in his shoulders and arms. Not from lifting Larry, but from wanting to hit him and resisting the urge.

"Ease down, Wallace. He didn't mean anything."

Wallace didn't say anything, he just pulled Larry closer to him, leaning over to put his face next to Larry's. A square of yellow light fell across his face. The muscle along the edge of his jaw was jutting out, throbbing like it would pop out of his face. There was a scar under the bone of his jawline. A scar that disappeared into the collar of his jacket.

Wallace nearly put his face nose to nose with Larry. "I-am-not-afraid-of-anything." Each word was squeezed out.

I stepped up close to him. He was bent down to intimidate Larry, so I could whisper in his ear. "Nice scar, Wallace."

He jumped like I'd hit him. He released Larry so suddenly that Larry stumbled. He whirled, one big hand raised to smash my face. At least he'd let go of Larry.

He swung at me. I swept his arm to one side and past me. He stumbled. I brought my knee up into his stomach hard. It took a lot not to follow through and really hurt him. He was a cop. One of the good guys. You don't beat up on them. I stepped back, out of reach, and hoped that one near miss had cooled him down. I could have hurt him badly in the initial rush, but now he'd be ready. Harder to hurt.

He was nearly a foot taller than me and outweighed me by more than a hundred pounds. If the fight turned serious, I was in trouble. I hoped I wouldn't regret my gallant gesture.

Wallace ended on all fours near the shrubs by the house. He got to his feet quicker than I wanted him to, but he stayed half bent over, hands on his knees. He looked up at me. I wasn't sure what his expression meant, but it wasn't completely hostile. It was more a considering sort of look, as if I'd surprised him. I get that look a lot.

"You all right now, Wallace?" Granger asked.

Wallace nodded. Hard to talk after a good gut shot.

Granger glanced at me. "You all right, Ms. Blake?"

"I'm fine."

He nodded. "Yes, you are."

Larry moved up beside me. He was standing too close. If Wallace came back at me, I would need more room to maneuver. I knew that Larry meant it to as a show of support. After we got Larry's shooting up to speed, we'd have to work on some basic hand-to-hand techniques.

Why was I training him to shoot before I taught him to fight? Because you don't arm wrestle vampires. You shoot them. He would live through a beating from Officer Wallace. He wouldn't live through a vampire attack. Not if he couldn't shoot.

"Were you with him when he got that scar?" I asked.

Granger shook his head. "His first partner didn't make it."

"Vampire got him?"

He nodded.

Wallace stood up sort of slow. He arched his back just a bit, as if working the kinks out. "Nice shot," he said.

I shrugged. "It was my knee, not my fist."

"Still a good shot. I don't have any excuses good enough for what I just did."

"No," I said, "you don't."

He just looked down at the ground, then up. "I don't know what made me do it."

"Let's take a little walk." I started off into the dark without looking back, as if I had no doubt he'd follow me. This technique works more often than you think it would.

He followed me. He had stopped to pick up his flashlight, but bravely turned it off.

I stopped just short of the woods and stared off into the trees, letting my eyes adjust to the dark. I didn't look at anything in particular. I let my eyes just sort of see everything. I was looking for movement. Any movement. The tree limbs moved fitfully in the spring wind, but it was a general movement like ocean waves. The trees weren't what worried me.

Wallace tapped the darkened flashlight against his thigh. A soft *whap, whap*. I wanted to tell him to stop but didn't. If it comforted him, I could live with it.

I let the silence stretch between us. The wind picked up, filling the night with a rushing, hurrying sound. You could smell the rain on the wind.

He gripped the flashlight in both hands. I could hear his intake of breath above the wind. "What was that?"

"The wind," I said.

"Are you sure?"

"Pretty much."

"What do you want?" he asked.

"Is this the first vamp you've gone after since your partner's death?"

He looked at me. "Granger told you?"

"Yeah, but I saw your neck. I was pretty sure what had done it."

I wanted to tell him it was okay to be scared. Hell, I was scared, but he was a cop and a man, and I didn't know him well enough to know how he'd take a pep talk from me. But I had to know if he'd follow me into those woods. I had to know if I could depend on him. If he stayed this scared, I couldn't.

"What happened?" I asked. Maybe talking about it right now was the wrong thing to do, but ignoring it wasn't working very well.

He shook his head. "Headquarters says you're in charge, Ms. Blake. Fine, I'll do what I'm told. But I don't have to answer personal questions."

It was too much trouble to shrug out of the overall, and I really didn't want my arms trapped. I undid one button on my blouse and spread the cloth.

"What are you doing?"

"How good's your night vision?"

"Why?"

"Can you see the scar?"

"What are you talking about?" He sounded suspicious. Suspicious that I was crazy, maybe.

My night vision would have picked it up, but most people don't have my eyes. "Give me your hand."

"Why?"

"I am about to give you a once-in-a-lifetime offer. Just give me your damn hand."

He did, sort of hesitatingly, glancing back at the waiting men.

His hand was cold to the touch. He was one scared puppy. I traced his large, blunt fingers along my collarbone. The moment he touched the scar tissue, his hand jerked like he'd had an electric shock. I pulled my hand away, and he traced the scar again on his own.

He took his hand back, slowly, rubbing his fingers together like he was remembering the feel of my skin. "What did that?"

"Same thing that did your neck. A vampire that wasn't neat with its food."

"Jesus," he said.

"Yeah," I said. I rebuttoned my blouse. "Tell me what happened, Wallace. Please."

He looked at me for a moment longer, then nodded. "Harry, my partner, and me, we got a call that someone had found a body with its throat torn out." He made the words very bland, ordinary, but I knew he was seeing it in his head. Watching it all happen again behind his eyeballs.

"It was a construction site. Just us in the middle of the place with our flashlights. There was a sound like wind whistling, and something hit Harry. He went down with a man on top of him. He screamed, and I had my gun out. I fired into the man's back. I hit him solid three, four times.

He turned on me and his face was bloody. I didn't have time to wonder why, 'cause he jumped me. I emptied my gun into him before I hit the ground."

He took a deep breath, big hands twisting back and forth on the flashlight. He was looking off into the trees, too, but not for vampires, or at least not for this one.

"He ripped my jacket and shirt like they were paper. I tried to fight him, but . . ." He shook his head. "He caught me with his eyes. He caught me with his eyes, and when he tore into my neck, I wanted him to do it, wanted it worse than I've ever wanted anything in my life."

He turned a little away from me, as if not meeting my eyes wasn't enough. "When I woke up, he was just gone. Harry was dead. The girl was dead. I was alive."

He turned to me finally, looked me straight in the eyes and said, "Why didn't he kill me, Ms. Blake?"

I looked into his earnest eyes and didn't have a good answer. "I don't know, Wallace. He wanted to make you one of them, maybe. I don't know why you and not Harry. You ever catch him?"

"The local master sent his head in a box to the station. The note apologized for his uncivilized behavior. That's what the note said, 'uncivilized behavior.'"

"It's hard to look at it as murder when you feed off humans yourself."

"Do they all do that? Feed off people?"

"I've never met one that didn't."

"Can't they eat animals?"

"Theoretically, yes. In practice it seems to lack certain nutrients." Truth was, feeding was too close to sex for most vamps. They weren't into bestiality, so they didn't feed off animals. I didn't think the sex analogy would go over well with Officer Wallace.

"Can you do this, Wallace?"

"What do you mean?"

"Can you go out into the dark and hunt vampires?"

"It's my job."

"I didn't ask if it was your job. I asked if you can go out into that darkness and hunt vampires."

"You think there's more than one?"

"Always best to assume so," I said.

He nodded. "Yeah, I guess so."

"Scared?" I asked.

"Are you?"

I looked off into the windswept night. The trees tossed and moaned in the wind. There was movement everywhere. Soon there would be rain, and what light the stars gave would be gone.

"Yeah, I'm scared."

"But you're a vampire hunter," he said. "How can you do this night after night if it scares you?"

"Doesn't it scare you to know that every time you pull over some yahoo for a traffic violation that he could be armed? You walk up on that car and never know."

"It's my job."

"And this is my job."

"But you're scared?"

"Down to my toes."

Larry called, "The sheriff's back. He's got the warrant."

Wallace and I looked at each other. "You got silver bullets?" I asked.

"Yes."

I smiled. "Then let's go. You'll be fine," I said. I believed it. Wallace would do his job. I would do my job. We would all do our jobs. And come morning, some of us would be alive and some of us wouldn't. Of course, maybe there was just the one newly dead vampire to deal with. If so, we might all see the sunrise. But I hadn't lived this long assuming the best. Assuming the worst was always safer. And usually truer.

15

I'D GOTTEN USED to the sawed-off shotgun that I had at home. Yeah, it is illegal, but it's easy to carry and makes mincemeat out of vampires. What more could a modern vampire hunter want? The Ithaca pump action 12 gauge was close.

"Why don't I get a shotgun?" Larry asked.

I just looked at him. He looked serious. I shook my head. "When you can handle the nine, we'll talk about shotguns."

"Great."

Oh, for the enthusiasm of youth. Larry was only four years younger than I was. Sometimes it seemed like a million.

"He's not going to shoot us in the back by accident, is he?" Deputy Coltrain asked.

I smiled, not sweetly. "He promised not to."

Coltrain looked at me like he wasn't sure I was kidding.

Sheriff St. John joined us at the edge of the woods. He had a shotgun, too. I had to trust that he knew how to use it. Wallace had the shotgun from their unit. His partner Granger had a wicked-looking rifle, like something a sniper would carry. It looked like the wrong tool for tonight's job, and I had said so. Granger had just looked at me. I'd shrugged and let it go. It was his neck and his gun.

I looked around at them. They looked at me. Waiting for me to give the word.

"Everybody got their holy water?" I asked.

Larry patted his coverall pocket. Everyone else nodded, or mumbled yes.

"Remember the three rules of vampire hunting. One: Never, ever look them in the eyes. Two: Never, ever give up your cross. Three: Aim for the head and heart. Even with silver ammo, it won't be a killing blow anywhere else." I felt like a kindergarten teacher sending her kiddies off to a hostile playground. "Don't panic if you get bitten. The bite can be cleansed. As long as they don't mesmerize you with their eyes, you can still fight."

I looked at them, all silent, all taller than me, even Larry by an inch or two. They could all arm wrestle me and win. So why did I want to order them all into the house where'd they'd be safe? Heck, we could all go inside. Have a nice cup of hot cocoa. Tell the Quinlans their little girl would be fine. I mean, liquid diets are in with teens. Right?

I took a deep breath and let it out slow. "Let's do it, boys. We're wasting starlight." Either nobody got my John Wayne reference, or nobody thought it was funny. Hard to tell which.

I had to let St. John lead the way into the black trees. I didn't know the area. He did. But I didn't like him taking point. I didn't like it at all. I wanted to bring him back to his wife. His high school sweetheart. Five years married and still in love. Jesus, I didn't want to get him killed.

The trees closed around us. St. John threaded his way through them like he knew what he was doing. There was very little undergrowth this time of year. It made it easier, but there is still an art to going through thick woods, especially in the dark. You can't really see even with a flashlight. You have to sort of give yourself over to the trees the way you give yourself to water when you swim. You don't really concentrate on the water, or even on your own body. You concentrate on the rhythm of your body cutting, sliding through the cool liquid. For the forest you find a rhythm, too. You concentrate on sliding your body through the natural openings. Finding the place where the forest itself will let you through. If you fight it, it will fight you back. And, just like water, it can kill you. Anyone who doesn't believe that the forest is a deadly place has never been lost in one.

St. John knew how to move, and so did I. I was pretty pleased at that, actually. I'd been a city girl for a long time. Larry stumbled into me. I had to brace, or we'd have both gone down.

"Sorry," he said, pushing himself away from me.

"How ya doing up there, vampire hunter?" Coltrain called. He was bringing up the rear. I had to go second to back up St. John, and I wouldn't let Larry take rear. Coltrain had wanted it. Said he and the sheriff would guard our ass. Fine with me.

"Yell a little louder," Wallace said. "I don't think the vampire heard you."

"I don't need no statie telling me how to do my job."

"It knows we're here," I said.

That stopped them. They both looked at me. Granger, who was just ahead of Wallace, looked at me, too. I had everyone's attention.

"Even if the vampire is only a few weeks old, its hearing is incredibly acute. It knows we're here. It knows we're coming. It doesn't matter if we're quiet or have a brass band. It's all the same. We won't surprise it in the dark." It would probably surprise us, but I didn't add that part aloud. We were all thinking it anyway.

"We are wasting time here, Deputy," St. John said.

Coltrain didn't apologize or even look sorry. Wallace did. "I'm sorry, Sheriff. It won't happen again."

St. John nodded and turned without another word and led us farther into the woods.

Coltrain made a small humphing sound but let it go. Whatever he said, I didn't think Wallace would rise to bait again. At least I hoped not. I didn't care if he was scared; we had enough problems without fighting among ourselves.

The trees rustled and swayed around us. Last year's dead leaves crunched underfoot. Someone cursed softly behind me. The wind blew in a wild gust, streaming my hair back from my face. Up ahead the quality of darkness was different. We were approaching the clearing.

St. John stopped just short of the tree line. He glanced back at me. "How do you want to do this?"

I could taste the rain on the wind coming closer. If possible, I wanted us out of here before it came. Visibility sucked as it was.

"We kill it, and we get the hell back to the house. It's not a hard plan."

He nodded, as if I'd said something profound.

Wish I had.

A figure stepped in front of us. One minute nothing, the next there he was. Darkness and shadows, magic. He grabbed St. John as he went for his gun and threw him out into the clearing in a high looping arch.

I shot the vampire in the chest at almost point-blank

range. He collapsed to his knees. I caught a glimpse of the whites of his eyes, like he couldn't believe it. I had to pump the shotgun to jack another shell in place.

Granger's rifle exploded behind me like a cannon. Someone screamed. I shot the vampire between the eyes. His head splattered into the leaves. I turned with the shotgun to my shoulder before the body hit the ground.

Larry was on the ground with a vamp on top of him. I had a glimpse of long brown hair before his cross flared to life in a brilliant flash of blue-white fire. She flung herself backwards with a scream, scrambling into the dark. Gone.

A vamp with long blonde hair held Granger in her slender arms, head pressed to his neck. I couldn't use the shotgun. They were pressed too close together. At this range I'd kill them both.

I dropped the shotgun into Larry's surprised lap. He was still lying on the ground, blinking. I drew the Browning and fired into the vampire's broad chest. She jerked but didn't let go of Granger. The vampire looked at me, the man still clasped to her chest. She hissed at me. I fired a round into her gaping mouth. It blew the back of her head out.

The vamp shuddered. I fired a second round into her head. She let go of Granger and fell to the leaves in convulsions. Granger just lay there. In the dark I couldn't see his face or neck. Dead or alive, I'd done all I could.

Larry was on his feet, shotgun awkward in his hands.

There was a scream, low and pain-filled. Wallace was on the ground with a slender-bodied vamp on top of him. Fangs sunk in his arm. The bone broke with a loud, brittle snap. He screamed again.

I had a glimpse of Coltrain standing, frozen, just beyond. There was movement behind him. I stared straight at it, waiting for the vampire to take shape from the shadows, but something gleamed. A dull silver blade flashed into sight. I stared straight at it, but I lost a second somehow. The next thing I knew the blade tip exploded from Coltrain's throat. I lost another second, blinking at shadows, and the vampire tore the blade from his throat and was gone. It scuttled through the trees like nothing human, unbelievably fast, like a nightmare seen from the corner of your eye.

Larry raised the shotgun to his shoulder, aimed in Wallace's direction. I grabbed it from him, and something smashed into my back and rode me into the leaves. A hand pressed my face into the dry, crackling leaves. A second hand ripped the back of my coverall so violently it wrenched one shoulder. There was an explosion just behind my head, and the vampire was gone. I rolled over, ears ringing.

Larry was standing over me with his arm extended, gun out. Whatever he'd shot was gone out in the dark.

My left shoulder was hurt, but not as badly as it might be if I didn't get up. I struggled to my feet. The vampires were gone.

Wallace was sitting up, cradling his arm. Coltrain lay on the ground without moving. A sound behind us. I turned, Browning pointed. Larry was turning too, but too slow. I sighted down the barrel, and it was St. John.

"Don't shoot. It's me."

Larry held his gun two-handed pointed at the ground. "Sweet Jesus," he said.

Amen. "What happened to you?"

"The fall knocked me out. I followed the sound of shots," St. John said.

A gust of wind slapped against us. It smelled so strongly of rain I almost felt it on my skin.

"Check Granger's pulse, Larry," I said.

"What?" Larry looked shell-shocked.

"See if he's alive." It was a messy job, and I'd have done it myself, but I trusted me more than Larry to keep the vampires away. He'd saved me once tonight, but I still trusted me more.

St. John walked past us. He touched Wallace, who nodded. "My arm's broke, but I'll live." St. John went to Coltrain's still form.

Larry knelt by Granger. He switched his gun to his left hand, not the best thing to do, but I understood. Hard to check for a pulse in the dark on a throat warm with blood; better to use your dominant hand.

"I've got a pulse." He looked up, his broad smile a dim whiteness in the dark.

"Coltrain's dead," St. John said. "God help me, he's dead." He raised a hand and the skin glistened with blood, black in the dim light. "He's nearly decapitated. What did this?"

"Sword," I said. I'd seen it. Watched it happen. But all I could remember was a black shape larger than a human being. Or larger than most. A shadow with a sword was all I'd seen, and I'd been looking right at it.

Something flowed across my skin, and it wasn't the wind. Power filled the spring night like water. "There's something old out here," I said.

"What are you talking about?" St. John said.

"An ancient vampire. It's here. I can feel it." I searched the darkness, but nothing moved but the trees, the wind. There was nothing to see. Nothing to fight. But it was here and it was close. Sword in hand, maybe.

Granger sat up so suddenly that Larry fell back into the leaves with a squeak. The big man's eyes turned to me. I saw his hand go for his gun, and I knew what the vampire was doing.

I pointed the Browning at his head and waited. I had to be sure.

Granger didn't hunt for his dropped rifle. He drew his sidearm and pointed it very slowly, as if he didn't want to do it. He pointed it at Larry from less than a foot away.

Wallace yelled, "Granger, what the fuck are you doing?"

I fired.

Granger jerked; the gun wavered, then his hand came back up. I fired again, and again. His hand fell slowly to the ground, gun still in it. He fell straight back into the leaves.

"Granger!" Wallace was screaming, crawling toward his partner. Shit.

I got there first and kicked the gun out of his hand. If he'd twitched, I'd have shot him again. He didn't twitch. He just lay there, dead.

Wallace tried to cradle him one-handed. "Why'd you shoot him? Why?"

"He was going to kill Larry. You saw it."

"Why?"

"The vamp that bit him. His master is out here. And he's a powerful son of a bitch. He used him."

Wallace had Granger's bloody head in his lap, his own ravaged arm pressed to Granger's chest. He was crying.

Shit.

A sound rode the rising wind. A sharp, furious barking. A woman's scream, high and clear, cut across the sound.

"Oh, God," I whispered.

"Beth." St. John was on his feet running before I could say anything.

I grabbed Wallace's shoulder, pulling on his jacket. He looked up.

"What's happening?"

"They're in the house," I said. "Can you walk?"

He nodded. I helped him to his feet.

Another scream came. It wasn't the same scream. A man this time, or a boy.

"Stay with him, Larry. Get to the house as soon as you can."

"What if they're trying to split us up?" Larry asked.

"Then it's going to work," I said. "Shoot anything that moves." I touched his arm, as if that would make him more real, keep him safe. It wouldn't, but it was all I had. I had to go for the house. Larry had signed up to be a monster slayer. The Quinlans and Beth St. John hadn't.

I holstered the Browning, kept a two-handed grip on the shotgun, and threw myself into the trees. I ran, not trying to see where I was going. Rushing through openings in the trees that I wasn't sure were there, but they were. I jumped over a log and nearly fell but caught myself and kept running. A branch slashed my face, bringing tears to my eye. The forest that had seemed passable before was now a maze of roots and branches that grabbed and tripped. I was running blind. It was not a good way to stay alive with vampires in the dark. I spilled out onto the Quinlans' lawn on my knees, shotgun tightly gripped.

The front door was open. Light spilled in a warm rectangle. Shots sounded from inside the house. I got to my feet and ran for the light.

The poodle lay broken by the door, crumpled like someone had tried to force it into a ball.

The doors to the living room were open. A second shot sounded. I went in to the left of the door, wall at my back, shotgun ready.

Mr. and Mrs. Quinlan were huddled in the far corner with their crosses held out before them. The metal glowed with a white-hot light like burning magnesium.

The thing in front of them didn't look much like a vampire. It looked like a skeleton with muscle and flesh stretched over a bone frame. It was stretched impossibly thin and tall. A sword rode its back, gleaming and wide as a scimitar. Coltrain's killer?

St. John was firing into the brown-haired vamp from the woods. She had long brown hair parted in the middle, straight and lovely, framing a face that was blood-smeared and stretched wide over fangs.

I had a glimpse of Beth St. John on the floor behind her. She wasn't moving.

St. John kept firing into the vampire's body. She just kept coming. Blood blossomed on the front of her jean jacket. His gun clicked, empty. The vampire staggered, then fell to her knees. She fell forward on all fours, and you could see that her back was so much raw meat. She lay gasping on the floor while St. John reloaded.

I got to my feet, trying to keep an eye on the door just in case this wasn't all. I walked towards the Quinlans and the thing that stood in front of them. I needed a better angle before I used the shotgun. Didn't want to catch them in the shot pattern.

The thing turned on me. I had a glimpse of a face that was neither human nor animal, but stretched thin and alien with fangs and blind, glowing eyes. It shrank, and skin flowed over the bare flesh, covered the nearly naked bone. I'd never seen anything like it. When I aimed the shotgun, I was looking into what could have passed for a human face. Long white hair framed a fine-boned face, and it ran—if running was the word for that blur of motion. It ran like some of them flew, almost like it was doing something else altogether, but I had no better word for it. Some of them flew; this one ran. It was gone before I could pull the trigger.

I was left staring at the open door where the barrel had followed its movement. Could I have fired? Had I hesitated? I didn't think so, but I wasn't sure. It was like in the woods when Coltrain died, like I'd missed a few seconds. The vampire had to be our killer, but the only thing I'd seen clearly in the woods had been the sword.

St. John shot into the fallen vampire. He fired until his gun clicked empty again. The gun went click, click, click.

I walked over to him. The vampire's head was bloody meat and heavier, wetter things. There was no face left. "It's dead, St. John. You killed it."

He just stared at it, down the barrel of his empty gun. He was shaking. He collapsed to his knees suddenly, as if he just couldn't stand any longer. He crawled over to his wife, gun left behind him on the carpet. He cradled her in his arms, half-lifting, rocking her. She was soaked with blood. Her throat was so much raw meat on one side.

St. John was making a high, keening sound deep in his throat.

The Quinlans's crosses had stopped glowing. They stood still clinging to each other, blinking as if blinded by the light.

"Jeff—he took Jeff," Mrs. Quinlan said.

I looked at her. Her eyes were too wide. "He took Jeff."

"Who took Jeff?" I asked.

"The big one," Mr. Quinlan said. "That thing, that thing told Jeff to take his cross off, and Jeff did it." He looked at me with startled eyes. "Why did he do that? Why did he take it off?"

"The vampire caught him with his eyes," I said. "He couldn't help himself."

"If his faith had been stronger, he wouldn't have given in," Quinlan said.

"It wasn't your son's fault."

Quinlan shook his head. "He wasn't strong enough."

I turned away from him. Which put me staring at St. John. He had folded as much of his wife's body into his lap and arms as he could. He rocked her, eyes distant. He wasn't seeing this room. He'd gone somewhere deep inside. Someplace better. I hoped.

I went for the door. I didn't have to see this. Watching St. John rock his wife's body was not part of my job description. Honest.

I sat down on the stairs where I could see the door, the hallway, and the stairs as far as the landing. St. John started singing in a strange, broken voice. It took me a few minutes to figure out what he was singing. It was "You Are So Beautiful." I got up and went for the outer door. Larry and Wallace were just limping up onto the porch.

I just shook my head and kept walking. I was almost to the driveway before I couldn't hear the singing. I stood there taking deep breaths, letting them out slowly. I concentrated on my breathing, concentrated on the sound of frogs and wind. I concentrated on anything but the sound that was building in my throat. I stood there in the dark, in the open, knowing it was dangerous, and not sure I cared. I stood there until I was sure I wasn't going to start screaming. Then I turned and went back to the house.

It was the bravest thing I'd done all night.

16

DETECTIVE FREEMONT SAT on one end of the Quinlans' couch and I perched on the other. We were as far away from each other as we could get and share it. Only pride kept me from taking a chair. I wouldn't flinch under her cool cop eyes. So I stayed nailed to my end of the couch, but it was an effort.

Her voice was low and careful, every word enunciated, as

if she thought she might yell if she rushed the words. "Why didn't you call and tell me you had a second vampire kill?"

"Sheriff St. John called the state cops. I assumed you'd be told."

"Well, I wasn't."

I stared up into her cool eyes. "You're twenty minutes away with a crime scene unit looking into a possible vampire kill. Why wouldn't they send you over to a second vampire scene?"

Freemont's eyes shifted to one side, then back to me. Her cool cop eyes had melted just a little. It was hard to read for sure, but she looked uneasy. Maybe even scared.

"You haven't told them it was a vampire kill, have you?"

Her eyes flinched.

"Shit, Freemont. I know you don't want the Feds to steal your case, but withholding information from your own people . . . Bet your superiors aren't happy with you."

"That's my business."

"Fine. Whatever plan you've got, more power to you, but why are you pissed at me?"

She took a deep, shaking breath and blew it out like a runner trying to get that extra kick. "How sure are you the vampire used a sword?"

"You saw the body," I said.

She nodded. "A vampire could have ripped the neck apart."

"I saw a blade, Freemont."

"The ME will either back you up, or not."

"Why don't you want this to be vampires?"

She smiled. "I thought I had this case all solved. Thought I'd make an arrest this morning. I didn't think it was vampires."

I stared at her. I wasn't smiling. "If it wasn't vamps, then what was it?"

"Fairies."

I stared at her for a heartbeat. "What do you mean?"

"Your boss, Sergeant Storr, called me. Told me what you'd found out about Magnus Bouvier. He's got no alibi for the time of the killings, and even you think he could have done it."

"Because he could have done it, doesn't mean he did," I said.

Freemont shrugged. "He ran when we tried to question him. Innocent people don't run."

"What do you mean, he ran? If you were there questioning him, how could he run?"

Freemont settled back into the couch, hands clasped together so tightly her fingers were mottled. "He used magic to cloud our minds, and made his escape."

"What sort of magic?"

Freemont shook her head. "What do you want me to say, Ms. Preternatural Expert? Four of us sat there in his restaurant like idiots while he just walked out. We didn't even see him get up from the table."

She looked at me, no smiles. Her eyes were back to that neutral coolness. You could stare all day at someone with eyes like that and keep all your secrets safe.

"He looked human to me, Blake. He looked like a nice, normal guy. I wouldn't have picked him out of a crowd. How did you know what he was?"

I opened my mouth, and closed it. I wasn't exactly sure how to answer the question. "He tried to use glamor on me, but I knew what was happening."

"What's glamor, and how did you know he was using a spell on you?"

"Glamor isn't exactly a spell," I said. I always hated explaining preternatural things to people who had no skill in the area. It was like having quantum physics explained to me. I could follow the concepts, but I had to take their word for it on the math. The math was beyond me, hated to admit it, but it was. But not understanding quantum physics wouldn't get me killed. Not understanding preternatural creatures might get Freemont killed.

"I'm not stupid, Blake. Explain it to me."

"I don't think you're stupid, Detective Freemont. It's just hard to explain. I was riding with two uniforms in St. Louis. They were transporting me from a crime scene, playing taxi.

The driver spotted this guy just walking along. He pulled over, put him up against a car. The guy was carrying a weapon, and was wanted in another state for armed robbery. If I'd been in a room with him, I'd have noticed the gun, but just passing by in a car, no way. I wouldn't have seen it Even his partner asked him how he spotted him. He couldn't explain so that we could do it, but he knew how to do it."

"So it's practice?" Freemont said.

I sighed. "In part, but hell, Detective, I raised the dead for a living. I have some preternatural abilities. It gives me a leg up."

"How the hell are we supposed to police creatures, Ms. Blake? If Bouvier had pulled a gun, we'd have sat there and let him shoot us. We just sort of woke up and he wasn't there anymore. I've never seen anything like it."

"There are things you can do to protect yourself from fairie glamor," I said.

"What?"

"A four-leaf clover will break glamor, but it won't keep the fey from killing you by hand. There are other plants you can wear, or carry that break glamor: Saint-John's-wort, red verbena, daisies, rowan, and ash. My choice would be an ointment made of either four-leaf clovers or Saint-John's-wort. Spread it on your eyelids, mouth, ears, and hands. It'll make you proof against glamor."

"Where do I get this stuff?"

I thought about that for a second. "Well, in St. Louis I'd know where to go. Here, try health-food stores and occult shops. Any fairie ointment will be hard to find because we don't have any fairies native to this country. Ointment from four-leaf clovers is very expensive, and rare. Try for the Saint-John's-wort."

She sighed. "Will this ointment work on any mind control, like for vamps?"

"Nope," I said. "You could drop a vamp in a whole tub of Saint-John's-wort and it wouldn't give a damn."

"What do you do against vampires, then?"

"Keep your cross, avoid eye contact, pray. They can do things that'll make Magnus look like an amateur."

She rubbed her eyes, smearing eye shadow on the ball of her thumb. She suddenly looked tired. "How do we protect the public against something like that?"

"You don't," I said.

"Yes, we do," she said. "We have to; it's our job."

I didn't know what to say to that, so I didn't try. "So you thought it was Magnus because he ran, and he doesn't have an alibi?"

"Why else would he run?"

"I don't know," I said. "But he didn't do it. I saw the thing in the woods. It wasn't Magnus. Hell, I've only heard about vampires forming from shadows. I'd never seen it before."

She looked at me. "You've never seen it before. That's not comforting."

"It wasn't meant to be. But since it wasn't Magnus, you can call off the warrant."

She shook her head. "He used magic on police officers while committing a crime. That's a class C felony."

"What was his crime?"

"Escaping."

"But he wasn't under arrest."

"I had a warrant for his arrest," she said.

"You didn't have enough for a warrant," I said.

"Helps to know the right judge."

"He didn't kill those kids, or Coltrain."

"You pointed the finger at him," she said.

"Just an alternate possibility. With five people dead, I couldn't afford to be wrong."

She stood. "Well, you got your wish. It was vampires, and I don't know why the hell Magnus Bouvier ran from us. But just using magic on a police officer is a felony."

"Even if he was innocent of the original crime you were trying to bring him in on?" I asked.

"Felonious use of magic is a serious crime, Ms. Blake. There's a warrant for his arrest. You see him, you remember that."

"I know Magnus isn't nice people, Detective Freemont. I don't know why he ran, but if you put out the word that he used magic on cops, someone'll shoot him."

"He's dangerous, Ms. Blake."

"Yeah, but so are a lot of people, Detective. You don't hunt them down and arrest them for it."

She nodded. "We've all got prejudices, Ms. Blake; makes us all wrong once in a while. At least here we know what did it."

"Yeah," I said. "We know what did it."

"Do you know when the girl's body was taken?" she asked. She got a notebook out of her coat pocket. Down to business.

I shook my head. "No. It was just gone when I went up."

"What made you think to check on the body?"

I looked at her. Her eyes were pleasant and unreadable. "They'd gone to a lot of trouble to make her one of them. I thought they might try to get her. They did."

"The father's making noises that he asked you to stake her body before you went out after the vampires. Is that true?" Her voice was soft, matter-of-fact. But she was paying attention to the answers. She didn't take as many notes as Dolph did. The notebook seemed to be more something to do with her hands than anything else. I was finally seeing Freemont doing her job. She seemed good at it. That was reassuring.

"Yeah, that's true."

"Why didn't you stake the girl when the parents requested it?"

"I had a father. A widower. His daughter and only child got bit. He wanted her staked. I did it that night, right away. Next morning he's in my office crying, wanting me to undo it. Wanting me to bring her back as a vampire." I leaned back into the couch, hugging myself. "You put a stake through a new vamp's heart, and it's dead for good."

"I thought you had to take a vampire's head to be sure."

"You do," I said. "If I had staked the Quinlan girl, I would have taken out her heart, cut off her head." I shook my head. "There isn't much left."

She drew something on her note pad. I couldn't see what. I was betting it was a doodle and not a word. "I see why you wanted to wait, but Mr. Quinlan is talking about suing you."

"Yeah, I know."

Freemont raised her eyebrows. "Just thought you'd want to know."

"Thanks."

"We haven't found the boy's body yet."

"I don't think you will," I said.

Her eyes didn't look pleasant anymore. They looked narrow and suspicious. "Why?"

"If they wanted to kill him, they could have done it here, tonight. I think they want to make him one of them."

"Why?"

I shrugged. "I don't know. But usually when a vampire takes this personal an interest in a family, there's a reason for it."

"You mean a motive?"

I nodded. "You've seen the Quinlans. They're devout Catholics. The church sees vampirism as suicide. Their children will be damned for all eternity if they become vampires."

"Worse than just killing them," she said.

"To the Quinlans, I think so."

"You think the vampires will be back to get the parents?"

I thought about that for a minute. "Hell, I don't know. I mean, before vampires were legal you had some cases where a master vamp would take out entire families. Sometimes befriend them first. Sometimes just for revenge for some slight. But since they've been legal, I don't know why the vamp would do it. I mean, the vampire can take them to court. What could the Quinlans have done that was bad enough for this?"

The doors opened. Freemont turned, a frown already in place. Two men appeared in the doorway. They were both dressed in dark suits, dark ties, white shirts. Standard federal issue. One was short and white, the other tall and black. That alone should have made them look different, but there was a sameness to them, like the same cookie cutter had been used no matter how well cooked the outside was.

The shorter of the two flipped his badge at us. "I'm Spe-

cial Agent Bradford, this is Agent Elwood. Which one of
you is Detective Freemont?"

Freemont walked towards them with her hand out. Showing she was unarmed and friendly. Yeah, right. "I'm Detective Freemont. This is Anita Blake."

I appreciated being included in the introductions. I stood
up and joined the foursome.

Agent Bradford looked at me for a long time. Long
enough that it got on my nerves. "Is there something wrong,
Agent Bradford?"

He shook his head. "I attended Sergeant Storr's lectures at
Quantico. The way he talked about you, I thought you'd be
bigger." He smiled when he said it, halfway between
friendly and condescending.

A lot of scathing comebacks came to mind, but never get
in a pissing contest with the Feds. You'll lose. "Sorry to disappoint you."

"We've already talked with Officer Wallace. He makes
you sound taller, too."

I shrugged. "Hard to make me sound shorter."

He smiled. "We'd like to speak with Detective Freemont
in private, Ms. Blake. But don't go far; we'll want a statement from you and your associate, Mr. Kirkland."

"Sure."

"I took Ms. Blake's statement personally," Freemont said.
"I don't think we need her any more tonight."

Bradford looked at her. "I think we'll be the judge of
that."

"If Ms. Blake had called me in when there was only one
body on the ground, there wouldn't be two dead policemen,
and a dead civilian," Freemont said.

I just looked at her. Somebody's ass was going to be in a
sling, and Freemont didn't want it to be hers. Fine.

"Don't forget the missing boy," I said. Everyone looked
at me. "You want to start pointing fingers, fine; there's
enough blame to go around. If you hadn't chased me off earlier, I might have called you in, but I did call the state police.
If you'd told your superiors everything I told you, they'd

have connected the two cases, and you'd have been here anyway."

"I had enough men with me to cover the house and the civilians," Freemont said. "Not including me cost lives."

I nodded. "Probably. But you'd have come down here and kicked me out again. You'd have taken St. John and his people out in the dark with five vampires, one of them ancient, when all you've seen is pictures of vampire kills. They'd have slaughtered you, but maybe, just maybe, Beth St. John would be alive. Maybe Jeff Quinlan would still be here."

I stared up at her, and watched the anger drain from her eyes. We looked at each other. "It took both of us to fuck this one up, Sergeant." I turned back to the two agents. "I'll wait outside."

"Wait," Bradford said. "Storr said that sometimes the legal vampire community will help on a case like this. Who do I talk to down here?"

"Why would they hunt down one of their own?" Agent Elwood asked.

"This kind of shit is bad for business. Especially right now with Senator Brewster's daughter getting killed. Vampires don't need any more bad publicity. Most of them like being legal. They like the fact that killing them is murder."

"So who do I talk to?" Bradford asked.

I sighed. "In this area, I don't know. I'm not a hometown girl."

"How do I go about finding out who to talk to?"

"I might be able to help you there."

"How?"

I shook my head. "I know someone who might know a name. I'm not trying to give you a hard time here, but a lot of the monsters don't like dealing with cops. It just hasn't been that long ago that the police shot them on sight."

"So you're saying the vampires will talk to you and not to us?" Elwood said.

"Something like that."

"That makes no sense. You're a vampire executioner. Your job is to kill them. Why would they believe you and not us?" he asked.

I didn't know how to explain it, and wasn't sure I wanted to. "I also raise zombies, Agent Elwood. I think they sort of consider me one of the monsters."

"Even though you're their version of an electric chair."

"Even though."

"That's not logical."

I laughed then; I couldn't help it. "God, has anything that happened here tonight been logical?"

Elwood gave a very small smile. I pegged him as the newer of the two. I don't think he'd gotten over the thought that FBI agents don't smile.

"You wouldn't be withholding information from the FBI, would you, Ms. Blake?" Bradford asked.

"If I come up with a vampire in this area that will talk to you, I'll give you the name."

Bradford stared at me. "How about if you come up with any vampires in this area, you give us the names. Let us worry about whether they'll talk to us or not."

I looked at him for a heartbeat and lied. "Sure." If I expected the monsters to help me, I couldn't give them all over to the cops. Only a select few.

He looked like he didn't believe me, but couldn't quite call me a liar to my face. "When we find the vampires responsible, we'll be sure to call you in for the kill."

That was more than Freemont had been willing to do. The night was looking up. "Beep me any time."

"We'll talk to Sergeant Freemont now, Ms. Blake." I was dismissed. Fine with me. He offered his hand. I took it. We shook. Agent Elwood and I shook. Everyone smiled. I left.

Larry was waiting out in the entryway. He got up off the stairs where he'd been sitting. "What now?"

"I need to make a phone call."

"Who to?"

Two more men with "Federal Agent" tattooed on their foreheads walked up the hallway from the direction of the kitchen. I shook my head and went out the door into the cool windy night. The place was swarming with cops. I'd never seen so many federal agents in my life. But hey, the very first vampire serial killer was news. Everyone would want a piece. Watching everyone mill around on the carefully tended lawn, I suddenly wanted to go home. To just pack up and go home. It was still early. Hours and hours left of darkness. It only seemed like it had been an eternity since we left the graveyard. Hell, there'd be time to go back and look at Stirling's boneyard before dawn.

I got in the jeep that Bayard had loaned us. I'd use the nifty portable phone it came with.

Larry got in the passenger side.

"Private call."

"Come on, Anita."

"Out, Larry."

"Out in the dark with the vampires." He blinked his big blue eyes at me.

"The place is lousy with cops. I think you'll be safe. Out."

He got out, grumbling under his breath. He could grumble all he wanted to. Larry wanted to be a vampire hunter, fine; but he didn't have to be as intimately involved with the monsters as I was. I was trying to keep him as out of it as I could. Not easy, but worth the effort.

I'd lied to the nice agents. It wasn't the fact that I raised zombies that got me in good with the vampires. It was the fact that the Master of the City, of St. Louis, had the hots for me. Was maybe in love with me, or at least thought he was.

I knew the number by heart, which was a bad sign all on its own. "Guilty Pleasures, where your darkest fantasies come true. This is Robert. How may I help you?"

Great; Robert, one of my least favorite vampires. "Hi, Robert, this is Anita. I need to speak to Jean-Claude."

He hesitated, then said, "I'll transfer you to his office phone. It's a new system, so if I disconnect you, call back."

The phone clicked before I could answer. A moment of silence, and the voice came on the line. You can criticize a lot about Jean-Claude, but he gives good phone.

"Good evening, *ma petite*." That was it, all he said, but even over the buzzing phone his voice was like fur inside my skull.

"I'm near Branson. I need to contact the Master of the City down here."

"No 'Good evening, Jean-Claude, how are you doing?'? Just down to business. How terribly rude, *ma petite*."

"Look, I don't have time for games right now. Some vampires down here are on the rampage. They've kidnapped a young boy. I want to find him before they can make him one of them."

"How young is the boy?"

"Sixteen."

"In centuries past, *ma petite*, that was not considered a child."

"It isn't legal age right this minute."

"Did he go willingly?"

"No."

"You know that for a fact, or were you merely told he was kidnapped?"

"I talked to him before. He didn't go willingly."

Jean-Claude sighed. The sound slithered down my skin like cool fingers. "What do you want of me, *ma petite*?"

"I want to talk to the Master of the City down here. I need the name. I'm assuming you do know who the Master is down here?"

"Of course, but it is not that simple."

"We only have three nights to save him, and a hell of a lot less if they just want a snack."

"The Master will not talk to you without a guide to take you in."

"Send someone, then."

"Who? Robert? Willie? Neither of them is powerful enough to be your escort."

"If you mean they can't protect me, I can protect myself."

"I know you can take care of yourself, *ma petite*. You have made that abundantly clear. But you do not look as dangerous as you are. You might have to shoot one or two to teach them their place. If you got out alive, they would not help you."

"I want to get this boy back intact, Jean-Claude. Work with me here."

"*Ma petite* . . ."

I had an image of Jeff Quinlan's brown eyes. His room with its cowboy wallpaper. "Help me, Jean-Claude."

He was silent for a moment. "I am the only one powerful enough to be your escort. Do you wish me to drop everything and rush down to you?"

It was my turn to be quiet. Put like that, it didn't sound right. It sounded like a big favor. I didn't want to be indebted to him. But I'd probably live through owing him a favor. Jeff Quinlan might not.

"Fine," I said.

"You want me to come help you?"

I gritted my teeth and said, "Yes."

"I will fly down tomorrow night."

"Tonight."

"*Ma petite, ma petite*, what am I to do with you?"

"You said you'd help me."

"And I will, but these things take time."

"What things?"

"It might be helpful if you thought of Branson as a foreign country. A potentially hostile foreign country where I am working to get us safe passage. There are customs to be observed. If I barge in, it will be seen as a declaration of war."

"Isn't there any way to start tonight?" I asked. "Short of starting a war?"

"Perhaps, but if you wait one more night, *ma petite*, we can enter much more safely."

"We can take care of ourselves. Jeff Quinlan can't."

"That is his name?"

"Yeah."

He took a deep breath and let it out in a sigh that made me shiver. I would have told him to stop that, but it would have amused him, so I didn't.

"I will fly down tonight. How do I contact you?"

I gave him the name of my hotel and then, with a sigh, my beeper number.

"I will call you when I arrive."

"How long will it take you to fly this far?"

"Anita, do you think I am going to fly myself down, as a bird would?"

I didn't like the faint amusement in his voice, but I answered truthfully. "It was a thought."

He laughed, and it raised goose-bumps on my arms. "Oh, *ma petite, ma petite*, you are precious."

Just what I wanted to hear. "So how are you getting here?"

"My private jet."

Of course, he had a private jet. "When can you be here?"

"I will be there as soon as I can, my impatient flower."

"I prefer *ma petite* to flower."

"As you like, *ma petite*."

"I want to see the Master of Branson tonight before dawn."

"You have made that abundantly clear, and I will try."

"Do more than try."

"You are feeling guilty about this boy; why?"

"I'm not feeling guilty."

"Responsible, then," he said.

I sat there, not sure what to say. He was right. "I don't suppose you read my mind just then?"

"No, *ma petite*, just your voice and your impatience."

I hated that he knew me that well. Hated it. "Yeah, I feel responsible."

"Why?"

"I was in charge."

"Did you do all you could to keep him safe?"

"I had hosts put at every entrance."

"Someone let them in, then?"

"They had a doggie door that exited through the garage, into the house wall. They didn't want to cut a hole through any of the outer doors."

"Was there a child vampire among them?"

"No."

"Then how?"

I described the thin, skeletal vampire. "It was almost a form change. He changed back in seconds. Once he changed back, he could have passed for human in dim light. I've never seen anything like it."

"I've only seen the ability once," he said.

"You know who it is, don't you?"

"I will be with you as soon as I am able, *ma petite*."

"You sound serious all of a sudden; why?"

He gave a small laugh, but this one was bitter, like swallowing broken glass. It hurt just to hear it. "You know me too well, *ma petite*."

"Just answer the question."

"Did the boy who was taken look younger than his years?"

"Yeah; why?"

Silence thick enough to slice was the only answer.

"Talk to me, Jean-Claude."

"Have there been any other young boys gone missing?"

"Not to my knowledge, but I haven't asked."

"Ask," he said.

"How young?"

"Twelve, fourteen, older if they look young enough."

"Like Jeff Quinlan," I said.

"I fear so."

"Is this vampire into more than just kidnapping?"

"What do you mean, *ma petite*?"

"Murder, not just biting them, but murder."

"What sort of murder?"

I hesitated. I didn't discuss ongoing police investigations with the monsters.

"I know you do not trust me, *ma petite*, but it is important. Tell me of these deaths, please."

He didn't say please very often. I told him. Not in great detail, but enough.

"Were they violated?"

"What do you mean, violated?" I asked.

"Violated, *ma petite*, violated. There are other words for it, but none better for children."

"Oh," I said. "I don't know if they were sexually assaulted. They were still clothed."

"There are things that can be done without removing clothing, *ma petite*. But the abuse would have happened before the killings. Systematic abuse over a period of weeks or months."

"I'll find out if they were assaulted." An idea occurred to me. "Would this vamp ever do a girl?"

"By 'do,' you mean sex?"

"Yeah."

"If pressed for company, he would take a young girl, pre-pubescent, but only if he could find nothing else."

I swallowed hard. We were talking about children like they were things, objects. "No, this girl looked like a woman. She didn't look young."

"Then, no, he would not willingly touch her."

"What do you mean, willingly? What other choice would there be?"

"His master could order him to do it, and he might, if he feared the master enough. Though I cannot think of many people that he would fear enough to do something he found repugnant."

"You know this vampire. Who is he? Give me a name."

"When I arrive, *ma petite*."

"Just give me the name."

"So you can give it to the police?"

"That is their job."

"No, *ma petite*. If it is who I think it is, it will not be a matter for the police."

"Why not?"

"Put simply, he is too dangerous and too exotic to be revealed to the general public. If mortals found out we could have among us such things, they might turn on us all together. You must be aware of that nasty law floating around the Senate."

"I'm aware."

"Then you must understand my caution."

"Maybe, but if more people die because of your caution, it's going to help Brewster's law get passed. You think about that."

"Oh, I am, *ma petite*. Trust that I am. Now farewell. I have much to do." He hung up.

I sat there staring at the phone. Damn him. What did he mean by exotic? What could this new vampire do that others couldn't? He could slim himself down enough to fit through a doggie door. Maybe it made Houdini jealous, but it was hardly a crime. But I remembered its face. Not human. Not even just a corpse's face. It had been something else altogether. Something different. And I remembered those few seconds I lost, twice. Me, the great vampire hunter, helpless as any civilian for just a heartbeat. With vampires, a heartbeat was enough.

Visions of such things would get you talking of demons, which Quinlan had done briefly. The police ignored him, and I didn't back up his story. Quinlan had never met a real demon, or he wouldn't have made the mistake. Once you've been in the presence of demons, you never forget it. I'd rather fight a dozen vampires than one demonic presence. They don't give a shit about silver bullets.

17

IT WAS AFTER 2:00 A.M. before we got back to the grave-yard. The Feds had kept us forever, like they didn't believe we were telling them the whole truth. Fancy that. I hated being accused of concealing evidence when I wasn't. Made me want to lie to them just so they wouldn't be disappointed. I think Freemont had painted a less than charitable picture of me. That'll teach me to be generous. But it seemed petty to point fingers at each other, and say she did it, when Beth St. John's blood was still wet on the carpet.

The wind that had all but promised rain had drifted away. The thick clouds that had obscured the woods while we were playing tag with vampires were suddenly gone. The moon rode high and two days past full. Since dating Richard, I'd paid more attention to the lunar cycles. Fancy that.

The moon sailed the shining night sky, gleaming like it had been polished. The moonlight was so strong it cast faint shadows. You didn't need a flashlight, but Raymond Stirling had one. A big freaking halogen torch that filled his hand like a captive sun.

I watched him start to point it at Larry and me. I raised an arm and said, "Don't point it at us. You'll ruin our night vision." It wasn't very diplomatic, but I was tired, and it had been a long night.

He hesitated in mid-motion. I didn't have to see his face to know he didn't like it. Men like Raymond give orders better than they take them.

He clicked off the light. Good for him. He waited with Ms. Harrison, Bayard, and Beau gathered around him. He was the only one with a flashlight. I bet that his entourage wasn't worried about night vision, and would have liked to have had a light.

Larry and I were still wearing the coveralls. I was getting tired of mine. What I really wanted to do was go back to the hotel and sleep. But once Jean-Claude arrived I wouldn't be sleeping anyway; might as well work. Besides, Stirling was my only paying client. Well, yeah I do get money for killing vampires if it's a legal kill, but it's not a lot of money. Stirling was financing this trip. He deserved his money's worth, I guess.

"We've been waiting for a very long time, Ms. Blake."

"I'm sorry that the death of a young girl inconvenienced you, Mr. Stirling. Shall we go up?"

"I am not unsympathetic to another's loss, Ms. Blake, and I resent the implication that I am." He stood there in the moonlit dark, very straight, very commanding. Ms. Harrison and Bayard moved a little closer, showing support. Beau just stood there, looking sort of amused behind Stirling's back. He was wearing a black slicker with a hood. He looked like a phantom.

I looked up at the clear, sparkling sky. Looked at Beau. He grinned broadly enough for his teeth to flash in the moonlight. I just shook my head and let it go. Maybe he'd been a Boy Scout, always prepared and all that.

"Fine, whatever you say. Let's get this over with." I didn't wait for them. I just walked past them and started up.

Larry, at my side, said, "You're being rude."

140

I glanced at him.

"Yeah, I am."

"He is a paying client, Anita."

"Look, I don't need you to chastise me, okay?"

"What's wrong with you?"

I stopped. "What we just left is what's wrong with me. I'd think it'd bother you a little more, too."

"It bothers me, but I don't have to take it out on everyone else."

I took a deep breath and let it out slow. He was right. Damn. "Alright, you've made your point. I'll try to be nicer."

Stirling marched up to us, entourage in tow. "Are you coming, Ms. Blake?" He walked past us, his back ramrod-straight.

Ms. Harrison stumbled, and only Bayard's grab on her elbow kept her from falling flat on her butt. She was still wearing her high heels. Maybe it was against the executive secretary code to wear tennis shoes.

Beau followed with his black slicker flapping around his long legs. It made a distinctive *slap-slap* sound that was most irritating.

Okay, maybe everything was irritating right now. I was feeling decidedly grumpy. Jeff Quinlan was out there somewhere. He was either already dead or had one bite by now. It wasn't my fault. I'd told his father to put a piece of the host in front of every entrance. I would have thought of the doggie door if I'd seen it, but I'd never gone that far into the house. Even I would have thought it was paranoid to guard the doggie entrance. But I would have done it, and Beth St. John would be alive.

I'd dropped the ball. I couldn't bring Beth St. John back, but I could save Jeff. And I would. I would. I didn't want to avenge him by killing the vampire that killed him. For once I wanted to be in time. For once I wanted to save someone and leave revenge for someone else.

Was Jeff being violated, right this minute? Was that thing I'd seen in the Quinlans' living room doing more than just biting his neck? God, I hoped not. I was pretty sure I could bring Jeff back from a vampire bite, but combine that with rape by a monster, and I wasn't so sure. What if I found him and there wasn't much left to save? The mind is a surprisingly fragile thing sometimes.

I prayed as we walked up the hill. I prayed and felt a measure of calm return. No visions. No angels singing. But a feeling of peace flowed over me. I took a deep breath, and something hard and tight and ugly in my heart let go. I took it as a good sign that I'd get to Jeff in time. But part of me was skeptical. God doesn't always save someone. Often He just helps you live through the loss. I guess I don't entirely trust God. I never doubt Him, but His motives are too beyond me. Through a glass darkly and all that. Just once I'd like to see through the damn glass clearly.

The moon shone down on the top of the hill like silver fire. The air was almost luminescent. The rain was gone, giving its blessing somewhere else. Heaven knows we could have used the rain, but personally I was just as glad I didn't have to walk the raw dirt in a downpour. Mud would have been just too perfect.

"Well, Ms. Blake, shall we begin?" Stirling asked.

I glanced at him. "Yeah." I took a breath and swallowed the blunt things I wanted to say. Larry was right. Stirling was a pain in the ass, but he wasn't who I was mad at. He was just a convenient target.

"Mr. Kirkland and I will walk the graveyard. But you need to stay here. Other people moving around are very distracting." There; that was diplomatic.

"If you were going to make us stand here like an audience, you could have said so at the bottom of this mountain. And saved us the walk."

So much for diplomacy. "Would you have liked me telling you to stay at the bottom of the hill where you couldn't see what we were doing?"

He thought about that for a minute. "No, I suppose I wouldn't have liked it."

"Then what are you complaining about?"

"Anita," Larry said very softly under his breath.

I ignored him. "Look, Mr. Stirling, it has been a really

rough night. I am just out of niceness right now. Please, just let me do my job. The faster I get this done, the sooner we go home. Okay?"

Honesty. I was hoping profound honesty would work. It was about all I had left.

He hesitated a minute, then nodded. "All right, Ms. Blake. Do your job, but know this. You have been decidedly unpleasant. It better be pretty spectacular."

I opened my mouth, and Larry touched my arm. He gripped my arm not too hard, but hard enough. I swallowed what I was going to say and walked away from all of them. Larry trailed after me. Brave Larry.

"What's the matter with you tonight?" he asked when we were out of earshot of Stirling and Co.

"I told you."

"No," he said, "it isn't just the murder tonight. Hell, I've seen you kill people and be less upset afterwards. What's wrong?"

I stopped walking and just stood there for a minute. He'd seen me kill people and be less upset. Was that true? I thought about it for a heartbeat. It was true. That was pretty damn sad.

I knew what was wrong. I'd seen too many slaughtered people in the last few months. Too much blood. Too much killing. I'd done some of the killing. Not all of it had been sanctioned by the state. I also wanted to be looking for Jeff Quinlan. I couldn't do anything until Jean-Claude arrived. I really couldn't. But I felt like my job was interfering with my police work. Was that a bad sign? Or a good one?

I took a deep breath of the cool mountain air. I let it out very slowly, concentrating on just breathing, in and out, in and out. When I felt calm again, I looked at Larry.

"I'm just a little on edge tonight, Larry. I'll be alright."

"If I said a little on edge with a surprised lilt in my voice, would you get mad?"

I smiled. "Yeah, I would."

"You've been in a blacker mood than usual since you talked to Jean-Claude. What's up?"

I stared into his smiling face and didn't want to tell him.

He wasn't that much older than Jeff Quinlan, four years. He could still have passed for a high-schooler. "Fine," I said, and told him.

"A vampire pedophile; isn't that against the rules?"

"What rules?"

"That you can only be one kind of monster at a time."

"It kind of caught me off guard, too."

A strange look flashed across his face. "Sweet Jesus, Jeff Quinlan is with that thing." He looked at me, all the horror, all the pain, or as much as he could imagine, flowing across his face. "We have to do something, Anita. We have to save him." He turned as if to go back down the mountain.

I grabbed his arm. "We can't do anything until Jean-Claude arrives."

"But we can't just do nothing."

"We aren't doing nothing. We're doing our job."

"But how can we . . ."

"Because we can't do anything else right now."

Larry looked at me for a second, then nodded. "Okay; if you can be calm, so can I."

"Good man."

"Thanks. Now show me this nifty trick you've been talking about. I've never heard of anyone who could read the dead without raising them first."

Truthfully, I didn't know if Larry could do it. But telling him he might not be able to was not going to help his confidence. Magic, if that was the right word, often rises and falls on your own belief in your abilities. I've seen very powerful people completely crippled by self-doubt.

"I'm going to walk the cemetery." I tried to think of how to put it into words. How do you explain something that you don't fully understand yourself?

I have always had an affinity with the dead. Even as a small child, I always knew if the soul had fled the body. I remember my great-aunt Katerine's funeral. I'm named after her, my middle name. She was my father's favorite aunt. We went early to view the body and make sure everything was ready. I felt her soul hovering above the coffin. I looked up expecting to see it, but there was nothing for my eyes to hold onto. I've never seen a soul. I've felt them, but I've never seen one.

I know now that Aunt Katerine's soul hung around a long time. Most souls leave within three days, some leave instantly, some don't. My mother's soul was gone by the time the funeral arrived. I didn't feel her there. There was nothing but a closed coffin and a blanket of pink roses over the coffin, as if the coffin would get cold.

It was at home where I felt my mother hovering close. Not her soul, not really, but some piece of her that couldn't let go immediately. I would hear her footsteps in the hall outside my bedroom as if she was coming to kiss me good night. She moved through the house for months, and I found it comforting. When she finally left, I was ready to let her go. I never told my father. I was only eight, but even then I knew that he couldn't hear her. Maybe he heard other things. I don't know. My father and I never talked much about my mother's death. It made him cry.

I'd been able to sense ghosts long before I could raise the dead. What I was about to do was just an extension of that, or maybe a combination of both skills. I don't know. But it was like trying to explain that there was a soul hovering over Aunt Katerine's coffin. Either you knew the soul was there or you didn't. Words didn't quite cover it.

"Can you see ghosts?"

"You mean right now?"

I smiled and shook my head. "No, just in general."

"Well, I knew the Calvin house wasn't haunted, no matter how many stories people made up. But there was a little cave near town that had something in it. Something not nice."

"Was it a ghost?"

He shrugged. "I never tried to find out, but nobody else seemed able to feel it."

"Do you know when the soul leaves the body? I mean, can you tell it?"

"Sure." He said it like, Couldn't everybody do that?

I had to smile. "Good enough. I'm just going to do it. I don't know what you'll see, if anything. I know that Raymond is going to be disappointed because he won't see anything, unless he's a lot more talented than he looks."

"What are you going to do, Anita? They never talked about 'walking a cemetery' in college."

"It's not like a magic spell, a few words or gestures and it works. It isn't anything like that." I struggled to put into words something that we had no vocabulary for. "It's closer to psychic ability than magic. It's not physical. It's not a muscle to move, or even a thought. It's . . . I just do it. Let me get started; then if I can, I'll bring you in or try and talk to you while I do it. Okay?"

He shrugged. "I guess so. I still don't understand what the heck you're doing, but that's okay. I usually don't know what's going on."

"But you always figure it out," I said.

He grinned. "I do, don't I?"

"You bet."

I stood in nearly the dead center of the raw earth. Not so long ago I was afraid of what I was about to do. It wasn't really frightening in and of itself. I was scared of the fact that I could do it at all. It wasn't a very human thing to be able to do. But then, lately I'd been rethinking exactly what made you human, and what made you one of the monsters. Once I'd been very sure of myself, and everyone else. I wasn't so sure anymore. Besides, I'd been practicing.

Of course, I'd been practicing in empty graveyards where there was nothing but me and the dead. Okay, night insects, but anthropods never bothered my concentration. People did.

Even with my back turned, I could feel Larry like a warm presence behind me. It bugged me. "Can you move back farther?"

"Sure; how far?"

I shook my head. "As far as you can get and still be in sight."

He raised his eyebrows. "Do you want me to go over and wait with Mr. Stirling?"

"If you can stand it."

"I can stand it. I schmooze clients better than you do."

That was the God's honest truth. "Great. When I call you over, come slowly. I've never tried to talk to someone while I do this."

"Whatever you say." He gave a laugh that was almost nervous. "I can't wait to see this."

I let that go, and turned away. I walked away from him. When I glanced back, he was walking to the others. I hoped Larry wouldn't be disappointed. I still wasn't sure if he'd be able to even sense anything. I turned my back on all of them. Seeing them huddled there would distract me, that much I was sure of.

The top of the mountain had been stripped. It was like standing on the edge of the world looking down. The moonlight bathed everything in a soft glow. It was so bright up here near the sky without any trees to hide it that the air itself glowed with diffused light. A gentle wind traced just about head-high. It smelled green and fresh, almost as if the rain had actually fallen. I closed my eyes and let the wind touch my skin, ruffle my hair. There was almost no sound but the singing of insects from below. Nothing but the wind, me, and the dead.

I couldn't tell Larry exactly how to do it, because I wasn't completely sure myself. If it was a muscle, I would move it. If it was a thought, I would think it. If it was a magic word, I would say it. It is none of those things. It is like my skin opens up. All my nerve endings naked to the wind. My skin grew cool. It's like a cool wind enamates from my body. It isn't really wind. You can't see it. You can't feel it, or no one else can. But it's there. It's real.

The cool fingers of "wind" stretched outward from me. Within a ten- to fifteen-foot radius I would be able to search the graves. As I moved, the circle would move with me, searching.

I raised my arm and waved. I didn't turn around to see if Larry saw me. I stayed tight inside my private circle. I was holding it in, trying not to start searching the dead until Larry got over here. I was hoping he'd be able to sense what was going on. Seemed logical that it would be easier to figure out if he saw it from the beginning.

I heard his footsteps on the dry earth. They seemed thunderously loud, as if I could hear every grain of dirt under his shoes.

He stopped behind me. "Jesus, what is that?"

"What?" My voice sounded distant and loud at the same time.

"Wind, a cold wind." He sounded a little scared. Good. You should always be a little afraid when you do magic. It's when you start taking it for granted that you get in trouble.

"Come closer, but don't touch me." I wasn't sure on that last, but it sounded like a good idea. Better cautious than not.

He came slowly, one hand held out like he was feeling the wind against his skin. "Jesus, Mary, and Joseph. Anita, it's coming from you. The wind is coming from you."

"Yes," I said.

His eyes were wide. He looked like his voice sounded, a little scared.

"If I stood right next to Stirling, he wouldn't feel a thing. None of them would."

Larry shook his head. "How could they miss it?" His hand hovered just off my body, almost touching but not quite. "It's colder, or stronger, or something the closer I get to your body."

"Interesting," I said.

"What now?" he asked.

"Now, I touch the dead." I let go of it, like unclenching a hand. The fingers of "wind" stretched downward. How does it feel to go through solid earth and touch the dead beneath? Like nothing human. It was as if the invisible fingers could melt through the dirt searching for the dead. This time we didn't have to search far. The earth was disturbed, and the dead lay on top of the raw land.

I'd never tried this in anything but a well-organized cemetery. Where each grave, each body, was distinct. The wind touched Larry like a stone in a stream. The power rippled around him. He was alive, and it disturbed us. But we'd been practicing, and we could work around him.

I was standing on top of bones. Under the earth where

eyes could not see. I tried to step off them, and only stepped on more. The earth was thick with bodies, like raisins in a pudding. No eating around them.

I stood on top on a raft of bones in a sea of dry, red earth. Everywhere I touched was a body—a piece of bone. There was no clear space. No breathing space. I stood there, huddled in on myself, trying to sort through what I was sensing.

The rib cage just to the left belonged with the thighbone yards away. The wind leaked out and touched piece after piece. I could have put the skeleton back together like a giant jigsaw puzzle. That was what my power would do if I tried to raise it.

I moved, stepping on the dead, and everywhere I walked I put bodies together. The pieces stayed separate, but I remembered.

Larry moved with me. He moved surprisingly smoothly through the power, like a swimmer leaving the smallest possible ripples behind.

A ghost flared to life like a pale, dancing flame. I walked towards it. It rose like a swaying snake, watching me without eyes. There was that thread of hostility that some ghosts seem to feel towards the living. A jealousy. But if I'd been tied to some forsaken piece of earth for a hundred years or more, I might be hostile, too.

"What is that?" Larry whispered.

"What do you see?" I asked.

"I think it's a ghost. I've just never seen one materialize before." He reached out as if to touch it.

I grabbed his wrist before he could ever have reached. I felt his power flare to life in a rush of wind that should have poured my hair back from my face.

The circle suddenly widened, like a camera lens spreading wide. The dead awoke under our combined power like twigs touched by fire. Our power spread over them, and they gave up their secrets. Bits of muscle withered to bone, gaping skulls, all the pieces were there. All we had to do was call them forth. Two more ghosts rose from the ground like smoke. It was a lot of active ghosts for this small and this old a cemetery. And they were all angry at being disturbed. The level of hostility was unusual.

Combining our powers hadn't doubled the circle—it had quadrupled it.

The nearest ghost stood like a white pillar of flame. It was strong, powerful. A full-blown ghost in a graveyard that hadn't seen a burial in over two hundred years.

I stared at it. Larry stared at it. As long as we didn't touch it, we were safe. Heck, we were safe even if we did touch it. Ghosts can't cause physical harm, not really. They can grab you, but if you ignore them they fall away. If you pay attention, they can be bothersome. Frightening, but if a spirit causes real harm it isn't just a ghost. Demon, evil sorcerous dead, but not a normal ghost.

Staring at the wavering shape, I wasn't at all sure this was a normal ghost. Ghosts wear out. They fade to haunts, which don't usually materialize, hot spots that can give you a jolt, then just shivery places. Ghosts do not last forever. These looked pretty damn solid. For ghosts.

"Stop!" a man's voice yelled.

Larry and I turned towards the voice. Magnus Bouvier scrambled up the side of the mountain opposite from where we had walked up. His hair fell across his face, hiding everything but his eyes from the moonlight. His eyes glowed in the dark, reflecting lights I could not see.

"Stop!" He was waving his hands. His long-sleeved shirt was untucked over jeans. He hit the circle of wind and froze. He put his hands up as if he was trying to touch it.

Two people in one night who could sense the power. Unusual, but sort of cool. If Magnus hadn't been on the run from the police, we could have sat down and had a nice talk about it.

"We told you to stay off this land, Mr. Bouvier," Stirling said.

Bouvier looked at him, turning his head slowly as if concentrating on anything besides the feel of power was hard.

"We've tried being nice about this," Stirling said. "We are not going to be nice any longer. Beau."

The pump action on a shotgun is a very distinctive sound.

I turned towards the sound, gun in hand. I don't remember thinking about it. I was just looking down the barrel of a gun at Beau. He was cradling a shotgun in his arms, not aimed at anything. That saved him. I know if it had been pointed near us, I'd have shot him.

I was still seeing double. I could see the graveyard behind my eyes where there is no optic nerve. The cemetery was mine. I knew the bodies. I knew the ghosts. I knew where all the pieces lay. I stared down the gun, seeing Beau and the shotgun, but inside my head the dead still reached out for their scattered parts.

The ghosts were still real. The power had agitated them. They'd dance and sway on their own for a while. But they'd fade back into the ground. There was more than one way to raise the dead, but not permanently.

I couldn't look away from the shotgun to see what Bouvier was doing. "Anita, please don't raise the dead." His surprisingly deep voice held a note of pleading.

I fought an urge to glance at him. "Why not, Magnus?"

"Get off my land," Stirling said.

"This is not your land."

"Get off my land or you will be shot for trespassing."

Beau glanced my way. "Mr. Stirling?" He was being very careful that the shotgun stayed loose, and harmless, in his hands.

"Beau, show him we mean business."

"Mr. Stirling," he said again, with a little more urgency in his voice.

"Do what I pay you for," Stirling said.

He started to raise the shotgun to his shoulder, but slowly, watching me.

"Don't do it," I said. I let my breath out all the way until my body was still and quiet. There was nothing but the gun and what I was aiming at.

Beau lowered the shotgun.

I took a breath and said, "Put it on the ground, now."

"Ms. Blake, this is none of your business," Stirling said.

"You are not going to shoot someone for trespassing on a piece of land while I watch."

Larry had his gun out too, now. It wasn't pointed at anybody in particular, which I was grateful for. Pointed guns have a tendency to go off if you don't know what you're doing.

"On the ground, Beau, now. I won't ask a third time."

He laid the shotgun on the ground.

"I pay your salary."

"You don't pay me enough to get killed."

Stirling made an exasperated sound and moved forward as if he would pick up the gun himself.

"Don't touch it, Raymond. You'll bleed just as easy as anybody else."

He turned to me. "I cannot believe that you would hold me at gunpoint on my own property."

I lowered my gun arm just a touch; it gets shaky if you hold a shooting poise too long. "I cannot believe that you had Beau come up here armed. You knew my little show would attract Bouvier. You knew it and planned for it. You cold-blooded son of a bitch."

"Mr. Kirkland, are you going to let her talk to me like that? I am a client."

Larry shook his head. "I'm with her on this one, Mr. Stirling. You were going to ambush that man. Murder him. Why?"

"Good question," I said. "Why are you so afraid of the Bouvier family? Or is it just him that you're afraid of?"

"I am afraid of no one. Come along; we will leave you to your new friend." He marched away, and the others followed. Beau sort of hesitated.

"I'll bring the shotgun down for you," I said.

He nodded. "Figured that."

"And you better not be waiting down there with another gun."

He looked at me for a long minute. At both of us. He shook his head. "I'm going home to my wife."

"You do that, Beau," I said.

He walked away, black slicker flapping against his legs. He hesitated, then said, "I'm out of it from now on. Money doesn't spend if you're dead."

I knew a few vampires that would argue with him, but I said, "Glad to hear it."

"I just don't want to get shot," he said. He walked away down the slope, out of sight.

I stood there with the Browning pointed skyward. I turned in a slow circle, surveying the mountaintop. We were alone, the three of us. So why didn't I want to put my gun up?

Magnus took a step up the slope and stopped. He raised slender hands towards the power-charged air. He trailed fingertips down it, like it was water. I felt the ripples of his touch shiver down my skin, tremble through my magic.

No, I wasn't putting my gun up yet.

"What was that?" Larry asked. His gun was still out, pointed at the ground.

Bouvier moved his gleaming eyes to Larry. "He is not a necromancer, Anita, but he is more than he seems."

"Aren't we all," I said. "Why didn't you want me to raise the dead, Magnus?"

He stared up at me. His eyes were full of glinting lights like reflections in a pool, but the reflections were of things that were not there.

"Answer me, Magnus."

"Or what?" he asked. "You'll shoot me?"

"Maybe," I said.

The slope made him shorter than I was, so I was looking down on him. "I didn't believe anyone could raise dead this old without a human sacrifice. I thought you'd take Stirling's money, try, fail, and go home." He took a step forward, trailing his hands through the power again, as if he were testing it. As if he weren't sure he could cross into it. The touch made Larry gasp.

"With this power you can raise some of them, maybe enough of them," Magnus said.

"Enough for what?" I asked.

He stared up at me, as if he hadn't meant to speak aloud. "You mustn't raise the dead on this mountain, Anita, Larry. You must not."

"Give us a reason not to," I said.

He smiled up at me. "I don't suppose just because I asked."

I shook my head. "Not hardly."

"This would be so much easier if glamor worked on you." He took another step up the slope. "Of course, if glamor worked on you, we wouldn't be here, would we?"

If he wouldn't answer one question, I'd try another one. "Why'd you run from the police?"

He took another step closer, and I backed up. He'd done nothing overtly threatening, but there was something about him as he stood there, something alien.

There were images in his eyes that made me want to glance behind to see what was reflecting in his eyes. I could almost see trees, water . . . It was like the things you see out of the corner of your eye, except in color.

"You told the police my secret; why?"

"I had to."

"You really think I did those awful things to those boys?" He took another step, moving into the flow of power, but he didn't slip easily as Larry had. Magnus was like a mountain, huge, forcing the power to go wide around him, as if he filled more space magically than could be seen with the naked eye.

I pointed the Browning two-handed at his chest. "No, I don't."

"Then why point a gun at me?"

"Why all this fey magic shit?"

He smiled. "I performed a lot of glamor tonight. It's like a high."

"You feed off your customers," I said. "You don't just do it for business. You siphon them; that's fucking unseelie court."

He gave a graceful shrug. "I am what I am."

"How'd you know the victims were boys?" I asked.

Larry moved to my left, gun pointed carefully at the ground. I'd yelled at him for pointing guns at people too soon.

"The police said so."

"Liar."

He smiled gently. "One of them touched me. I saw it all."

"Convenient," I said.

He reached out towards me. "Don't even think it."

Larry pointed his gun at Magnus. "What's going on, Anita?"

"I'm not sure."

"I can't allow you to raise the dead here. I am sorry."

"How are you going to stop us?" I asked.

He stared at me, and I felt something push against my magic, like something large swimming just out of sight in the dark. It made me gasp.

"Freeze, right there, or I will pull this trigger."

"I haven't moved a muscle," he said softly.

"No games, Magnus; you're too damn close to being dead."

"What did he just do?" Larry asked. There was a fine tremor in his two-handed grip.

"Later," I said. "Clasp your hands on top of your head, Magnus, slowly, very slowly."

"Are you going to take me in, as they say on television?"

"Yeah," I said. "You've got a better chance of getting to the jail alive with me than with most of the cops."

"I don't think I'll go with you." Staring down two guns, and he still sounded sure of himself. He was either stupid or knew something I didn't. I didn't think he was stupid.

"Tell me when to shoot him," Larry said.

"When I shoot him, you can shoot him, too."

"Okay," Larry said.

Magnus looked from one to the other of us. "You would take my life for such a small thing?"

"In a heartbeat," I said. "Now clasp your hands slowly on top of your head."

"If I don't?'

"I don't bluff, Magnus."

"Do you have silver bullets in those guns?"

I just stared at him. I could feel Larry shift slightly beside me. You can only point a gun so long without getting tired, or antsy.

"I'll bet they're silver. Silver isn't very effective against fairies."

"Cold iron works best," I said. "I remember."

"Even normal lead bullets would be better than silver. The metal of the moon is a friend to the fey."

"Hands, now, or we find out how fairie flesh holds up to silver bullets."

He raised his hands slowly, gracefully upward. His hands were above shoulder level when he threw himself backwards, falling down the slope. I fired, but he kept on rolling down the earth, and somehow I couldn't quite see him. It was like the air blurred around him.

Larry and I stood at the top of the slope and fired down on him, and I don't think either of us hit him.

He scrambled down the raw earth faster than he looked because he got harder to see even in the moonlight until he vanished into the underbrush left near the midpoint on that side.

"Please tell me he didn't just go poof," Larry said.

"He didn't just go poof," I said.

"What did he do, then?"

"How the hell do I know. This wasn't covered in Fairies 301." I shook my head. "Let's get out of here. I don't know what's going on, but whatever it is, I think we lost our client."

"You think we lost our hotel rooms?"

"I don't know, Larry. Let's go find out." I clicked the safety on the Browning but left it out in my hand. I'd have left the safety off, but that didn't seem wise while stumbling down a rocky mountainside even in the moonlight.

"I think you can put the gun up now, Larry." He hadn't put his safety on.

"You aren't."

"But I've got the safety on."

"Oh." He looked a little sheepish, but he clicked the safety on and holstered it. "You think they would have really killed him?"

"I don't know. Maybe. Beau would have shot at him, but see how much good it did us."

"Why does Stirling want Magnus dead?"

"I don't know."

"Why did Magnus run from the police?"

"I don't know."

"It makes me nervous when you keep answering all my questions with 'I don't know.' "

"Me, too," I said.

I glanced back once just before we lost sight of the mountaintop. The ghosts twisted and flared like candle flames, cool white flames. I knew something else I hadn't known before tonight. Some of the bodies were nearly three hundred years old. A hundred years older than Stirling had told us they were. A hundred years makes a lot of difference in a zombie raising. Why had he lied? Afraid I'd refuse, maybe. Maybe. Some of the bodies were Indian remains. Bits and pieces of jewelry, animal bone, stuff that wasn't European. The Indians in this area didn't bury their dead, at least not in simple graves. And this wasn't a mound.

Something was going on, and I didn't have the faintest idea what it was. But I'd find out. Maybe tomorrow after we got new hotel rooms, gave back the nifty jeep, rented a new car, and told Bert we no longer had a client. Maybe I'd let Larry break the news to him. What are apprentices for if they can't do some of the grunt work?

Okay, okay, I'd tell Bert myself, but I wasn't looking forward to it.

18

STIRLING AND CO. were gone when we trudged down off the mountain. We drove the Jeep back to the hotel. I was frankly surprised they hadn't taken the Jeep with them and left us to walk. Stirling didn't strike me as a man who liked having guns pointed at him. But then, who does?

Larry's room was first down the hall. He hesitated with

his room card in the lock. "You think the rooms are paid for tonight, or do we pack?"

"We pack," I said.

He nodded, and shoved the card in its little slot. The door handle turned, and in he went. I went to the next door and put in my own card. There was a connecting door between the rooms. We hadn't unlocked it, but it was there. Personally I liked my privacy, even from my friends. And especially from my coworkers.

The room's silence flowed around me. It was wonderful. A few minutes of quiet before I faced Bert and told him all that money had just flown the coop.

The room was a suite with an outer room and a separate bedroom. My apartment wasn't much bigger. There was a bar set into the left-hand wall. Being a teetotaler, that was a real plus for me. The walls were a soft pink with a delicate pattern of gilt-edged leaves, the carpet a deep burgundy. The full-sized couch was a purple so dark it looked nearly black. A love seat matched it. Two armchairs were done in a purple, burgundy, and white floral pattern. All exposed wood was very dark and highly polished. I had suspected I had some kind of honeymoon suite until I saw Larry's room. It was nearly a mirror of mine, but done in shades of green.

A cherrywood desk that looked like a genuine antique sat against the far wall. The connecting door was beside it but opened opposite so you wouldn't accidentally bump the desk. Monogrammed stationery graced the desk, along with a second telephone line for your modem I guess.

I don't know if I'd ever stayed in a room this expensive. I doubted seriously if Beadle, Beadle, Stirling, and Lowenstein would want to pick up the tab now.

A sound jerked me around. The Browning sort of materialized in my hand. I was staring down the barrel at Jean-Claude. He stood in the doorway leading to the bedroom. The shirt had long, full sleeves that had been gathered in three puffs down the length of the arm to end in a spill of cloth that framed his long, pale fingers. The collar was high and tied with a white cravat that spilled lace down the front of him tucked into a vest. It was black and velvety with pinpricks of silver on it. Thigh-high black boots fit his legs like a second skin.

His hair was nearly as black as the vest, making it hard to tell where the curls ended and the velvety cloth began. A silver and onyx stickpin that I'd seen before pierced the white lace at his chest.

"Well, *ma petite*, are you going to shoot me?"

I was still standing there with the gun pointed at him. He had not moved. He had been very careful to do nothing that could be taken as threatening. His blue, blue eyes stared at me. Serious, waiting.

I pointed the gun at the ceiling and let out a breath I hadn't realized I was holding. "How the hell did you get in here?"

He smiled then, and pushed away from the doorjamb. He walked into the room with that wonderful gliding motion of his. Part cat, part dancer, part something else. Whatever the "else" was, it wasn't human.

I put the gun away, though I wasn't sure I wanted to. It made me feel better having it in my hand. Trouble was, a gun wouldn't help me against Jean-Claude. Oh, if I was going to kill him it would, but that's not what we were doing lately. Lately we were—dating. Can you stand it? I wasn't sure I could.

"The desk clerk let me in." His voice was very mild, amused, whether with himself or with me it was hard to tell.

"Why would he do that?"

"Because I asked him to." He walked around me like a shark circling its prey.

I didn't turn with him. I stared straight ahead and let him circle me. It would only amuse him if I kept him in sight. The hairs at the back of my neck stood up. I took a step forward and felt his hand fall back. He'd been about to touch my shoulder. I didn't want him to touch me.

"You used mind tricks on the desk clerk?"

"Yes," he said. That one word was full of so much more. I turned towards him so I could see his face.

He was staring at my legs. He raised his face to mine, and somehow that one quick gaze took in my entire body. His midnight blue eyes looked even darker than usual. We weren't sure how I was able to meet his gaze. I was beginning to suspect that being a necromancer had more fringe benefits than just being good with zombies.

"Red becomes you, *ma petite*." His voice had grown softer, deeper. He moved closer to me, not touching. He knew better than that, but somehow his eyes showed where his hands wanted to be. "I like this very much."

His voice was soft and warm, and far more intimate than his words. "Your legs are wonderful." His words were growing softer. A whisper in the dark that hovered around my body like a line of warmth. His voice was always like that, touchable. He still had the best voice I'd ever heard.

"Stop it, Jean-Claude. I'm too short to have wonderful legs."

"I do not understant this modern obsession with height." He ran his hands just above my hose, so close I could almost feel it like a breath of warmth against my skin.

"Stop it," I said.

"Stop what?" His voice was utterly mild, harmless. Ri—ight.

I shook my head. Asking Jean-Claude not to be a pain in the ass was like asking rain not to be wet. Why try?

"Fine, flirt all you want, but keep in mind that you're here to save the life of a young boy. A young boy who may be being raped while we sit here and waste time."

He sighed deeply and walked towards me. Something must have shown on my face because he sat down in the other chair, not trying to come closer. "You have a habit, *ma petite*, of taking all the fun out of seducing you."

"Yippee," I said. "Now, can we get down to business?"

He smiled his lovely, perfect smile. "I had arranged to meet with the Master of Branson tonight."

"Just like that," I said.

"Isn't that what you wanted me to do?" he asked. His voice held that amused edge again.

"Yeah. I'm just not used to you giving me exactly what I ask for."

"I would give you anything you wanted, *ma petite*, if you would only let me."

"I wanted you out of my life. You don't seem to want to do that."

He sighed. "No, *ma petite*, I do not want to do that." He let it go at that. No accusations about me wanting to be with Richard instead of him. No vague threats on Richard's life. It was sort of odd.

"You're up to something," I said.

He turned, eyes wide, long fingers pressed to his heart. "*Moi?*"

"Yeah, you," I said. I shook my head and let it go. He was up to something. I knew him well enough to know the signs, but I also knew him well enough to know that he wouldn't tell me until he was good and ready. Nobody kept a secret like Jean-Claude, and nobody else had as many of them. There was no deceit in Richard. Jean-Claude lived and breathed it.

"I've got to change and pack before we can leave."

"Change your lovely red skirt, why? Because I like it?"

"Not just that," I said, "though admittedly it's a plus. I can't wear my inner pants holster with the skirt."

"I will not argue that having a second gun will help our show of force tomorrow night."

I stopped and turned. "What do you mean, tomorrow night?"

He spread his hands wide. "It is too close to dawn, *ma petite*. We cannot even drive to the master's lair before the sun rises."

"Dammit," I said softly and with feeling.

"I did my part, *ma petite*. But even I cannot stop the sun from rising."

I leaned against the back of the love seat, hands gripping the edge hard enough to hurt. I shook my head. "We're going to be too late to save him."

"*Ma petite, ma petite.*" He knelt in front of me, staring up at me. "Why does this boy bother you so very much? Why is his life so precious to you?"

I stared down into Jean-Claude's perfect face, and had no answer. "I don't know."

He laid his hands on top of my hands. "You're hurting yourself, *ma petite*."

I moved my hands out from under his, crossing my arms over my stomach. Jean-Claude remained kneeling, a hand on either side of me. He was entirely too close to me, and I was suddenly very aware of how short the skirt was.

"I have to go pack," I said.

"Why? Don't you like your room?" Without moving, he seemed closer somehow. I could feel the line of his body against my legs like heat.

"Move," I said.

He leaned backwards, sitting on his heels, forcing me to move past him. The hem of my skirt brushed his cheek as I walked past. "You are such a pain in the ass."

"So nice of you to notice, *ma petite*. Now, why are you leaving this lovely room?"

"A client's paying for the room, and he's not a client anymore."

"Why ever not, *ma petite*?"

"I pulled a gun on him."

His eyes widened, his face a perfect mask of surprise. The mask slipped and he stared at me with ancient eyes. Eyes that had seen much but still didn't know what to make of me. "Why would you do that?"

"They were going to shoot a man for trespassing."

"Was he trespassing?"

"Technically, yeah."

Jean-Claude just looked at me. "Does he not have the right to protect his own land?"

"No, not if it means killing people. A piece of land isn't worth killing over."

"Protecting our lands has been a valid excuse for slaughter since the beginning of time, *ma petite*. Did you suddenly change the rules?"

"I wasn't going to stand there and watch them kill a man for walking on a piece of ground. Besides, I think it was a setup."

"A setup? You mean a plot to kill the man."

"Yeah."

"Were you part of this plot?"

"I may have been bait. He could feel my power over the dead. It called to him."

"Now that is interesting. What is this man's name?"

"You give me the name of the mystery vampire first."

"Xavier," he said.

"Just like that. Why wouldn't you give me the name earlier?"

"I do not want the police to have it."

"Why not?"

"I explained all that. Now, the name of the man you saved tonight."

I stared at him, and didn't want to give it to him. I didn't like how interested he was in the name. But a deal was a deal. "Bouvier, Magnus Bouvier."

"I do not know the name."

"Should you?"

He just smiled at me. It meant nothing and everything.

"You are an irritating son of a bitch."

"Ah, *ma petite*, how can I resist you when you whisper such sweet endearments to me?"

I glared at him, which made him smile wider. There was just the faintest hint of fang peeking into view.

Someone knocked on the door. Probably the manager telling me to get out. I walked to the door. I didn't bother looking through the peephole, so I was caught off guard by who was outside. It was Lionel Bayard.

Had he come to throw us out in person?

I stood there for a second, looking at him. He spoke first, clearing his throat nervously. "Ms. Blake, may I speak with you for a moment?"

He was being awfully polite for someone who had come to kick us out. "I'm listening, Mr. Bayard."

"I really don't think the hallway is the place to discuss this."

I stepped to one side, ushering him into the room. He stepped past me, hands smoothing his tie. His gaze flicked to Jean-Claude, who was standing now. Jean-Claude smiled at Bayard. Pleasant, charming.

"I didn't realize you had company, Ms. Blake. I can come back."

I closed the door. "No, Mr. Bayard, it's all right. I told Jean-Claude about our misunderstanding this evening."

"Ah, yes, uh . . . " Bayard looked from one to the other of us, as if not sure what to say.

Jean-Claude didn't so much sit in the chair as fold his body around it. The movement was almost catlike. "Anita and I have no secrets from one another, Mr. . . . "

"Bayard, Lionel Bayard." He walked over and offered his hand to Jean-Claude. Jean-Claude raised an eyebrow but took the offered hand.

The handshake seemed to make Bayard feel better. A normal gesture. He didn't know what Jean-Claude was. How he could look at him and think him human was beyond me. I'd only seen one vampire that could have passed for human, and he hadn't been human at all. Bayard turned back to me, adjusting his glasses, which didn't need adjusting. That nervous little gesture again. Something was up

"What's up, Bayard?" I asked. I'd closed the door and was leaning to one side of it, arms crossed over my stomach.

"I'm here to offer our most sincere apologies for earlier tonight."

I just stared at him. "You're apologizing to me?"

"Yes. Mr. Stirling was overzealous. Why, if you had not been there to bring us all to our senses, a great tragedy might have occurred."

I tried to keep my face blank. I wanted to frown at him, or look confused. "Stirling's not mad at me?"

"On the contrary, Ms. Blake. He's grateful to you."

I didn't believe that. "Really," I said.

"Oh, yes. In fact, I've been authorized to offer you a bonus."

"Why?"

"To make up for our behavior tonight."

"Your behavior was fine," I said.

He smiled modestly. His act was about as sincere as faux pearls, but not half so realistic.

"How much is the bonus?"

"Twenty thousand," he said.

I stayed leaning against the wall, staring at him. "No."

He blinked at me. "Excuse me?"

"I don't want the bonus."

"I'm not authorized to go higher than twenty thousand, but I could speak with Mr. Stirling. Perhaps he would go higher."

I shook my head and pushed away from the wall. "I don't want more money. I don't want the bonus at all."

"You aren't quitting on us, are you, Ms. Blake?" He was blinking so fast I thought he'd pass out. Me quitting bothered him. A lot.

"No, I'm not quitting. But you're already paying an enormous fee. You don't need to pay more."

"Mr. Stirling is just very anxious that he has not offended you."

I let that one go. Too easy. "Tell Mr. Stirling I'd have thought better of his apology if it had been delivered in person."

"Mr. Stirling is a very busy man. He would have come himself, but he had pressing business."

I wondered how often Bayard had to apologize for the big man. I wondered how often the apology was for telling a fellow flunkie to shoot someone. "Fine, you've delivered the message. Tell Mr. Stirling that it isn't the gunfight that's going to make me bail. I read the cemetery tonight. Some of the corpses are closer to three hundred than two hundred. Three hundred years, Lionel; that's an old zombie."

"Can you raise them?" He had stepped closer, hands fidgeting with his lapels. He was close to invading my space. I'd have rather had Jean-Claude next to me.

"Maybe. The question isn't can I, but will I, Lionel."

"What do you mean?"

"You lied to me, Lionel. You underestimated the age of the dead by nearly a century."

"Not deliberately, Ms. Blake, I assure you. I merely repeated what our research department told me. I did not deliberately mislead you."

"Sure."

He reached out almost like he wanted to touch me. I moved back, just enough. He seemed terribly intense. He let his hand drop. "Please, Ms. Blake, I did not lie on purpose."

"The problem, Lionel, is that I'm not sure I can raise zombies this old without a human sacrifice. Even I have my limits."

"So nice to know," Jean-Claude said softly.

I frowned at him. He smiled.

"You will try, won't you, Ms. Blake?"

"Maybe. I haven't decided yet."

He shook his head. "We will do anything to make this oversight up to you, Ms. Blake. It is entirely my fault that I did not double-check the research department's findings. Is there anything that I can do personally to make it up to you?"

"Just leave. I'll call your office tomorrow to discuss details. I may need some extra . . . paraphernalia to attempt the raising."

"Anything, anything at all, Ms. Blake."

"Fine; I'll call." I opened the door and stood by it. I thought it was enough of a hint. It was. Bayard went to the door and almost backed out, apologizing as he went.

I closed the door and stood there for a minute.

"That little man is up to something," Jean-Claude said.

I turned and looked at him. He was still curled in the chair, looking scrumptious.

"I didn't need vampiric powers to tell me that."

"Neither," he said, "did I." He rose from the chair easily. If I'd curled up in a chair like that, I'd have been stiff.

"I've got to tell Larry that he can stop packing. I don't understand why we're still hired, but we are."

"Can anyone else raise the graveyard?"

"Not without a human sacrifice, maybe not even then," I said.

"They need you, *ma petite*. From the little man's anxiety, they must need the dead raised very badly."

"Millions of dollars are at stake."

"I do not think money is all that is at stake," he said.

I shook my head. "Me either."

He came to join me by the door. "What extra paraphernalia will you need to raise a three-hundred-year-old corpse, *ma petite*?"

I shrugged. "A bigger death. I'd originally thought to use a couple of goats." I opened the door.

"What are you thinking about using now?"

"An elephant, maybe," I said.

We were out in the hall and he was staring at me.

"I'm kidding. Honest. Besides, elephants are an endangered species. I was thinking maybe a cow."

Jean-Claude stared down at me for a long space of moments, his face very serious. "Remember, *ma petite*, I can tell if you are lying."

"What's that supposed to mean?"

"You meant the elephant comment."

I frowned up at him. What could I say? "Okay, but just for a minute. I wouldn't really do in an elephant. I'm telling the truth."

"Yes, *ma petite*, I know."

I hadn't really meant the crack about the elephant. Not really. It was just the biggest animal I could think of on short notice. And if I was going to attempt to raise several three-hundred-year-old corpses, I was going to need something big. I didn't think a cow would do. Hell, I didn't think a herd of cows would do it. I just hadn't thought of a good alternative yet.

But no elephants, I promise. Besides, can you imagine trying to slit the throat of an elephant? The logistics of just getting one to hold still while you killed it were mindboggling. There's a reason why most sacrifices are our size or smaller. Makes it easier to hold them down.

"We can't just leave Jeff with that monster," Larry said. He was standing in the middle of his forest green carpet. Jean-Claude was sitting in the corner of the green patterned couch. He was looking amused, like a cat that had found a very interesting mouse.

"We aren't leaving him," I said. "We just can't go looking for him tonight."

He whirled and pointed a finger at Jean-Claude. "Why, because he says so?"

Jean-Claude's smile widened. Definitely amused.

"Check the time, Larry. It'll be dawn soon. All the vampires will be asnooze in their coffins."

Larry shook his head. The look on his face reminded me of me. Stubborn, not wanting to accept it. "We have to do something, Anita."

"We can't talk to vampires during daylight hours, Larry. That's just the way it is."

"And what happens to Jeff today, while we wait for the sun to go down?" His pale skin had gone almost white. His freckles looked like brown ink spots. His pale blue eyes glittered like angry glass. I'd never seen Larry so mad. Hell, I'd never seen him angry.

I glanced at Jean-Claude; he just looked at me. I was on my own. Wasn't I always. "Xavier will have to sleep. He won't be able to harm Jeff once the sun rises."

Larry shook his head. "Will we get him back in time?"

I wanted to say "Sure," but I wouldn't lie. "I don't know. I hope so."

His soft, Howdy-Doody face was set in very stubborn lines. I looked at him and understood why so many people underestimate me. He looked so harmless. Hell, he was sort of harmless, but he was armed now, and learning how to be dangerous. And in his face for the first time I saw a grim purpose building. I'd planned on leaving him behind when I went to talk to the Master of Branson. Looking at him now, I wasn't sure he was going to let me do that. He'd had his first vampire hunt tonight. I'd managed to keep him out of the rough stuff until now. But it wasn't going to last. I'd been hoping he'd give up the idea of hunting vampires. Staring into his glittering eyes, I realized I was the one who was fooling myself. In his own way Larry was as stubborn as I was. Frightening thought, that. But for tonight he was safe.

"You couldn't just comfort me? Tell me we'll find him?" Larry asked.

I smiled. "I try not to lie to you, if I can avoid it."

"For once," Larry said, "I'd have liked to have heard the lie."

"Sorry," I said.

He took in a deep breath and let it out slow. His anger was gone just like that. Larry didn't know what it was to hold onto his rage. He didn't brood over things. One of the main differences between us. I never forgave anyone for anything. A character flaw to be sure, but hell, everyone's got to have at least one.

There was a knock on the door. Larry went for the door.

Jean-Claude was suddenly standing by me. I hadn't seen him move. Hadn't heard his leather boots slither over the carpet. Nothing. Magic. My heart was suddenly thudding in my throat.

"Stomp your feet or something when you do that."

"Do what, *ma petite*?"

I glared up at him. "That wasn't a mind trick, was it?"

"No," he said. That one word slithered across my skin like a low creeping breeze.

"Damn you," I said softly and with feeling.

He smiled. "We've been over that, *ma petite*; you are too late."

Larry had closed the door. "There's a guy out in the hall says he's with Jean-Claude."

"A guy or a vampire?" I asked.

Larry frowned. "Not a vampire, but if you mean human I wouldn't go that far."

"You expecting company?" I asked.

"Yes, I am."

"Who?"

He stalked to the door and put a hand on the doorknob. "Someone I believe you've already met." He opened the door with a flourish, stepping to one side to let me have a clear view.

Jason stood in the open door, smiling, relaxed. He was my height exactly, not something you find in a man often. Straight blond hair barely touched the top of his collar; his eyes were the innocent blue of spring skies. The last time I'd seen him he'd been trying to eat me. Werewolves will do that sometimes.

He was dressed in an oversized black sweater that hit him almost at mid-thigh. He'd had to roll the sleeves over his wrists. His pants were leather, laced up the side from waist to mid-calf, where the laces vanished into boots. The lacings were loose enough that there was a pale line of flesh all the way down.

"Hello, Anita."

"Hi, Jason. What are you doing here?"

He had the grace to look embarrassed. "I'm Jean-Claude's new pet."

He said the last word like it was alright. Richard wouldn't have said it that way.

"You didn't tell me you brought company," I said.

"We are going to be calling on the Master of the City. We must make a good show of it."

"So a werewolf, and what . . . me?"

He sighed. "Yes, *ma petite*, whether you bear my marks or not, most consider you my human servant." He raised a hand. "Please, Anita, I know you are not my human servant in the technical sense. But you have helped me defend my territory. You have killed to protect me. That is the best definition of what a human servant does."

"So, what? I have to pretend to be your human servant on this visit?"

"Something like that," he said.

"Forget it."

"Anita, I need a show of strength here. Branson was part of Nikolaos's territory. I gave it up because the population density could support another group. But it was still my land, and now it's not. Some view that as weakness rather than practicality."

"So without any marks at all you've finally got me to play servant for you. You manipulative son of a bitch."

"You asked me down here, *ma petite*." A thread of warmth cut through his words. He stalked towards me. "I am doing you a favor, do not forget that."

"I don't think you'll let me forget," I said.

He made a harsh sound, as if he had no words for his anger. "Why do I put up with you? You insult me at every turn. There are many who would give their souls for what I offer you."

He stood in front of me, eyes like dark sapphires, skin white as marble. His skin glowed like there was a light inside him. He looked like some kind of live sculpture made of light, jewels, and stone.

He was impressive and scary, but I'd seen it before. "Cut the vampire powers shit, Jean-Claude. It's almost dawn; don't you have a coffin to crawl into somewhere?"

He laughed, but it wasn't pleasant, it was bitter like the touch of steel wool. Something to irritate rather than entice. "Our luggage has not arrived, has it, my wolf?"

"No, master," Jason said.

"Your coffin hasn't arrived?" I asked.

"Either I have chosen a very lax skycab, or . . ." He let the words trail off, face bland and pleasant.

"Or what?" Larry asked.

"*Ma petite.*"

"You think the local master took your coffin," I said.

"A punishment for entering her territory without observing all the social niceties." He looked at me when he said it.

"I suppose that's my fault," I said.

He gave that infuriating shrug. "I could have said no, *ma petite.*"

"Stop being so civilized about it."

"Would you be happier if I was angry?" His voice was very mild when he said it.

"Maybe," I said. It would have made me feel less guilty, but I didn't say that out loud.

"Go to the airport and find our luggage if you can, Jason. Bring it back to Anita's room."

"Wait a minute. You are not moving into my room."

"It is nearly dawn, *ma petite.* I have no choice. Tomorrow we will find other accommodations."

"You planned this."

He gave a short, bitter laugh. "Even my deviousness knows some bounds, *ma petite.* I would not willingly be without my coffin this close to dawn."

"What are you going to do without your coffin?" Larry asked. He looked anxious.

Jean-Claude smiled. "Do not fear, Lawrence, all I need is darkness, or rather lack of sunlight. The coffin itself is not absolutely necessary, simply more secure."

"I've never known a vampire that didn't sleep in a coffin," I said.

"If I am underground in a secure place, I forego my coffin. Though truthfully, once daylight finds me I am insensible and could sleep on a bed of nails and not know it."

I wasn't sure I believed him. He worked harder than most at passing for human.

"You will see the truth of my words soon enough, *ma petite*."

"That's what I'm afraid of," I said.

"You can sleep on the couch if you prefer, but I am telling you truly that once full daylight arrives I will be harmless, helpless if you like. I would be unable to molest you even if I wanted to."

"And what other fairy tales am I supposed to believe? I've seen you move around after dawn, hidden from light, but you worked just fine."

"After eight hours or so of sleep, if it is still daylight I can move around, true, but I doubt you will stay abed for eight hours. You have clients or something, a murder investigation, some business that will take you out and about."

"If I leave you alone, who'll see that some maid doesn't come in, pull the curtains back and French fry you?"

The smile widened. "Concern over my well-being. I am touched."

I looked at him. He looked pleasant, amused, but it was a mask. His expression when he didn't want you to know what he was thinking, but didn't want you to know that he didn't want you to know. "What are you up to?"

"For once, *ma petite*, nothing."

"Yeah, right."

"If I find the coffin, I'll need to rent a truck," Jason said.

"You can use our Jeep," Larry said.

I glared at him. "No, he can't."

"Think of it as expediency, *ma petite*. If Jason must rent a truck, then I may have to spend another day in your bed. I know you do not want that." There was amusement in his voice, and an undercurrent of something else. It might have been bitterness.

"I'll drive," Larry said.

"No, you won't," I said.

"It's almost dawn, Anita. I'll be alright."

I shook my head. "No."

"You can't treat me like a kid brother forever. I can drive the Jeep."

"I promise not to eat him," Jason said.

Larry held out his hand for the keys. "You have to trust me sometime."

I just looked at him.

"I promise to shoot anything, human or monster, that threatens me while I'm gone." He made the Boy Scout sign, three fingers to heaven. "You can bail me out of jail and explain that I was just following orders."

I sighed. "Alright, dammit." I gave him the keys.

He grinned at me. "Thanks."

I shook my head. "Just hurry back, okay?"

"Anything you say."

"Just get out of here, and be careful."

Larry left with Jason trailing behind. I stared at the door after it closed, wondering if I should have gone with them. Knowing that Larry would have gotten mad, but mad was better than dead. Hell, it was a simple errand; go to the airport and pick up a coffin. What could go wrong with less than an hour of darkness left? Shit.

"You cannot protect him, Anita."

"I can try."

Jean-Claude gave that infuriating shrug that meant anything you wanted it to mean, and nothing at all. "Shall we retire to your room, *ma petite*?"

I opened my mouth to tell him he could bunk with Larry, but didn't say it. I didn't really believe he'd munch on Larry, but I was sure he wouldn't munch on me. "Sure," I said.

He looked a little surprised, as if he'd expected an argument. But I was all out of argument tonight. He could have the bed. I'd take the couch. What could be more innocent? Biker Nuns from Hell, but besides that.

19

I COULD FEEL dawn pressing against the windows like a cool hand when we got back to my room. It was very near. Jean-Claude smiled at me. "The first time I manage to share a hotel room with you, and there is no time." He gave an elaborate sigh. "Things never work as I plan with you, *ma petite.*"

"Maybe that's a hint," I said.

"Perhaps." He glanced at the closed drapes. "I must go, *ma petite*. Until darkness." He shut the bedroom door a little hurriedly. I could feel the coming light pressing around the building. I'd noticed over the years of hunting vamps that I'd become aware of dawn, and sunset. There had been times when I'd struggled from disaster to disaster just to stay alive until that soft growing pressure of light could sweep the sky and save my cookies. For the first time I wondered what it would be like to see it as a danger instead of a blessing.

After he'd closed the door I realized my suitcase was in the bedroom. Damn. I hesitated, and finally knocked. No answer. I opened the door just a crack, then farther. He wasn't in there. Water ran in the bathroom. A line of light showed under the door. What did vampires do in bathrooms? Better not to know.

I grabbed my suitcase from the floor and carried it out before the bathroom door could open. I did not want to see him again. I did not want to see what happened to him when the sun rose.

When the sun had risen enough to pulse against the closed drapes like pale lemon liquid, I changed into a t-shirt and jeans. I had a robe with me, but if I was going to greet both Larry and Jason I wanted to be wearing some pants.

I called down for extra blankets and a pillow. No one bitched that it was a quarter past dawn, and a strange time to need bedclothes. They just brought the stuff. True class. The maid didn't even glance at the closed bedroom door.

I spread the blanket on the couch and stared at it. It was a pretty couch but didn't look terribly comfortable. Oh, well, virtue had its punishments. Of course, maybe it wasn't virtue that kept me out of the bedroom. If it had been Richard curled up in the next room, then only moral fortitude would have kept me out. With Jean-Claude . . . I had never seen him after dawn when he was dead to the world. I wasn't sure I wanted to see. I knew I didn't want to cuddle up next to him while the warmth left his body.

There was a knock on the door. I hesitated. It was probably Larry, but then again . . . I went to the door with the Browning naked in my hand. Beau had had a shotgun last night. Paranoia, or caution; hard to tell the difference sometimes.

I stood to one side of the door and said, "Yes."

"Anita, it's us."

I hit the safety and put the barrel of the Browning down the front of my jeans. It was too big a gun to wear in an inner pants holster, but for temporary holding, that worked.

I opened the door.

Larry leaned against the doorjamb, looking rumpled and tired. He had a McDonald's sack in one hand, and four cups shoved into one of those Styrofoam holders. Two of the cups held coffee, the other two sodas.

Jason had a large leather suitcase under each arm, a battered, much smaller suitcase in his right hand, and a second McDonald's bag in his left. He didn't look the least bit tired. A morning person, even after no sleep at all. It was disgusting. His eyes flicked to the gun shoved in my waistband. He noticed, but he didn't comment. Point for him.

Larry never even blinked at the gun.

"Food?" I asked.

"I didn't eat much last night. Besides, Jason was hungry, too," Larry said. He came inside, putting the drinks and food on the wet bar. None of us drank; good to use the bar for something.

Jason walked through the door sideways with the suitcases and food, but there was no effort to it. He wasn't straining one little bit to carry it all.

"Showoff," I said.

He sat the luggage on the floor. "This isn't even close to showing off," he said.

I locked the door behind them. "I suppose you can bring the coffin up single-handedly."

"No, but not because it's heavy. It's just too long. The balance isn't right."

Great. Super werewolf. Though for all I knew, all lycanthropes could lift that much weight. Maybe Richard could lift coffins with one arm. It was not a comforting thought.

Jason started laying food out on the bar. Larry had already climbed onto one of the bar stools. He was pouring sugar into one of the coffees.

"Did you just leave the coffin in the lobby?" I asked. I had to lay the Browning on the bar to sit down. I was just too short-waisted to have it down my pants.

Larry sat the unopened coffee in front of me. "It's missing."

I stared at him. "You found the suitcases but not the coffin?"

"Yep," Jason said, as he finished dividing the food into three piles. He'd pushed some of it in front of both of us, but the lion's share was in front of him.

"How can you eat this early in the morning?"

"I'm always hungry," he said. He looked at me sort of expectantly.

I let it slide. It was too easy.

"Come on, I fed you that one," he said.

"You don't seem particularly worried," I said.

He shrugged, and slid onto a bar stool. "What do you want me to say? I've seen some weird shit since I became a werewolf. If I got hysterical every time something went wrong, every time someone I knew died, I'd be in the loony bin by now."

"I thought fights for dominance in the pack, except for pack leader, weren't to the death," I said.

"People forget," he said.

"I'll have to talk to Richard when I get back in town. He hasn't been mentioning any of this."

"Nothing to mention," Jason said. "Just business as usual."

Great. "Did anybody see who took the coffin?"

Larry answered, his voice sluggish even with the caffeine and sugar. There's only so much you can do on no sleep at all. "No one saw anybody take it. In fact, the only guy left from the night shift said, 'I just turned away for a second, and it wasn't there. Just the luggage standing there by itself.'"

"Shit," I said.

"Why take the coffin?" he asked. He drank most of his coffee. His Egg McMuffin sat untouched in front of him. They'd put hotcakes in front of me with a little tub of syrup beside it.

"Your breakfast is getting cold," Jason said.

He was enjoying himself too much. I frowned at him, but I opened my coffee. I didn't want the food. "I think the master is flexing a little muscle. What do you think, Jason?" I kept my voice casual.

He smiled at me around a mouthful of food, swallowed, and said, "I think whatever Jean-Claude wants me to think."

Maybe my voice had been too casual. I should really give up on subtlety; I just wasn't good enough at it. "Did he tell you not to talk to me?"

"No, just to be careful what I said."

"He says jump, and you say how high; is that it?"

"That's it." He ate a bite of scrambled egg, his face peaceful.

"Doesn't that bother you?"

"I don't make the rules, Anita. I'm not an alpha anything."

"And it doesn't bother you?" I asked.

He shrugged. "Sometimes, but there's nothing I can do about it. Why fight it?"

"I don't understand that at all," Larry said.

"Me either."

"You don't have to understand it," he said. He couldn't have been more than twenty, but the look in his eyes wasn't young.

It was the look of someone who'd seen a lot, done a lot, and not all of it nice. It was the look I was dreading to see on Larry's face someday. They were nearly the same age; what had people been doing to Jason to give him such jaded eyes?

"What do we do now?" Larry asked.

"You're the vampire experts. I'm just Jean-Claude's pet."

He said it like it didn't bother him. It would have bothered me. I shook my head. "I'm going to call the cops, then get some sleep."

"What are you going to tell them?" Jason asked.

"I'm going to tell them about Xavier."

"Did Jean-Claude say you could tell the cops?"

I looked at him. "I didn't ask for permission."

"Jean-Claude wouldn't like you bringing in the police."

I just stared at him.

He blinked at me. "Don't do it just because I said that, please."

"He knows you pretty well for someone who's only met you twice," Larry said.

"Three times," I said. "Two out of three times, he's tried to eat me."

Larry's eyes widened a little. "You're kidding."

"She just looks so tasty," Jason said.

"I've had about enough of you," I said.

"What's wrong? Jean-Claude and Richard both tease you."

"I'm dating both of them," I said. "I'm not dating you."

"Maybe you've got a thing for monsters. I can be just as scary as the next guy."

I stared at him. "No," I said, "you can't. That's why you're not alpha. That's why you're Jean-Claude's pet, because you aren't scary enough."

Something flowed through his pale blue eyes. Something angry and dangerous. Sitting there with his forkful of scrambled eggs, and a Coke in one hand, he was suddenly different. It was hard to put into words, but it raised the hair on the back of my neck.

"Ease down, wolf boy," I said. My voice was soft, careful. I was sitting less than a foot away from him. At this distance he could jump me easy. The Browning was an inch away from my right hand, but I knew better. I might grab the gun, but I'd never get it pointed in time. I'd seen him move before, and I wasn't quick enough. Lack of sleep was making me trusting, or stupid. Same thing.

A low, trickling growl rumbled out of him. My pulse beat a little faster.

Larry's gun was suddenly pointing past my nose at the werewolf's face. "Don't," Larry said. His voice was low and even, and very damn serious.

I eased back off the bar stool, bringing the Browning with me. Didn't really want Larry's gun to go off right next to my face.

I pointed my gun at Jason's chest, one-handed, almost casual. "Don't ever threaten me again."

Jason stared at me. His beast lurked just behind his eyes like a wave rushing towards the shore.

"You start going furry, and I won't wait to find out if you're bluffing," I said.

Larry had one knee on the bar stool, gun still pointed nice and steady. I hoped he didn't fall off the bar stool and accidentally shoot Jason. If he shot him, I wanted it to be on purpose.

Jason's shoulders relaxed. His hands unclenched, leaving the fork and the drink on the bar. He closed his eyes and sat very still for nearly a full minute. Larry and I waited, guns still pointed. Larry's eyes flicked to me. I shook my head.

Jason opened his eyes and let out a deep, sighing breath. He looked normal again, that tension drained away. He grinned. "I had to try."

I took another step back, putting my back to the wall. Out of reach, I lowered the gun. Larry hesitated, but followed my lead.

"So you tried; now what?"

He shrugged. "You're dominant to me."

"Just like that," I said.

"Would you be happier if I made you fight me?"

I shook my head.

"But I backed her up," Larry said. "She didn't do it alone."

"Doesn't matter. You're loyal to her, would risk your life for her. There's more to being dominant than just muscle, or guns."

Larry looked puzzled. "What do you mean, dominant? I feel like I'm missing part of the conversation."

"Why are you working so damn hard at not being human, Jason?" I asked.

He smiled and went back to his breakfast.

"Answer me, Jason."

He finished off his eggs and said, "No."

"What's going on?" Larry said.

"Mind games," I said.

Larry made an exasperated noise. "Someone explain to me why we had to pull a gun on someone who's supposed to be on our side."

"Jean-Claude keeps telling me Richard isn't any more human than he is. Jason's little display helps emphasize that. Doesn't it, wolf-boy?"

Jason ate the rest of his food like we weren't there.

"Answer me," I said.

He turned on the bar stool, putting his elbows behind him. "I have too many masters now, Anita. I don't need another one."

"And I've got too many monsters messing with me right now. Don't add yourself to the list, Jason."

"Is it a short list?" he asked.

"Gets shorter all the time," I said.

He smiled and slid off the bar stool. "Is anybody tired but me?"

Larry and I stared at him. The werewolf didn't look tired—more than I could say for us mere humans.

Jason wasn't going to answer my questions, and they weren't important enough to shoot him over. Stalemate.

"Fine; where are you sleeping?" I asked.

"If you trust me not to eat him, in Larry's room."

"No way," I said.

"You want me here, with you?"

"I told him he could stay in my room on the ride over," Larry said.

"That was before he pulled the werewolf crap," I said.

Larry shrugged. "You've got the Master of the City tucked into your bed. I think I can handle one werewolf."

I didn't think so. But I didn't want to discuss it in front of the werewolf. "No, Larry."

He was instantly angry. "What do I have to do to prove myself to you?"

"Stay alive," I said.

"What's that supposed to mean?"

"You're not a shooter, Larry."

"I was willing to shoot him." Larry pointed to the smiling werewolf.

"I know."

"Because I'm not trigger-happy, you don't trust me to handle myself?"

I sighed. "Larry, please. If Jason turned furry in the middle of the day and killed you, I couldn't live with myself."

"And if he kills you?" Larry said.

"He won't."

"Why not?" Larry asked.

"Because Jean-Claude would kill him. If he hurt you, I'd kill him, but I don't know if Jean-Claude would avenge you. Jason's more frightened of Jean-Claude than he is of me. Aren't you, Jason?"

Jason had sat down on the end of the couch on my blanket. "Oh, yes."

"I don't know why," Larry said. "You're the one who kills for Jean-Claude. He never seems to kill anyone on his own."

"Larry, who would you be more afraid of, Jean-Claude or me?"

"You wouldn't hurt me," he said.

"If you had to face one of us, which would you prefer?"

Larry looked at me for a long time. The anger drained away, replaced by something tired and old in his eyes. "Him."

"For God's sake, why?" I asked.

"I've seen you kill a lot of people, Anita. A lot more than

Jean-Claude. He might try to frighten me to death, but you'd just kill me."

My mouth was open, just a little. "If you really believe that I'm more dangerous than Jean-Claude, then you haven't been paying attention."

"I didn't say you were more dangerous. I said you'd kill me quicker."

"That's why I'm not as afraid of Anita as I am of Jean-Claude," Jason said.

Larry looked at him. "What do you mean?"

"All she'll do is kill me, quick, neat. Jean-Claude wouldn't kill me quick, or easy. He'd make sure it hurt."

The two men stared at each other. Each one's logic was sound as far as it went. I was with Jason. "If you really believe what you're saying, Larry, then you haven't seen enough vampires."

"How am I ever going to see enough vampires if you keep me at arm's length, Anita?"

Had I really kept him out of it that much? Had I overprotected him? Let him see my ruthlessness but not Jean-Claude's?

"And I'm going to the master's tomorrow night. You are not leaving me behind anymore."

"You're right," I said. The answer seemed to surprise both of them.

"If you really believe that I'd kill someone quicker than Jean-Claude would, I have overprotected you. You have to understand how dangerous they are, Larry. How deadly, or someday I won't be around and you'll get killed."

I took a deep breath and let it out slowly. My stomach was tight with fear. Fear that Larry would get killed because I'd kept him out of it. It was something I hadn't anticipated.

"Come on, Jason," Larry said.

Jason stood up.

"No. Tomorrow you can be ass-deep in vampires with me watching. Until you understand how dangerous the monsters are, I don't want you alone with them."

His eyes were angry and hurt. I'd undercut his confidence, his self-esteem. But . . . what else could I do?

Larry turned abruptly on his heel and left. He didn't argue. He didn't say good-bye. He slammed the door behind him, and I fought an urge to follow him. What could I say? I leaned my forehead against the door, and whispered, "Damn."

"Do I get the couch?" Jason asked.

I turned and leaned against the door. I still had the Browning in my hand, though I wasn't sure why anymore. I was getting tired, sloppy. "No, I get the couch."

"Where do you want me, then?"

"I don't care; just not near me."

He ran his hands down the edge of the blanket, running the cloth between his fingers. "If you're really sleeping out here, I'd just as soon have the bed."

"It's taken," I said.

"How big is the bed?"

"King-size, but what difference does it make?"

"Jean-Claude won't mind if I share with him. He'd prefer it was you, but . . . " He shrugged.

I looked at him, at his tranquil, pleasant face. "Is this the first time you've shared a bed with Jean-Claude?"

"No," he said.

It must have shown on my face, because he lowered the high neck of the sweater enough for me to see two fang marks. I pushed away from the wall and walked closer. Close enough to see that the bite was almost healed.

"Sometimes he likes a snack when he first wakes up," Jason said.

"Jesus," I said.

Jason let go of the collar, and it slid over the bite like it wasn't there. The same way you'd hide a hickey. Jason sat there looking harmless. He was exactly my height, and had the face of a knowledgeable angel.

"Richard didn't let Jean-Claude snack on him," I said.

"No," he said.

"No. That's all you have to say."

"What do you want me to say, Anita?"

I thought about that for a second. "I want you to be outraged. Angry."

"Why?"

I shook my head. "Go to bed, Jason. You're making me tired."

He went into the bedroom without another word. I didn't peek to see if he changed into a wolf and curled up on the carpet, or if he crawled into bed beside the corpse. None of my business, or at least nothing I wanted to see.

20

I PUT THE Browning under the pillow with the safety on. At home with the gun in the special holster I'd added to the headboard of the bed, the safety would have been off. But I'd look pretty silly if I accidentally shot myself during the night—day—trying to protect myself from werewolves.

The Firestar I put under the couch cushion, safety on. Normally it would have been in my luggage, but I was feeling just a little insecure.

The knives were in the luggage. Things weren't quite dangerous enough to wear the wrist sheaths to bed. Besides, they weren't very comfortable, not to sleep in, anyway.

I had just settled down for a long day's sleep when I realized I hadn't called Special Agent Bradford. Damn. I threw the blanket back and padded to the telephone in nothing but a t-shirt and undies. Yes, the Browning came with me. Doesn't do you a damn bit of good to have a weapon if it isn't with you.

I dialed the number and got no answer. Fancy that. Didn't everyone work twenty-four hours a day? I had his beeper number. Could the news about Xavier wait? Would even having the name help them? Agent Bradford had made it very clear that I was persona non grata. First, Freemont had blackballed me; second, the Quinlans were threatening to sue everybody unless I was kept away from the case. I'd done such a bang-up job protecting their family, they didn't

want a repeat. They seemed to think I'd get their son killed.
Fancy that.

I had Bradford's beeper number. He'd given strict orders
that if I found out anything I was to tell him, and only him.
Made me not want to tell him a bloody thing. But who was
I to say the FBI didn't have a vampire file somewhere?
Maybe the name would mean something to them. Maybe it
would help them find Jeff. Besides, Jean-Claude hadn't told
me not to give Xavier's name to the cops. I used the beeper
number. I left my phone number. Now I could either go back
to bed, and let his return call wake me, or I could sit in the
chair for a few minutes and wait. I waited.

The phone rang in under five minutes. I like a man who
returns his pages promptly. I said "Hello," in case it wasn't
him. It was.

"Special Agent Bradford. This number was on my
beeper." His voice was rough with sleep.

"This is Anita Blake."

A moment of silence, then, "Do you know what time it
is?"

"I haven't been to bed yet, so yeah, I know what time it
is."

Another silence. "What do you want, Ms. Blake?"

I took a deep breath and let it out slow. Getting mad
would not be helpful. "I have a possible name for the vampire that's been slaughtering kids."

"What's the name?"

"Xavier."

"Last name?"

"Vampires don't have last names, as a general rule."

"Thank you for the name, Ms. Blake. How did you get
it?"

I thought about that for a few seconds. I couldn't think of
a really good answer. "It sort of fell into my lap."

"Why don't I believe that, Ms. Blake? I thought I'd made
myself clear this evening. You are not to involve yourself in
this case, in any way."

"Look, I didn't have to call, but I want Jeff Quinlan back

alive. I thought the FBI might be able to use the name of the vampire who took him."

"I want to know how you got the name," he said.

"An informant."

"I'd like to talk to this informant," he said.

"No," I said.

"Are you withholding information from a federal investigation, Ms. Blake?"

"No, Agent Bradford, I am going out of my way to share information."

He was quiet again. "Alright, Ms. Blake, you're right. Thank you for the name. We'll run it in the computers."

"This vampire has a history of harming preadolescent boys. He's a pedophile."

"Good lord, a vampire pedophile." He finally sounded genuinely interested in what I was saying. "And he has the Quinlan boy."

"Yeah," I said.

"I would really like to talk to this source of yours," he said.

"He's a little shy around the police."

"I could insist, Ms. Blake. We've got reports that a private jet flew in last night, and a coffin got unloaded. It's registered to a J. C. Corporation. They seem to own a lot of vampire-related, St. Louis-based businesses. Do you know anything about that, Ms. Blake?"

Lying to the FBI seemed like a bad idea, but I wasn't sure what they'd do with the truth. The Feds were investigating vampire crime, and suddenly a new vamp shows up in town. The least they would do was question him. The worst . . . well, there was the vampire in Mississippi that had been accidentally transferred to a cell with a window. The sun rose, and . . . French fried vampire. An ACLU lawyer had sued the cops' asses, and won, but that didn't bring the vamp back. Admittedly the dead vamp was one of the newly dead. Jean-Claude would have escaped fairly easily, but just escaping from the law by using vampire powers would get a warrant for his arrest. Sort of like what was happening to Magnus.

Besides, a vampire had killed a cop last night. The police might not be terribly careful with any vampire right now. The police are only human, after all.

"You still there, Blake?"

"I'm here."

"You didn't answer my question."

"Where was the coffin delivered?" I asked.

"It wasn't. It just disappeared."

"So what do you want from me?"

"There was some luggage that went with it. The luggage was picked up a little while ago by two young men. The description of one of them sounds a lot like Larry Kirkland."

"Is that so?"

"That's so."

We both sat on our ends of the phone waiting for someone to say something. "I could send some agents down to your hotel room."

"There are no coffins in my hotel room, Agent Bradford."

"You sure of that, Blake?"

"My hand to God."

"Do you know who runs this J. C. Corporation?"

"No." It was the truth. Until Bradford told me about it, I'd never heard of the J. C. Corporation. It would only have been an educated guess if I'd said Jean-Claude owned it. Okay, I was fooling myself, but so what?

"Do you know where the coffin was delivered?" he asked.

"Nope."

"Would you tell me if you knew?"

"If it would help find Jeff Quinlan, you bet."

"Alright, Blake, but no more helping. Stay the fuck out of this case. When we find the vampires we'll call you in, and you can do your job. You're a vampire hunter, not a cop. Try to remember that."

"Fine," I said.

"Good. Now I'm going back to sleep. I suggest you do the same. We'll find the vampires today, Blake. And let's just say I don't believe everything Freemont said. We'll call you in for the kill."

"Thanks."

"Good night, Blake."

"Good night, Bradford."

We hung up. I sat there for a minute, just letting it all sink in. If they found Jean-Claude in my room, what would they do? I'd seen the cops pop a comatose vampire in a body bag, transport it to the station house, and wait for nightfall to question it. I'd thought it was a bad idea because the vamp would wake up pissed. It did. I ended up killing it. I've always felt bad about that particular kill. It was an out-of-state job. The local cops invited me in to advise them. Once we found the vamp, they stopped listening to my advice. Reminded me of now. That vampire had also just been brought in for questioning.

I was suddenly tired. It was like the entire night just hit me in one grinding wave. Sleep dragged at me. I had to go to sleep. I couldn't help Jeff Quinlan, or anybody else, until I'd had a few hours of sleep. Besides, maybe the Feds would find him. Stranger things had happened.

I left a wake-up call with the desk for noon, and cuddled under the blanket. The Browning was lumpy under the pillow. At least I couldn't feel the Firestar under the couch cushion. I half wished I'd packed Sigmund, my stuffed toy penguin, but somehow having Jean-Claude or Jason find me sleeping with a stuffed toy bothered me almost as much as them trying to eat me. What price machismo?

21

SOMEONE WAS BANGING on the door. I opened my eyes to a room filled with soft, indirect sunlight. The curtains in here weren't nearly as thick as the ones in the bedroom. Which was why I was out here and Jean-Claude was in there.

I struggled into the jeans I'd left on the floor and yelled, "I'm coming."

The banging stopped, then it sounded like they kicked the door. Was this a federal wake-up call? I went to the door with the Browning in my hand. Somehow I didn't think the FBI would be so rude. I stood to the side of the door and asked, "Who is it?"

"It's Dorcas Bouvier." She kicked the door again. "Open this damn door."

I peeked through the little peephole. It was Dorcas Bouvier, or her evil twin. She didn't have a weapon in sight. I was probably safe. I put the Browning under the t-shirt in the waistband of my pants. The t-shirt was a large and fell to mid-thigh. It hid the gun and then some.

I unlocked the door and stood to one side. Dorcas shoved the door open, leaving it swinging open behind her. I closed and locked the door, leaning against it watching her.

Dorcas stalked through the room like some sort of exotic cat. Her waist-length, chestnut hair swung like a curtain as she moved. She finally turned and glared at me with those sea-green eyes that were a mirror of her brother's. The pupil had spiraled downward to a pinpoint, leaving the irises floating and making her look almost blind.

"Where is he?"

"Where's who?" I asked.

She glared at me and went for the bedroom door. I couldn't get there in time to stop her, and I wasn't willing to shoot her yet.

When I came up behind her she was two steps into the bedroom, back rigid, staring at the bed. It was worth staring at.

Jean-Claude lay on his back with the wine-dark sheets pulled up to mid-chest. One shoulder and a pale, pale arm were stretched across the dark sheets. In the semidarkness his hair blended with the pillow to leave his face white and nearly ethereal.

Jason lay on his stomach. The only things under the sheet were one leg and, barely, his buttocks. If he was wearing clothes, I couldn't tell. He raised up on his elbows and turned to us. His yellow hair had fallen into his face, and he blinked like he'd been deeply asleep. He smiled when he saw Dorcas Bouvier.

"It isn't Magnus," she said.

"No," I said, "it isn't. You want to talk outside?"

"Don't go on my account," Jason said. He rolled onto one elbow. The silken sheet slid across his hips as he moved.

Dorcas Bouvier turned on her heel and marched out of the room. I closed the door to the sound of Jason's laughter.

Dorcas looked shaken, embarrassed even. Good to see. I was embarrassed, too, but didn't know what to do about it. Trying to explain your way out of situations like this never works. People are always willing to believe the worst of you. So I didn't try. I just stood there looking at her. She wouldn't meet my eyes.

After a nice uncomfortable silence that caused heat to wash up her face, she said, "I don't know what to say. I thought my brother was in there. I . . . " She met my eyes finally. She was already regaining her composure, her surety of purpose. You could watch it solidify in her eyes. She was here for more than rousting her brother out of my bed.

"Why in the world would you think Magnus was here?"

"May I sit down?"

I motioned her to a seat. She sat in one of the chairs, spine very straight, perfect posture. My stepmother, Judith, would have been proud. I leaned on the arm of the couch because I couldn't sit down with the Browning down my pants. I wasn't sure how she'd take me being armed, so I didn't want to show the gun. Some people freeze up around firearms. Go figure.

"I know Magnus was with you last night."

"With me?" I said.

"I don't mean . . . " Heat crept up her face again. "I don't mean *with* you. I mean I know you saw him last night."

"He tell you that?"

She shook her head, making her hair slide like fur over her shoulders. It was eerily reminiscent of Magnus. "I saw you together."

I studied her face, trying to read past the embarrassment. "You weren't there last night."

"Where?" she asked.

I frowned at her. "How did you see us?"

"You admit you saw him last night, then," she said. Her eagerness came back in a rush.

"What I want to know is how you saw us together."

She took a deep breath. "That's my business."

"Magnus said his sister was better at visions than he was. Is that true?"

"What didn't he tell you?" she asked. She was angry again. Her emotions seemed to collide, spinning too fast over her face and voice.

"He didn't tell me why he ran from the police."

She looked down at her hands, folded in her lap. "I don't know why he ran. It doesn't make any sense." She looked back up at me. "I know he didn't kill those children."

"I agree," I said.

Surprise showed on her face. "I thought you told the police he did it."

I shook my head. "No, I told them he could have done it. I never said he did it."

"But . . . The detective was so sure. She said you'd told her."

I cursed softly under my breath. "Detective Freemont?"

"Yes."

"Don't believe everything she tells you, especially about me. She doesn't seem to like me very much."

"If you didn't tell them, then why are they so sure Magnus did these horrible things? He would have no reason to kill these people."

I shrugged. "Magnus isn't wanted for the killings anymore. Didn't anybody tell you that?"

She shook her head. "No. You mean he can come back home?"

I sighed. "It's not that simple. Magnus used glamor on the police to escape. That's a felony all on its own. The cops will kill him on sight, Ms. Bouvier. They don't mess around where magic is concerned. Can't say I blame them."

"I saw the two of you talking outside under the sky."

"I did see him last night."

"Did you tell the police?"

"No."

She stared at me, "Why not?"

"Magnus is probably guilty of something, or he wouldn't have run, but he deserves better treatment than he's getting."

"Yes," she said, "he does."

"What made you think he'd be in my bed?"

She looked down at her lap again. "Magnus can be very persuasive. I can't remember the last time a woman told him no. I apologize for assuming that about you." She stopped, glanced towards the bedroom, then back to me. She blushed again.

I was not going to explain how I ended up with two males in my bed. Surely it was obvious from the blanket and pillow that I'd slept out here. Surely.

"What do you want from me, Ms. Bouvier?"

"I want to find Magnus before he gets himself killed. I thought you could help me. How could you have betrayed Magnus to the police? Surely you know what it's like to be different."

I wanted to ask if it showed, if she could see "Necromancer" written across my forehead, but I didn't. If the answer was yes, I wasn't sure I wanted to know.

"If he hadn't run away, they would have simply questioned him. They didn't have enough to arrest him. Do you have any idea why he ran?"

She shook her head. "I've tried to think of something, anything, but it doesn't make any sense to me, Ms. Blake. My brother is a little amoral, but he's not a bad man."

I wasn't sure you could be a little amoral, but I let it slide. "If he turns himself in to me, I'll walk him into the police station. But short of that, I don't know what I can do."

"I've been everywhere I can think of, but he's just not there. I even checked the mound."

"The mound?" I asked.

She stared up at me. "He didn't tell you about the creature?"

I thought about lying to see if I could get information, but the look in her eyes told me I'd blown it. "He didn't mention any creature."

"Of course; if he had told you, the police would be down there with dynamite. Dynamite won't kill it, but it would screw our magical wards six ways to Sunday."

"What creature?" I asked.

"Is there anything Magnus told you that you didn't tell the police?" Dorcas asked.

I thought about that for a second. "No."

"He was right not to tell you."

"Maybe, but I'm trying to help him now."

"Do you have a guilty conscience?" she asked.

"Maybe," I said.

She looked at me. Her pupils had resurfaced, and she looked almost normal. Almost. "How can I trust you?"

"You probably can't. But I do want to help Magnus. Please talk to me, Ms. Bouvier."

"I have to have your word that you won't tell the police. I am serious, Ms. Blake. If the police interfere, they could loose the thing and people would die."

I debated but couldn't see any reason the police would need to know. "Okay, I give you my word."

"I may not have Magnus's way with glamor, but an oath to one of the fey is a serious matter, Ms. Blake. Lying to us tends to go badly."

"Is that a threat?"

"Think of it as a warning." The air moved between us like heat rising off a road. Her eyes swirled like miniature whirlpools.

Maybe I should have shown her my gun. "Don't threaten me, Dorcas. I'm not in the mood."

The magic seemed to seep away like water running into a crack in the rocks. You knew it was still there, below the surface. But for someone who had been threatened by werewolves and vampires, she paled in comparison. Magnus seemed to have most of the talent in the family. On the scale of scariness, Magnus was up there.

"Just so we understand each other, Ms. Blake. If you tell

the police and they let loose the creature, the deaths will be on your head."

"Alright, I'm impressed; now tell me about it."

"Did Magnus tell you about our ancestor, Llyn Bouvier?"

"Yeah, he was the first European in this area. He married into the local tribe. Converted them to Christianity. He was also fey."

She nodded. "He brought another fey with him."

"A wife?" I asked.

"No, he had captured one of the less intelligent fairies. He imprisoned it in a magically constructed box. It escaped and slaughtered nearly the entire tribe we're descended from. He finally managed to contain it with the help of an Indian shaman, or priest, but he never regained control over it. The best he could do was to imprison it."

"What kind of fairie did he bring over?"

"Bloody Bones isn't just the name of our bar," she said. "It's short for Rawhead and Bloody Bones."

My eyes widened. "But that's a nursery boggle; why would your ancestor want to capture one? They don't have any treasure, or wishes, to give out. Or am I wrong on that?"

"No, you're quite correct. Bloody Bones has no riches or gentle magic to grant wishes."

"Then why capture it?"

"Most children born of human and fairie blood don't have a lot of magic."

"That's what the legends say," I said, "but Magnus proves that wrong."

"Llyn Bouvier made a sort of pact for himself and his descendants. We would all have fey power, at a price."

She was dragging this out, and I was tired. "Just tell me, Ms. Bouvier. The suspense is getting irritating."

"Has it ever occurred to you that this might be embarrassing for me to admit?" she asked.

"No; if that's the case, I apologize."

"My ancestor imprisoned Bloody Bones so he could make a potion of its blood. But the potion had to be remade periodically, retaken, or his magic deserted him."

I stared at her. "How did the other fey take this little idea?"

"He was forced to flee Europe, or they would have killed him. It is forbidden among us to use each other like that."

"I can see why."

"His barbaric act gave us glamor. Power. But it was still purchased by blood, Ms. Blake. After Rawhead and Bloody Bones was imprisoned, my ancestor gave up his potion. He finally saw it as evil. Though his power faded, his children had the power of fairie in their blood. So here we are," she said.

"So you've got Rawhead and Bloody Bones hidden in some magic box somewhere?" I asked.

She smiled, and it made her face seem suddenly young and lovely. I had no way of judging her age. I couldn't see a line on her face. "When the magic failed the first time, Rawhead and Bloody Bones grew to its full size. It is bigger than a person, almost as big as a giant. It is imprisoned in a mound of earth and magic."

"You say it nearly wiped out an entire tribe way back when?"

She nodded.

I sighed. "I have to see where it's imprisoned."

"You promised . . . "

"I promised not to tell the police, but you've just told me there's a giant-sized creature capable of mass destruction imprisoned near here. I have to see that it's secure, that it's not going to break out and start slaughtering people."

"I assure you, Ms. Blake, our family has managed for centuries. We know what we're doing."

"If I can't tell the cops, I have to see for myself."

She stood up, trying to use her height to intimidate me. She wasn't even close. "And you'll bring the police, right? Do you think I'm that stupid?"

"I won't bring the cops, Ms. Bouvier, but I have to see it. If it does break out and I didn't warn the cops, then it would be my fault that no one was prepared."

"You can't prepare for Bloody Bones," she said. "It is immortal, Ms. Blake, truly immortal. It cannot die. You could cut off its head and it would not die. The police can do nothing but make things worse."

She had a point. "I still need to see for myself."

"You are a stubborn woman."

"Yeah, I can be a real pain in the ass, Ms. Bouvier. Let's not dance, just take me to see the prison, and if it's secure I'll leave you to it."

"If it's not secure enough for you?" she asked.

"We contact a witch and see what she recommends."

She frowned. "You wouldn't just go to the police?"

"If my home was robbed, I'd call the cops. If I need help with magic, I call somebody who can do magic."

"You are a strange woman, Ms. Blake. I don't understand you."

"There's a lot of that going around," I said. "Do I get to see where Rawhead and Bloody Bones is buried, or not?"

"Alright, I'll show you."

"When?"

"Without Magnus we're shorthanded at the bar, so not today. Come to the bar around three tomorrow. I'll take you from there."

"I have a coworker that I'd like to bring along," I said.

"One of those in the bedroom?"

"No."

"Why do you want to bring him?"

"Because I'm training him, and when will he ever get to see fey magic again?"

She seemed to think about it for a minute, then nodded. "Alright, you may bring one other person with you, but no more."

"Trust me, Ms. Bouvier, one is plenty."

"My friends call me Dorrie," she said. She held out her hand.

"I'm Anita." I shook her hand. She had a nice, firm grip for a woman. Sexist but true. Most women don't seem to know how to give a good handshake.

She held my hand longer than she had to. When she took her hand back, I remembered Magnus's clairvoyance. Dorrie turned those wide, eerie eyes to me. She held her hand to her chest like it hurt. "I see blood, and pain, and death. It follows you like a cloud, Anita Blake."

I watched horror seep into her eyes. Horror at the brief glimpse she'd had of me, my life, my past. I didn't look away. If you're not ashamed, you don't need to look away. Sometimes I would prefer a different line of work, but it's what I do, who I am.

The look faded from her eyes, and she blinked. "I won't underestimate you, Anita."

Dorrie looked normal again, or as normal as she had when she first came in, which wasn't very. Now for the first time I looked at her and wondered if I was seeing what was really there. Was she using glamor on me now, to appear normal? To appear less powerful than she was?

"I'll return the favor, Dorrie."

She flashed me that lovely smile again that made her seem young and vulnerable. Illusion, maybe? "Until tomorrow, then."

"Until tomorrow," I said.

She left, and I locked the door behind her. So Magnus's family were the guardians of a monster. Had that had something to do with why he ran? Dorrie didn't think it was a reason. She should know. But there was a feeling in the room of power gently moving on the air currents. A faint whiff of magic traced the air like perfume, and I hadn't known it until just before she left. Maybe Dorrie was just as good with glamor as Magnus, just more subtle. Could I really trust Dorrie Bouvier? Hmmm.

Why had I asked if Larry could go along? Because I knew it would please him. It might even make up for treating him so badly in front of Jason. But standing there, sensing Dorrie Bouvier's power hanging like a ghost in the air, I wasn't sure it was a good idea. Oh, hell, I knew it wasn't, but I was going, and Larry would go, too. He had a right to go. He even had a right to endanger himself. I couldn't keep him safe forever. He was going to have to learn to take care of himself. I hated it, but I knew it was true.

I wasn't ready to cut the apron strings, but I was going to have to lengthen them a bit. I was going to give Larry the proverbial rope. Here was hoping he didn't hang himself.

22

I **SLEPT MOST** of the day, and when I woke up, I discovered that nobody would let me come play. Everybody was running scared of the Quinlan lawsuit, and I was persona non grata everywhere I tried to go. Agent Bradford sent me packing, and threatened to have me jailed for obstruction of justice and hampering a police investigation. That's gratitude for you. The day was a bust. The only person who would talk to me was Dolph. All he could tell me was that they hadn't found any sign of Jeff Quinlan, or his sister's body. No one had seen Magnus either. The cops were questioning people, searching for clues, while I twiddled my thumbs, but neither of us came up with anything useful.

I watched darkness fall with a sense of relief; at least now we could get on with it. Larry had gone back to his room. I hadn't asked. Maybe he wanted to give me some privacy with Jean-Claude. Scary thought, that. At least Larry was talking to me. Nice that someone was.

I opened the drapes and watched the glass turn black. I'd brushed my teeth in Larry's room today. My own bathroom was suddenly off limits. I just didn't want to see Jason naked, and I certainly didn't want to see Jean-Claude. So, I borrowed part of Larry's room for the day.

I heard the bedroom door open but didn't turn. Somehow I knew who it was. "Hello, Jean-Claude."

"Good evening, *ma petite.*"

I turned. The room was almost in darkness. The only light was from the streetlights outside, and the glowing sign of the hotel. Jean-Claude stepped into that faint glow. His shirt had a collar so high it covered his neck completely. Mother-of-pearl buttons fastened the high collar so that his face was framed by the white, white fabric. There must have been a dozen buttons gleaming down the pleated front of his shirt. A black waist-high jacket that was almost too black to be seen hid the sleeves. Only the shirt's cuffs showed; wide and stiff, covering half his hand. He raised a hand to the light and the cuffs bent back underneath to give his hand a full range of motion. His tight black pants were stuffed into another pair of black boots. They came all the way up his legs, so that he was encased in leather; black on black buckled straps held the soft leather in place.

"Do you like it?" he asked.

"Yeah, it's spiffy."

"Spiffy?" There was an edge of humor to that one word.

"You just can't take a compliment," I said.

"My apologies, *ma petite*. It was a compliment. Thank you."

"Don't mention it. Can we go get your coffin now?"

He stepped out of the light, so I couldn't see his face. "You make it sound so simple, *ma petite.*"

"Isn't it?"

Silence then, so thick the room felt empty. I almost called out to him; instead I walked to the bar and turned on the track lighting above it. The soft white light glowed in the dark like a lighted cave. I felt better with the light. But with my back to where I thought he should be, I couldn't sense Jean-Claude. The room felt empty. I turned and there he was, sitting in one of the chairs. Even when I looked at him, there was no sense of movement. It was like a stop-action picture waiting for the switch to go on.

"I wish you wouldn't do that," I said.

He turned his head and looked at me. His eyes were solid darkness. The faint light picked up blue sparks from them. "Do what, *ma petite?*"

I shook my head. "Nothing. What's so complicated about tonight? I feel like you're not telling me everything."

He stood in one smooth motion almost like he skipped part of the process, and was just suddenly on his feet. "It is within our rules for Serephina to challenge me tonight."

"Is that the master's name, Serephina?"

He nodded.

"You don't think I'll tell the cops?"

"I will take you to her, *ma petite*. There will be no time for your impatience to make you foolish."

If I'd been stuck here all day with nothing much to do, but

had had the name, would I have tried to find her on my own? Yeah, I would have.

"Fine, let's go."

He paced the room, smiling and shaking his head. *"Ma petite,* do you understand what it will mean if she challenged me tonight?"

"It means we fight them, right?"

He stopped pacing and came into the light. He slid onto one of the bar stools. "There is no fear in you, none."

I shrugged. "Being afraid doesn't help. Being prepared does. Are you afraid of her?" I looked at him, trying to read that lovely mask.

"I do not fear her power. I believe us to be near equals in that, but let us say I am wary. All things being equal, I am still in her territory with only one of my wolves, my human servant, and Monsieur Lawrence. It is not the show of force I would have chosen to confront her after two centuries."

"Why didn't you bring more people? More werewolves, anyway."

"If I had had time to negotiate more of an entourage I would have, but with the rush . . ." He looked at me. "There was no time to bargain."

"Are you in danger?"

He laughed, and it wasn't entirely pleasant. "Am I in danger, she asks. When the council asked me to divide my lands, they promised to set in place someone of power equal to or less than mine. But they did not expect me to enter her territory so unprepared."

"Who are they? What council?"

He cocked his head to one side. "Have you really come among us so long and not heard of our council?"

"Just tell me," I said.

"We have a council, *ma petite.* It has existed for a very long time. It is not so much a governing body as a court, or police, perhaps. Before your courts made us citizens with rights, we had very few rules, and only one law. Thou shall not draw attention to yourself. That's the law that Tepes forgot."

"Tepes," I said, "Vlad Tepes? You mean Dracula?"

Jean-Claude just looked at me. His face was perfectly blank, no expression. He looked like a particularly lovely statue, if a statue's eyes could glitter like sapphires. I could not read that expressionless face, nor was I meant to.

"I don't believe you."

"About the council, our law, or Tepes?"

"The last part."

"Oh, I assure you we did kill him."

"You make it sound like you were around when it happened. He died in, what, the 1300s?"

"Was it 1476, or was it 1477?" He made a great show of trying to remember.

"You are not that old," I said.

"Are you sure, *ma petite?*" He turned that unnervingly blank face to me; even his eyes went dead and empty. It was like looking at a well-constructed doll.

"Yeah, I'm sure."

He smiled, and sighed. Life, for lack of a better word, rushed back into his face, his body. It was like watching Pinocchio spring to life.

"Shit."

"So nice to know that I can still unnerve you from time to time, *ma petite.*"

I let that go. He knew exactly the effect he had on me. "If Serephina is your equal, then you take care of her, and I'll shoot everybody else."

"You know it will not be that simple."

"It never is."

He stared at me, smiling.

"Do you really think she'll challenge you?"

"No, but I wanted you to know that she could."

"Is there anything else I need to know?"

He smiled wide enough to flash a little bit of fang. He looked wonderful in the light. His skin was pale but not too pale. I touched his hand. "You're warm."

He glanced up at me. "Yes, *ma petite;* what of it?"

"You've slept an entire day. You should be cold to the touch until after you've fed."

He just looked at me with his drowning eyes.

"Shit," I said. I went for the bedroom. He didn't try to stop me. He didn't even try. It made me nervous. I was half-running by the time I hit the door.

All I could see was a pale outline on the bed. I turned on the switch by the door. The overhead light was glaring, and merciless.

Jason lay on his stomach, blond hair bright against the dark pillows. He was naked except for a pair of vibrant blue bikini briefs. I walked towards the bed, staring at his back, willing him to breathe. When I was almost at the bed I could see him breathe. Something tight in my chest loosened.

I had to kneel on the edge of the bed to reach him. I touched his shoulder. He moved under my hand. I rolled him onto his side, and he didn't try to help. He was totally passive. He stared up at me with heavy-lidded eyes. Two thin crimson lines flowed down his neck. Not a lot of blood, at least not spilled onto the sheets. I had no way of knowing how much he'd lost. How much Jean-Claude had taken.

Jason smiled at me. It was a slow, lazy smile.

"Are you alright?"

His hand slid around my waist as he rolled onto his back.

"I'll take that as a yes." I tried to back off the bed, but his arm was firm around me, holding me. He pulled me down to his chest. I pulled the Browning on the way down. He could have stopped me, but he didn't try.

I shoved the gun against his ribs. My other hand was pressed to his bare chest, trying to hold my face a little above his. He raised his face towards mine.

"I will pull this trigger."

He stopped with his face inches from mine. "I'll heal."

"Is one kiss worth getting a hole punched in your side?"

"I don't know," he said. "Everyone else seems to think so." His face moved towards me slowly, giving me plenty of time to decide.

"Jason, release her, now." Jean-Claude's voice filled the room with whispers like tiny echoes.

Jason let me go. I slid off the bed, the gun still naked in my hand.

"I need my wolf tonight, Anita. Try not to shoot him until after we've seen Serephina."

"Tell him to stop hitting on me," I said.

"Oh, I shall, *ma petite,* I shall."

Jason lay back against the pillows. He raised one knee, his hands laying across his stomach. He looked relaxed, lascivious, but his eyes stayed on Jean-Claude.

"You are almost the perfect pet, Jason, but do not provoke me."

"You never said she was off limits."

"I am saying it now," Jean-Claude said.

Jason sat up on the bed. "I'll be a perfect gentleman from now on."

"Yes," Jean-Claude said, "you will." He stood there in the doorway, still lovely to look at, but dangerous. You could feel it building in the room, whispering through his voice. "Leave us for a moment, *ma petite.*"

"We don't have time for this," I said.

Jean-Claude looked at me. His eyes were still a solid midnight blue; the whites had drowned. "Are you protecting him?"

"I don't want him hurt because he got out of hand with me."

"Yet you would have shot him."

I shrugged. "I never said I was consistent, just serious."

Jean-Claude laughed. The abrupt change in mood made both Jason and me jump. His laughter was rich and thick as chocolate, as if you could pull it from the air and eat it.

I glanced at Jason. He was watching Jean-Claude the way a well-trained dog will watch its master, looking for clues to what its master wanted next.

"Get dressed, my wolf, and you, *ma petite,* you must change as well."

I was wearing black jeans and a royal blue polo shirt. "What's wrong with what I'm wearing?"

"We must make a show of it tonight, *ma petite.* I would not ask if it were not important."

"I am not wearing a dress tonight."

He smiled. "Of course not. Just something a little more

stylish. If your young friend does not have anything suitable, I believe he and Jason are about the same size. I'm sure we could find something."

"You'll have to talk to Larry about that."

Jean-Claude looked at me for a heartbeat. "As you like, *ma petite*. Now, if you would leave Jason to dress? I will stay in here until you have chosen more appropriate attire."

I wanted to argue. I didn't like being told what to wear, or what not to wear. But I let it go. I'd been around vampires enough to know they admired the spectacular, or the dangerous. If Jean-Claude said we needed to make a show of it, maybe he was right. It wouldn't kill me to dress up a little. It might get us all killed to refuse. I just didn't know the rules in this situation. I suspected that there weren't any.

I hadn't packed with meeting a master vampire in mind, so my choices were sort of limited. I settled for a crimson blouse with a high collar and a spill of lace down the front. There was even a little frilly cuff at each sleeve. It looked like a cross between a Victorian blouse and a business shirt. It would have looked very conservative if it hadn't been screaming vermillion red. I hated the idea of wearing it, because I knew Jean-Claude would like it. Except for the color, it looked like something he might wear.

I put the all-purpose black jacket over the blouse. With both guns, both knives, and a cross around my neck inside the blouse, I was ready to go.

"Ma petite, may we come out?"

"Sure."

He opened the door and took it all in with a glance. "You look splendid, *ma petite*. I appreciate the makeup."

"I look pale in crimson without it."

"Of course; do you have other shoes?"

"I only have the Nikes and high heels. I move better in the Nikes."

"The blouse was more than I hoped for; keep your jogging shoes. They are black, at least."

Jason walked out of the bedroom. He was wearing black leather pants tight enough that I knew he wasn't wearing the underwear anymore. The top was vaguely oriental with one of those upright collars and one black button, the kind where a loop of thread comes over the button. The sleeves were full, and the collar was a soft shining blue that matched his eyes to perfection. It was embroidered in yellow so dark it looked gold, and darker blue thread. The sleeves, collar, and edge of the fabric were embroidered black on black. When Jason moved, the shirt gaped just a little, enough to show glimpses of his bare stomach. Soft black boots rode up over his knees.

"Well, I know who your tailor is," I said. I was going to be woefully underdressed.

"If you would fetch Monsieur Kirkland. When he is dressed, we can go."

"Larry may not want to change."

"Then he won't. I will not force him."

I looked at him, not quite sure I believed him, but I got Larry. He agreed to go into the bedroom and see what other goodies were in the luggage, but he didn't promise to change.

He came out still wearing dark blue jeans and Nikes. He had changed his t-shirt for a silk dress shirt that was a rich, vibrant blue. It made his eyes look even bluer than usual. A black leather jacket that was just a touch big in the shoulders hid his shoulder holster. I guess it was an improvement over the oversized flannel he'd been wearing. The collar of the shirt was spread over the jacket so that it framed his face.

"You should see some of the stuff in there," Larry said. He shook his head as if he still couldn't believe it. "I wouldn't even know how to get into some of it."

"You look nice," I said.

"Thanks."

"Can we go now?" I asked.

"Yes, *ma petite,* we can go. It will be interesting to meet Serephina after two centuries."

"I know this is old home week for you, but let's remember why we're here," I said. "Xavier has Jeff Quinlan. Who knows what he's doing to him? I want him home safe. It's the second night. We have to get to him tonight, or find someone else who can."

Jean-Claude nodded. "Then let us be off, *ma petite*. Serephina awaits us." He sounded almost eager, like he was looking forward to seeing her. For the first time I wondered if he and Serephina had been lovers. I knew Jean-Claude wasn't a virgin. I mean, get real. But knowing he had lovers and meeting one were two different things. I realized with a start that it would bother me.

He smiled at me, almost as if he knew what I was thinking. The whites of his eyes had reappeared. It made him look almost human. Almost.

23

JEAN-CLAUDE WALKED across the parking lot in his boots and jacket, looking like someone should be snapping his picture, or asking for an autograph. The rest of us followed like his entourage. Which was what we were, whether I liked it or not. But to save Jeff Quinlan I could do a little bootlicking. Even I will toady a little if it's in a good enough cause.

"You driving, or do I get directions to Serephina's house now?" I asked.

"I will tell you where to turn when it is time."

"You think I'm going to run to the cops with directions to her house?"

"No," he said. That was all he said.

I frowned at him, but we all got in the Jeep. Guess who got the front seat.

We drove out onto the main road, the Strip. The traffic was bumper-to-bumper. If traffic is bad, it can take a couple of hours to drive the four miles that make up the Strip. Jean-Claude had me turn on a small road. It looked like a driveway leading to yet another theater, but it turned out to be an access road. If you knew your way around the smaller roads, you could avoid most of the congestion.

You would never know from the main drag of Branson but just out of sight, over the next hill, is the real Ozarks. Mountains, forests, houses where people who don't make their living off tourists live. On the Strip it was all neon and artifice; within fifteen minutes we were surrounded by trees, on a road that wound through the Ozark Mountains.

Darkness closed around the Jeep. The only light was a spill of stars pressed against the blackness, and the tunnel of my own headlights.

"You seem to be looking forward to seeing Serephina, even with the coffin missing," I said.

Jean-Claude turned in his seat as far as the seat belt would allow. I'd insisted everybody wear seat belts, which amused the vampire. I guess it was silly to have a dead man buckle up, but hey, I was driving.

"I believe Serephina still thinks of me as the very young vampire she knew centuries ago. If she thought me a worthy opponent, she would have confronted me or my minions directly. She would not have simply stolen the coffin. She is overconfident."

"Speaking as one of your minions," Larry called from the back seat, "are you sure you're not the one who's overconfident?"

Jean-Claude glanced back at him. "Serephina was centuries old when I met her. The limit of a vampire's powers is well established after two or three centuries. I know her limits, Lawrence."

"Stop calling me Lawrence. The name's Larry."

Jean-Claude sighed. "You have trained him well."

"He came that way," I said.

"Pity."

Jean-Claude made this sound like a hostile family reunion, or is that an oxymoron? I hoped he was right, but one thing I've learned about vampires—they keep pulling new rabbits out of their cloaks. Big, fanged, carnivorous bunnies that'll eat your eyeballs if you're not paying attention.

"What's wolf-boy in the back going to do?"

"I do what I'm told," Jason said.

"Great," I said.

We drove in silence. Jean-Claude rarely sweats small talk, and I wasn't in the mood. We could all have a nice little visit, but out there somewhere Jeff Quinlan had woken to a second night in Xavier's tender care. Sort of ruined the mood for me.

"The turn is just ahead to your right, *ma petite.*" Jean-Claude's voice made me jump. I had sunk into the silence and the dark hush of the highway.

I slowed the Jeep. Didn't want to miss the turnoff. A gravel road, like a hundred other gravel roads, spilled off the main road. There was nothing to make it stand out. Nothing special.

The road was narrow with trees growing so close on either side it was like driving through a tunnel. The naked branches of trees curved around us like interlocking pieces of a wall. The headlights slid over the nearly naked trees, bouncing when the Jeep eased over a pothole. Naked wooden fingers tapped the roof of the Jeep. It was damn near claustrophobic.

"Geez," Larry said. He had pressed his face to the dark glass as far as the seat belt would allow. "If I didn't know there was a house down this road, I'd turn back."

"That is the idea," Jean-Claude said. "Many of the older ones value their privacy above almost all else."

The headlights picked up a hole that stretched across the entire road. It looked like a gully wash where rainwater had eaten the road away over decades.

Larry leaned over the back of the seat, straining against his seatbelt. "Where'd the road go?"

"The Jeep can make it," I said.

"Are you sure?" he asked.

"Pretty sure," I said.

Jean-Claude had settled back into the seat. He seemed totally relaxed, almost detached, like he was listening to music I couldn't hear, thinking thoughts that I never would understand.

Jason leaned forward, putting a hand on the back of my seat. "Why wouldn't she pave the road? She's been here almost a year."

I glanced back at Jason. It was interesting to find out that he knew more about Jean-Claude's business than I did.

"This is her moat," Jean-Claude said. "Her barrier against the curious. Many find our new status hard to accept and still closet themselves away."

The wheels slid over the edge. It was like driving into a crater. Miraculously, the Jeep crawled out the other side. If we'd been in a car, we'd have had to walk.

The road climbed upward for about a hundred yards, and suddenly on the right-hand side of the road was an opening. It didn't look big enough to drive the Jeep through, not without scratching the paint job to hell. The only thing that really told you it was a clearing was the moonlight pulsing against the darkness of the trees. That much moonlight meant something was there. Grass had grown over a scattering of gravel that might once have been a driveway.

"Is this it?" I asked, just to make sure.

"I believe so," Jean-Claude said.

I eased the Jeep into the trees and listened to branches slap the sides. I hoped Stirling's company owned the Jeep, and wasn't just renting. We crawled free of the trees with a last metallic *scritch*. An acre of open land spread out before us, silver-edged with moonlight. The grass was butchered short like someone had bush-hogged it last fall, and left it naked and unfinished through the winter. There was a neglected orchard behind the house. The land rose in a gentle slope up towards the foot of a mountain. Just beyond the bush-hogged grass was forest, thick and untouched.

A house sat in the middle of the gentle rise. The house was silver-grey in the moonlight. Curling flecks of paint clung here and there, like the last sad remnants of an accident victim's clothes. A large stone porch graced the front of the house, hid the door and windows in a well of shadow.

"Turn off the lights, *ma petite.*"

I looked at that dark porch and didn't want to hit the lights. The moonlight should have penetrated those shadows.

"*Ma petite,* the lights."

I hit the lights. The moonlight bathed us like a wash of

visible air. The porch stayed dark and still like a cup of ink. Jean-Claude undid his seat belt and slid out. The boys followed suit. I got out last.

Large, flat stones were set in the grass, forming a curving sidewalk to the foot of the steps that led up to the porch. There was a large picture window to one side of the peeling door. The glass was jagged. Someone had nailed plywood behind the broken window to keep out the night air.

The smaller window on the other side of the door was intact, but so covered in grime it was blind. The shadows were viscous, and seemed thick enough to touch. It reminded me of the darkness that the sword had come swinging out of. But it wasn't as thick. I could see through this darkness. There was nothing there but shadows.

"What's with the shadows?" I asked.

"A parlor trick," Jean-Claude said. "Nothing more." He glided up the steps without a backward glance. If he was worried, it didn't show. Jason glided up the steps behind him. Larry and I just walked up. It was the best we could do. The shadows were colder than they should have been, and Larry shivered beside me. But there was no sense of power to it. As Jean-Claude had said, a parlor trick.

The screen door had been ripped off its hinges. It lay on the porch, torn and forgotten. Even with the protection the porch offered, the inner door was warped and peeling, exposed to too much weather. Leaves lay in piles at the edges of the porch railings where the wind had blown them.

"Are you sure this is it?" Larry asked.

"I am sure," Jean-Claude said.

I understood the question. If it hadn't been for the shadows, I'd have said the house was deserted. "The shadows would discourage any casual passersby," I said.

"Well, I wouldn't come trick-or-treating," Larry said.

Jean-Claude glanced back at us. "Our hostess comes."

The pitted, broken door opened. I had expected a haunted-house *screech* of rusty hinges but the door opened smoothly. A woman stood in the doorway. The room behind her was dark, her body silhouetted against the room and the night. But even in the dark I knew two things: she was a vampire, and she wasn't old enough to be Serephina.

The vampire was only a few inches taller than I was. She raised an unlit candle in one hand. The hairs on the back of my neck stood at attention, as a trickle of power slid through the room. The candle flared to life, leaving stars dancing across my night vision.

The vampire had brown hair, cut so short the hair on either side of her head had been shaved. Silver stud earrings glittered up the curve of her ears. One long earring dangled from her left ear. It was a green enamel leaf on a silver chain. She wore a red leather dress that was so tight on top, it was how I'd known in the dark she was a girl. The skirt of the dress fell to her ankles, loose once you got past the hips. A leather formal; wow.

She grinned at us, flashing fangs. "I'm Ivy." Her voice had an edge of laughter to it, but unlike Jean-Claude's laugh that always felt vaguely sexual, or fattening, hers felt sharp as broken glass, meant to hurt, terrify, not titillate.

"Enter our dwelling, and be welcome." The words sounded too formal, like a rehearsed speech, or an incantation that you don't understand.

"Thank you, Ivy, for your most generous invitation," Jean-Claude said. He was suddenly holding her hand. I hadn't seen him reach for it. I hadn't seen him move. It was like I'd missed a frame of the film. From the look on Ivy's face, so had she. She looked pissed.

Jean-Claude raised her hand, very slowly, towards his lips. He never took his eyes off her. The way you bow to someone on the dojo mat, because if you look away they may spill you on your ass.

A line of wax trickled down the side of the white candle. She was holding it in her bare fist, no candle holder. Jean-Claude slowly raised her hand and laid his lips on the back of it. The wax dripped faster than it should have.

He released her hand in time for her to save herself, but she stood there and let the line of hot wax drip down her skin. Only the faintest flicker in her eyes showed that it hurt.

She left the wax to harden on her hand. A faint redness spread from the line of wax. She ignored it.

No more wax dripped from the candle. Usually when a candle runs that soon, it keeps running. The wax made a little golden pool at the top of the candle, like a drop of water under tension.

I glanced from one vampire to the other and shook my head. Does the term "childish" mean anything to you? I didn't say it out loud, though. For all I knew, this was some kind of ancient vampire ritual. Though I doubted it pretty damn sincerely.

"Aren't your companions going to come inside?" Ivy stepped aside with a swish of leather skirts, holding the candle high, lighting our way.

Jean-Claude stepped to the other side of the door so we would have to walk between the two vampires to get into the house. I trusted Jean-Claude not to munch on me. I even trusted him to keep Ivy from munching on me. But I didn't like how much fun Jean-Claude was having. Made me nervous. I've never been around vampires that were having a good time when it didn't get ugly.

Jason walked between them, into the house. Larry glanced at me. I shrugged and walked inside. He followed at my heels, trusting that if I went inside it would be okay. It probably would be. Probably.

24

THE DOOR CLOSED behind us, and I don't think anybody closed it, not with hands anyway. Safe or not, these little displays of power were getting on my nerves.

The air in the room was utterly still, stale. It smelled musty, dry, with an undertaste of mildew. You knew even with your eyes closed that these rooms had been empty for a very long time. There was an open archway to the left that led into a smaller room. I could see a bed, complete with bedspread and pillows, so covered in dust it looked grey. A vanity sat in one corner with its mirror reflecting the empty room.

There was no furniture left in the living room. The wooden floor was dust-coated. The hem of Ivy's dress trailed in the thick dust as she moved towards a door in the far wall. A thin line of light showed under that door. Golden and thicker than electricity. I was betting on more candles.

The door opened before Ivy reached it. A rich wave of light spilled out, brighter than it should have been because we'd been in the dark so long. A male vamp stood framed in the light. He was short, slender, with a face too young to be handsome, more pretty. He was so newly dead that his skin still held the tan he'd picked up at the beach, or lake, or some other sun-soaked place. He looked frightfully young to be dead. He had to be eighteen, anything younger and it was illegal, but he still looked delicate and half-finished. Jailbait forever.

"I'm Bruce." He seemed vaguely embarrassed. Maybe it was the clothes. He was dressed in a pale grey tux complete with tails, and a charcoal grey strip down the outside leg of the pants. His gloves were white and matched what could be seen of his shirt. His vest was a silky grey. His bow tie and cummerbund were a red that matched Ivy's dress. They looked like they were going to the prom.

Two man-sized candelabra stood on either side of the door, filling the room with moving, golden light. The room beyond was twice the size of the living room, and had probably been the kitchen once upon a time. But unlike the front rooms, there'd been some redecorating.

A Persian carpet was spread across the floor. The colors were so bright it looked like stained glass. Wall hangings covered the two longest walls. On one wall a unicorn fled from a pack of hounds. The other hanging was a battle scene so dimmed with age that parts of the figures had vanished into the cloth. Bright silken drapes covered the far end of the room, hung from the ceiling with heavy cords. A door opened to the left of the drapes.

Ivy sat the candle she'd been holding in an empty sconce on the candelabra. She moved in front of Jean-Claude. She had to tilt her head up to look him in the eyes. "You are beautiful." She ran her fingers along the edge of his jacket. "I thought they'd lied. That nobody could be that beautiful." She fingered the mother-of-pearl buttons, starting at his neck and working down. Jean-Claude moved her hand when she reached the last button before the shirt disappeared into his pants.

Ivy seemed to find that amusing. She stood on tiptoe, leaning her hands and forearms on his chest. Her mouth was tilted towards him, kissable. "Do you fuck as good as you look? They said you did. But you're sooo pretty. Nobody could be that good a lay."

Jean-Claude laid his fingers on either side of her face, cradling her jawline. He smiled at her.

Her red lips curved into a smile. She pressed against him, letting her full weight rest against his body.

Jean-Claude kept his light touch on her face as if she wasn't leaning full out against him.

Her smile began to fade, slipping from her face like the sun sinking below the earth. She slid slowly down to stand flat-footed in front of him. Her face was blank and empty in the cradle of his hands.

Bruce the vampire jerked her back by one arm. Ivy stumbled and would have fallen if he hadn't caught her. She looked around bewildered, as if she expected to be elsewhere.

Jean-Claude wasn't smiling now. "It has been a long time since I was anyone's meat that wanted me. A very long time."

Ivy stood half-collapsed in Bruce's arms. Her face was harsh with fear. She pushed away from Bruce to stand straight and alone. She tugged at the red dress as if to settle it into place. The fear was mostly gone from her face; just a certain tightness remained around the eyes.

"How did you do that?"

"Centuries of practice, little one."

Anger made her eyes dark. "You aren't supposed to be able to capture another vampire with your gaze."

"You aren't?" he asked, his voice lilting with amazement.

"Don't you laugh at me."

I had some sympathy for her frustration. Jean-Claude can be such a pain in the ass when he wants to be.

"You were told to lead us somewhere, children; do so."

Ivy stood in front of him, hands balled into fists. Her anger spilled into her eyes, and the brown irises bled onto the whites of her eyes until she looked blind. Her power breathed through the room, creeping along the skin, raising the tiny hairs on my body as if a finger had been run just above them.

My hand started for the Browning. Old habits.

"No, Anita, that is not necessary," Jean-Claude said. "This little one cannot hurt me. She shows her fangs, but unless she wishes to die on this lovely carpet she had best remember who and what I am."

"I am the Master of the City!" His voice thundered through the house, echoing in the room until the air was so thick with echoes that it was like breathing his words.

When the sound died, I was shaking. Ivy had pulled herself together. She still looked angry, but her eyes had bled back to normal.

Bruce had laid a hand on her shoulder, as if he wasn't sure she would listen to reason. She shook off his hand and motioned gracefully towards the open door.

"We are to take you downstairs. Others await you there."

Jean-Claude gave a low theatrical bow, never taking his eyes from her. "After you, my sweet. A lady should always walk before a gentleman, never behind."

She smiled, suddenly pleased with herself again. "Then your human lady can walk beside me."

"I don't think so," I said.

She turned innocent brown eyes to me. "Are you not a lady, then?" She stalked towards me with an exaggerated sway of her hips. "Did you bring us someone who is not a lady, Jean-Claude?"

I heard him sigh. "Anita is a lady. Walk beside her, *ma petite,* but carefully."

"What does it matter what these assholes think of me?"

"If you are not a lady, then you are a whore. You do not want to know what would happen to a human whore within these walls." He seemed tired as he said it, as if he'd been there, done that, and hadn't had a good time.

Ivy smiled at me, giving me a big dose of brown eyes. I met her gaze and smiled.

She frowned. "You are human. You can't meet my gaze, not like that."

"Surprise, surprise," I said.

"Shall we go?" Jean-Claude said.

Ivy frowned again, but she stepped into that open door, and down a step or two, one hand on her dress to keep the hem from tripping her feet. She turned and looked back at me. "Are you coming?"

I asked Jean-Claude, "How careful do I need to be?"

Larry and Jason came to stand beside me.

"Defend yourself if they offer violence first. But do not shed the first blood, or strike the first blow. Defend, but do not attack, *ma petite.* We are playing games tonight, unless you make it more; the stakes are not that high."

I scowled at him. "I don't like this."

He smiled. "I know, but bear with us, *ma petite.* Remember the human you wish to save, and control that wonderful temper of yours."

"Well, human?" Ivy said. She was waiting for me on the steps. She looked like an impatient child, petulant.

"I'm coming," I said. I did not run to catch up with the waiting vampire. I walked at a normal pace, though the weight of her gaze made my skin itch. I stopped at the head of the stairs and peered downward. Cool, damp air pushed against my face. The smell was thick, enclosed, and mildewed. You knew there would be no windows, and somewhere water was eating the walls. A basement. I hated basements.

I took a deep breath of the fetid air and walked down the steps. They were the widest stairs I'd ever seen in a basement. The wood felt new and raw, like they hadn't taken time to stain or sand it. There was enough room for the two of us to share a step. I didn't want to share a step. Maybe she wasn't a threat to Jean-Claude, but I had no illusions about what she could do to me. She was a baby master, not full grown yet, but the power was there bubbling under the surface, crawling along my skin. I stopped a step above her, waiting for her to go down.

Ivy smiled. She could smell my fear. "If we are both ladies, then we should walk together. Come, Anita." She held out a hand to me. "Let us go down together."

I didn't want to be that close to her. If she tried to jump me, there wouldn't be time to do much. I might get a weapon out in time, I might not. It irritated me that I wasn't supposed to show a weapon first. And scared me. One of the things that's kept me alive is shooting first and asking questions later. Doing it the other way around was no way to stay alive.

"Is Jean-Claude's human servant afraid of me?" She stood there framed against the darkness beyond, smiling. The basement was like a great black pit behind her.

But she couldn't sense vampire marks, or she'd have known I wasn't his servant. She wasn't as hot as she thought she was. I hoped.

I ignored the outstretched hand, but walked down those two steps. My shoulder brushed her bare skin, and it felt like worms were crawling down my arm. I kept walking down the steps into the dark beyond, left hand in a death grip on the railing. I heard her high heels clattering down the steps to catch up with me. I could feel her irritation like heat rising from her skin. I heard the menfolk following us, but didn't look behind to check. We were playing chicken tonight. It was one of my best games.

We went down the steps together like horses pulling a carriage, my left hand on the railing, her hands lifting her dress. I kept up a pace that made gliding effortlessly impossible, unless she could levitate. She couldn't.

She grabbed my right arm and whirled me around to face her. I couldn't go for a gun. Because I was wearing wrist sheaths, I couldn't even go for a knife. I stood there nearly face to face with an angry vampire and couldn't reach a weapon. All that could save me was her not killing me. Trusting my life to Ivy's beneficence seemed like a bad bet.

Her anger spilled along my skin. Heat flowed down her body. I could feel her hand, hot, even through the leather jacket. I didn't try to pull away; things that can bench-press Toyotas don't let go. Her touch didn't burn, because it wasn't that kind of heat, but it was hard to convince my body that it wouldn't hurt eventually. Years of warnings, don't touch, it's hot. Heat flared along my body like I was standing next to a fire. If she hadn't been doing it unintentionally, it would have been impressive. Hell, it was still impressive. Give her a few centuries and she'd be scary as hell, as if she wasn't already.

I could still meet her eyes, drowning deep and glowing with their own light. That was going to do me a hell of a lot of good when she ripped my throat out.

"If you hurt her, Ivy, our truce is over." Jean-Claude glided down the steps to stand just above us. "You do not want the truce to be over, Ivy." He ran his fingertip along the edge of her jaw.

I felt the jolt of power jump from him, to her, to me. I gasped, but she let me go. My arm was numb at my side like it'd gone to sleep. I couldn't have held a gun. I wanted to ask what the hell he'd done, but didn't. As long as I got the use of my arm back, we could argue about it later.

Bruce pushed between us, hovering over Ivy like a worried boyfriend. Watching his face, I realized that was accurate. I was betting she'd brought him over.

Ivy pushed him away so hard that he went tumbling backwards down the stairs, lost in the thicker darkness. Everything seemed to be working on her just fine. I could barely feel my fingertips.

Heat rushed over me like a scalding wind, and swept outward into the dark. Torches flared to life in sconces along the walls with a *whoosh* and a shower of sparks. A large kerosene lamp suspended from the ceiling filled with fire.

Its glass chimney exploded in a shower of glass, its flame burning naked on the wick.

"Serephina will make you clean up your mess," Jean-Claude said. He made it sound like she'd spilled her milk.

Ivy walked down the rest of the steps in a hip-swinging glide. "Serephina will not care. Broken glass and flame have so many uses." I didn't like the way she phrased that.

The basement was black. Black walls, black floors, black ceiling. It was like being in a great dark box. Chains hung from the walls, some with what looked like fur on the cuffs. Straps dangled from the ceiling like obscene decorations. There were . . . devices placed throughout the room. I recognized some of them. A rack, an iron maiden, but most of it was like looking at bondage paraphernalia. You were pretty sure what the point was, but not how it worked. There were always more holes than I could figure out what to do with, and nothing ever seemed to come with instructions.

There was a drain in the floor, and a thin trickle of water ran down it. But I was betting that the drain wasn't there just for water.

Larry moved down the steps to stand beside me. "Are those what I think they are?"

"Yeah, they're torture devices." I forced my hand to make a fist, and another one. The feeling was coming back.

"I thought they weren't going to harm us," he said.

"I think it's supposed to scare us."

"It's working," he said.

I didn't like the decor much either, but I could feel my hand. I could have held a gun if I had to.

A door that I hadn't even seen opened to the left. A secret panel. A vampire came through the door. He had to bend nearly double to make it through the door frame. He unfolded, impossibly tall and thin, cadaverous. He had not fed tonight, and was wasting no power on looking pretty. His skin was the color of old parchment and clung to the bones of his face like a thin film barely covering his skull. His eyes were sunken and dull in his head, the dead blue of fish eyes. His sickly hands were long and bony with impossibly long fingers, like white spiders sticking from the sleeves of his black coat.

He stalked into the room with the edges of his black coat sweeping behind him like a cloak. He was dressed entirely in black; only his skin and the short cut white hair on his head betrayed him. As he moved through the black room, it looked like his head and hands were floating on their own.

I shook my head to clear the image. When I looked back, he seemed a touch more normal. "He's using his powers to make himself look frightening," I said.

"Yes, *ma petite,* he is." There was something in his voice that made me turn and look at him. His face was its usual lovely mask—but in his eyes, for just a second, I saw fear.

"What's going on, Jean-Claude?"

"The rules have not changed. Do not draw a weapon. Do not strike the first blow. They cannot harm us unless we break these rules."

"Why are you suddenly scared?"

"That is not Serephina," he said. His voice was very bland when he said it.

"What's that supposed to mean?"

He threw back his head and laughed. The sound reverberated through the room, echoing and outwardly joyous. But I could taste it on the back of my tongue, and it was bitter. "It means, *ma petite,* that I am a fool."

25

JEAN-CLAUDE'S LAUGHTER faded away in bits and pieces, like the sound was clinging to the walls. "Where is Serephina?" he asked.

Ivy and Bruce walked out of the room. I didn't know where they were going, but it had to be better than this. How many torture rooms could a house this size have? Don't answer that.

The tall vampire looked at us with his dead-fish eyes. There was no pull, nothing; it was like looking into the eyes of a corpse.

His voice, when it came, was almost shocking. It was rich and deep, resonant, but not with vampiric powers. It was the voice of an actor, or an opera singer. I watched it come out of the thin, lipless mouth and it still looked like a parlor trick, like the mouth should move out of sync with the words, but they didn't.

"You must pass through me before she will see you."

"You surprise me, Janos." Jean-Claude glided down the steps. I guess we were going down. Pity. "You are more powerful than Serephina. How is it you do her bidding?"

"When you have seen her, you will understand. Now come, all of you, join us. The night is young, and I want to see you all naked and bleeding before dawn."

"Who is this guy?" I asked. I could use my hand again; might as well smart off.

Jean-Claude stopped on the last step. Jason moved up, one step behind him. Larry and I stayed a little behind that. I don't think either of us was too eager to go down.

The vampire turned his dead eyes on me. "I am Janos."

"Dandy, but the rules say you can't bleed us, or anything else. Or did I miss something?"

"You miss very little, *ma petite,*" Jean-Claude said.

"You will not be harmed against your will," Janos said. "You must all consent for any harm to befall you."

"Then we're safe," I said.

He smiled, the skin of his face stretching like paper. I half-expected bone to break through, but it didn't. The smile was nicely hideous.

"We shall see."

Jean-Claude took that last step, and moved farther into the room. Jason followed, and after a moment's hesitation so did I. Larry followed me like a trooper.

"This room is your idea, Janos," Jean-Claude said.

"I do nothing without my master's consent."

"She cannot be your master, Janos. She is not powerful enough."

"Yet, here I am, Jean-Claude. Here I am."

Jean-Claude walked around the dark wood of the rack, trailing a pale hand over it. "Serephina was never much for torture. She was many things, but not sadistic." Jean-Claude came to stand in front of Janos. "I think you are master here and she is your stalking horse. She is known as master so all the challenges come her way. When she dies, you will find another puppet."

"I promise you, Jean-Claude, she is my master. Think of this room as my reward for being a faithful servant." He looked around the room with a proprietary smile, like a storekeeper admiring well-stocked shelves.

"What do you plan for us in this room of yours?"

"But wait a few moments, my impatient boy, and all will be revealed."

It was odd to have someone call Jean-Claude "boy," as if he were a much younger cousin that Janos had watched grow up. Had Janos known him when he was a little vampire? Freshly dead?

A woman's voice: "Where are you taking me? You're hurting me." Ivy and Bruce dragged a young woman through the side door. Literally dragged her. She had let her legs collapse, trying to use them like a dog does when you try to take it to the vet. But she only had two legs and a vampire on each arm. She wasn't having much luck slowing them down.

She had straight blonde hair that barely touched the tops of her shoulders. Her eyes were large and blue, and the makeup she'd started the night with was smeared from crying.

Ivy seemed to be having a good time. Bruce had very wide eyes. He was afraid of Janos. Hard not to be, I guess.

The girl stared wordlessly at Janos for a second, then screamed. Ivy cuffed her absently like you'd swat a barking dog. The girl whimpered and fell silent, staring at the floor, fresh tears trailing down her cheeks.

There was only Janos and the two youngsters in the room with us. I was betting we could take them. Two more vampires came in, but they didn't drag in the next girl. She walked in, eyes glittering with anger, back very straight, hands in fists at her sides. She was short, a little heavy, but not quite fat, as if a good burst of growth would take care of the weight. Her hair was a nondescript brown, glasses framed small brown eyes, freckles dusted her face. The personality that radiated from that face was not nondescript. I liked her instantly.

"Oh, Lisa," she said, "get up." She sounded embarrassed as well as angry.

The blonde girl, Lisa, just cried harder.

The two vamps that were guarding the second girl were not young. They were both tall, around six feet, dressed in black leather, one with her long yellow hair in a braid down her back, the other with black hair falling free around her face. Their bare arms were muscled and firm. They looked like female bodyguards from some bad spy movie.

The power that radiated from the two of them was not a B movie effect. It crept through the room like a current of water, thick and cool. When the line of power poured over my body it took my breath away. The power crawled into my bones and made them ache. Larry gasped behind me.

I glanced at him just to make sure he was gasping for the same reason I was. No new monsters behind us, just the power of the two new vamps.

"What are you guys doing, running a halfway house for all vampires over five hundred years?" I asked.

Everyone turned towards me. The two female vamps smiled, most unpleasantly. They looked at me like I was a piece of candy and they wondered what sort of center I had. Soft and gooey, or hard with a nut in the middle? I'd had men undress me with their eyes, but I'd never had anything trying to picture what I'd look like with my skin off. Yikes.

"Do you have something to add?" Janos asked.

"You can't just drag a couple of underage girls in here and expect us to do nothing."

"On the contrary, Anita, we expect you to do many things."

I didn't like the phrasing of that. "What's that supposed to mean?"

"First, the young women aren't underage, are you, girls?"

The second girl just glared at him. Lisa shook her head, still staring at the floor.

"Tell her your ages," Janos said.

Neither of them answered. Ivy yanked hard enough to make the blonde girl cry out.

"Eighteen. I'm eighteen." She collapsed on the floor in a sobbing heap, and the vampires let go of her so she could do it.

One of the female vamps said, "Your age, now." Her voice was like quiet thunder, a warning of the coming storm.

The second girl's eyes widened behind her glasses. "I'm nineteen." There was fear now peeking out from behind her anger.

"Fine; they're over eighteen, but an unwilling human is still an unwilling human, regardless of age," I said.

"Would you play policeman here, Anita?" Janos asked. He sounded amused.

"I won't just stand here and watch you hurt them."

"You have a high opinion of yourself, Anita. Confident. I like that. Always so much more entertaining to break someone strong. The weaklings fold and cry and snivel, but the brave ones, they almost demand that you hurt them." He stalked towards me, reaching out one white spider-hand. "Do you want me to hurt you?"

I remembered Jean-Claude's warning not to use weapons, but fuck it, I was going for the Browning.

Jean-Claude was just suddenly there, holding Janos's wrist. Janos seemed impressed. Truthfully, so was I. I hadn't seen him move, and apparently neither had Janos. A nifty trick, that.

I let my hand relax away from the gun, though I was pretty sure that drawing it would make me feel better. But the purpose of tonight's exercise was not to make me feel better, it was to stay alive.

"No harm to any of us; that was the promise," Jean-Claude said.

Janos drew his wrist from Jean-Claude's grasp slowly, almost lingeringly, as if he enjoyed it. "Once Serephina's promise is given, she keeps it."

"Then why are the young women here?"

"Those two"—he motioned to Larry and me—"would truly not stand by and watch harm come to strangers?" He sounded surprised, but not unhappy about it.

"Sadly, yes," Jean-Claude said.

"And if they join the fray, you will come in to protect her?" Janos asked.

"If I must."

Janos smiled, and I could hear his skin creak with the strain of holding in his bones. "Splendid."

I saw a tremor run through Jean-Claude's back, as if he had been caught off guard. I was just plain confused.

"The two young women came willingly into our house. They knew what we were, and agreed to help us entertain guests."

I glanced at the second girl. "Is that true?"

One of her vampire guards touched her shoulder, lightly, but it was enough. "We came willingly, but we didn't know . . ." The vampire's hand squeezed. The girl's face crumbled in pain but she made no sound.

"They came of their own free will, and they are of the age of consent," Janos said.

"So what happens now?" I asked.

"Ivy, chain that one over there." He pointed as he said it to some fur-lined manacles to the left of the door. Ivy and Bruce picked up the girl, pulled her to her feet, and led her stumbling to the wall.

"Her back facing the room, please."

I stepped next to Jean-Claude and whispered, though I knew within reason they'd hear, "I don't like this."

"Nor I, *ma petite.*"

"Can we stop it without breaking the truce?"

"Not unless they offer harm to us directly, no."

"What happens if I break the truce?"

"They will try to kill us, most likely."

There were five vampires in the room, three of them older than Jean-Claude. We would die. Dammit.

The blonde girl sobbed and struggled, pulling at her arms as the vampires chained her to the wall. She screamed and pulled so violently that without the fur lining she'd have bloodied her wrists.

A woman stepped into the room from the side door. She was tall, taller than Jean-Claude. Her skin was the color of coffee with two creams. Her dark hair fell in long cornrows to her waist. She was dressed in a black, patent leather body suit. It left very little to the imagination. She strode hard on her heels, a very human walk. But she wasn't human.

"Kissa," Jean-Claude said. "You are still with Serephina." He sounded surprised.

"Not all of us have your luck." Her voice was thick like honey. There was a smell like spices in the air, and I wasn't sure if it was her perfume or illusion.

Her high-boned face was empty of makeup and still she was beautiful—though I wondered what she'd look like if she weren't clouding my mind. Because surely no human could have radiated the raw sexuality that clung to Kissa like a touchable cloud.

"I am sorry you are here, Kissa."

She smiled. "Don't pity me, Jean-Claude. Serephina has promised you to me, before Janos breaks that beautiful body of yours."

Six vampires, four of them older than Jean-Claude. The odds were not going in our favor.

"Chain the other girl there." Janos motioned to a matching set of manacles to the right of the door.

The girl shook her head. "No way." She just refused to go, and she struggled better than the blonde. She threw her body on the ground and used every inch of it, not to fight, just not to go.

Two vampires several centuries old, powerful enough to make my teeth hurt, and they had to pick her up from both ends and carry her to the wall. She'd finally started to scream, one loud, ragged, rage-filled sound after another. The dark-haired vamp pinned her to the wall, and the other one chained her.

"I can't just watch this," Larry said. He was standing very

close to me; maybe he didn't know the vampires would hear his whispers.

It didn't really matter. "Neither can I."

We were going to get ourselves killed; might as well take as many of them with us as we could.

Jean-Claude turned around, as if he could smell us going for our guns. *"Ma petite,* Monsieur Kirkland, do not go for your weapons. They are treading legalities. The women have come to help entertain. They will not kill them."

"You're sure of that?" I asked.

He frowned. "I am sure of nothing anymore, but I believe that they will keep their word. The women are frightened and a little bruised, but they are not harmed."

"This isn't harm?" Larry asked. He looked outraged, and I couldn't blame him.

I answered him. "Vampires have a very unique sense of what's harmful, don't they, Jean-Claude?"

He met my gaze. "I see accusation in your eyes, but remember this, *ma petite,* you asked me to bring you here. So do not blame this particular problem on me."

"Is our entertainment so boring?" Janos asked.

"We were discussing whether to kill you all now, or later," I said, my voice very matter-of-fact.

Janos gave a low chuckle. "Please do break the truce, Anita. I would love to have an excuse to get you on one of my novelties. I think you would take a long time to break. Then again, it is sometimes the braggarts who break first."

"I don't brag, Janos. I tell the truth."

"She believes what she says," Kissa said.

"Yes, she has a disturbing hint of truth to her," Janos said. "Most tasty."

The blonde, Lisa, has stopped struggling against the chains. She sagged in them, nearly incoherent with crying. The other girl, now that she was chained, stood very still, but a fine trembling had started in her arms and hands. She balled her hands into fists, but could not stop the trembling.

"The women came for a little adventure. They are certainly getting their money's worth," Janos said.

The two female vamps opened panels in the black walls.

They each took out a long coil of whip. Neither of the girls could see. I was glad.

I couldn't stand and watch, I couldn't. It would kill something inside me to just stand and watch, even if it meant I died. I'd at least go down fighting, and I'd take some of them with me. Better than nothing. But before we all committed suicide, I'd try to talk. "If you're not trying to goad us into breaking the truce, then what the hell do you want?"

"Want?" Janos said. "Want? Why, many things, Anita."

I was beginning to hate the way he said my name, sort of half-amused, and intimate, like we were friends, or close enemies.

"What do you want, Janos?"

"Shouldn't you be negotiating for your people?" he asked Jean-Claude.

"Anita does well enough on her own," Jean-Claude said.

Janos gave another rictus smile. "Very well. What do we want?"

The vampires went to the girls. They held up the whips so the two girls could see them.

"What is that?" the blonde asked. "What is that?" Her voice was high and bubbly with fear.

"It's a whip," the second girl said. Firm and clipped, her voice did not betray her the way her trembling body did.

The two vampires backed away, just enough for good whipping distance, I guess.

"What the bloody hell do you want?" I asked.

"Are you familiar with the term 'whipping boy'?" Janos asked.

"It was a person used by royalty to be beaten in the place of the royal heir."

"Very good; so few young people have a sense of history."

"What does the history lesson have to do with anything?"

"The girls are whipping boys for your two young men," Janos said.

The two vampires snaked the whips along the floor, and cracked them nearly in unison, but neither whip touched the girls. The second girl screamed, a short, clipped sound, when the whip whistled into the wall next to her. The blonde just sank against the wall, sobbing, "Please, please, please," over and over in a ragged voice.

"Don't hurt them," Larry said. "Please."

"Would you take her place?" Janos asked.

I finally understood where we were heading. "You can't hurt us without our cooperation. You treacherous son of a bitch."

He smiled. "Answer me, lad. Would you take her place?"

Larry nodded.

I grabbed his arm. "No."

"Surely it is his choice," Janos said.

"Let go of my arm, Anita."

I stared at his eyes, searching to see if he understood what he was doing. "You don't know what a whip will do to human flesh. You don't know what you're offering."

"We can remedy that," Janos said.

The vampires ripped the backs of the girls' blouses with a harsh, quick tearing.

The blonde screamed.

"We can't just watch," Larry said.

He was right; whether I liked it or not, he was right.

"I've seen what a whip can do," Jason said suddenly. "Don't hurt them."

I stared at him. "You don't strike me as the self-sacrificing kind."

He shrugged. "We all have our moments."

"Would it make this an easier choice if I swore that if your young man takes the girl's place we will not cripple him?"

"How about kill him?" I said. "You can die of shock from a whipping."

"No killing, no crippling. We simply want our pound of flesh, and a quart of blood."

Something must have shown on our faces, because he laughed. "Figuratively speaking, of course. You will wear scars until you die, but no greater harm."

"This is ridiculous," I said. "We aren't going to do this."

"If we pull our guns, can we take them?" Larry asked.

I looked away from his earnest eyes. He touched my arm. "Anita?"

"We can take some of them with us," I said.

"But we'll still be dead, and once we're dead who'll help the girls?"

I shook my head. "There's got to be a better way."

Larry looked at Jean-Claude. "Will he keep his word? Will they not kill me?"

"Janos's word has always been reliable, or at least it was a couple of centuries ago."

"Can we trust them?" Jason asked.

"No," I said.

"Yes," Jean-Claude said.

I glared at him.

"I know you would rather shoot it out, but you would only succeed in getting us all killed. Or perhaps some of us made into vampires."

Larry touched my shoulders. He made me look at him. "It's alright."

"It's not alright," I said.

"Fine, but it's the best we can do right now."

"Don't do this."

"I don't have a choice," he said. "Besides, I'm a big boy, remember? I can take care of myself."

I hugged him. I didn't know what else to do.

"I'll be alright," he whispered.

I just nodded. I didn't trust my voice, and I try never to lie to my friends. He would not be alright. I knew it. He knew it. We all knew it.

Jason walked away from us towards the vampires. "Oh, no, my good shapeshifter, we don't want you chained to a wall."

"But you said . . ."

"I said you could save the girls, but not like that. Let the human take his lashes. All you must agree to is satisfying the desires of my two helpers, Bettina and Pallas."

Jason stared at the two vampires. They'd turned to face us. I suddenly tried to see them from the viewpoint of a twenty-year-old male. They were chesty, slim waisted; if

Pallas's face was a little too witchy-looking for my taste, and Bettina's eyes too small, that was just me. Neither of them was pretty, or even beautiful; they were handsome in the way that some tall, leggy women are. Handsome in a good way, if they had been human.

Jason frowned. "It seems I'm getting the better deal here."

"Would it make any difference if I said you had to do it here in this room, on the floor, in front of everyone?" Janos asked.

Jason thought about that for a minute. "If I say no, does the girl get whipped?"

Janos nodded.

"Then I agree," he said, but his voice was soft and uncertain. Being lascivious in private was one thing; doing it in public was different.

"Come then, shapeshifter, let the show begin." Janos made a sweeping motion with his white hands.

Jason glanced back at Jean-Claude like a kid on the first day of school wondering if the bullies were really going to hurt him. Jean-Claude gave no comfort. His face was as still and unreadable as a painting. He gave a small nod that could have meant anything from "It will be alright" to "Just do it."

I watched Jason's shoulders rise with a deep breath, and heard him blow it out like a runner before a race. Why is it that most things you might willingly do under other circumstances become distasteful when you have no choice?

"Have you ever been with one of us?" Janos asked.

Jason shook his head.

Janos put a long-fingered hand on Jason's shoulder. Jason didn't seem to enjoy that. Couldn't blame him. "There are many pleasures that await you, my young shapeshifter. Things that no human or wereanimal can give to you. Sensations that only the dead can offer."

The two female vampires had stepped to the far end of the room in a clear space on the black floor. The whips lay coiled at the feet of the two girls, as if they were a reminder of what would happen if anyone chickened out.

If Jason wanted to fuck a few vampires, that was fine with

me. Besides, he wasn't mine to protect. But the sex wasn't going to last forever. I couldn't let them have Larry. I couldn't stand by and watch him be tortured. I just couldn't. But if I pulled down the room, then even if we got out of the basement—highly doubtful all on its own—we'd have every vamp in the place after our ass. There would be more; there were always more. But what had Jean-Claude said? If they broke the truce first, we could draw weapons. It had possibilities.

The one with long blonde hair had undone her braid. She shook out her hair like it was a thick curtain of yellow waves. It hid her face for a moment, and she seemed softer, more human. Maybe it was illusion. Whatever, Jason touched that thick hair, wadded his hands into it, then slid his hands around her waist. If he was going to have to do it, it looked like he was going to have fun while he did. Nice to see someone who enjoys his work.

The dark-haired vamp came in from behind, pressing her leather-clad body against him. Jason was short enough that his face was about breast level for both of them. He buried his face in the blonde's chest. She unlaced the front of her leather vest, peeling it back so he could suck her breasts.

I turned away. I was never much for voyeurism. Had an embarrassing tendency to blush. Ivy and Bruce moved along the wall to stand near the corner next to the threesome. Bruce was fascinated and embarrassed, but he kept looking. There was no embarrassment on Ivy's face. She moved along the wall, her back pressed to it, hands feeling their way along. Her red lipsticked mouth was partially open. She slid down the wall, the red dress bunching around her thighs as she went to all fours. Watching them move along the wall brought my gaze back to the entertainment.

Jason's shirt was gone. Wearing nothing but his leather pants and his black boots, he matched the two vampires. He was on his knees, his back arched so he was cradled against the brunette behind him. She smoothed her hands down his naked chest. He turned, giving her his lips. The kiss was long and deep, and full of more probing than anybody but your doctor should be doing.

The blonde was sitting with her legs wide open in front of them, undoing Jason's pants. She'd already done something to her leather pants so that the crotch was open. She was a natural blonde. Why was I surprised?

Ivy stretched out a hand to pull at the other vampire's long yellow hair.

"Ivy," Janos said, "you were not invited."

She pulled her hand back but didn't back away. She was as close to the action as she could get and not be part of it. Bruce was still pinned to the wall, open-mouthed and a little sweaty, but he didn't seem to want to come closer.

Janos stood very calmly watching. He had a tight grin on his face, and for the first time there was some light in those dead-fish eyes. He was enjoying himself.

Jean-Claude was half-leaning, half-sitting against a metal frame that held the rough outline of a body. He was watching the show, but his face was still unreadable, a beautiful mask.

He saw me looking at him, but there was no change in his eyes. He was as closed and solitary as if he were standing in an empty room. He wasn't breathing that I could see. Did he have a heartbeat when he held himself so still? Or did everything stop?

Kissa stood by the door that we hadn't been through. She had her arms crossed over her stomach. For someone that had wanted to jump Jean-Claude's bones so badly, she didn't seem to like the show much. Or maybe she was the guard to keep Larry and me from running screaming from the room.

Larry had backed as far away from the action as he could get. He was pressed up against the wall, trying to find something to look at, but his eyes kept being drawn back to the other end of the room. It was like trying not to watch a train wreck. You didn't want to see it happen, but if it was going to happen you didn't quite want to look away either. When would you ever get the chance to see it again? A ménage à trois made up of two vampires and a werewolf couldn't be that common a sight for Larry. It wasn't even a common sight for me.

The two girls still chained to the wall couldn't see what was going on. Probably just as well.

A low moan broke from the other side of the room. It made me glance back. Jason's pants had been pulled partially down to reveal most of the smooth expanse of his buttocks. His arms were braced, leaving only his lower body touching the woman. His body rose and fell rhythmically. The blonde vampire writhed under him, another low moan escaping her throat. Her breasts spilled out of her black leather vest like an offering as she did a sort of sit-up to meet Jason's mouth.

The brunette licked a slow, pink tongue along his spine. His back convulsed with the sensation, or maybe it was another sensation. The effect looked the same.

I turned away, but the image was burned on my mind. I felt heat crawl up my neck. Damn. Larry's eyes widened and I watched the color drain from his face, until his skin was the surprised white of paper and his eyes too big for his face.

I fought it for a minute, but I turned back to see, like Lot's wife risking it all for one last forbidden glimpse. Jason had collapsed, his face lost in the blonde's hair. Her face was turned to the room. Her skin had thinned until you could see every bone in her face. Her full lips had thinned back, making her teeth look longer. She no longer had enough lips to hide her fangs.

The brunette knelt just behind them, her knees between both their legs. She lowered her hands from her face, and one half of that handsome face rotted away. She ran her hand through her long dark hair and it came away in clumps.

She turned her face towards the rest of us. The skin sloughed off the bones on the left side of her face and fell to the floor with a thick wet plop.

I swallowed hard enough that it hurt going down and backed up to stand by Larry. He wasn't white anymore; he was green.

"My turn now," one of the vampires said. My face turned back to the scene at the end of the room, almost against my will. I couldn't stand to watch, and couldn't stand to look away.

Jason rose in a sort of push-up motion. He caught a glimpse of the blonde's face and his shoulders tensed, the line of his spine tightening. He pulled away from her slowly, coming to his knees.

The brunette ran her fingers down his naked back. Her flesh sloughed away, leaving a trail of greenish slime behind. A tremor ran through his body that had nothing to do with sex.

From across the room I could see Jason's chest rise and fall faster and faster, as if he was hyperventilating. He stayed staring straight ahead, making no move to turn and look behind him, as if it would go away if he didn't look.

The brunette wrapped her decaying arms around his shoulders, leaned her rotted face next to his, and whispered something.

Jason struggled away from them, crawling against the wall. His bare chest was covered in bits of her flesh. His eyes were impossibly wide, showing too much white. He couldn't seem to get enough air. A strand of something thick and heavy slid slowly down his neck onto his chest. He batted at it like you would swat at a spider that you found crawling along your skin. He was pressed into the black wall with his pants nearly to his thighs.

The blonde rolled off her back and crawled towards him, reaching a hand out that was nothing but bones with bits of dried flesh. She seemed to be decaying in dry ground. The brunette was wet. She lay back on the floor, and some dark fluid rushed out from her to pool beneath her body. She'd undone her own leather shirt, and her breasts were like heavy bags of fluid.

"I'm ready for you," the brunette said. Her voice was still clear and solid. No human voice should have come out of those rotting lips.

The blonde grabbed Jason's arm, and he screamed.

Jean-Claude sat there watching, motionless, unmoved.

I found myself walking towards them. It surprised even me. I kept waiting for the smell that should have accompanied the rotting flesh, but with every step the air was clean.

I stood beside Jean-Claude and said, "Is this illusion?"

He wouldn't look at me. "No, *ma petite*, it is not an illusion."

I poked him in the arm, and it was hard and firm as wood. It didn't feel like flesh at all. "Is this illusion?"

"No, *ma petite*." He looked at me at last, and his eyes were solid drowning blue. "Both forms were real." He stood, and even standing next to him I could not see him breathe.

The brunette was on all fours reaching for Jason with a hand that fell into wet pieces as it moved. Jason screamed and pressed himself into the wall as if he wanted to crawl through it. He hid his face like a child ignoring the monster under his bed, but this was no child, and he knew the monsters were real.

"Help him," I whispered, and I wasn't sure which of us I was talking to.

"I shall do what I can," Jean-Claude said. I was staring at him when I heard the next words in my head. His lips never moved. "If they break the truce first, *ma petite*, then you are free to slaughter everyone in this room."

I stared at him, but his face betrayed nothing. Only the echo of him inside my head told me I hadn't hallucinated it. There was no time to bitch about the fact that he'd invaded my head. Later, we could argue later.

"Janos." That one word reverberated through the room until it echoed up the soles of my feet like a deep bass drum.

Janos turned to look at Jean-Claude, his skeletal face set in a pleased expression. "You rang?"

"I challenge you." The three words were bland; they fell like off-key notes jangling along my nerves. If the tone bothered Janos, you couldn't tell it.

"You cannot prevail against me," Janos said.

"That remains to be seen, does it not?" Jean-Claude asked.

Janos smiled until the skin nearly snapped. "If by some miracle you best me, what do you want?"

"Safe passage for all my people." I cleared my throat. "And the two girls."

"And if I win," Janos said, "what do I get?"

"What do you want?"

"You know what we want."

"Say it," Jean-Claude said.

"You give up your safe passage. We get you, to do with as we like."

Jean-Claude gave a small nod. "So be it." He pointed at the rotting vampires. "Get them away from my wolf."

Janos smiled. "They will not hurt him, but if you fail . . . I'll make a gift of him to my two beauties."

A low sound like a swallowed scream crawled from Jason's throat. The brunette's hand started the crawl down his stomach to his privates. He screamed and pushed her away, but unless he resorted to violence he was trapped. And if we broke the truce first we were dead, but if they broke the truce . . .

Jean-Claude and Janos had moved back to the center of the room. They stood a few yards apart. Jean-Claude stood with his feet spaced as if he was bracing for a fight. Janos stood with his feet together, easy, unconcerned.

"You will lose everything, Jean-Claude; what are you up to?"

Jean-Claude just shook his head. "Challenge has been offered and accepted; what are you waiting on, Janos? Are you afraid of me at long last?"

"Afraid of you? Never, Jean-Claude. Not a hundred years ago, not a moment ago."

"Enough talk, Janos." His voice had gone low and soft, yet it carried through the entire room, and crawled up the black walls to rain down in drops of sound that were dark and anger-filled.

Janos laughed, but the sound had none of the touchable qualities of Jean-Claude's voice. "Let us dance." Silence fell so abruptly on the room I thought I'd gone deaf. Then I realized I could still hear my own heartbeat, the blood rushing in my own head. Waves of something rose between the two master vampires like heat rising off summer pavement. What poured along my skin wasn't heat, it was . . . power.

A whirling, rushing storm of power. I'd felt Jean-Claude go up against other vampires, and I'd never felt anything like this. My hair streamed in a wind that was coming from the two.

Jean-Claude's face was thinning down, his white skin glowing like polished alabaster. His eyes were blue flames that bled sapphire fire down every vein under his skin. His bones glowed gold. His humanity was folding away, and it wouldn't be enough. He would lose.

Unless they broke the truce first.

Kissa stood by the door, still guarding it. Her dark face was impassive. She was no help to me. The two rotted things still crawled over Jason. Only Ivy and Bruce were still standing. Bruce looked scared, Ivy looked excited. She watched the two master vamps with half-parted lips, her lower lip drawn under with concentration or excitement.

I'd been able to meet her eyes, and that had bothered her—a lot.

I crossed the room behind Jean-Claude. When I passed him, the current of power lashed out and curled around me like an arm. I kept walking and it slipped away, but my skin shivered where it had touched me. The shit was going to hit the fan unless I could stop it.

Kissa watched me move past her with narrowed eyes. I ignored her. One master vampire at a time. I walked past Bruce and stopped in front of Ivy. She stared past me at the two masters, ignoring me.

I opened my mouth. As I spoke, the silence split apart and sound came back to me ears with a nearly painful clap like a tiny sonic boom.

"I challenge you."

Ivy blinked at me as if I'd just appeared. "What did you say?"

"I challenge you," I said. I kept my face blank and tried very hard not to think about what I was doing.

Ivy laughed. "You are mad. I am a master vampire. You cannot challenge me."

"But I can meet your eyes," I said. I let a small smile play along my lips. I tried to keep my mind blank, no thought to betray me, no fear to leak out, but of course once I thought of fear it was there curling in my stomach.

She laughed, high and tinkling like broken glass. It nearly cut skin just to hear it. What the hell was I doing?

The wind rushed against my back, nearly flinging me into her. I glanced back in time to see Jean-Claude stagger and a splash of blood spill from his hand. Janos hadn't broken a sweat yet.

Whatever I was doing, I'd better do it fast.

"After Jean-Claude loses, I'm going to ask Janos to make him fuck me. Your master is going to be everybody's meat, and so will you."

My eyes flicked to the rotted things clawing at Jason. Incentive enough. I turned back to Ivy and met her brown eyes. "You won't do shit. You can't even outstare one puny human being."

She glared at me. Her anger was instantaneous, like fire springing out of a match. I watched the brown of her irises spread across her eyes from a space of less than ten inches. Her eyes were shining pools of dark light. My pulse threatened to choke me, and a little voice in my head was screaming, "Run away, run away." I stood there and stared her down.

She was a master vampire but a young one. A hundred years from now she'd have eaten me for breakfast, but right now, tonight, maybe, just maybe, she wouldn't.

She hissed at me, flashing her fangs.

"Oh, that's impressive," I said. "Like a dog showing its teeth."

"This dog could tear your throat out." Her voice had gone low and evil crawling along my spine, until I spent most of my effort not to shiver.

I didn't trust my voice not to shake, so I spoke low, and soft, and very clear. "Try it; see how far you get."

She darted forward, but I saw her move, felt her come for me. I threw myself backwards away from her, but she grabbed my arm and lifted me off my feet with her elbow braced so that she could hold me aloft. Her strength was incredible. She could have crushed my arm and I couldn't have done a damn thing about it.

Kissa was suddenly there. "Put her down, now!"

Ivy put me down. She threw me across the room. Air rushed past me, the world blurring so quickly it was like being blind. The air stopped rushing, and down I came.

26

FALLING DOES NOT cover the speed and abruptness of being thrown from less than ten feet high. I smacked into the wall and tried to slam my arms and hands against it to take some of the momentum before my head smacked into it. I slid down the wall, though slid implies something slow, and there was nothing slow about it. I collapsed at the base of the wall in a crumbled, breathless heap, blinking at bright jarring images that didn't quite make pictures yet.

The first image that came clear was a rotted face with a patch of long, dark hair dangling from its scalp. The vamp's tongue rolled behind broken teeth; something black and thicker than blood spilled with a plop out of her mouth.

I pushed to my knees and found skeletal arms wrapped around my shoulders. The blonde's dried, fang filled mouth whispered in my ear. "Come to play." Something hard and stiff poked my ear. It was her tongue. I scrambled away, but claws caught in my jacket. Hands that should have been weak as dried sticks were like steel bands.

"They broke the truce, *ma petite*. I cannot hold him long."

I had a moment to glance up and find Jean-Claude on his knees with both hands extended towards Janos. Janos still stood, but he did nothing else. I had a few moments, nothing more.

I stopped trying to get free of the two vampires. They swarmed over me, and in the mess of arms and legs and body fluids, I drew the Browning. I fired it point-blank into the rotted one's chest. She staggered, but didn't go down. Fangs sank into my back, and I screamed.

A gun exploded from across the room, but there was no

time to look. Jason was suddenly there, pulling the blonde off me. I fired into the rotting skull of the brunette. She finally collapsed onto the floor in a puddle of liquid and jerking limbs.

I turned back to Jean-Claude and found him nearly prone on the floor, a pool of blood in front of him. He had one arm still held outward towards Janos.

Janos made a small, flicking motion, and blood flew in an arc from Jean-Claude's body. He collapsed to the floor, and power rushed outward, blowing back my hair. The world suddenly stank of rotting corpses.

I gagged and pulled the trigger on that long black body.

Janos turned. It seemed like slow motion, as if I had all the time in the world to aim and fire again, but somehow he was facing me when I pulled the trigger the second time. The bullet took him squarely in the chest. He staggered, but didn't go down.

I sighted on that round, skeletal head. His white hand came up and slashed the air. And impossibly, I felt like some invisible claw had slashed my arm. I fired, but my aim was a little off. The bullet grazed the side of his face.

He slashed at me again, and I saw blood start to drip down my hands. Scare tactics. It didn't hurt that much, not nearly as much as it would hurt if he got his hands on me for real.

A second gun sounded, and Janos staggered as a bullet took him in the shoulder. Larry was behind him, gun out.

My vision faded, as if fog was rolling in behind my eyes. I lowered my aim to the larger target of his upper body and pulled the trigger again. I heard Larry's bullet go high and wide into the wall behind me.

A startled, "Hey!" let me know Jason was still back there.

I saw Janos go for the door, like watching slow motion through a fog so thick I could barely see. I fired twice more and knew I hit him at least once. When he was out of the room I fell forward onto all fours, and waited for my vision to clear. Hoped it would clear.

Through my ruined vision I saw Jean-Claude still lying motionless in a pool of his own blood. The question that

came into my head was, Is he dead? A stupid question about
a vampire, but it was still the first thing I thought of.

I glanced behind me and found Jason scattering bits of the
two female vampires around the floor. He was tearing at
them with his bare hands, cracking their bones and throwing
them far away from each other, as if by sheer destruction he
could wash away what they'd done to him.

Bruce lay on his back by the wall. Blood had soaked into
his tuxedo. I couldn't tell for sure, but he looked dead. Ivy
and Kissa were nowhere to be seen.

Larry was still standing across the room, gun extended, as
if he didn't realize that Janos was gone. He was frowning.
Everybody was up, everybody was moving except Jean-
Claude. Shit.

I crawled towards him, not trusting myself to stand with
my vision so spotty. It seemed to take a long time to reach
him, as if more than my eyesight wasn't working quite right.

My vision was mostly clear by the time I got to him. I
knelt in a thick pool of his blood and stared down at him.
How do you tell if a vampire is dead? Sometimes he didn't
have a pulse, or a heartbeat, or didn't breathe. Shit, again.

I holstered the Browning. There was nothing here right
now to shoot, and I needed my hands. I bled on my shirt and
looked at my hands for the first time. It looked like fingernails had scraped down both of them, a little deeper than
normal, but they'd heal. Probably wouldn't even be a scar.

I touched Jean-Claude's shoulder and the flesh was soft,
very human. I rolled him over onto his back. His hand
flopped against the floor with a bonelessness that only the
dead have. Some trick of the night had made his face beautiful again. The most human I'd ever seen it, except for the
fact that no one was that pretty.

I checked for the big pulse in his neck. I held my fingers
against his cooling skin, and felt nothing. Something like
tears welled against my eyes, and my throat was tight. But I
wouldn't cry, not yet. I wasn't even sure I wanted to.

When is dead, dead for a vampire? Is there such a thing
as CPR for the undead? Hell, he breathed some of the time.

He had a heart, and it beat most of the time. Not beating couldn't be a good thing.

I positioned his head, pinched his nose closed, and blew a breath into his mouth. His chest rose with it. I tried two more breaths, but he didn't breathe on his own. I unbuttoned his shirt and found the spot above his breastbone, and pressed, one, two, three, four, all the way to fifteen compressions. Two breaths.

Jason staggered over to me, then collapsed to his knees. "Is he gone?"

"I don't know." I pumped with everything I had in me, hard enough to break ribs on a human being, but he wasn't human. He lay there, his body moving only when I moved it, as loose and boneless as only the dead can be. His lips were half-parted, his closed eyes edged with the black lace of his thick eyelashes. His curling black hair still framed his pale face.

I'd pictured Jean-Claude dead. I'd even thought about killing him myself once or twice, but now that his death was a fact I didn't know how to feel. It didn't seem fair somehow. I'd brought him here. I'd asked him to come, and he came. And now he was dead, well and truly dead. And it was partially my fault, partially my doing. If I killed Jean-Claude, I wanted to actually pull the trigger and watch his eyes as he died. Not like this.

I stared down at him. I thought about no more Jean-Claude. This beautiful body rotting at last in the grave it so richly deserved. I shook my head. I couldn't let that happen, not if I could save him. I only knew one thing that all dead respected, craved. Blood. I tried to breathe life into him one more time, with one difference. I smeared my blood on his mouth first. My lips touched his, and I tasted the sweet, metallic taste of my own blood.

Nothing.

Larry knelt beside us. "Where did Janos go?"

He hadn't been able to see through the fog, but I didn't have time to explain. "Watch the door; shoot anything that comes through."

"Can I let the girls go?"

"Sure." I'd forgotten about the girls. I'd forgotten about Jeff Quinlan. I'd have traded them all for Jean-Claude to blink his eyes at me. Not if the choice had been offered to me as an either-or, but just now they were strangers. He wasn't.

"More blood, maybe," Jason said softly.

I looked at him. "You offering?"

"Neither of us can feed him back to full strength without dying, but I'll help," he said.

"You fed him once tonight already. Can you donate twice?"

"I'm a werewolf. I heal quick. Besides, my blood has more kick to it than a human's, more power."

I really looked at him then. He was covered in slime. A big black smear covered most of one cheek. His blue eyes didn't look wolfish; they looked haunted, hurt. There are things that harm a lot more than physically.

I took a deep breath and slid one of my knives out of its sheath. I sliced my left wrist. The pain was sharp and immediate. I placed the wound against Jean-Claude's lips. Blood welled into his mouth. Blood filled his mouth like wine pouring into a cup. It seeped out the corner of his mouth and slid down his cheek. I stroked his throat to make him swallow the blood.

How he'd laugh to know I'd finally opened a vein for him. More blood spilled from his unresponsive lips. Dammit.

I breathed into his mouth and got a taste of my own blood. I made his chest rise, breathing in my own blood. I thought one word at him: Live, live, live.

A shudder ran through the body. The throat convulsed, swallowed. I pulled back from him. He caught my wrist as I moved it back from his chin. His grip hurt. I could feel that unnatural strength that could break bone. His eyes were still closed; only the grip on my wrist let me know we were making progress.

I put a hand on his chest. He wasn't breathing on his own yet. No heartbeat. Was that bad? Good? Indifferent? Hell, I didn't know.

"Jean-Claude, can you hear me? It's Anita."

He raised up in a small motion and pressed my bleeding wrist to his mouth. He bit me, and I gasped. He used both hands to press my wrist to his mouth and sucked me. In the middle of sex it might have felt good; now it just hurt.

"Damn," I said.

"What's wrong?" Larry asked.

"It hurts," I said.

"I thought it was supposed to feel good," the blonde girl said.

I shook my head. "Not unless you're under hypnotic control."

"How long will this take?" Larry asked.

"As long as it takes," I said. "Watch the door."

"Which one?"

"Oh, hell, just shoot anything that comes through it." I was feeling light-headed. How much had he drank?

"Jason, I'm getting a little woozy here." I tried to pull my wrist free, but his hands were like iron forged to my skin. "I can't get him off."

Jason pulled at the pale hands, but couldn't budge them. "I could tear the fingers off one at a time and get you loose, but . . ."

"Yeah, Jean-Claude would be pissed." Dizziness was coming in waves, nausea starting to build in the pit of my stomach. I had to get him off me.

"Let go of me, Jean-Claude. Let go of me, dammit!"

His eyes were still closed, his face blank. He fed like a baby with single-minded determination, but this baby was draining my life away. I could feel it going down my arm. My heart was beginning to pound in my ears as if I'd been running, pumping the blood faster. Feeding him faster. Killing me faster.

Spots were dancing in front of my eyes. The darkness beginning to eat the light. I drew the Browning.

"What are you doing?" Jason asked.

"He's going to kill me."

"He doesn't know what he's doing."

"I'll still be dead."

"Something's moving around at the head of the stairs," Larry called.

Great. "Jean-Claude, let go of me, now!"

I pressed the barrel of the gun to the flawless skin of his forehead. Darkness was eating my vision in great moving bites. Nausea burned up my throat.

I leaned over him and whispered, "Please, Jean-Claude, let me go. It's your *ma petite,* let me go." I sat back up.

"Vampires coming," Larry said. "Hurry up."

I stared down at that beautiful face locked on my arm, eating me alive, and squeezed. His eyes flew open. I moved my whole finger to keep from squeezing down.

He lay his head back onto the floor, still holding my wrist but no longer feeding. His mouth was crimson with my blood. The gun was still pointed at him.

"Ah, *ma petite,* haven't we done this before?"

"The gun," I said, "but not this." I drew my wrist from his reluctant hands and sat back with the Browning cradled in my lap. Nausea and darkness flew inside my head like clouds driven by the wind.

I saw Larry crouched by the foot of the stairs, gun out. But it was like looking down a tunnel, distant and not as important as it should have been.

Jason lay down on the bloody floor. I blinked at him. "The neck hurts less," he said, just as if I'd asked. Jean-Claude crawled on top of him. Jason turned his head to one side without being asked. Jean-Claude pressed his bloodstained mouth over the big pulse in Jason's neck. I saw the muscles in his mouth and jaw as he sank fangs into the tender skin.

Even if I'd known the neck hurt less, I wouldn't have offered it. It looked too much like sex. The wrist at least let me pretend we weren't doing something intimate.

"Anita!"

I turned back to the stairs. Larry was crouched there, alone, with his gun. The two girls had moved back away from the door. The blonde was having hysterics again. Couldn't really blame her.

I shook my head, lifted the Browning in a teacup grip, and pointed it at the door. I needed the extra arm to steady me.

There was a faint tremor to my arms that wasn't going to help my aim much.

Power breathed through the room, prickling along my skin. You could almost smell it like perfumed sheets in the dark. I wondered if Jean-Claude and I had given off that kind of power when he'd fed off me. I hadn't noticed it.

Something white appeared in the doorway. It took me a second to figure out what it was. A white handkerchief tied to a stick.

"What the fuck is that?" I asked.

"A flag of truce, *ma petite.*"

I didn't look away from the stairs to that thick, honey-dipped voice. Jean-Claude sounded better, or worse, than ever, each word like fur rubbing along my tired body. His voice was thick enough to wrap around all the aches and pains. He could make them go away. I just knew it.

I swallowed and lowered the gun towards the floor. "Stay the fuck out of my head."

"My apologies, *ma petite.* I can taste you in my mouth, feel your frantic heartbeat like a treasured memory. I will curb my enthusiasm, but with effort, Anita, with great effort." He sounded like I had let him have just a little sex, and he wanted more.

I glanced at him. He was sitting beside Jason's half-naked body. Jason was staring at the ceiling, eyes heavy-lidded like he was half-asleep. Blood trickled from two new puncture wounds in his neck. He didn't look like he'd felt much pain. In fact, it looked like it had felt good. I'd taken the edge off Jean-Claude's need, and Jason had gotten a smoother ride. Bully for him.

"May we talk?" A voice from the hallway, a man's. I couldn't place it. Hell, I was having trouble focusing on anything, let alone who the disembodied voices belonged to.

"Anita, what do you want me to do?" Larry asked.

"It's a flag of truce," I said. My words felt slurred, though they sounded clear enough. I felt almost drunk, or drugged. It was a bad drunk, a dangerous downer.

Magnus stepped into the doorway. For a second I thought I was seeing things. It was so damned unexpected. He was dressed all in white from his tux to his shoes. The cloth seemed to shine against his dark skin. His long hair was tied back with a loose white ribbon. He had the handkerchief-coated stick gripped in one hand. He walked down the steps in a graceful, almost dancelike movement. It wasn't a vampire's glide, but it was close.

Larry kept his gun trained on him. "Stay where you are," Larry said. He sounded a little scared, but like he meant it. The gun was pointed nice and steady.

"We've discussed the fact that silver bullets don't work on the fey."

"Who says this gun has silver bullets?" Larry said.

It was a good lie. I was proud of him. I was certainly too gone to have thought of it.

"Anita?" Magnus looked past Larry like he wasn't there, but he didn't come down those last few steps.

"I'd do what he says, Magnus. Now what do you want?"

Magnus smiled and spread his arms away from his body. To show he was unarmed, I guess. But I knew, and Larry knew, that weapons weren't what made him dangerous. "I mean you no harm. We know that Ivy broke the truce first. Serephina offers her most sincere apologies. She asks that you come directly to her audience chamber. No more tests. We have all been unforgivably rude to a visiting master."

"Do we believe him?" I asked of no one in particular.

"He speaks the truth," Jean-Claude said.

Great. "Let him pass, Larry."

"You sure that's a good idea?"

"No, but do it anyway."

Larry pointed his gun at the floor, but he didn't look happy. Magnus walked down the stairs, smiling, mostly at Larry. He walked past him and made a show of giving him his back. It was almost enough to make me wish Larry would shoot him.

He stopped a few feet in front of the rest of us. We were all still on the floor, sitting, or in Jason's case, lying. Magnus looked down at us, amused, or bemused.

"What the hell are you doing here?" I asked.

Jean-Claude glanced at me. "You seem to know each other."

"This is Magnus Bouvier," I said. "What are you doing here, with them?"

He loosened the tie at his collar and spread the stiff cloth. I was pretty sure what he was trying to show me, but I couldn't see from the floor. I wasn't at all sure I could stand without falling over. "If you want me to take a peek, you're going to have to come down here."

"With pleasure." He knelt in front of me less than two feet away. He had two healing bite marks on his neck.

"Shit, Magnus. Why?"

He looked at me, eyes flicking to my bloody wrist. "I might ask you the same thing."

"I donated blood to save his life. What's your excuse?"

He smiled. "Nothing half as nice as that." Magnus undid the ribbon and let his hair fall like a curtain around his shoulders. He looked at me with his turquoise blue eyes, and crawled on all fours towards Jean-Claude. He moved like he had muscles in places that people didn't. It was like watching a great cat move. People just didn't move like that.

He knelt in front of Jean-Claude, so close they were almost touching. He swept his hair to one side and offered his neck.

"No," Jean-Claude said.

"What's going on?" Larry asked.

It was a good question. I didn't have a good answer. I didn't even have a bad one.

Magnus slipped off his white jacket and let it slide to the floor. He undid the cuff to his right wrist and pushed the cloth back. He offered his bare wrist to Jean-Claude. The skin was smooth and unbroken. Jean-Claude took his hand and raised the skin to his lips.

I almost looked away, but in the end I didn't. Looking away is like lying to yourself. You pretend it isn't happening, but it is.

Jean-Claude brushed his lips across the skin, then released Magnus's hand. "The offer is generous, but I would be drunk indeed if I added your blood to theirs."

"Drunk?" I asked. "What the fuck are you talking about?"

"Ah, *ma petite,* you do have a way with words."

"Shut up."

"Losing a quantity of blood makes you grumpy," he said.

"Fuck off."

He laughed, and the sound was sweet. It had a taste just outside description, like some forbidden candy that was not just fattening but poisonous. But what a way to go.

Magnus stayed kneeling, staring at the laughing vampire. "You won't taste me?"

Jean-Claude shook his head, as if he didn't trust himself to speak. His eyes glittered with suppressed laughter.

"The blood has been offered." Magnus crawled back towards me. His hair had spilled forward on one side so one eye was lost, glittering like a jewel through his hair. Eyes just weren't supposed to be that color. He crawled up to me until our faces were inches apart. "A pint of blood, a pound of flesh." He whispered it, leaning in towards me as if for a kiss.

I leaned back, away from him, and overbalanced. I ended up on my back on the floor. It was not an improvement. Magnus crawled over me, still on all fours, hovering. I pressed the Browning into his chest.

"Back off, or bite it."

Magnus crawled backwards, but not very far. I sat up, keeping the gun on him one-handed. The barrel wavered a lot more than normal. "What was that all about?"

Jean-Claude said, "Janos spoke of taking blood and flesh from us this night. As an apology, Serephina offers us blood, and flesh."

I stared at Magnus, still on all fours, still looking feral and dangerous. I lowered the gun. "No, thanks."

Magnus sat back on the floor, smoothing his hands through his hair, brushing it back from his face. "You have refused Serephina's peace offerings. Do you refuse her apology as well?"

"Take us to Serephina, and you will have done what was asked of you," Jean-Claude said.

Magnus looked at me. "What of you, Anita? Are you content that I take you to Serephina? Do you accept her apology?"

I shook my head. "Why should I?"

"Anita is not a master," Jean-Claude said. "It is my vengeance, my pardon, you should be asking."

"I am doing what I was told," he said. "She challenged Ivy to a test of wills. Ivy lost."

"I didn't throw her across the room," I said.

Jean-Claude frowned. "She resorted to brute force, *ma petite*. She could not win by force of will or vampire wiles against a human being." He looked suddenly very serious. "She lost . . . to you."

"So?"

"So, *ma petite*, you declared yourself a master, and proved that claim."

I shook my head. "That's ridiculous; I'm not a vampire."

"I did not declare you a master vampire, *ma petite*. I said you were a master."

"A master what? Human being?"

It was his turn to shake his head. "I do not know, *ma petite*." He turned to Magnus. "What does Serephina say?"

"Serephina says to bring her."

Jean-Claude nodded and stood like he was pulled by strings. He looked fresh and new, if a little bloodstained. How dare he look so good when I felt like shit?

He looked down at Jason and me. His strange good humor had returned. He smiled down at me, and even with blood staining his mouth he was beautiful. His eyes glittered with some amusing secret. He was full of himself in a way I'd never seen before.

"I do not know if my companions are able to walk. They're feeling a little drained." He chuckled at his own joke, putting a hand in front of his eyes, as if it was too funny even for him.

"You are drunk," I said.

He nodded. "I believe I am."

"You can't be drunk on blood."

"I've drunk deep of two mortals, but neither of you are human."

I didn't want to hear this. "What the hell are you talking about?"

"Necromancer with a chaser of werewolf; a drink to make any vampire giddy." He giggled. Jean-Claude never giggled.

I ignored him, if you can ignore an intoxicated vampire. "Jason, can you stand?"

"I think so." His voice was thick, heavy but not sleepy, more the languor after sex. Maybe I was glad my bite had hurt.

"Larry?"

Larry walked over to us, glancing at Magnus, gun naked in his hand. He didn't look happy. "Can we trust him?"

"We're going to," I said. "Help me stand up, and let's get out of here before fangface busts a gut."

Jean-Claude was doubled over with laughter. He seemed to think "fangface" was outrageously funny. Ye gods.

Larry helped me stand, and after a second of dizziness I was okay. He offered a hand to Jason without being asked. Jason swayed on his feet, but stayed standing.

"Can you walk?"

"If you can, I can," he said.

A man after my own heart. I took a step, another, and was on my way across the room. Jason and Larry followed. Jean-Claude staggered to his feet, still laughing softly.

Magnus was standing at the foot of the stairs, waiting for us. He had the jacket slung over one arm. He'd even found the ribbon to tie back his hair.

Jason walked wide around the torn bodies of his two would-be lovers and picked his shirt off the floor. The shirt covered the mess on his chest, but the goo was still on his face, and his hair was stiff and nearly as dark as his pants.

Even the back of Jean-Claude's clothes and hair were thick with congealing blood. I had my own share of blood and goop. Good thing I wore mostly black tonight; didn't show dirt as badly. The crimson blouse was looking a little worse for wear.

Larry was the only one without any blood or gore on him. Here was hoping he could keep up the good work.

The two girls had hidden under the stairs while we discussed things. I was betting it was the brown-haired girl's idea to hide. Lisa seemed too scared to think, let alone do anything smart. Not that I could blame her, but hysteria gets you nowhere but dead.

The brown-haired girl walked over to Larry. The blonde came along for the ride, her hands dug so tightly into the other one's torn blouse it would have taken surgery to remove them.

"We just want to go home now. Can we do that?" Her voice was a little breathy, but for the most part solid. I stared into her brown eyes and nodded.

Larry looked at me.

"Magnus," I said.

He raised his eyebrows, still waiting by the stairs like a tour guide, or a butler ready to escort us up. "You called?"

"I want the girls to leave now, safe."

He glanced at them. "I don't see why not. Serephina had us collect them mostly for your benefit, Anita. They've served their purpose."

I didn't like the way he said that last. "Safe, Magnus, no more harm. Are we clear on what that means?"

He smiled. "They walk out the door, and go home. Is that clear enough for you?"

"Why so cooperative all of a sudden?"

"Would letting them go be apology enough?" Magnus asked.

"Yeah, if they go free, unharmed. I'll accept her apology."

He nodded. "Then consider it done."

"Don't you have to check with your master first?"

"My master whispers sweetly to me, Anita, and I obey." He smiled while he said it, but there was a tightness around his eyes, an involuntary flexing of his hands.

"You don't like being her lap dog."

"Perhaps, but there's not much I can do about it." He started up the stairs. "Shall we go up?"

Jean-Claude paused at the bottom of the stairs. "Do you need some help, *ma petite?* I have taken quite a bit of your blood. You do not recover as quickly as my wolf."

Truthfully, the stairs looked longer going up than they had coming down. But I shook my head. "I can make it."

"Of that, *ma petite,* I have no doubt." He stepped close to me, but did not whisper; instead I felt him in my mind. "You are weak, *ma petite.* Let me help you."

"Stop doing that, dammit."

He smiled and sighed. "As you like, *ma petite.*" He walked up the steps like he could have flown, barely touching them. Larry and the girls went up next; none of them seemed tired. I slogged up after them. Jason brought up the rear. He looked hollow-eyed. It may have felt good, but donating that much blood is still rough, even on the temporarily furry. If Jean-Claude had offered to carry him up the stairs, would he have agreed?

Jason caught me looking, but he didn't smile; he just stared back. Maybe he'd have said no, too. Weren't we all just being uncooperative tonight?

27

THE SILKEN DRAPES had been drawn aside. A throne sat in the far right hand corner. There was no other word for it; "chair" just didn't cover that golden, bejeweled thing. Cushions were scattered on the floor around it, heaped like they should be covered with harem girls, or at least small pampered dogs. Nothing sat on them. It was like an empty stage waiting for the actors to appear.

A small wall-hanging on the back wall had been pushed aside to reveal a door. The door had been wedged open with a triangular piece of wood. The spring air poured through the open door, chasing back the smell of decay. I started to say "Come on, girls," but the wind changed. It blew harder, colder, and I knew it wasn't wind at all. My skin prickled, the fine muscles along my arms and shoulders twitching with it.

"What is that?" Larry asked.

"Ghosts," I said.

"Ghosts? What the hell are ghosts doing here?"

"Serephina can call ghosts," Jean-Claude said. "It is a unique ability among us."

Kissa appeared in the doorway. Her right arm hung loose at her side. Blood dripped down her arm in a slow, heavy line.

"Your handiwork?" I asked.

Larry nodded. "I shot her, but it didn't seem to slow her down much."

"You hurt her."

Larry widened his eyes. "Great." He didn't sound great when he said it. Wounded master vampires get cranky as hell.

"Serephina bids you come outside," Kissa said.

Magnus dropped to the cushions, boneless as a cat. He looked like he'd curled up there before.

"You aren't coming?" I asked.

"I've seen the show," he said.

Jean-Claude walked towards the door. Jason had moved up beside him, but back a couple of steps like a good dog.

The two girls were holding onto Larry's jacket. He had been the one who unchained them. They'd seen him shoot the bad guys. He was a hero. And like all good heroes, he'd get himself killed protecting them.

Jean-Claude was suddenly at my side. "What is wrong, *ma petite?*"

"Can the girls go out the front?"

"Why?"

"Because whatever's out there is big and bad, and I want them out of it."

"What's wrong?" Jason asked. He stood a little to one side. He was flexing his hands, closed, open, closed, open. He'd seemed a lot more relaxed thirty minutes ago, but then, weren't we all?

Jean-Claude turned to Kissa. "Was this one right?" He motioned to Magnus. "Are the girls free to go?"

"They may go; so says our master."

He turned to the girls. "Go," he said.

They looked at each other, then at Larry. "Alone?" the blonde said.

The brown-haired one shook her head. "Come on, Lisa, they're letting us go. Come on." She looked at Larry. "Thank you."

"Just go home," he said. "Be safe."

She nodded and started for the far door with Lisa clinging to her. They left the door to the room open, and we watched them walk out the front. Nothing swooped down upon them. No screams cut the night. What do you know?

"Are you ready now, *ma petite?* We must pay our respects." He took a step forward, looking at me. Jason already stood at his side, nervous hands and all.

I nodded and fell into step behind Jean-Claude. Larry stayed at my side like a second shadow. I could feel his fear like a trembling against my skin.

I understood why he was scared. Janos had beaten Jean-Claude. Janos was afraid of Serephina, which meant she could take Jean-Claude without raising a sweat. If she could take the vampire that was on our side, she wouldn't find us much of a challenge. If I was smart, I'd shoot her as soon as I saw her. Of course, we were here to ask for her help. It sort of cut my options

The cool wind played in our hair like it had little hands. It was almost alive. I'd never felt any wind that could make me want to brush it off, like an overly amorous date. But I wasn't afraid. I should have been. Not of the ghosts, but of whatever had called them up. But I felt distant and faintly unreal. Blood loss will do that to you.

We walked out the door and down two small stone steps. Rows of small, gnarled fruit trees decorated the back of the house. There was a wall of darkness just beyond the orchard. It was a thick wall of shadows, so black that I couldn't see through it. The naked tree branches were framed against the blackness.

"What is that?" I asked.

"Some of us can weave shadows and darkness around us," Jean-Claude said.

"I know. I saw it when Coltrain was killed, but this is a freaking wall."

"It is impressive," he said. His voice was very bland, matter-of-fact. I glanced at him, but even in the bright moonlight I couldn't read his face.

A sparkle of white light showed behind the blackness. Beams of cold, pale light pierced the darkness. The light ate away at the dark like paper burns, the blackness crumbling, vanishing as the light consumed it. When the last of the darkness had shredded away, a pale figure stood among the trees.

Even from this distance you wouldn't have mistaken her for human, but then she wasn't trying to pass. A pale, white luminescence swirled above her head, a glowing cloud, yards across like colorless neon. Vague figures darted out from it, then swirled back.

"Is that what I think it is?" Larry asked.

"Ghosts," I said.

"Shit," he said.

"My thoughts exactly."

The ghosts flowed out into the trees. They hung on the dead branches like a froth of early blossoms, if blossoms could move and writhe and glow.

The strange wind blew against my face, sending my hair streaming backwards. A long, thin line of phosphorescent figures whirled out. The ghosts came sweeping towards us, low to the ground.

"Anita!"

"Just ignore them, Larry. They can't actually hurt you as long as you keep moving and ignore them."

The first ghost was long and thin with a wide, screaming mouth that looked like a smoke ring. It hit me at mid-chest; the shock ran through me like electricity. The small muscles in my arms jerked with it. Larry gasped.

"What the hell was that?" Jason asked.

I took a step forward. "Keep walking and ignore them."

I didn't mean to, but my pace took me ahead of Jean-Claude. The next ghost swept over my face. There was a moment of smothering but I kept walking and it passed.

Jean-Claude touched my arm. I stared into his face and wasn't sure what I saw. He was definitely trying to tell me something. He stepped out in front of me, still staring at me.

I nodded, and let him lead. It didn't cost me anything.

"I don't like this," Larry said in a singsong voice.

"Me either," Jason said. He was batting at a tiny swirl of whiteness like a tame mist. The more he swatted at it, the more solid it became. A face was forming out of the mist.

I walked back to Jason and grabbed his arms. "Ignore it."

The small ghost perched on his shoulder. It had a large, bulbous nose and two half-formed eyes.

Jason's arms tensed under my hands. "Every time you notice them, you give them power to manifest themselves," I said. A ghost hit me in the back. It was like a lump of moving ice in the center of my body. It crawled out the front of my body like a cold rope being pulled through me. The sensation was unnerving as hell, but it wasn't permanent. It didn't even really hurt.

The ghost dived into Jason's chest, and he cried out. Only my grip on his arms kept him from clawing at the thing. Every muscle in Jason's body twitched like a horse being eaten alive by flies. He sagged when the ghost was through him, looking at me with horror-filled eyes. It was nice to know he could be scared. The vampires seemed to have taken some of his courage with their rotting arms. Couldn't blame him. I'd have had screaming fits, too.

Larry jumped when a ghost popped through him, but that was all. His eyes were a little wide, but he knew where the danger lay, and it wasn't the ghosts.

Jean-Claude came to stand near us. "What is wrong, my wolf?" There was an undercurrent of warning, anger. His pet was not living up to his reputation.

"We're fine," I said. I squeezed Jason's hand; his eyes were still wide, but he nodded. "We'll be fine."

Jean-Claude walked towards the distant white figure once more, his movement graceful, unhurried, as if he wasn't as scared as the rest of us. Maybe he wasn't. I pulled Jason with me. Larry had moved to my back. The three of us walked like normal human beings behind Jean-Claude. We looked like good little soldiers except for the fact that I was holding the werewolf's hand. His hand was sweating against my skin. Couldn't afford to have a hysterical werewolf. My right hand was still free to go for a gun, or a knife. We'd hurt them once; if they didn't behave themselves, we could finish the job. Or at least go down trying.

Jean-Claude led us among the naked trees with the ghosts crawling over the bare branches like phantom snakes. He stopped a few feet away from the vampire. I almost expected him to bow, but he didn't. "Greetings, Serephina."

"Greetings, Jean-Claude." She was dressed in a simple white dress that fell in folds of shining cloth over her feet. White gloves covered her arms almost completely. Her hair was grey with streaks of white, left unadorned save for a headband of silver and pearls. It wasn't a headband, probably called a coronet or something. Her face was lined with age. Delicate makeup had been added, but not enough to hide the fact that she was old. Vampires didn't age. That was the whole point, wasn't it?

"Shall we go inside?" she asked.

"If you like," he said.

She gave a faint smile. "You may escort me inside, as you did of old."

"But it is not olden days, Serephina. We are both masters now."

"I have many masters serving me, Jean-Claude."

"I serve only myself," he said.

She stared at him for a space of heartbeats, then nodded. "You have made your point. Now be a gentleman."

Jean-Claude took a deep enough breath that I heard it sigh from his lips. He offered her his arm, and she slid one gloved hand through it, her hand resting on his wrist.

The ghosts floated downward behind her like a great flowing train. They brushed past the rest of us with a skin-prickling rush, then floated upward, hovering about ten feet off the ground.

"You may walk with us," Serephina said. "They will not molest you."

"Comforting," I said.

She smiled again. It was hard to tell in the moonlight and ghostly glow, but her eyes were pale, maybe grey, maybe blue. You didn't need to see the color to not like the look in them.

"I have looked forward to meeting you, necromancer."

"Wish I could say the same."

The smile didn't widen, and didn't fade; it didn't move at all. It was like her face was a well-constructed mask. I raised my glance to her eyes, for just a moment. They didn't try to suck me under, but there was an energy in them, a deep burning that pushed at the surface of her being like a banked fire; move a log just wrong, and the flames would come licking out and burn us all up. I couldn't judge her age; she was stopping me. I'd never met anyone that could actually stop me—trick me into believing them younger, yes, but not just glare at me and keep me from doing it.

She turned and walked through the door. Jean-Claude helped her up the steps, as if she needed it. The easy distance of the blood loss was receding, leaving me real, and alive, and wanting to stay that way. Maybe it was Jason's hand warm in my own. The sweat on his palm. The reality of him. I was suddenly scared, and she hadn't done a damn thing to me.

The ghosts flowed into the house, some pouring through the door, some sliding through the walls. Watching them pull free of the wood, you almost expected a sound, like a plop, but it was utterly quiet. The undead make no noise.

The ghosts bounced along the ceiling like helium-filled balloons, poured down the walls in back of the throne like milky water. They were translucent near the candle flames, like bubbles.

Serephina sat down in the corner on her throne. Magnus curled in the cushions at her feet. There was a flash of anger in his eyes, there, and gone. He wasn't enjoying being Serephina's boy toy. That got him an extra point in my book.

"Come sit by me, Jean-Claude," Serephina said. She motioned to the cushions on the opposite side from Magnus. They'd have made an interesting pair.

"No," Jean-Claude said. That one word was warning

enough. I drew my hand slowly from Jason's. If we really were going to fight, I'd need both hands.

Serephina laughed, and with that sound her power broke open and crashed on us poor humans.

The power rode down on me like pounding horses. My whole body vibrated with it. My mouth was too dry to swallow, and I couldn't quite get a full breath of air. She didn't have to touch me to hurt me. She could just sit on her throne and throw power at me. She could grind my bones into dust from a nice safe distance.

Something touched my arm. I jerked and turned, and it felt like slow motion. It has hard to focus on Jean-Claude's face, but once I did, the grinding power receded like the ocean pulling back from the shore.

I took a deep, shuddering breath, then another; every breath was firmer. "Illusion," I whispered. "Fucking illusion."

"Yes, *ma petite.*" He turned from me and went to Larry and Jason, who were still standing spellbound.

I looked back at the throne. The ghosts had formed a glowing nimbus around her; most impressive. But not nearly as impressive as her eyes. I had one wild glimpse of eyes that seemed to go on forever, then I stared at the hem of her white dress as hard as I could.

"Can you not meet my gaze?"

I shook my head. "No."

"Can you really be that powerful a necromancer when you cannot even meet my eyes?"

I wasn't just not meeting her eyes. I was hunched over. I straightened but didn't move my eyes. "You're only about six hundred years old." I raised my eyes slowly, inch by inch up the white dress until I could see her chin. "How the hell did you get to be this powerful in that amount of time?"

"Such bravado. Meet my eyes and I will answer you."

I shook my head. "I don't want to know that badly."

She chuckled, and the sound was low and dark. It slid down my spine like something loathsome and half-alive. "Ah, Janos, Ivy, so good of you to join us."

Janos glided through the door with Ivy at his side. Janos

looked more human than he had since I'd first met him. His skin was pale but fleshy. His face was still thin, and he couldn't have passed for completely human, but he looked less monstrous. He also looked healed.

"Shit."

"Is something wrong, necromancer?" Serephina asked.

"I hate to waste that many bullets."

She gave that low chuckle again. It made my skin feel tight. "Janos is very talented."

He walked past us. I could see bullet holes in his shirt. At least I'd ruined his wardrobe.

Ivy looked dandy. Had she run when the shooting started? Had she left Bruce to die?

Janos went down on one knee among the cushions. Ivy knelt with him. They stayed there, head bent, waiting for her to notice them.

Kissa moved to stand beside Magnus, bleeding, her arm held close to her side. But she glanced from the two kneeling vampires to Serephina, and back again. She looked . . . worried.

Something was up. Something unpleasant.

She left them kneeling, and said, "What business brings you to me, Jean-Claude?"

"I believe you have something that belongs to me," he said.

"Janos," she said.

Janos rose to his feet and went back out the door. He was out of sight only a moment, then came back carrying a large cloth sack like something Santa Claus would have carried. He untied the cord that held it shut and emptied the contents on the floor at Jean-Claude's feet. Splinters of wood, none of them big enough to make a decent stake, fell into a medium-sized pile. The wood was dark and polished where it wasn't white with new cuts.

"With my compliments," Janos said. He shook the last bits of wood out of the sack and knelt back on the steps.

Jean-Claude stared down at the splintered wood. "This is childish, Serephina. Something I would have expected from you centuries ago. Now . . ." He motioned at the ghosts, at everything. "How have you managed to subdue Janos? You feared him once."

"State your business, Jean-Claude, before I grow impatient and challenge you myself."

He smiled and gave a graceful bow, arms out to his sides like an actor. When he raised up, the smile was gone. His face was like a beautiful mask. "Xavier is in your territory," he said.

"Did you truly think I would feel the presence of your pet necromancer, and not sense Xavier? I know he is here. If he challenges me, I will deal with him. Speak the rest of your business, or was that it? Did you come all this way to warn me? How touching."

"I realize you are more powerful than Xavier now," Jean-Claude said, "but he is slaughtering humans. Not just the attack on the missing boy's home, but many deaths. He has gone back to cutting up his pets. He draws attention to us all."

"Then let the council kill him."

"You are master in this territory, Serephina; it is your task to police it."

"Do not presume to tell me my duties. I was centuries old when you died. You were nothing but a catamount for any vampire that wanted you. Our beautiful Jean-Claude." She made beautiful sound like a bad thing.

"I know what I was, Serephina. Now I am Master of the City and follow the council's laws. We are not to allow humans to be slaughtered in our territories. It is bad for business."

"Let Xavier kill hundreds. There are always more," she said.

"Nice attitude," I said.

She turned her attention to me, and I wished I hadn't said anything. Her power pulsed against me, like a great beating heart.

"How dare you disapprove of me," Serephina said. I heard the rustle of her silk dress as she stood. No one else moved, and I heard her dress slither across the cushions, sliding along the floor, as she came closer. I did not want her to touch me.

I stared up the line of her body, and saw her gloved hand strike outward. I gasped. Blood dripped down my hand.

"Shit!" It was a deeper cut than Janos had managed, and it hurt more. I met her eyes, anger making me brave, or stupid. Her eyes were pure white, like captive moons shining from her face. Those eyes called to me. I wanted to fling myself into her pale arms, to feel the touch of those soft lips, the sharp sweet caress of her teeth. I wanted to feel her body cradling mine. I wanted her to hold me like my mother once had. She would take care of me forever, and never leave, never die, never desert me.

That stopped me. I stood very still. I was standing at the edge of the pillows. The hem of her dress spilled at my feet. I could have reached out a hand and touched her.

Fear pounded my heart in my head. I could taste my pulse on my tongue.

She spread her arms wide. "Come to me, child, and I will always be with you. I will hold you forever."

Her voice was everything good; warmth, food, shelter from all the things that hurt, all the disappointment. I knew in that moment that all I had to do was step into her arms and all the bad things would go away.

I stood there with my hands balled into fists. My skin ached to have her touch me, hold me. Blood still dripped down my hand from where she'd cut me. I rubbed my fingers into the cut, making the pain sharp.

I shook my head.

"Come to me, child. I will be your mother forever."

I found my voice. It sounded rusty, choked, but it came. "Everything dies, bitch. You aren't immortal, none of you are."

I felt her power waver like a pebble thrown in a pool, and I moved back a step, then another. It took everything I had left not to run from that room, and to keep running. To run and run and run. Away from her.

I didn't run. In fact, I stayed about two steps back, looking around. People had been busy. Janos stood next to Jean-

Claude. They weren't trying their vampire wiles on each
other, but the threat was open, and there. Kissa stood to one
side, blood pooling on the pillows at her feet. There was a
look on her face that I couldn't read. It was almost amazement. Ivy was standing now, staring at me, smiling, pleased
that I'd nearly fallen into Serephina's arms.

I wasn't pleased. No one had ever come closer, not even
Jean-Claude. I was beyond scared. My skin was cold. I had
broken her hold over me, but it was temporary. She might
not be able to trick me with her mind, but I'd felt her mind
brush mine. If she wanted me, she could have me. It wouldn't
be pretty. No illusions, no tricks, just brute fucking force and
she could have me. I would never run into her arms, but she
could crush my mind. That she could do.

The knowledge was almost calming. If there was nothing
I could do to prevent it, might as well not worry about it.
Worry about the things you can control; the rest will either
work themselves out, or they'll kill you. Either way, no
more worries.

"You are quite right, necromancer," Serephina said. "We
are all mortal in this room. Vampires can live a long, long
time. It makes us forget that we are mortal. But immortality
eludes even us."

It wasn't a question, and I agreed with everything she
said, so I just looked at her.

"Janos told me you had an aura of power, necromancer.
He said he used it against you as he would another vampire.
I did it just now when I slashed your hand. I have never
known a human that could be harmed so."

"I don't know what you mean about an aura of power."

"It is what allowed you to slip my magic. No human
could have withstood me, and few vampires."

"Glad I could do something to impress you."

"I never said I was impressed, necromancer."

I shrugged. "Fine, maybe you don't give a damn about
humans, or keeping a low profile. I don't know about your
council, or what they'll do to you for not helping us. But I
do know what I'll do."

"What are you babbling about, human?"

"I am the vampire executioner for this state. Xavier and his crew took a young boy. I want him back, alive. You help me get him back alive, or I go to the courts and get a death warrant on you."

"Jean-Claude, talk to her, or I will kill her."

"She has the weight of human law behind her, Serephina."

"What is human law to us?"

"The council says that it rules us as it rules the humans. Refusing the human laws is the same as breaking with the council."

"I don't believe you."

"You can taste the truth of my words. I could never lie to you, not two hundred years ago, not now." His voice was very calm, very sure.

"When did this new law go into effect?"

"When the council saw the benefit of being mainstream. They want the money, the power, the freedom to walk the streets in safety. They don't want to hide anymore, Serephina."

"You believe what you say; that much is true," she said. She looked down at me, and the weight of that gaze even with me looking away was like a giant hand mashing me down. I stayed on my feet, but it was an effort. You should bow down to such power. Grovel before it. Worship it.

"Stop it, Serephina," I said. "Cheap mind tricks won't work, and you know it." The cold lump in my stomach wasn't so sure.

"You fear me, human. I can taste it on the back of my tongue."

Oh, goody. "Yeah, you scare me. You probably scare everybody in this room. So what?"

She drew herself up to every inch of her tall, thin frame. Her voice was suddenly soft, breathing down my skin like fur. "I will show you."

She gestured outward with one gloved hand. I tensed, waiting for another cut, but it never came. A scream cut the air and whirled me around.

Blood ran down Ivy's face. Another cut appeared on her

bare arm. Two more on her face. Long, slicing wounds with every gesture that Serephina made.

Ivy shrieked. "Serephina, please!" She fell to her knees among the bright cushions, one hand outstretched towards the master vampire. "Serephina, master, please."

Serephina walked around her, one gliding movement at a time. "If you had held your temper, they would all be ours now. I knew their hearts, their minds, their deepest fears. We would have broken them all. They would have broken the truce and we could have feasted on them to our blood's content."

She was almost even with me. I wanted to move back away from her, but she might see it as a sign of weakness. Her dress brushed my leg, and I didn't care. I did not want her to touch me. I moved back, and she caught my wrist. I hadn't even seen her move.

I stared at that silk-gloved hand as if a snake had just coiled around my wrist. Hell, I'd have rather had the snake.

"Come, necromancer; help me punish this bad vampire."

"No, thanks," I said. My voice sounded shaky. It matched the fluttering in my gut. She hadn't done anything to me yet except touch me, but touch makes all powers stronger. If she tried a mind trick now, I was finished.

"Ivy would have taken great delight in your pain, necromancer."

"That's her problem, not mine." I was staring very hard at the silky cloth of Serephina's dress. I had a terrible urge to looks upward, to meet her eyes. I didn't think it was her power, just my own morbid compulsion. It's hard to be tough when you're staring at someone's body and being led around by the hand like a child.

Ivy lay on the floor, half-propped on her arms. Her lovely face was a mass of deep cuts. Bone gleamed in the candlelight from one cheek. Her right arm had a cut that showed muscle twitching and bloody.

Ivy stared up at me, and behind the pain was a hatred strong enough to light a match. The anger rose from her in slapping waves.

Serephina knelt beside her, drawing me down with her. I

glanced back at Jean-Claude. Janos had a white spider-hand on his chest. Larry mouthed the word "gun." I shook my head. She hadn't hurt me yet. Not yet.

The hand jerked my arm hard enough to wrench my head around to face her. We were eye to eye, suddenly, horribly. What I saw in her eyes wasn't horrible. Her eyes, which I would have sworn were some pale shade, looked solid wood brown. My mother's eyes.

I think she meant for it to be comforting, or seductive. It wasn't. My skin went cool with fear. "Stop it."

"You don't want me to stop," she said.

I tried to pull my arm out of her grasp. I might as well have tried to move the sun to a different part of the sky. "All you can offer me is death. My dead mother in your dead eyes." I stared into those brown eyes that I never thought to see this side of heaven. I yelled at my mother's eyes, because I couldn't look away. Serephina wouldn't let me, and I couldn't fight her on that, not while she touched me.

"You're a walking corpse, and everything else is just lies."

"I am not dead, Anita." There was an echo of my mother's voice in her words. She raised her other hand as if to caress my cheek.

I tried to close my eyes. Tried to look away. I couldn't. A strange paralysis was sliding over my body, like the feeling you get just on the edge of sleep when your body weighs a thousand pounds and every movement is nearly impossible.

That hand came for me in slow motion, and I knew if she touched me I would fall into her arms. I would cling to her and cry.

I remembered my mother's face the last time I'd seen her. The coffin had been dark wood covered in a blanket of pink roses. I knew Mommy was in there, but they wouldn't let me see. No one could see. Closed coffin, they said, closed coffin. Every adult in my life was having hysterics. The room was full of screams, sobbing. My father collapsed to the floor. He was useless to me. I wanted my mother. The latches on the coffin were silver. I opened them, and I heard a cry behind me. I didn't have much time. The lid was heavy, but I shoved it upward and it moved. I got a glimpse of white satin, and shadows. I raised my arms over my head with every ounce of strength and got a glimpse of something.

My Aunt Mattie grabbed me back. The lid clanged shut, and she snapped the lock back in place, dragging me away. I didn't struggle; I'd seen enough. It was like looking at one of those pictures that you know must look like something, but your eyes can't make sense of it. It took me years to make sense of it. But what I saw wasn't my mother. Couldn't be my beautiful mother. It had been a husk, something left behind. Something to hide in a dark box and let rot.

I opened my eyes, and Serephina had pale grey eyes. I pulled my wrist from her suddenly loose grasp and said, "Pain helps."

I stood and stepped away from her, and she didn't stop me. Which was good, because I was shaking all over, and it wasn't from the vampire. Memories have teeth, too.

She stayed kneeling by Ivy, and said, "Most impressive, necromancer. I will help you find this boy you seek."

Her sudden cooperation was unnerving. "Why?"

"Because since I attained my full powers, no one has ever slipped my illusions twice in one night. No one living or dead."

She grabbed Ivy by one bloody arm and pulled her into her lap to bleed on the white dress. Ivy gasped. "Remember this, young master vampire: This mortal did what you could not. She stood against me and won." She tossed her suddenly away, sending her sprawling across the floor. "You are not worthy of my sight. Get out."

Serephina stood. The fresh blood stood out in scarlet relief against her white dress and gloves. "You have impressed us. Now go, all of you." She turned and walked back to her throne. She didn't sit down. She stood with her back to us, one hand on the chair arm. Perhaps it was my imagination, but she seemed tired. Her ghosts flowed down to meet her in a swirling white mist. There weren't as many individual shapes as before, as if the phantoms had lost some of their solidity.

"Go," she said without turning around.

The back door was open, but Jean-Claude walked to the doorway that led out the front. I wasn't going to argue. I just wanted out. I didn't give a damn which door we took.

We walked coolly, calmly towards the door. I wanted to run. Larry stood next to me, and I could see the pulse in his throat jumping with the effort not to bolt. Jason reached the door a little ahead of us, but he waited and turned and motioned us through like a doorman, or a butler.

I caught a glimpse of his eyes, too wide, scared, and knew what the gesture had cost him. We went through; he followed. Jean-Claude brought up the rear. The doors slammed behind us, and we walked out. Just like that.

But for the first time I knew that I'd been let go. I hadn't fought my way out, or bluffed my way out. She could be impressed all she wanted, but she had allowed us to go. Being allowed to leave was not the same thing as winning.

I would never go back into that house voluntarily. I would never be near her willingly. Because I'd been impressive tonight, but I couldn't keep it up. Even now I knew that she could have me. This vampire had my ticket. Had a lie almost worth my immortal soul.

Damn.

28

JASON WALKED PAST me into the hotel room. He headed straight for the bathroom. "I'm taking a shower." It was pushy, but he did smell like a decayed corpse. We'd driven back with all the windows rolled down. Most of the time if you stink, you can't smell someone else. I had some of the rotted stuff on me, but I could still smell Jason. Some smells are too unique to ever really go away.

"Wait," Larry said.

Jason turned, but not like he was happy.

"Use my shower." He held up a hand before I could say anything. "It's an hour until dawn. If we want everybody tucked in before that, it makes sense to use both bathrooms."

"I thought we'd all sleep in this room tonight," I said.

"Why?" he asked.

Jean-Claude stood by the love seat looking lovely and unhelpful. Jason just looked impatient.

"Safety in numbers," I said.

Larry shook his head. "Alright, but I can take the werewolf next door and let him shower. Or don't you trust me to even do that?" He was getting angry again.

"I trust you, Larry. You did good tonight."

I expected a smile. I didn't get it. He looked very serious. "I killed that vampire Bruce."

I nodded. "I thought we were going to have to kill everything in the room."

"So did I." He sank into one of the chairs. "I've never killed anyone before."

"It was a vampire. It's not the same thing as killing a person."

"Yeah, right. And how many corpses have you given CPR to lately?"

I glanced at Jean-Claude smiling at me. I shrugged. "Just one. Can you give us some privacy here?" I asked.

"I will hear what you are saying no matter where I stand in this room," Jean-Claude said.

"Illusion is all; just back off," I said.

Jean-Claude bowed his head slightly and took Jason to one side of the room, near the windows. I knew he'd hear everything, but at least he wouldn't be standing over us.

"You don't really believe he's dead, do you?" Larry asked.

"You saw what happened to those two vampires," I said. "They are just rotting corpses; everything else is illusion."

"You think he ever looks like that?"

I looked at Jean-Claude's back for a minute. "I'm afraid I do."

"How can you date him after seeing that?"

I shook my head. "I don't know."

"Corpse or not, you tried to keep him alive." He reacted to the look on my face. "Alive, undead, whatever you want to call it, you tried to preserve it. You were scared he was really dead."

I just looked at him. "So?"

"So, I killed another living being, or undead being. Hell, Anita, Bruce was so newly dead he seemed human."

"Probably why one bullet to the chest finished him."

"How am I supposed to feel about that?"

"Killing him, you mean?"

"Yeah."

"They are monsters, Larry. Some of them are prettier than others, but they are monsters. Never doubt that."

"You can honestly tell me that you think Jean-Claude is a monster." It was more statement than question.

I almost looked at the monster in question, but I didn't. I'd looked at him enough for one night. "Yeah, I do."

"Now, ask her if she thinks she's a monster." Jean-Claude leaned on the back of the love seat, his arms crossed over his chest.

Larry looked a little startled, but he said, "Anita?"

I shrugged. "Sometimes."

Jean-Claude smiled. "See, Lawrence? Anita thinks we're all monsters."

"Larry's not," I said.

"Give him time."

That was a little too close to the truth. "I asked for privacy, or did you forget?"

"I forget nothing, *ma petite*, but time grows short. My wolf is not the only one that needs a bath. Only our young friend is still fresh."

I looked at Larry. There wasn't a drop of blood on him. He was the only one who hadn't wrestled with vampires tonight. He shrugged. "Sorry; I just couldn't get anybody to bleed on me tonight."

"Don't joke, Larry," I said. "With Serephina I think you'll get another chance."

"Sadly, true, *ma petite*."

"How long can you go without a coffin?" I asked.

He smiled. "Concern over my well-being. I am touched."

"Don't give me crap. I opened a freaking vein for you tonight."

"If I have not thanked you for saving my life tonight, *ma petite,* my apologies."

I looked at him. He looked pleasant, amused, but it was a mask. His expression when he didn't want you to know what he was thinking, but didn't want you to know that he didn't want you to know. "Don't mention it."

"I will remember that you saved me, *ma petite.* You could have been free of me. Thank you."

It sounded sincere enough. "You're welcome."

"I need to get this crud off me," Jason said. He sounded just a touch frantic. I was betting he'd be trying to scrub off more than just dirt. But memories don't wash that easily. More's the pity.

"Go on, both of you. Jason can scrub up in Larry's room. It's only practical."

Larry grinned at me. "Thanks."

"I meant it when I said you did good tonight."

I finally got the smile I'd expected. "Come on, Jason, hot water and fresh towels await." Larry held the door for Jason and gave me a little salute. Geez.

Alone again with Jean-Claude. Would this night never end? "You never answered my question about the coffin," I said.

"I will be alright for another night or two."

"How did Serephina go from being your equal in power to being what we saw tonight?"

He shook his head. "I truly do not know, *ma petite.* She surprised me badly. She did not have to let us go tonight. As long as she did not harm us, we could have been her guests for the day."

"Are you surprised she let us go?" I asked.

"Yes," he said.

Jean-Claude pushed away from the love seat. "Take your shower, *ma petite.* I will await the young men's return."

"I thought you could go next, wash the blood out of your hair."

He put a hand up to the back of his hair. He grimaced at the feel of it. "Distasteful, but I want a bath, *ma petite*. It takes longer than a shower, so you go first."

I looked at him for a long moment.

"If you do not hurry, I will not have time for a bath before dawn. I would hate to sleep on your clean sheets covered in blood."

I took a deep breath and let it out slowly. "Fine; just be sure you stay out of the bathroom."

"My word of honor that I will not barge in on you."

"Yeah, right." Though, strangely enough, I believed him. Jean-Claude had been trying to seduce me for a long time. A frontal assault just wasn't his style. I went to take my shower.

29

RONNIE HAD DRAGGED me into Victoria's Secret. I had pointed out that no one would see my underwear or my nightclothes except other women in the gym locker room. Ronnie had replied, "You'll see them." The logic escaped me but she had talked me into a robe.

It was burgundy, the color of wine-dark peonies. It glowed against my pale skin and matched some of the bruises blossoming on my back. Nothing like getting thrown into a wall to give you a little color. The bite mark on my back wasn't very deep. Hard for humanoid fangs to sink in from that angle. The fang marks on my wrist were deeper. They were two neat little holes, almost dainty. It didn't hurt as much as it should have. Maybe vampires did have painkillers in their saliva, or maybe it was the fangs.

I still couldn't believe that I'd let him sink fangs into me. Shit.

I pulled the robe closer around me. The material was heavy enough to be cozy on a winter evening, and had wide silky cuffs, and more silk lining the edges. It looked vaguely Victorian, a little masculine. I looked delicate in it, like a Victorian doll that hadn't gotten completely dressed yet. I put on an oversized black t-shirt under the robe. It ruined some of the effect, but it beat the heck out of wearing nothing but a robe and underwear out to greet the boys.

I retrieved the Browning from the back of the stool where it had sat during my shower. I carried it with me to the bedroom, and hesitated. I always went armed. Hell, I slept with a gun, but I didn't feel like slipping on a holster. I put the Browning away and settled for slipping the Firestar into the robe pocket. Made the cloth hang funny, but if something nasty came through the door I was ready for it.

Jean-Claude was standing at the window when I opened the bedroom door. He had opened the drapes, and was leaning against the window's edge staring out into the darkness. He turned when the door opened, though I knew he'd heard me before that.

"Ma petite, you look lovely."

"It's the only robe I own," I said.

"Of course," he said. His face had that amused mask on it again; this time I would have liked to know what he was thinking. His midnight blue eyes were very intense; they didn't match the nonchalant expression. Maybe I didn't want to know what he was thinking.

"Where are Larry and Jason?"

"They have come and gone," he said.

"Gone?"

"Jason had a sudden craving, and Larry drove him in the Jeep."

I just looked at him. "There is such a thing as room service."

"It is the wee hours of the morning, *ma petite.* The room service menu is somewhat limited. Jason has donated blood twice to me tonight; he needed protein." Jean-Claude smiled. "It was either take-out, or he could eat Larry. I thought you'd prefer take-out."

"Very funny. You shouldn't have sent them alone."

"We are safe from Serephina tonight, *ma petite,* and as long as they stay in town, safe from Xavier."

"How can you be so sure?" I crossed my arms over my stomach.

He leaned his back against the window and looked at me. "Your Monsieur Kirkland handled himself well tonight. I think you worry unnecessarily about him."

"One night of heroics doesn't keep you safe," I said.

"It will be dawn soon, *ma petite;* even Xavier cannot bear the light of day. All the vampires will be seeking shelter. They will have no time to chase our young men."

I stared at him, trying to read past his pleasant face. "I wish I was as sure as you seem to be."

He smiled then, and pushed away from the wall. He slid out of his jacket and let it fall to the rose-colored carpet.

"What are you doing?"

"Undressing."

I jerked a thumb at the bedroom, "Undress in there."

He began unbuttoning his shirt.

"In the other room, right now," I said.

He pulled the white shirt out of his pants, working the last few buttons as he walked towards me. The flesh of his chest and stomach had more color than the shirt. He was pumped up and human-looking on blood, part of it mine. The dried bloodstains that had soaked through the shirt marred the pale perfection of his body.

I expected him to try to kiss me, or something, but he walked past me. The back of the shirt was brownish with dried blood. He peeled it off his skin with a sound like tearing. He dropped the shirt on the carpet and walked into the bedroom.

I stood there staring after him. There had been white scars on his back. At least I thought that's what they were. Hard to tell through all the blood. He left the bedroom door open, and in a few minutes I heard water running in the bathtub.

I sat down in one of the straight-back chairs. I wasn't sure what else I was supposed to do. Water ran for a long time, then silence, then sloshing water. He was in the tub. He hadn't closed the bathroom door first. Great.

"Ma petite," he called.

I sat there for a minute, unwilling to move.

"Ma petite, I know you are there. I can hear you breathing."

I walked to the edge of the bedroom door, very careful not to look inside. I leaned my back against the wall and crossed my arms. "What do you want?"

"There seem to be no clean towels."

"What am I supposed to do about it?"

"Could you call down to housekeeping and have some sent up?"

"I guess so."

"Thank you, *ma petite.*"

I stomped over to the phone, pissed. He'd known there were no clean towels before he got into the tub. Hell, I'd known there were no clean towels, but I'd been so busy listening to him splash around in the water I hadn't thought of it.

I was as mad at me as I was at him. He was always a tormenting son of a bitch. I was supposed to watch myself around him better than this. I was in a hotel room that looked like a freaking bridal suite with Jean-Claude all naked and soapy in the next room. After what I'd seen with Jason, there shouldn't have been this much sexual tension in the air, but there was. Maybe it was habit, or maybe Larry was right. I just didn't believe that Jean-Claude was a rotting corpse.

I called for more towels.

They would be happy to bring some up. No one bitched about the time. No one questioned. You can always tell how much you're paying for a room by how little they complain.

A maid brought me four big, soft towels. I looked at her for a full minute, hesitating. I could have her take the towels into Jean-Claude.

She said, "Ma'am?"

I took the towels, said thanks, and closed the door. I just couldn't let a strange woman see that I had a naked vampire in my tub. I wasn't even sure the vampire part was what made it embarrassing. Good girls do not end up with naked male anything in their bathtubs at four something in the morning. Maybe I wasn't a good girl. Maybe I never had been.

I hesitated at the bedroom door. The room was dark. The only light came from the bathroom, spilling in an oblong across the carpet.

I crushed the towels to my chest, took a deep breath, and stepped into the room. I could see the bathtub from here, but mercifully not all of it. I had a glimpse of white porcelain and a mound of white bubbles. Just seeing the bubble bath made the muscles in my shoulders relax a little. Bubbles can hide a multitude of sins.

I stopped at the bathroom door.

Jean-Claude lay back against the edge of the tub. His black hair was wet and had obviously been cleaned. Strands of it clung to his bare shoulders. His arms lay propped on the edge of the bathtub, his head resting against the dark tile of the wall. One pale hand was suspended in midair as if reaching for something, but the hand was utterly limp. His eyes were closed, making black half-moons against his pale cheeks. Beads of water clung to his face and what I could see of his body. He looked almost asleep.

His knee came up through the mound of bubbles, a surprising glimpse of bare wet skin. He turned his head and opened his eyes. The midnight blue of his eyes seemed darker. Maybe it was the way the water made his hair seem heavier, blacker.

I took a shallow breath and said, "Here are the towels."

"Could you place them here, please?" He gestured with that one half-suspended hand.

"Here" was the closed top of the toilet, which was close enough to the tub for grabbing. "I'll put them on the edge of the sink."

"I'll drip water all over the floor getting them from there," he said. His voice was neutral, no vampiric tricks, almost no tone at all.

He was right, and I was being silly. He wouldn't grab me and ravish me. If that'd been the plan, he could have done that years ago.

I placed the towels on the stool, eyes studiously anywhere but the tub.

"You must have questions about tonight," he said.

I glanced at him. The water on his naked torso caught the light like quicksilver. Suds clung to his chest, just under one nipple. I had a horrible urge to brush off the bubbles. I stepped back until I was standing by the far wall.

"It's not like you to offer answers," I said.

"I am feeling generous tonight." His voice had that quality that voices get when they are edging towards sleep.

"If you weren't naked in a tub of bubble bath, would you be offering to answer questions?"

He smiled then, a quick, familiar expression. "Perhaps not, but if I must answer your ravenous curiosity, isn't it more fun this way?"

"Fun for whom?"

"Both of us, if you would only admit it."

That got a smile from me, and I didn't want to smile. I didn't want to be enjoying watching him all soapy and wet. I wanted to be afraid of him, and I was, but I also wanted him. Wanted to run my hands down his wet flesh, wanted to touch what lay under those bubbles. I didn't want intercourse. I couldn't imagine that with him, but I wanted to do a little exploring. I hated that. He was a corpse; surely what I'd seen tonight convinced me of that.

"You're frowning, *ma petite;* why?"

"I asked you if the two rotting vampires were illusion, you said no. I asked if your form was real, you said yes. Both forms are real, you said."

"That is true," he said.

"Are you a rotting corpse?"

He settled lower in the warm, soapy water, drawing his arms into it, until only his head showed above the surface of the water. "That is not one of my forms."

"That isn't an answer."

He raised a pale hand from the water, a handful of bubbles cupped like a snowball. "There are different vampiric abilities, *ma petite;* you know that."

"What's that have to do with it?"

He raised his other hand and began to play with the bubbles, trailing them from hand to hand. "Janos and his two female companions are a different type of vampire than I am. Than most of us are. They are much rarer. If you ever see me as a rotted corpse, I will be well and truly dead. They can rot and reform, and it makes them much harder to kill. The only true surety is fire."

"Volunteering an awful lot of information, aren't you?"

He lowered his hands in the water, washing the soap away. He sat up a little straighter; suds clung to his body. "Perhaps I am afraid you will think that what happened with Jason would happen with us."

"We will never test that theory," I said.

"You sound so sure of that," he said. "Your lust perfumes the air, and yet you truly believe that we will never make love. How can you want me almost as much as I want you, yet be sure we will never know each other's bodies?"

I wasn't sure I had an answer for that one. I slid down the wall and sat with my knees drawn up to my chest. The pocket with the gun in it clunked against the wall. I moved the gun to a better position and said, "We just won't, Jean-Claude, not ever. I just can't." A part of me regretted that, but only part.

"Why, *ma petite?*"

"Sex is about trust. I'd have to trust someone implicitly to have sex with them. I don't trust you."

He stared at me with his blue, blue eyes, looking all scrumptious and wet. "You mean that, don't you?"

I nodded. "Yeah, I do."

"I do not understand you, *ma petite*. I try, but still I do not."

"You're pretty much a riddle to me, too. If that's any comfort."

"It isn't. If you were a woman who had casual lusts, we would have been in bed long ago." He sighed and sat up even straighter in the water so it hit him just above the waist. "Of course, if you were a woman of casual appetites, I don't think I would love you."

"You enjoy the chase, the challenge," I said.

"True, but it is more than that with you, if only you would believe me." He leaned forward, drawing his knees to his naked chest, rounding his shoulders to hug himself. White scars dribbled down his back from his shoulders to vanish into the water, not a lot of them, but enough.

"What made the scars on your back? Unless it was a holy item, you should have been able to heal them."

He laid his cheek on his knees so he could look at me. He looked younger, more human, vulnerable suddenly. "Not if the injury occurred before I died."

"Who whipped you?"

"I was the whipping boy for an aristocrat's son."

I stared at him. "You're telling me the truth, aren't you?"

"Yes."

"Is that why Janos chose whips tonight, to remind you where you came from?"

"Yes."

"You weren't born into the aristocracy?"

"I was born in a house with a dirt floor, *ma petite.*"

I looked at him. "Yeah, right."

He raised his head. "If I was going to make something up, *ma petite,* it would be more romantic, more entertaining than being a French peasant."

"So you were a servant in the castle?"

"I was their only son's constant companion. When he had clothes made, so did I. His tutor was my tutor. His riding instructor, mine. I learned swordplay and dancing and the proper way to eat at table. And when he was bad I was punished, because he was their only child, their only heir to an old family name. People speak of child abuse now." He leaned back in the tub, cuddling down into the warm water. "They complain of spanking. They have no idea what true abuse is. When I was a boy, parents thought nothing of taking a horse whip to a misbehaving child, or beating them bloody. Even the aristocrats beat their children. It was normal.

"But he was the only heir, the only child. So they paid money to my parents and took me. The lady of the manor chose me because I was fair of face. When the vampire who made me sought me out, she said my beauty called to her."

"Wait a minute."

He turned his head to give me the full weight of those dark blue eyes. I worked hard at not looking away.

"This gorgeous body and face is all vampire illusion, right? I mean, no one's this beautiful."

"I told you once that it was not my power that made you see me as you do, not most of the time at any rate."

"Serephina said you were a catamount for any vampire that would have you. What did she mean?"

"Vampires kill for food, but they bring others over for many reasons. Some for money, wealth, even title, love, but I was brought over for lust. When I was young and weak, they passed me around among them. One would grow tired of me, but there was always another."

I stared at him, horrified. "You're right. If you were going to make up a story, this wouldn't be it."

"The truth is so often disappointing, or ugly; don't you find that, *ma petite?*"

I nodded. "Yeah. Serephina was old. I thought vampires weren't supposed to age."

"Whatever age we die at is the age we remain."

"Did you know Serephina when you were young?"

"Yes."

"Did you sleep with her?"

"Yes."

"How could you let her touch you?"

"I was given to her as a gift by a master that makes even her new and improved powers seem weak. I had very little choice." He stared at me. "She knows what you want. Your greatest need, your most treasured wish, and she'll make it come true, or seem to. What did she offer you, *ma petite?* What could she offer you that nearly won you tonight?"

I looked away then; I didn't want to meet his eyes. "What did she offer you all those years ago?"

"Power."

I looked up at that. "Power?"

He nodded. "Power to escape them all."

"But you had to have the ability to be a master vampire inside you from the beginning. No one can give that to you," I said.

He smiled, but it wasn't a happy smile. "I know that now, but then I thought only she could save me from an eternity of . . ." His words trailed off and he submerged, leaving only a few black locks floating on the top of the water. He sat up with a loud breath of air, blinking the water from his eyes. The water had clumped his thick, dark eyelashes. He ran his hands through his wet hair, and it trailed over his shoulders.

"Your hair wasn't this long when we first met."

"You seem to prefer longer hair on your men."

"If you're dead, how can your hair grow?"

"That is a question for you to answer," he said. He ran his hands through his hair again, squeezing the ends out. He reached out a hand for a towel.

I scrambled to my feet. "I'll leave you to get dressed."

"Have Jason and Larry returned?" he asked.

"No."

"Then I won't be getting dressed." He stood, drawing the towel towards him. I had a glimpse of one side of his pale naked body, water streaming from it. The towel moved into view just in time. I fled.

30

I HUDDLED IN the straight-back chair farthest from the bedroom. But I was staring at the doorway. Shit. I wanted to run from the room, but why? It wasn't Jean-Claude I didn't trust. It was me. Fuck.

I touched the gun in my robe pocket. It was smooth and hard and reassuring, but it wouldn't help me now. Violence I understood; sex gave me more problems.

I honestly didn't want to sleep with him, but part of me was hoping for another glimpse of naked flesh. A long line of naked thigh, perhaps. Or maybe . . . I put the palms of my hands over my eyes, as if I could get the image out of my head by just pressing.

"Ma petite?" His voice sounded closer than the bathroom.

I didn't want to look, as if, just as Grandma Blake had said, I'd be struck blind. I felt him standing in front of me. Felt the movement of air. I lowered my hands a millimeter at a time. He was kneeling in front of me, one of the thick white towels wrapped around his waist.

I lowered my hands to my lap. Beads of water still clung to his skin. He'd combed his hair, but it was wet, slicked back, leaving his face plainer, more unadorned than normal. His eyes seemed bluer without his hair to frame them.

He put a hand on each chair arm and raised himself up. His lips brushed mine in a soft, nearly chaste kiss. He moved back from me, letting go of the chair.

I could taste my heart in my throat, and it wasn't fear.

Jean-Claude touched my hands, lifted them up. He placed my hands on his bare shoulders. The skin was warm, smooth, wet. He held my wrists in his hands, lightly, very lightly. I could have pulled away at any time. He ran my hands down his slick body.

I pulled my hands free. He said nothing, did nothing. He stayed kneeling, looking at me. Waiting. I could see the pulse in his neck jumping against the skin, and I wanted to touch it.

I slid my hands across his shoulders and lowered my face to his. He started to move into me for a kiss, but I slid my hand along his jaw and turned his head away. I touched lips to his neck and slid my mouth down his skin, until I could taste his pulse beating against my tongue. He tasted of perfumed soap, water, and clean skin.

I slid from the chair to the floor, kneeling in front of him. He was taller now, but not too tall. I licked water off his chest, and let myself do something I'd wanted to do for months. I ran my tongue over his nipple, and he shuddered against me.

I licked water off the center of his chest and ran my hands along his waist up the damp curve of his back.

He pulled the sash of my robe, and I didn't protest. I let his hands slide under the robe, around my waist, with nothing but the t-shirt between his flesh and mine. He ran his hands up my sides, his thumbs playing over my rib cage. The gun swung heavily in the loose cloth. It was annoying.

I raised my face to his. His arms slid behind my back, pressing me against the long wet line of his body. The towel was perilously loose.

His lips brushed mine; then the kiss became something more. Harder, nearly bruising, with his arms locked behind my shoulders. My hands slid down his waist, rubbed the sliding top of the towel, and found it had already slipped. My hand touched the smooth top of his buttocks. Only the pressure of our bodies kept the towel in place.

He ate at my mouth and I felt something sharp, painful. I jerked back and tasted blood.

Jean-Claude let me go. He sat back on his heels, the towel gathered in his lap. "I am sorry, *ma petite*. I got carried away."

I touched my mouth and came away with a spot of blood. "You nicked me."

He nodded. "I am truly sorry."

"I'll just bet you are," I said.

"Do not go all self-righteous on me, *ma petite*. You have finally admitted to yourself, to me, that you feel the pull of my body."

I sat on the floor by the chair with my robe in disarray. The t-shirt had ridden up to my waist. I guess it was a little too late to protest my innocence.

"Fine, lust; you happy?"

"Almost," he said, and now there was something in his eyes. Something dark and drowning, and older than it should have been.

"I can offer you my mortal body, and more, *ma petite*. It can be between us much more than any human lover could offer."

"Would I lose a little blood each time?"

"That was an accident," he said.

I stared at him, all pale and damp, kneeling on the floor with the white towel bundled into his lap, leaving nearly every inch of him bare.

"This is the first time I've cheated on Richard," I said.

"You have been dating me for weeks," he said.

I shook my head. "But I haven't been cheating. *This* is cheating."

"Then have you been cheating on me, with Richard?"

I didn't know what to say to that. "Go get dressed."

"Do you really want me to dress?" he asked.

I looked away. I was embarrassed now and uncomfortable. "Yes, please."

He stood up, the towel gripped in his hands. I looked down at the floor and didn't have to see his face to picture the smile on it.

He walked away from me, and didn't bother moving the towel around behind him. Muscles moved under his skin from calf to waist. He walked naked into the bedroom, and I enjoyed the view.

I touched my finger to my tongue. It was still bleeding. That's what I got for French kissing a vampire. Even thinking about it made me nervous.

"*Ma petite?*" he called from the other room.

"Yeah."

"Do you have a blow dryer?"

"In my suitcase. Help yourself."

Thankfully, I'd dragged my suitcase into the bedroom beside the bathroom door. One point for laziness. I was spared another glimpse of his naked body. Now that hormones were receding, I was embarrassed.

I heard the dryer and wondered if he was standing naked in front of the bathroom mirror while he dried his hair. I was very aware that all I had to do was go to the doorway and I could see for myself.

I stood up, pulled my t-shirt down, tied my robe securely in place, and sat down on the couch. My back was to the bedroom. I wouldn't be seeing anything else. I took the Firestar out of my pocket and laid it on the coffee table in front of me. The gun sat there looking very solid, very black, and somehow accusatory.

The dryer stopped, and he called to me again. *"Ma petite?"*

"What?"

"Come talk to me as the sun rises."

I glanced up at the window he had opened. The sky outside was less black, not light yet, but not pure darkness anymore. I closed the drapes and went to the bedroom. I left the gun on the table. The Browning was in the bedroom anyway.

Jean-Claude had neatly folded the bedspread and blanket at the foot of the bed. Only the wine-dark sheet covered him. He lay with his black hair soft and curling over the dark pillows. The sheet was bunched at his waist. "You can join me if you like."

I leaned against the wall and shook my head.

"I'm not offering sex, *ma petite;* dawn is too close for that. I offer you your half of the bed."

"I'll take the couch; thanks anyway."

He smiled, a slow knowing curve of lips—his old arrogance peeking back out. It was almost comforting to know nothing had really changed. "It is not me that you do not trust. It is you."

I shrugged.

He raised the sheet in front of his chest, an almost protective gesture. "It comes." Fear in his voice.

"What comes?"

"The sun."

I glanced at the closed drapes against the far wall. They were double thick, but a line of greyish light edged them. "You'll be alright like this without your coffin?"

"As long as no one opens the drapes." He looked at me for a long moment. "I love you, *ma petite,* as much as I'm able."

I didn't know what to say. Saying I lusted after him didn't seem appropriate. Saying I loved him would be a lie.

The light grew stronger, a white edge around the curtains. His body slumped back against the bed. He rolled onto his side, one hand outstretched, the other curling the sheets against his chest. He stared at the growing light, and I could taste his fear.

I knelt beside the bed. I almost took his hand but didn't. "What happens now?"

"You want the truth, then watch." I expected his eyes to flutter, his voice to grow sluggish as if he were falling asleep. It didn't happen that way. He closed his eyes all at once. Pain flashed across his face. He whispered, "It hurts." His face went slack. I'd seen people die, watched the light fade from their bodies. Felt their souls slip away. That was what I saw. He died. The light grew against the drapes, and when it was a solid white line, he died. His breath went out of him in a long rattle.

I knelt beside the bed and stared. I knew dead when I saw it, and this was it. Shit.

I put my arms on the bed and propped my chin on them. I watched him, waiting for him to breathe, to twitch, something. But there was nothing. I reached out to his one outstretched arm. My fingers hovered above his skin, then I touched him. The skin was still warm, still human, but he did not move. I checked his wrist, and there was no pulse. No blood moved in this body.

Did he know I was here? Did he feel me touching him? I stared at him for what seemed like a long time. So this answered the question. Vampires were dead. Whatever animated them was like my own power, some sort of necromancy. But I knew death when I saw it. It gave necrophilia a whole new slant.

Had I only imagined that I felt the brush of his soul leave his body? Surely vampires had no souls—that was part of the point—but I'd felt something leave. If not a soul, what? If a soul, where did it go for the daylight hours? Who watched all the vampires' souls while they lay dead?

There was a knock at the door, probably the other boys. I stood up, pulling my robe in tight. I was cold, and wasn't sure why. I went to answer the door. The cut on my tongue had almost stopped bleeding.

31

I DREAMED. IN the dream, someone held me in their lap. Smooth dark arms wrapped around me. I looked up into my mother's laughing face. She was the most beautiful woman in the world. I snuggled against her body, and the clean smell of her skin was there. She'd always smelled of Hypnotique bath powder. She bent and kissed me on the lips. I had forgotten the taste of her lipstick, the way she brushed my mouth with her thumb, and laughed because she'd gotten bright red lipstick on my small mouth.

Her thumb came away with something brighter than lipstick. Blood dripped down her thumb. She'd pricked her skin with a safety pin. It was bleeding. She held her thumb out to me and said, "Kiss it, Anita, make it all better."

But there was too much blood. It ran down her hand. I stared up at her laughing face, and blood ran down it like rain. I woke sitting bolt upright on the velvet couch, gasping for breath. I could still taste her lipstick on my mouth, and the smell of Hypnotique bath powder clung to me.

Larry sat up on the love seat, rubbing at his eyes. "What's wrong? Did we get our wake-up call?"

"No, I had a bad dream."

He nodded, stretching, then frowned. "Do you smell perfume?"

I stared at him. "What do you mean?"

"Perfume or powder or something; do you smell it?"

I swallowed and nearly choked on my own pulse. "Yeah. I smell it."

I flung back the extra blanket and threw the lumpy pillow across the room.

Larry swung his legs off the love seat. "What is wrong with you?"

I went to the window and flung the drapes open. The bedroom door was closed, and Jean-Claude was safely inside. Jason was sleeping in there. I stood in the sunlight and let the heat sink into me. I leaned against the warm glass, and only then realized that I was wearing nothing but an oversized t-shirt and my undies. Oh, well. I stayed in the sunlight for a few minutes, waiting for my pulse to calm down.

"Serephina sent me a dream. The smell is my mother's perfume."

Larry came to stand beside me. He was wearing a pair of gym shorts and a green t-shirt. His curly red hair stuck up in all directions. His blue eyes squinted when he stepped into the light. "I thought only a vampire that had a connection with you, a hold on you, could invade your dreams."

"That's what I thought," I said.

"How could I smell perfume from your dream?"

I shook my head, forehead against the glass. "I don't know."

"Has she marked you?"

"I don't know."

He touched my shoulder, squeezing. "It'll be alright."

I stepped away from him to pace the room. "It won't be alright, Larry. Serephina invaded my dreams. No one but Jean-Claude has ever done that." I stopped, because that wasn't true. Nikolaos had done it. But that was after she'd bitten me. I shook my head. Either way, it was a very bad sign.

"What are you going to do?"

"Kill her."

"Murder her, you mean."

If Larry's earnest eyes hadn't been staring at me, I'd have said, "You bet." But it's hard to contemplate murder with someone staring at you like you've kicked their favorite puppy.

"I'll try to get a warrant," I said.

"If you can't?"

"If it's her or me, Larry, then it's her. Okay?"

Larry looked at me sadly. "What I did last night was murder. I know that, but I didn't go in planning to kill someone."

"You stay in this business long enough and you will."

He shook his head. "I don't believe that."

"Believe what you want, but it's still the truth. These things are too dangerous to play fair."

"If you really believe that, then how can you date Jean-Claude? How can you let him touch you?"

I shook my head. "I never said I was consistent."

"You can't defend yourself, can you?"

"Defend which one? Killing Serephina or dating Jean-Claude?"

"Either, both. Hell, Anita, if you're one of the bad guys you can't be one of the good guys."

I opened my mouth and closed it. What could I say? "I am one of the good guys, Larry. But I'm not going to be a martyr. If that means breaking the law, so be it."

"Are you going to get a warrant?" His face was very neutral as he asked. He looked older suddenly. Even with his orangey curls sticking up, he looked solemn.

I was watching Larry grow older before my eyes. Not in age, but in experience. The expression in his eyes was older than it had been a few months ago. Seen too much, done too much. He was still trying to be Sir Galahad, but Galahad had had God on his side. All Larry had was me. It wasn't enough.

"The only way I could get a death warrant is to lie," I said.

"I know," he said.

I stared at him. "Serephina hasn't broken any laws, yet. I won't lie about that."

He smiled. "Good. When do we meet Dorcas Bouvier?"

"Three."

"Have you figured out what you can sacrifice to raise the zombies Stirling wants done?" he asked.

"Nope."

He stared at me. "What are you going to tell Stirling?"

I shook my head. "I don't know yet. I wish I knew why he's so hot and heavy to kill Bouvier."

"He wants the land," Larry said.

"Stirling and Company have been saying the Bouvier family, not Magnus Bouvier. That means he's not the only one suing them. So killing Magnus won't solve their problems."

"So why do it?" Larry asked.

"Exactly," I said.

Larry nodded. "We need to talk to Magnus again."

"Preferably without Serephina around," I said.

"Amen to that," Larry said.

"I'd love to talk to Magnus, but before we tackle Mr. Bouvier again, I'd like to find some fairie ointment."

"Some what?"

"Didn't you take any classes on fairies?"

"It was an elective," he said.

"Fairie ointment makes you proof against glamor. Just in case whatever else Magnus is hiding is nastier than Serephina."

"Nothing nastier than that," he said.

"True, but just in case, he won't be able to work magic on us. In fact, it's not a bad precaution before we meet Dorrie. She may not be as scary as Magnus, but she shines, and I'd just as soon she didn't shine all over us."

"You think Serephina will find Jeff Quinlan?"

"If anyone can, she can. She seemed pretty confident she could take Xavier, but then Jean-Claude had been pretty confident he could take her last night. He was wrong."

He frowned. "So we're rooting for Serephina?"

It sounded wrong, put that way, but I nodded. "If it's a choice between a vampire that obeys most of the laws, and one that slaughters kids, yeah, we're on her side."

"You were talking about killing her just a little bit ago."

"I can stay out of her way until she saves Jeff, and kills Xavier."

"Why would she kill him?" Larry asked.

"He's killing people in her territory. She can say anything she wants, but that's a direct challenge to her authority. Besides, I don't think Xavier will give up Jeff without a fight."

"What do you think happened to him last night?" Larry asked.

I shook my head. "It doesn't do any good to dwell on it, Larry. We're doing all we can."

"We could tell the FBI about Serephina."

"One thing I've learned is that master vamps don't talk to the cops. Too many years of the cops killing them on sight, or trying to."

"Okay," he said, "but we've still got to come up with something big enough to kill for raising the cemetery tonight," he said.

"I'll think on it."

"You really have no idea what to do?" He sounded surprised.

"Short of a human sacrifice, Larry, I don't think I can raise several three-hundred-year-old corpses. Even I've got my limits."

He grinned. "Nice to hear you admit it."

I had to smile. "It'll be our little secret."

He put his hand out, and I slapped it. He slapped mine back, and I felt better. Larry had a way of making me smile. Friends will do that to you.

32

DORCAS BOUVIER WAS leaning on a car in the parking lot. Her hair gleamed in the sunlight, swirling as she moved, like heavy water. In jeans and a green tank top, she was flawless.

Larry tried not to stare at her, but it was hard work. Larry was wearing a blue t-shirt, jeans, white Nikes, and an oversized checked flannel shirt to hide his shoulder holster.

I was in jeans and a navy blue polo shirt, black Nikes, and an oversized blue dress shirt. I'd had to borrow it from Larry after my black jacket had gotten covered in vampire goop. Had to have something to hide the Browning. Makes people nervous if you go around with a naked gun. Larry and I looked like we'd dressed from the same closet.

Dorrie pushed away from the car. "Shall we go?"

"We'd like to talk to Magnus."

"So you can turn him into the cops?"

I shook my head. "So we can find out why Stirling is so hot to kill him."

"I don't know where he is," Dorcas said.

Maybe it showed on my face, because she said, "I don't know where he is, but if I did, I wouldn't tell you. Using magic on the police is a death penalty case. I won't turn him in."

"I'm not the police."

She looked at me, eyes narrowing. "Did you come to look at Bloody Bones, or to question me about my brother?"

"How did you know to be waiting here for us?" I asked.

"I knew you'd be on time." Her pupils swirled downward to pinpoints, like the eyes of an excited parrot.

"Let's go," I said.

She led us to the back of the restaurant where it nearly touched the woods. A path began at the edge of the clearing. It was barely wide enough for a man. Even though we walked single file, the branches whipped at my shoulders. The new green leaves rubbed like velvet along my cheek. The path was deep and rutted down to naked tree roots in places, but weeds were beginning to encroach on the path, as if it wasn't used as much as it once had been.

Dorrie moved down the uneven path with an easy, swinging stride. She was obviously familiar with the path, but it was more than that. The tree limbs that caught on my shirt didn't get caught in her hair. The roots that threatened to trip me didn't slow her down.

We'd found ointment at a health food store. So the bushes moving for her and not for us was real, not illusion. Maybe glamor wasn't the only thing to worry about. Which was why the Browning was loaded with nonsilver bullets. I'd had to go out and buy some special for the occasion. Larry was loaded up too, and for the first time I wished he had two guns. I still had the Firestar with silver ammo, but Larry was out of luck if a vamp jumped us. Of course, it was broad daylight. I was more worried about fairies than vamps right this minute. There was salt in our shirt pockets, not a lot, but you didn't need much, just enough to throw on the fey or the thing being magicked. Salt disrupted fey magic. Temporarily.

A breeze came up the path. It grew into a wind in one fit-

ful gust. The air smelled clean and fresh. You hoped the beginning of time smelled like that; like fresh bread, clean
laundry, childhood memories of spring. It probably smelled
like ozone and swamp water. Reality almost always smells
worse than daydream.

Dorrie stopped and turned back to us. "The trees across
the path are just illusion. They're not solid."

"What trees?" Larry asked. I cursed silently. It would
have been nice to keep the ointment a secret.

Dorrie took two steps back towards us. She stared at my
face from inches away, then made a face like she'd seen
something unclean. "You're wearing ointment." She made it
sound like a very bad thing.

"Magnus did try to bedazzle us twice. Nothing wrong
with being cautious," I said.

"Well, our illusions won't matter to you, then." She took
off at a faster pace, leaving us to stumble after her.

The path led into a clearing that was nearly a perfect circle. There was a small mound in the center with a white
stone Celtic cross in the middle of a mass of vibrant blue
flowers. Every inch of ground was covered with bluebells.
English bluebells, thick and fleshy, bluer than the sky. The
flowers never grew in this country without help. They never
grew in Missouri without more water than was practical. But
standing in the solid mass of blue surrounded by trees, it
seemed worth it.

Dorrie stood frozen nearly knee-deep in the flowers. She
was staring open-mouthed, a look of horror on her lovely
face.

Magnus Bouvier knelt in the flowers on top of the mound,
near the cross. His mouth was bright with fresh blood.
Something moved around him, in front of him. Something
more felt than seen. If it was illusion, the ointment should
have taken care of it. I tried looking at it out of the corner of
my eye. Sometimes peripheral vision works better on magic
than straight-on sight.

From the corner of my eye I could see the air swimming
in something that was almost a shape. It was bigger than a
man.

Magnus turned and saw us. He stood up abruptly, and the swimming air blinked out like it had never been. He wiped a sleeve across his mouth.

"Dorrie . . ." His voice was soft and strangled.

Dorrie clawed her way up the hill. She screamed, "Blasphemy!" and smacked him. I could hear the slap all the way across the clearing.

"Ouch," Larry said. "Why is she mad?"

She hit him again, hard enough to sit him down on his butt in the flowers. "How could you? How could you do such a vile thing?"

"What did he do?" Larry asked.

"He's been feeding off Rawhead and Bloody Bones just like his ancestor," I said.

Dorrie turned to me. She looked haggard, horrified, as if she had caught her brother molesting children. "It was forbidden to feed." She turned back to Magnus. "You knew that!"

"I wanted the power, Dorrie. What harm did it do?"

"What harm? What harm?" She grabbed a handful of his long hair and pulled him to his knees. She exposed the bite marks on his neck. "This is why that creature can call you. This is why one of the *Daoine Sidhe,* even a half-breed like you, is called by death." She let go so abruptly he fell forward on his hands and knees.

Dorrie sat down in the flowers and cried.

I waded into the flowers. They parted like water, but they didn't move. They were just never exactly where you were stepping.

"Jesus, are they moving out of the way?" Larry asked.

"Not exactly," Magnus said. He walked down the mound to stand at its base. He was wearing the white tuxedo from last night, or what was left of it. The smear of blood on his shirtsleeve was very bright against the whiteness.

We waded through the flowers that were moving and not moving, to join him in front of the mound.

He'd shoved his hair back behind his ears so his face was visible. And no, his ears weren't pointed. Where do these rumors get started?

He met my eyes without flinching. If he was ashamed of what he'd done, it didn't show. Dorrie was still weeping in the bluebells like her heart would break.

"So now you know," he said.

"You can't bleed a fairie, in the flesh or not in the flesh, without ritual magic. I've read the spell, Magnus. It's a doozy," I said.

He smiled at that, and the smile was still lovely, but the blood at the corner of his mouth ruined the effect. "I had to tie myself to the beastie. I had to give him some of my mortality in order to get his blood."

"The spell isn't meant to help you gather blood," I said. "It's to help the fairies kill each other."

"If it got some of your mortality, did you get some of its immortality?" Larry asked. It was a good question.

"Yes," Magnus said, "but that wasn't why I did it."

"You did it for power, you son of a bitch," Dorrie said. She came down the mound, sliding in the strange flowers. "You just had to do real glamor, real magic. My God, Magnus, you must have been drinking its blood for years, ever since you were a teenager. That's when your powers suddenly got so strong. We all thought it was puberty."

"Afraid not, sister dear."

She spit at him. "Our family was cursed, tied to this land forever in repentance for doing what you have done. Bloody Bones broke free last time someone tried to drink from his veins."

"It's been safely imprisoned for ten years, Dorrie."

"How do you know? How do you know that nebulous thing you called up hasn't been out scaring children?"

"As long as it doesn't hurt any of them, what's the harm?"

"Wait a minute," said Larry. "Why would it scare children?"

"I told you, it's a nursery boggle. It was supposed to eat bad children," I said. I had an idea, an awful idea. I'd seen a vampire use a sword, but was I absolutely sure of what I'd seen? No. "When the thing got out and started slaughtering the Indian tribe, did it use a weapon, or its hands?"

Dorrie looked at me. "I don't know. Does it matter?"

Larry said, "Oh, my God."

"It might matter a great deal," I said.

"You can't mean those killings," Magnus said. "Bloody Bones cannot manifest itself physically. I've seen to that."

"Are you sure, brother dear? Are you absolutely sure?" Dorrie's voice cut and sliced; she wielded scorn like a weapon.

"Yes, I'm sure."

"We'll have to have a witch look at this. I don't know enough about it," I said.

Dorrie nodded. "I understand. The sooner the better."

"Rawhead and Bloody Bones did not do those killings," Magnus said.

"For your sake, Magnus, I hope not," I said.

"What do you mean?"

"Because five people have died. Five people who didn't do a damn thing to deserve it."

"It's imprisoned by a combination of Indian, Christian, and fairie power," he said. "It's not breaking free of that."

I walked around the mound slowly. The fleshy flowers still moved out of the way. I'd tried watching my feet, but it was dizzying, because the flowers moved yet didn't, like trying to watch one of them bloom. You knew it did, but you could never watch the actual event.

I ignored the flowers and concentrated on the mound. I wasn't trying to sense the dead, so daylight was fine. There was magic here, lots of it. I'd never felt fairie magic before. There was something here that had a familiar taste to it, and it wasn't the Christianity. "Some kind of death magic went into this," I said. I walked around the mound until I could see Magnus's face. "A little human sacrifice, perhaps?"

"Not exactly," Magnus said.

"We would never condone human sacrifice," Dorrie said.

Maybe she wouldn't, but I wasn't so sure about Magnus. I didn't say it out loud. Dorrie was upset enough already.

"If it's not sacrifice, then what is it?"

"Three hills are buried with our dead. Each death is like a stake to hold old Bloody Bones down," Magnus said.

"How did you lose track of which hills belonged to you?" I asked.

"It's been over three hundred years," Magnus said. "There were no deeds back then. I wasn't a hundred percent sure the hill was the right hill myself. But when they raked up the dead, I felt it." He huddled in on himself as if the air had suddenly grown colder. "You can't raise the dead from that hillside. If you do it, then Bloody Bones will be loosed. The magic to stop it is complicated. Truthfully, I'm not sure I'm up to it myself. And I don't know any Indian shamans anymore."

"You have made a mockery of everything we stand for," Dorrie said.

"What did Serephina offer you?" I asked.

He looked at me, surprised. "What are you talking about?"

"She offers everyone their heart's desire. What was yours, Magnus?"

"Freedom and power. She said she'd find another guardian for Rawhead and Bloody Bones. She said she'd find a way for me to keep the power I'd borrowed from it without having to tend it."

"And you believed her?"

He shook his head. "I'm the only person in the family who has the power. We are the guardians forever as penance for stealing it, for letting it kill." He collapsed to his knees in the blue, blue flowers, his head bowed, hair spilling forward to hide his face. "I'll never be free."

"You don't deserve to be free," Dorrie said.

"Why did Serephina want you so badly?" I asked.

"She's afraid of death. She says drinking from something as long-lived as I am helps her keep death at bay."

"She's a vampire," Larry protested.

"But not immortal," I said.

Magnus looked up, strange aquamarine eyes glimmering out through his shining hair. Maybe it was the hair, or the eyes, or his being nearly covered in the strange moving, not moving flowers, but he didn't look very human.

"She fears death," he said. "She fears you." His voice was low and echoing.

"She nearly cleaned my clock last night. Why's she afraid of me?"

"You brought death among us last night."

"It can't be the first time," I said.

"She came to me for my long life, my immortal blood. Perhaps she will go to you next. Perhaps instead of running from death, she will embrace it."

The skin on my arms twitched, marching in gooseflesh up to my elbows. "She tell you that last night?"

"There is a power involved, hurting her old enemy Jean-Claude, but in the end, Anita, she wonders if your power would make the difference. If she drank you up, would she be immortal? Would you be able to keep death from her with your necromancy?"

"You could leave town," Larry said. I wasn't sure which of us he was speaking to.

I shook my head. "Master vampires don't give up that easy. I'll tell Stirling that I won't be raising his dead, Magnus. No one else can do it but me, so it won't get done."

"But they won't give back the land," Magnus said in his strange voice. "If they simply blow up the mountain, the result might be the same."

"Is that true, Dorrie?"

She nodded. "It could be."

"What do you want me to do?" I asked.

Magnus crawled through the flowers, peering at me through the shining curtain of his hair. His eyes were swirling bands of green and blue, whirling until I was dizzy. I looked away.

"Raise a handful of the dead. Can you do that?" he asked.

"No sweat," I said. "But will everybody's lawyers agree to that?"

"I'll see that they do," he said.

"Dorrie?" I asked.

She nodded. "I'll see to it."

I stared at Magnus for a moment. "Will Serephina really rescue the boy?"

"Yes," he said.

I stared down at him. "Then I'll see you tonight."

"No, I'll be well and truly drunk again. It's not foolproof, but it helps drown her out."

"Fine; I'll raise you a handful of dead. Keep your land safe."

"You have our gratitude," Magnus said. He looked feral, frightening, beautiful crouched in the flowers. His gratitude might be worth something if Serephina didn't kill him first.

Hell, if she didn't kill me first.

33

I CALLED SPECIAL Agent Bradford late in the day. They hadn't found Xavier. They hadn't found Jeff. They hadn't found any vampires that I needed to kill, and why the hell was I calling him? I was not on this case, remember? I remembered. And yes, the two youngest victims had been sexually assaulted, but not the same day they were killed. I probably should have brought Magnus in, but he was the only one who understood the spells on Bloody Bones. He wouldn't be any good to us locked up. Dorrie knew a local witch she trusted. I'd thought that maybe Bloody Bones was our killer. I'd never seen a vampire hide itself so completely from me as the one that killed Coltrain. I'd added it to my list of suspects, but hadn't told the cops. Now I was glad I hadn't. The sexual assault had Xavier written all over it. Besides, explaining that a nursery boggle from Scotland was committing murders on the ethereal plane sounded farfetched even to me.

The sky was thick with clouds that glowed like jewels. They shimmered and stretched across the sky like a gigantic gleaming blanket that some great beast had shredded with massive claws. Through the holes in the clouds, the sky peeked through black with a few diamond-chip stars bright enough to compete with the gleaming sky.

I stood on the hilltop staring up at the sky, breathing in the cool spring air. Larry stood beside me, looking up. His eyes reflected the glowing light.

"Get on with it," Stirling said.

I turned and looked at him. Him, Bayard, and Ms. Harrison. Beau had been with them, but I'd made him wait at the bottom of the mountain. I'd even told him if he so much as showed his face up top, I'd put a bullet in it. I wasn't sure Stirling believed me, but Beau had.

"Not an appreciator of nature's beauty, are you, Raymond?"

Even by moonlight I could see his scowl. "I want this over with, Ms. Blake. Now, tonight."

Strangely enough, I agreed with him. It made me nervous. I didn't like Raymond. It made me want to argue with him, regardless of whether I agreed. But I didn't argue. Point for me.

"I'll get it done tonight, Raymond; don't sweat it."

"Please stop calling me by my first name, Ms. Blake." He made the request through clenched teeth, but he had said "please."

"Fine. It'll be done tonight, Mr. Stirling. Okay?"

He nodded. "Thank you; now get on with it."

I opened my mouth to say something smart, but Larry said very softly, "Anita."

He was right, as usual. As much fun as it was to yank Stirling's chain, it was just delaying the inevitable. I was tired of Stirling, of Magnus, and of everything. It was time to do this job and go home. Well, maybe not straight home. I wouldn't leave without Jeff Quinlan, one way or another.

The goat gave a high, questioning bleat. It was staked out in the middle of the boneyard. It was a brown-and-white-spotted goat with those strange yellow eyes they sometimes have. It had floppy white ears and seemed to like having the top of its head scratched. Larry had petted it in the Jeep on the drive over. Always a bad idea. Never get friendly with the sacrifices. Makes it hard to kill them.

I had not petted the goat. I knew better. This was Larry's first goat. He'd learn. Hard or easy, he'd learn. There were two more goats at the bottom of the hill. One of them was even smaller and cuter than this one.

"Shouldn't we have the Bouviers' lawyers present, Mr. Stirling?" Bayard said.

"The Bouviers waived having their attorney present," I said.

"Why would they do that?" Stirling asked.

"They trust me not to lie to them," I said.

Stirling looked at me for a long moment. I couldn't see his eyes clearly, but I could feel the wheels inside his head moving.

"You're going to lie for them, aren't you?" he said. His voice was cold, repressed, too angry for heat.

"I don't lie about the dead, Mr. Stirling. Sometimes about the living, but never about the dead. Besides, Bouvier didn't offer me a bribe. Why should I help him if he doesn't throw money at me?"

Larry didn't call me on that one. He was looking at Stirling, too. Wondering what he'd say, maybe.

"You've made your point, Ms. Blake. Can we get on with it now?" He sounded reasonable, ordinary suddenly. All that anger, all that mistrust, had had to go somewhere. But it wasn't in his voice.

"Fine." I knelt and opened the gym bag at my feet. It held my animating equipment. I had another one that held vampire gear. I used to just transfer whatever I wanted into the bag. I bought a second bag after I showed up once at a zombie raising with the wrong bag. It was also illegal to carry vampire slaying stuff if you didn't have a warrant of execution on you. Brewster's law might change that, but until then . . . I had two bags. The zombie was my normal burgundy one; the vampire bag was white. Even in the dark, it was easy to tell them apart. That was the plan.

Larry's zombie bag was a nearly virulent green with Teenage Mutant Ninja Turtles on it. I was almost afraid to ask what his vampire bag looked like.

"Let me test my understanding here," Larry said. My words fed back to me. He knelt and unzipped his bag.

"Go ahead, " I said. I got out my jar of ointment. I knew animators who had special containers for the ointment. Crockery, hand-blown glass, mystical symbols carved into the sides. I used an old Mason jar that had once held Grandma Blake's green beans.

Larry fished out a peanut butter jar with the label still on it. Extra-crunchy. Yum-yum.

"We have to raise a minimum of three zombies, right?"

"Right," I said.

He stared around at the scattered bones. "A mass grave is hard to raise from, right?"

"This isn't a mass grave. It's an old cemetery that was disturbed. That's easier than a mass grave."

"Why?" he asked.

I laid the machete down beside the jar of ointment. "Because each grave had rites performed that would tie the dead individual to the grave, so that if you call it you have a better chance of getting an individual to answer."

"Answer?"

"Rise from the dead."

He nodded. He laid a wicked curved blade on the ground. It looked like a freaking scimitar.

"Where did you get that?"

He dipped his head, and I would have bet he was blushing. Just couldn't see it by moonlight.

"Guy at college."

"Where'd he get it?"

Larry looked at me, surprise plain on his face. "I don't know. Is something wrong with it?"

I shook my head. "Just a little fancy for beheading chickens and slitting a few goats open."

"It felt good in my hand." He shrugged. "Besides, it looks cool." He grinned at me.

I shook my head, but I let it go. Did I really need a machete to behead a few chickens, no, but the occasional cow, yeah.

Why, you may ask, didn't we have a cow tonight? No one

would sell Bayard one. He had the brilliant idea of telling the farmers why he wanted the cow. The God-fearing folk would sell their cows to be eaten, but not for raising zombies. Prejudiced bastards.

"The youngest of the dead here are two hundred years old, right?" Larry asked.

"Right," I said.

"We're going to raise a minimum of three of these corpses in good enough condition for them to answer questions."

"That's the plan," I said.

"Can we do that?"

I smiled at him. "That's the plan."

His eyes widened. "Damn, you don't know if we can do it either, do you?" His voice had dropped to an amazed whisper.

"We raise three zombies a night every night routinely. We're just doing them back to back."

"We don't raise two-hundred-year-old zombies routinely."

"True, but the theory's the same."

"Theory?" He shook his head. "I know we're in trouble when you start talking about theories. Can we do this?"

The honest answer was no, but the thing that dictated more than anything else what you could raise and what you couldn't was confidence. Believing you could do it. So . . . I was tempted to lie. But I didn't. Truth between Larry and me.

"I think we can do it."

"But you don't know for sure," he said.

"No."

"Geez, Anita."

"Don't get rattled on me. We can do this."

"But you aren't sure."

"I'm not sure we'll survive the plane ride home, but I'm still getting on the plane."

"Was that supposed to be comforting?" he asked.

"Yeah."

"It wasn't," he said.

"Sorry, but this is as good as it gets. You want certainty, be an accountant."

"I'm not good at math."

"Me either."

He took a deep breath and let it out slowly. "Alright, boss, how do we combine powers?"

I told him.

"Neat." He didn't look nervous anymore. He looked eager. Larry may have wanted to be a vampire executioner, but he was an animator. It wasn't a career choice, it was a gift, or a curse. No one could teach you to raise the dead unless you had the power in your blood. Genetics is a wonderful thing: brown eyes, curly hair, zombie raising.

"Whose ointment you want to use?" Larry asked.

"Mine." I'd given Larry the recipe for the ointment and told him which ingredients you couldn't mess with, like the graveyard mold, but there was room for experimentation. Every animator had their own special recipe. You never knew what Larry's ointment would smell like. For sharing powers you used the same ointment, so we were using mine.

For all I knew, we didn't have to use the same ointment, but I'd only shared my powers three times. Twice with the man who trained me as an animator. Each time we'd used the same ointment. I had acted as a focus all three times. Which meant I was in charge. Where I liked to be, right?

"Could I act as a focus?" Larry asked. "Not this time, but later?"

"If this comes up again, we'll try it," I said. Truth was, I didn't know if Larry had the power to be a focus. Manny, who taught me, couldn't do it. Very few animators could act as a focus. Those who could were mistrusted by the rest, and most wouldn't play with us. We would literally share our powers. A lot of animators wouldn't be willing to do that. There is a theory that you could permanently steal another's magic. But I don't buy it. Raising the dead isn't like a magic charm that someone can take with them, and leave you without. Animating is built into the cells of our bodies. It's part of us. You can't steal that.

I opened the ointment, and the spring air suddenly smelled like Christmas trees. I used a lot of rosemary.

The ointment was thick and waxy and always felt cool. Flecks of glowing graveyard mold looked like ground-up lightning bugs. I smeared ointment across Larry's forehead, down his cheeks. He untucked his t-shirt and raised it so I could dab it over his heart. Which is harder than it sounds with a shoulder holster on, but we'd both worn a gun apiece. I had left both knives and my backup gun in the Jeep. I touched his skin and could feel his heart pounding under my hand.

I handed Larry the Mason jar. He dipped two fingers into the thick ointment. He traced ointment over my face. His hand was very steady, face blank with concentration. Eyes utterly serious.

I unbuttoned the polo shirt and Larry slipped his fingers inside to touch my heart. His fingers rubbed the chain of my crucifix, spilling it out of my shirt. I slipped it back inside next to my skin. He handed the jar back to me, and I screwed the lid on tight. Wouldn't do to let it dry out.

I'd never heard of anyone doing exactly what we were about to attempt. Not the age part, but the scattered bodies. We only wanted three, but there weren't three intact bodies. Even doing them one at a time, it was chancy. How to raise just so much dead and no more when they were lying jumbled together? I had no names to use. No gravesite to encircle with power. How to do it?

It was a puzzlement.

But for now we just had to close the circle. One problem at a time.

"Make sure both of your hands have ointment on them," I said.

Larry rubbed his hands together like he was putting on lotion. "Aye, aye, boss; what next?"

I drew a deep silver bowl out of my bag. It gleamed in the moonlight like another piece of sky.

Larry's eyes widened.

"It doesn't have to be silver. There are no mystical symbols on it. You could use a Tupperware bowl, but the life of another living creature is going in here. Use something nice to show some respect, but understand that it doesn't have to be silver, or this shape, or anything. It's just a container. Okay?"

Larry nodded. "Why not have the other goats up here on top? It's going to be a trek to get them up here every time."

I shrugged. "First, they'd panic. Second, it seems cruel for them to watch their friends bite the dust, knowing they're next."

"My zoology prof would say you're humanizing them."

"Let him. I know they feel pain, and fear. That's enough."

Larry looked at me for a long moment. "You don't like doing it either."

"No. You want to help hold or feed the carrot?"

"Carrot?"

I dug a carrot, complete with leafy green top, out of the bag.

"Was that what you got in the grocery store while I waited in the car with the goats?"

"Yeah."

I held the carrot up in the air. The goat strained to the end of its picket line, towards the carrot. I let the goat lip the leafy top. It bleated and strained towards me. I let him get a little more leaf. His stubby little tail started wagging. Happy goat.

I handed Larry the silver bowl. "Put it on the ground under the throat. When the blood starts coming, catch as much as you can."

I had the machete behind my back in my right hand, carrot in my left. I felt like a child's dentist. No, nothing behind my back. Pay no attention to that huge needle. Except this needle was permanent.

The goat yanked most of the leaves off the carrot, and I waited while it snaked them up into its mouth. Larry knelt beside it, bowl on the ground. I offered the meat of the carrot to the goat. It got a taste of it, and I drew the carrot out, out, until the goat strained its neck out as far as it could, trying to get more of the hard orange flesh.

I laid the machete against the hairy throat, not cutting,

gentle. The neck vibrated against the blade, straining for the carrot. I drew the blade across the neck.

The machete was sharp, and I had practice. There was no sound, only the shocked, widened eyes, and blood pouring from the neck.

Larry picked up the bowl, holding it under the wound. Blood splashed down his arms onto the blue t-shirt. The goat collapsed to its knees. Blood filled the bowl, dark and glinting, more black than red.

"There's bits of carrot in the blood," Larry said.

"It alright," I said. "Carrot's inert."

The goat's head fell slowly forward until it touched the ground. The bowl sat under its throat, filling with blood. It had been nearly a perfect kill. Goats could be sort of pesky, but sometimes, like tonight, it all worked. Of course, we weren't done.

I laid the bloody knife against my left arm and sliced it open. The pain was sharp and immediate. I held the wound over the bowl, letting the thick drops mingle with the goat's blood.

"Give me your right arm," I said.

Larry didn't argue. He just held out his bare arm. I'd told him what would happen, but it was still a very trusting gesture. His face turned up to me was without any trace of fear. God.

I sliced his arm. He winced but didn't draw back. "Let it drip into the bowl."

He held his arm over the bowl. All the blood was red-black in the moonlight.

The beginnings of power trickled over my skin. My power, Larry's power, the power of a ritual sacrifice. Larry looked up at me with wide eyes.

I knelt beside him and laid the machete across the mouth of the bowl. I held out my left hand to him. He gave me his right. We clasped hands and pressed the wounds in our forearms together, letting the blood mingle. Larry held one side of the blood-filled bowl and I held the other. Blood trickled down our arms to drip off our elbows into the bowl, onto the bloody naked steel.

We stood still clasped together, still holding the bowl. I withdrew my hand from his slowly, then took the bowl from him. He followed my every movement like he always did. He'd be able to close his eyes and mimic me.

I walked to the edge of the circle I had in my mind and plunged my hand into the bowl. The blood was still amazingly warm, almost hot. I grasped the handle of the machete with my bloody hand and began using the blade to sprinkle blood as I walked.

I could feel Larry standing in the center of the circle that I walked like there was a rope stretched between us. As I walked, that rope stretched tighter and tighter like a rubber band being twisted. The power grew with each step, each drop of blood. The earth was hungry for it. I'd never raised the dead on ground that had seen death rituals before. Magnus should have mentioned that. Maybe he hadn't known. Charitable of me.

It didn't matter now. There was magic here for blood and death. Something that was eager for me to close the circle. Eager for me to raise the dead. Hungry.

I stood nearly where I'd begun. I was a sprinkle of blood away from closing the circle. The line of power between Larry and me was so tight it hurt. The potential power was frightening, and exhilarating. We'd awakened something old and long dormant. It made me hesitate. Made me not want to finish the circle. Stubbornness, and fear. I didn't completely understand what I was feeling. It was someone else's magic, someone's spell. We'd triggered it, but I didn't know what it would do. We could raise our dead, but it would be like walking a tightrope between the other spell and . . . something.

I felt old Bloody Bones in its barrow miles away. I felt it watching me, urging me to take that last step. I shook my head as if the fey creature could see me. I just didn't understand the spell well enough to risk it.

"What's wrong?" Larry asked. His voice sounded strangled. We were choking on unused power, and damned if I knew what to do with it.

I caught movement out of the corner of my eye. Ivy stood

at the edge of the mountain. She was wearing hiking boots with thick white socks folded over them, baggy black shorts, and a skin-tight neon pink top, with a checked flannel shirt over it. The chain of her dangling earring gleamed in the moonlight. She'd dressed herself tonight.

All I had to do was drop that last bit of blood, and the circle would close. And I could hold this circle against her, against them all. Nothing would cross it that I didn't want to cross it. Well, within reason. Demons and angels could probably cross it, but vampires couldn't.

I felt a surge of triumph from the thing trapped in its mound. It wanted me to close the circle. I tossed the bowl and machete behind me towards the center of the circle, away from the outer edge so no blood would fall on it. Ivy started towards me in a faster-than-light display, a blur of speed. I went for my gun, felt it slide from the holster, and she smashed into me. The impact knocked the Browning out of my hand. I hit the ground with nothing in my hands but air.

34

IVY REARED BACKWARDS, fangs flashing. Larry screamed, "Anita!" I heard the gun go off, felt the bullet hit her body. It hit her in the shoulder, twisted her body, but she turned back to me with a smile. She dug fingers into my shoulders and rolled us over, putting me on top, with one of her hands leeched to the back of my neck. She squeezed until I gasped.

"I'll snap her spine unless you throw that toy away," she said.

"She'll kill me anyway. Don't do it."

"Anita . . ."

"Now, or I'll kill her while you watch."

"Shoot her!" But there wasn't a clear shot. He'd have to

walk around me and fire point-blank. Ivy could kill me twice over before he got to us.

Ivy forced my neck lower. I braced my right arm on the ground. She'd have to break something to get me down to her. If she broke my neck, it'd be over; a broken arm would just hurt.

I heard something hit the ground, a dull, heavy thump. Larry's gun. Damn.

She pressed harder on the back of my neck. I dug the palm of my hand into the ground hard enough to leave an imprint.

"I can break that arm and bring you to me. Your choice: easy, or hard."

"Hard," I said between gritted teeth.

She grabbed for my arm, and I had an idea. I collapsed forward on top of her. It caught her off guard. I had a handful of seconds to pull the chain around my neck out of my shirt.

Her hand slid through my hair like a lover's, pressing my face against her cheek, not hard, almost gentle. "Three nights from now you'll like me, Anita. You'll worship me."

"I doubt that." The chain slid forward, the crucifix pooled against her throat. There was a blinding flash of white, white light. A rush of heat that singed my hair.

Ivy screamed and clawed at the cross, scrambling from underneath me.

I stayed on all fours with the cross dangling in front of me. The blue-white flames died away because it wasn't touching vampiric flesh anymore, but it glowed like a captive star, and she backed away from it.

I didn't know where my gun was, but the machete gleamed against the dark earth. I wrapped my hand around it and got to my feet. Larry was behind me with his own cross out, held in front of him to the length of its chain. The white light with its core of blue was almost painfully bright.

Ivy screamed, shielding her eyes. All she had to do was walk away. But she was frozen, immobile in the face of the crosses, and two true believers.

"Gun," I said to Larry.

"Can't find it."

Both guns were matte black so they wouldn't reflect light at night and make us a target; now it made them invisible.

We advanced on the vampire. She threw both arms up before her face and screamed, "Nooo!" She'd backed up nearly to the edge of the circle. If she ran, we wouldn't chase her, but she didn't run. Maybe she couldn't.

I shoved the machete up under her ribs. Blood poured down the blade onto my hands. I drove the blade upward into her heart. I gave it that last little wrench to slice it up.

Her arms fell away from her face slowly. Her eyes were wide, surprised. She stared down at the blade in her stomach, as if she didn't understand what it was doing there. The flesh of her neck was black where the cross had burned her.

She fell to her knees and I went with her, keeping my grip on the machete. She didn't die. I hadn't really expected her to. I jerked the blade out of her, doing more damage. She made a low gurgling sound, but stayed on her knees. Her hands touched the blood flowing out of her chest and stomach. She stared at the gleaming darkness as if she'd never seen blood before. The blood flow was already slowing; unless I killed her soon, the wound would close.

I stood over her and brought the machete back in a two-handed grip. I put everything I had into that downswing. The blade bit into her neck, down to the spine, catching on the bone.

Ivy stared up at me with blood streaming down her neck. I swung back for another chop, and she watched me do it, too hurt to run now. I had to struggle to get the blade out of the spine, and still she blinked up at me. If I didn't finish her, she'd heal even this.

I brought the blade down one last time and felt the last edge of bone give. The blade came out the other side, and her head slid off her shoulders in a spray of blood like a black fountain. That black blood poured over the circle and closed it.

Power filled the circle until we were drowning in it. Larry fell to his knees. The light from the crosses faded like dying stars. The vampire was dead, and the crosses couldn't help us now.

"What's happening?"

I could feel the power like water on every side, choking close. I was breathing it in, soaking it up through my skin.

I screamed wordlessly and fell to the ground. I fell through layers of power, and the moment I hit the ground I could feel the power below me, stretching downward, outward.

I was lying on top of bones. They twitched like something moving in its sleep. I crawled to my knees, hands digging into the earth. I touched a long, thin arm bone, and it moved. I scrambled to my feet, slow, too slow through the pressing air, and watched.

Bones slid through the earth like water, coming together. The earth heaved and rocked underfoot like giant moles were crawling.

Larry was on his feet now, too. "What's happening?"

"Something bad," I said.

I'd never seen the dead coalesce. They always came to the surface of the grave all in one piece. I'd never realized it was like putting together a macabre jigsaw puzzle. A skeleton formed at my feet, and flesh began to crawl over it, flow like clay, molding itself back to the bones.

"Anita?"

I turned to Larry. He was pointing at a skeleton at the far edge of the circle. Half the bones were on the outside of the circle. Flesh crawled over this side of the bones and pushed against the blood circle. The earth gave one last heave, and the magic poured out over the ground. I heard it pop inside my head like a release of pressure. The air spread out, not so drowning-thick. It poured over the hillside like invisible flame, and everywhere it touched the dead formed bodies.

"Stop it, Anita. Stop it."

"I can't." The killing magic in the ground had stolen the reins. All I could do was watch and feel the power spreading outward. Enough power to ride forever. Enough power to raise a thousand dead.

I knew when Rawhead and Bloody Bones burst its prison.

I felt the power sag as the thing escaped. Then the power lashed back into this bit of ground and drove us to our knees. The dead struggled from the earth like swimmers dragging themselves to shore. When nearly twenty dead stood waiting with empty eyes, the power flowed outward. I felt it seeking more dead, something else to raise. This I could stop. The fairie was gone, out of the loop; he had what he wanted.

I called the power back. I drew it into me, back through the ground, like pulling a snake by its tail out of a hole. I flung it into the zombies. Flung it into them and said, "Live."

The wrinkled flesh filled out. The dead eyes gleamed. The tattered clothing mended itself. Dirt fell away from a long gingham dress. A woman with midnight hair, dark skin, and Magnus's startled eyes looked at me. They all looked at me. Twenty dead, all over two hundred years old, and they could have passed for human.

"My God," Larry whispered.

Even I was impressed.

"Very impressive, Ms. Blake." Stirling's voice was wrenching, as if he shouldn't have been there. He was a different part of reality from the near-perfect zombies. The fairie was out, but I'd do my job, for what good it would do any of us.

"Which of you is a Bouvier?"

There was a murmur of voices, most of them speaking French. Nearly all of them were Bouviers. The woman introduced herself as Anias Bouvier. She looked very alive.

"Looks like you'll have to move your hotel," I said.

"Oh, I don't think so," Stirling said.

I turned and looked at him.

He had a big shiny silver gun out. A nickel-plated .45. He held it like it was a movie, kind of out in front of him, waist-high. A .45 is a big gun; you don't hit much from a waist shot. Or that's the theory. With it pointed at us, I wasn't eager to try the theory.

Bayard was pointing a .22 automatic vaguely in our direction. It didn't look like he'd held a gun before. Maybe he forgot and left the safety on.

Ms. Harrison had a nickel-plated .38 pointed very steadily at me. She stood with her legs apart, balanced on her ridiculous high heels. She held the gun in a two-handed grip like she knew what she was doing.

I flashed on her face. Her eyes in her thick makeup were a little wide, but she was rock steady. Steadier than Bayard and a better stance than Stirling. I hoped Stirling paid her well.

"What's going on, Stirling?" I asked. My voice was even, but there was an edge of power to it. I was still riding the power, enough power to put the zombies back in the ground. Enough power to do a lot of things.

He smiled visibly in the bright reflected light. "You've released the creature; now we shall kill you."

"Why the hell do you care if Bloody Bones is out?" I saw the guns and still didn't know why.

"It came into my dreams, Ms. Blake. It promised me all the Bouvier land. All of it."

"The fey breaking out won't get you the land," I said.

"It will with Bouvier dead. The deed that got us this hillside will be found to include all the land, once there's no one to fight it."

"Even with Magnus dead, you won't get the land," I said, but my voice didn't sound so sure.

"You mean his sister?" Stirling said. "She'll die just as easily as Magnus."

My stomach was tight. "Her children?"

"Rawhead and Bloody Bones loves children best of all," he said.

"You son of a bitch." It was Larry. He took a step forward, and Ms. Harrison's gun swung to him. I grabbed his arm with my free hand. I still had the machete in my hand. Larry stopped, and the gun stayed on him. I wasn't sure that was an improvement.

Tension sang down Larry's arm. I'd seen him angry, but never like this. The power responded to that anger. The zombies all turned to us in a rustle of cloth. Their glittering eyes, so alive, were waiting for us.

"Move in front of us," I whispered. The zombies began walking towards us. The closest ones moved in front of us immediately. I lost sight of the gun-toting trio. Here was hoping they'd lost sight of us.

"Kill them," Stirling said, loud, almost a yell.

I started to drop to the ground, still holding Larry's arm. He resisted. Gunfire exploded around us and he kissed dirt, flat.

With the side of his face pressed to the ground, he said, "What now?"

Bullets were hitting the zombies. The bodies jerked and twitched. Some of the very alive faces stared down, alarmed as holes appeared in their bodies. But there was no pain. The panic was reflex.

Someone was yelling; it wasn't us. "Stop it, stop it. We can't do this. We can't just kill them."

It was Bayard.

"It is late for an attack of conscience," Ms. Harrison said. It may have been the first time I'd heard her voice. She sounded efficient.

"Lionel, you are either with me, or against me."

"Shit," I muttered. I wormed forward, trying to see what was happening. I pushed aside a billowing skirt just in time to see Stirling shoot Lionel in the stomach. The .45 gave out a booming sound and nearly jerked itself out of Stirling's hand, but he held on. From less than ten inches away, you could shoot nearly anything with a .45.

Bayard collapsed to his knees, looking up at Stirling. He was trying to say something, but no sound came out.

Stirling took the gun from Bayard's hand and put it in his own jacket pocket. He turned his back on Bayard and walked out onto the hard, dry soil.

Ms. Harrison hesitated, but she followed her boss.

Bayard fell onto his side with a dark flood draining out of him. His glasses reflected the moonlight, making him look blind.

Stirling and Ms. Harrison were coming in after us. Stirling pushed among the dead as if they were trees and he was wading through. The dead didn't move for him. They stood there like stubborn, fleshy barriers. I hadn't told them to move, so they wouldn't.

Ms. Harrison had stopped trying to force her way through. Moonlight glinted on her shiny gun as she used a zombie's shoulder to sight on us.

"Kill her," I whispered.

The zombie she was using as a sighting post turned towards her. She made an exasperated sound, and the dead closed on her.

Larry looked at me. "What did you tell them?"

Ms. Harrison was screaming now. High, frightened shrieks. She fired her gun again and again. It clicked empty. Slow, eager hands and mouths latched onto her body.

"Stop them," Larry said. He grabbed my arm. "Stop them."

I could feel the hands tearing bits of flesh from Ms. Harrison. Teeth sank into her shoulder, tore that tender neck, and I knew when blood flowed into that mouth.

Larry was along for the ride. "Oh, God, stop it!" He was on his knees pulling at me, begging.

Stirling hadn't fired a shot. Where was he?

"Stop," I whispered.

The dead froze like automatons, stopped in mid-action. Ms. Harrison slid to the ground in a moaning heap.

Stirling came in from one side, the big gun pointed very steadily at us, out in a two-handed grip like it was supposed to be held. He'd made his way behind us while the zombies worked over Ms. Harrison. He was standing nearly on top of us. It took a lot of nerve to come that close to the zombies.

Larry's fingers dug into my arm. "Don't, Anita; please don't." Even staring down the barrel of a gun, Larry stuck to his morals. Admirable.

"If you say a word, Ms. Blake, I will kill you."

I just stared up at him. I was so close to him I could have reached out and touched his pants leg. The .45 was pointed very solidly at my head. If he pulled the trigger, I was gone.

"Careless of you not to have the zombies attack both of us."

I agreed with him, but all I could do was stare up at him. I still had the machete in one hand. I tried not to tighten my grip on it. Not to draw attention to it.

I must have made some betraying motion because he said, "Take your hand away from the knife, Ms. Blake, slowly."

I didn't do it. I stared up at him and his gun.

"Now, Ms. Blake, or . . ." He thumbed back the hammer on the gun. Not necessary but always dramatic.

I let go of the machete.

"Hand away from it, Ms. Blake."

I moved my hand away. I didn't move away from him and the gun. I wanted to, but I made myself be still. A few inches wouldn't make the gun less deadly, but it might make a big difference if I tried to jump him. Not my first choice, but if we ran out of other options . . . I wouldn't go down without a fight.

"Can you lay these zombies to rest, Mr. Kirkland?"

Larry hesitated. "I don't know."

Good boy. If he'd said no, Stirling might have killed him. If he'd said yes, he'd have killed me.

Larry let go of my arm and moved just a little away from me. Stirling's eyes flicked to him, back to me, but the gun barrel never wavered. Damn.

Larry was on his knees, still moving away from me, forcing Stirling to keep an eye on both of us. The .45 moved an inch from the center of my forehead, towards Larry. I took a breath and held it. Not yet, not yet . . . If I tried something too soon, I'd be dead.

Larry lunged for something on the ground. The .45 swung towards him.

I did two things at once. I slipped my left hand behind Stirling's leg and pulled, and I grabbed his groin with my right and shoved with all I was worth. I was doing the wrong thing to cause a lot of pain, but it tipped him over. He fell flat of his back with the gun swinging back towards me.

I'd hoped he'd drop the gun, or be slower. He didn't, and he wasn't. So I only had a split-second to decide whether to try to pull his privates out of his body, and cause as much pain as possible, or go for the gun. I went for the gun, not trying to grab it, but sweeping my hands into his arms. If I could control his arms, I could control the gun.

The gun went off. I didn't look. No time. Larry was either hit, or he wasn't. If he wasn't, I had to get that gun. Stirling's arms were on the ground, my hands keeping them there, but I had no leverage. He raised his arms off the ground, and I couldn't stop him. I shoved my feet into the ground and forced his arms over his head, but it had become a wrestling match now, and he outweighed me by sixty pounds.

"Drop the gun." Larry's voice behind me. I couldn't look. Couldn't take my attention from the gun. We both ignored him.

"I will shoot you," Larry said.

That got Stirling's attention. His eyes flicked to Larry; for just a moment his body hesitated. I kept my grip on his wrists and shoved myself forward, up his body. I dug my knee into his groin, trying to reach the ground through him. He let out a strangled cry. His hands spasmed.

I moved my hands up and touched the gun. His grip tightened. He wasn't letting go.

I came up beside Stirling's arms and braced his arms against my hip. I pulled the arm against my body, just one quick movement, and snapped his arm at the elbow. The hand went numb, and the gun fell into my hand.

I crawled away from him, the gun in one hand.

Larry was standing over us with a gun pointed at Stirling. Stirling didn't seem to care. He was rocking back and forth over the ground, trying to cradle both injuries at once.

"I had a gun. You could have just moved away from him," Larry said.

I just shook my head. I trusted Larry to shoot Stirling. I just hadn't trusted Stirling not to shoot Larry. "I had my hands on the gun. Seemed a shame to let it go," I said.

Larry pointed the gun at the ground, but kept a nice two-handed grip on it. "It's yours; you want it?"

I shook my head. "Keep it until we get to the car."

I looked up at the zombies. They were watching me with

calm eyes. There was blood on the mouth of the dark-haired woman. It had been her teeth that tore into Ms. Harrison's neck.

Ms. Harrison was lying very still on the ground. Passed out, at the very least.

The power was beginning to unravel at the edges. If I was going to put everybody back in the ground, it had to be now.

"Go back into the ground. Back to your graves. Go back, all of you, go back."

The dead walked upon the earth, moving among one another like children in a game of musical chairs. Then one by one they lay down upon the earth, and it swallowed them like water. The earth moved and buckled in waves, until they were all tucked out of sight.

There were no bones protruding from the earth. The earth was smooth and soft, as if the entire top of the mountain had been dug up and smoothed over.

The power shredded, flowing back into the ground, or wherever the hell it came from. We had to get down to the Jeep and start making phone calls. There was a rampaging fey on the loose. We at least had to get cops out to the Bouviers' place.

Larry knelt beside Ms. Harrison. He touched her neck. "She's alive." His hand came away stained with blood.

I looked at Stirling. He'd stopped rolling around and was just sort of huddled on his side, his arm held at an obscene angle. The look he gave me was part pain and part hate. If he ever got a second chance, I was dead.

"Shoot him if he moves," I said.

Larry got to his feet and pointed the gun dutifully at Stirling.

I went to check on Bayard. He lay on his side, half-crumpled around the wound in his belly. A wide black circle showed where his blood had soaked into the thirsty ground. I knew dead when I saw it, but I knelt on the far side of his body so I could keep an eye on Stirling. It wasn't that I didn't trust Larry. I just didn't trust Stirling.

There was no pulse in his neck. The skin was already cooling in the soft spring air. It hadn't been an instant death.

Lionel Bayard had died while we were fighting. He'd died alone, and he'd known he was dying, and that he'd been betrayed. It was a bad way to die.

I stood up and looked at Stirling. I wanted to kill him for Bayard, for Magnus, for Dorrie Bouvier, for her kids. For being a heartless son of bitch.

He'd witnessed me using zombies as a weapon. Using magic as a killing weapon was punishable by death. Self-defense was not an acceptable plea.

I stared very calmly across at Stirling and the unconscious Ms. Harrison, and realized that I could have crossed that ground and put a bullet in both of them, and slept just fine.

Sweet Jesus.

Larry glanced my way, gun still steady, but he'd taken his eyes off Stirling for a second. Not fatal, tonight, but I'd have to break him of it. "Is Bayard dead?"

"Yeah." I started back towards them, wondering what I was going to do. I didn't think Larry would let me shoot them in cold blood. Part of me was glad. Part of me wasn't.

Wind blew against my face. There was a rustling sound in the wind, like that made by trees or cloth. There were no trees on top of this mountain. I turned with the big .45 in a two handed grip, and Janos was just there, on the edge of the mountain. Staring at his skeletal face, I think I stopped breathing. He was dressed all in black; even his hands were hidden inside black gloves. For one wild moment he looked like a floating skull. "We have the boy," he said.

35

THE CROSSES WERE still in plain sight. They glowed with a soft white radiance. No burning light, not yet. We weren't in active danger, but the cross grew warm even through my shirt.

Janos put a hand in front of his eyes, the way I would

guard my eyes from the sun in the car. "Please put those away, so we may talk."

He hadn't asked us to take them off. I could live with tucking my cross in my shirt. It could come out again later. I spilled the chain back down my shirt one-handed, keeping the .45 ready. I realized then that I didn't know if the gun had silver ammo. Now was not the time to ask. Stirling would probably lie anyway.

Larry slipped his own cross out of sight. The glowing night was just a little dimmer.

"Alright, now what?" I asked.

Kissa came up behind him, Jeff Quinlan in front of her like a shield. His glasses were gone, and he looked even younger without them. She had his arm behind his back, at an angle that could be painful with just a tug.

He was wearing a cream-colored tuxedo with a cummerbund done two shades darker to match the bow tie. Kissa was in black leather. Jeff stood out against her in wonderful contrast.

I swallowed; my pulse threatened to choke me. What was going on? "You alright, Jeff?"

"I guess so."

Kissa gave a little tug.

He winced. "I'm okay." His voice was a little higher than it should have been, a little scared.

I held out my hand to him. "Come here."

"Not yet," Janos said.

I'd tried. "What do you want?"

"First drop your guns."

"If we don't?" I thought I knew the answer, but I wanted him to say it.

"Kissa will kill the boy, and you will have done all this for nothing."

"Help me," Stirling said. "She's mad. She attacked Ms. Harrison with zombies. When we tried to defend ourselves, she nearly killed us."

That was probably what he'd say in court, too. And a jury would believe him. They'd want to believe him. I would be the big, bad zombie queen, and he would be the innocent victim.

Janos laughed, his paper-thin skin threatening to split, but never quite doing it. "Oh, no, Mr. Stirling, I watched from the darkness. I saw you murder the other man."

Fear flashed across his face. "I don't know what you mean. We hired him in good faith. He turned on us."

"My master opened your mind to Bloody Bones. She freed him to whisper in your dreams about land, money, and power. All that you desire."

"Serephina sent Ivy to kill me, or rather for me to kill her. So she'd be sure to have Bloody Bones free," I said.

"Yes," he said. "Serephina told her she had to rid herself of the disgrace of losing to you."

"By killing me."

"Yes."

"What if she'd succeeded?"

"My master had faith in you, Anita. You are death come among us. A breath of mortality."

"Why'd she want the thing freed?" I seemed to be asking that a lot tonight.

"She wishes to taste immortal blood."

"This is all sort of elaborate for a little extra kick in your food."

He gave another rictus grin. "You are what you eat, Anita. Think upon it."

I did, and my eyes widened. "She thinks by drinking immortal blood, she'll be truly immortal?"

"Very good, Anita."

"It won't work," I said.

"We shall see," he said.

"What do you get out it?" I asked.

He cocked his skeletal head to one side, like a decaying bird. "She is my master, and she shares her bounty."

"You want immortality, too?"

"I want power," he said.

Great. "And it doesn't bother you that the thing will kill children? That it's already killed some?"

"We feed, Bloody Bones feeds, what does it matter?"

"And Bloody Bones is going to just let you feed off it?"

"Serephina has found the spell that Magnus's ancestor used. She controls the fairie."

"How?"

He shook his head and smiled. "No more delays, Anita. Drop the gun, or Kissa will taste him before your eyes."

Kissa ran a hand through Jeff's short hair, a caressing gesture. It pushed his head to one side, baring a long smooth line of neck.

"No!" Jeff tried to pull away, and Kissa yanked on his arm hard enough that he cried out.

"I will break the arm, boy," she growled.

The pain held him immobile, but his eyes were wide and terrified. He looked at me. He wouldn't plead, no begging, but his eyes did it for him.

Kissa's lips pulled back from her teeth in a flashy snarl, fangs visible.

"Don't," I said, and hated it. I tossed the .45 to the ground. Larry threw my gun down. Disarmed twice in one night. It was a record even for me.

36

"NOW WHAT?" I asked.

"Serephina awaits us at the party. She sent suitable clothing for you. You can change in the limousine," Janos said.

"What party?" I asked.

"The one we have come to invite you to. She is delivering Jean-Claude's invitation in person."

That didn't sound good. "I think we'll pass on the party."

"I don't think so," Janos said.

Another vampire stepped out of the trees. It was the brunette that had tormented Jason. She stalked forward in a long black dress that covered her from neck to ankle. She slid her arms around Janos, nuzzling his neck, giving us a glimpse of her pale back. Only a fine webbing of black straps covered her back. The dress moved like it would slide down her body at the least movement, but somehow it stayed in place. Fashion-plate magic. Her dark hair was in a looping braid to one side of her face. She looked good for someone I'd seen ripped to rotting bits of flesh.

I couldn't keep the surprise off my face.

"I thought she was dead," Larry said.

"So did I."

"I would never have risked Pallas if I truly thought your werewolf could kill her," Janos said.

A second figure came out of the dark woods. Long white hair framed a thin, fine-boned face. His eyes glowed blood-red. I'd seen vampires with glowing eyes before, but they always glowed the color of their irises. No one who had ever been human had red irises. He wore a proverbial black tux and tails, complete with a nearly ankle-length cape.

"Xavier," I said softly.

Larry looked at me. "This is the vampire that's been killing everyone?"

I nodded.

"Then what's he doing here?"

"That's how you found Jeff so quickly. You're working with Xavier," I said. "Does Serephina know?"

Janos smiled. "She is master of all, Anita, even him." He said the last like it impressed him.

"You won't get to munch on your fairie for long if the cops trace Xavier to you."

"Xavier was following orders. He was on a recruitment drive." Janos seemed to like saying that last bit like it was an in-joke.

"Why did you want Ellie Quinlan?"

"Xavier likes a bit of young boy now and then. It is his one weakness. He turned the girl's lover, and the boy wanted her with him forever. Tonight she will rise and feed with us."

Not if I could help it. "What do you want, Janos?"

"I was sent to make your life easier," he said.

"Yeah, right."

Pallas uncurled herself from Janos. She glided over to Stirling.

Stirling stared up at her, cradling his broken arm. It had to hurt like hell, but it wasn't pain on his face now, it was fear. He stared up at the vampire; all the arrogance had slipped away. He looked like a kid who'd discovered the thing under the bed was really there.

A third vampire moved out of the trees. It was the blonde half of the pair. She looked fine, like she'd never rotted right before our eyes. I'd never known a vampire that could look so dead, and not be.

"You remember Bettina," he said.

Bettina wore a black dress that left her pale shoulders bare. A throw of black cloth went over one shoulder and down the front of the dress. A gold belt held it in place, cinching her waist tight. Her yellow braid was wound in a crown atop her head.

She walked towards us, and her face was perfect. The dry, rotting skin had been a bad dream, a nightmare. I wish. Fire, Jean-Claude had said, fire was the only surety. I thought he'd meant just Janos.

Janos reached over and grabbed Jeff from Kissa. He gripped the boy's shoulders with both black-gloved hands. His fingers were longer than they should have been, as though they had an extra joint. Against the white of Jeff's jacket, you could tell that the index finger was as long as the middle finger. Another myth that was true, at least for Janos. Those long, strange fingers dug into Jeff just a little.

Jeff's eyes were so wide it looked painful.

"What's going on?" I asked.

Kissa was dressed in the same black vinyl outfit she'd had on in the torture room, though it couldn't be the exact same one, because the first one had Larry's bullet hole in it. She stood beside him, her hands in fists. She stood very still, as only the dead can, but there was a tension to her, a wariness. She wasn't happy. Her dark skin was strangely pale. She hadn't fed yet tonight. I could always tell . . . with most vampires. There are always exceptions.

Xavier moved in a shadow of that impossible blurring

speed past Stirling, to stand beside the still unconscious Ms. Harrison. Larry shook his head. "Did he just appear there, or did I see him move?"

"He moved," I said.

I expected Janos to send Kissa out to join the others, but he didn't. A figure crawled over the lip of the hill, dragging itself into sight like it hurt to move. Pale hands dug into the naked dirt, pale arms bare to the spring night. The head drooped towards the ground, short dark hair hiding the face. With one upward motion, the face raised into the moonlight. Thin, bloodless lips drew back from fangs. The face was ravaged with hunger. I knew the eyes were brown only because I'd seen them staring lifelessly at the ceiling of Ellie Quinlan's bedroom. There was no pull to her eyes, but down in the dark depths a flicker of something burned. It wasn't sanity; hunger, maybe. An animal's emotion, nothing human. Maybe after they'd let her feed for the first time, she'd have time for emotions; now everything had narrowed down to one basic need.

"Is that who I think it is?" Larry asked.

"Yeah," I said.

Jeff tried to run to her. "Ellie!"

Janos jerked him tight against his chest, one arm around his shoulders like an embrace. Jeff struggled against that arm, tried to run to his dead sister. I was with Janos on this one. The newly risen have a tendency to eat first and ask questions later. The thing that had once been Ellie Quinlan would have gladly torn out her baby brother's throat. She'd have bathed in the blood, and minutes, or days, or weeks later, she would realize what she'd done. She might even regret it.

"Go, Angela; go to Xavier," Janos said.

"A new name won't change who she was," I said.

Janos looked at me. "She is two years dead, and her name is Angela."

"Her name is Ellie," Jeff said. He'd stopped struggling, but he looked at his dead sister with fresh horror, as if just beginning to really see her.

"People will recognize her, Janos."

"We shall be careful, Anita. Our new angel will see no one that we do not wish."

"Well, isn't that cozy?" I said.

"It will be," he said, "once she has drunk her fill."

"I'm impressed that you dragged her this far without feeding her first."

"I did it." Xavier's voice was surprisingly pleasant. It was disturbing hearing that voice coming from that pale, ghostly face.

I looked at him, careful to avoid his gaze. "Impressive," I said.

"Andy brought her over, and I brought Andy over. I am her master."

Since Andy hadn't shown up, I was betting I'd killed him in the woods with Sheriff St. John. Probably not a good time to bring that up. "And who is your master?"

"Serephina, for now," Xavier said.

I glanced at Janos. "You haven't worked out which of you is top dog, have you?" I smiled.

"You waste our time, Anita. Our master awaits you eagerly. Let us finish this. Call our angel."

Xavier held out one pale hand. Ellie made a noise low in her throat, and scrambled on all fours over the raw dirt. The long black dress tangled around her legs. She tore at it impatiently. The cloth ripped like paper in her hands, the skirt shredding around her bare legs. She grabbed Xavier's hand like it was a lifeline. She bent over his wrist, and only his hand in her hair kept her from trying to feed on him.

"There is no sustenance for you from the dead, Angela," Janos said. "Feed on the living."

Pallas and Bettina knelt on either side of Stirling. Xavier fell gracefully beside Ms. Harrison, his black cape spread out around him like a pool of blood. He kept hold of Ellie's hair the whole way down, forcing her snarling face to touch the dirt. Her hands dug at his hands, mewling sounds crawling from her throat. Nothing that was human should have made sounds like that.

"Ms. Blake," Stirling said, "you're the law. You have to protect me."

"I thought you were going to see me in court, Raymond. Something about me attacking you and Ms. Harrison with zombies."

"I didn't mean it." He glanced up at the kneeling vampires, then back to me. "I won't tell. I won't tell anyone, Please."

I just looked at him. "Begging for mercy, Raymond?"

"Yes, yes, I'm begging."

"Like the mercy you showed Bayard?"

"Please."

Bettina caressed Stirling's cheek. He jerked like it had burned. "Please!"

Shit.

"We can't just watch," Larry said.

"You have another suggestion?"

"You never give anyone over to the monsters, not for any reason. It's a rule," he said.

It was my rule. I'd believed in it once, back when I'd been sure who the monsters were.

He was pulling the chain out from inside his shirt.

"Don't do this, Larry. Don't get us killed for Raymond Stirling."

His cross spilled out in the open air. It glowed like Serephina's eyes. He just looked at me.

I sighed, and brought out my own cross. "This is a bad idea."

"I know," he said. "But I can't just watch."

I stared at his earnest face, and knew it was true. He couldn't just watch. I could have. I might not have enjoyed it, but I could have let it happen. More's the pity.

"What are you doing with your little holy objects?" Janos asked.

"Stopping this," I said.

"You want them dead, Anita."

"Not like this," I said.

"Would you have me let you use your gun and waste all this blood?"

He was offering to let me shoot them. I shook my head. "I don't think that's an option anymore."

"It was never an option," Larry said.

I let that go; no need to disillusion him. I walked towards Pallas and Bettina. Larry walked towards Ellie and Xavier, cross held outward to the length of its chain, as if that made it work better. Nothing wrong with a little dramatic gesture, but I'd have to clue him in that it didn't really help. But later.

The cross's glow grew until it was like wearing a 100-watt lightbulb naked around your neck. I saw the world as a black circle outside the glow.

Xavier was on his feet facing Larry, but the others had crawled away from their prey, beaten by the light.

"Thank you, Ms. Blake," Stirling said. "Thank you." He grabbed my leg with his good hand, fawning over me. I fought an urge to shake him off.

"Thank Larry; I'd have let you die."

He didn't seem to hear me. He was nearly crying with relief, slobbering all over my Nikes.

"Back away from them, please." The voice was female and honey-thick.

I blinked over the glow of the cross and saw Kissa holding a gun. A revolver that looked like a Magnum; hard to tell in the glow. Whatever it was, it'd make a big hole.

"Move away from them, now."

"I thought Serephina didn't want me dead."

"Kissa will shoot your young friend."

I stopped in mid-breath and let it out. "If you kill him, I won't cooperate with whatever you have in mind for tonight."

"You misunderstand us, Anita," Janos said. "My master does not require your cooperation. Everything she wants from you can be taken by force."

I stared at him over the shining light. He had Jeff cuddled against him; most heartwarming.

"Take off your crosses and throw them far out into the trees," Janos said. He ran a gloved hand along both sides of Jeff's face, planting a kiss on his cheek.

"Now that we know you would give up your safety for both young men, we have one more hostage than is absolutely necessary." He put his hands on either side of Jeff's neck, just holding, not hurting, not yet.

"Take off your crosses and throw them into the woods. I will not ask a third time."

I stared at him. I didn't want to give up my cross. I glanced at Larry. He was still facing off against Xavier, his cross glowing bravely. Shit.

"Kissa, shoot the man."

"No," I said. I undid the chain. "Don't shoot him."

"Don't do it, Anita," Larry said.

"I can't watch them shoot you, not if I can stop it." I let the chain pool in my hand; the cross shone with a blue-white flame like burning magnesium. It was a bad idea to throw it away. A real bad idea. I tossed it into the woods. The cross glittered like a falling star and died out of sight in the dark.

"Now your cross, Larry," Janos said.

Larry shook his head. "You'll have to shoot me."

"We'll shoot the boy," Janos said. "Or perhaps I'll feed upon him while you watch." He pinned Jeff against himself with one arm, while his other hand dug into the boy's hair, holding him immobile, neck exposed.

Larry looked at me. "What do I do, Anita?"

"You have to decide this one for yourself," I said.

"They'll really kill him, won't they?"

"Yeah, they will."

He cursed under his breath and let the cross fall against his chest. He undid the chain and threw it out into the woods with a lot of force to it, as if he could throw his anger with it.

When the light from his cross died away, we stood there in the darkness. The moonlight that had seemed so bright before was a dim substitute.

My night vision returned in stages. Kissa stepped closer, the gun still pointed at us. The first time I'd seen her, she had exuded sexuality, power; now she was docile, quiet, as though some of her power had been drained away. She looked pale and drawn. She needed to feed.

"Why haven't they let you feed tonight?" I asked.

"Our master is not a hundred percent sure of Kissa's loyalty. It needed testing, didn't it, my dark beauty?"

Kissa didn't answer. She stared at me with large, dark eyes, but the gun never wavered.

"Feed, children, feed."

Pallas and Bettina walked over to Stirling. They stared at me over him. I stared back.

Stirling grabbed my leg. "You can't let them have me. Please, please."

Pallas knelt by him. Bettina walked around to the side I was on. She pulled Stirling's hand off my leg. The vampire's lower back brushed my legs. I took a step back, and Stirling started screaming.

Xavier and Ellie had already started to feed on the blessedly unconscious Ms. Harrison. Larry looked at me, hands out, empty, helpless.

I didn't know what to say.

"Don't touch me, don't touch me!" Stirling batted at Pallas with his good hand, and the vampire caught it easily, held it.

"At least put him under," I said.

Pallas looked up at me. "After he tried to kill you? Why show him mercy?"

"Maybe I don't want to hear him scream."

Pallas smiled. Her eyes flashed dark fire. "For you, Anita, anything."

She grabbed Stirling's chin, forcing him to meet her gaze.

"Ms. Blake, help me. Help . . ." The words died in his mouth.

I watched everything slide out of his eyes, until they were empty and waiting.

"Come to me, Raymond," Pallas said. "Come to me."

Stirling sat up, his one good arm embracing the vampire. He tried to use the broken arm, but it wouldn't bend at the elbow.

Bettina bent the broken arm backward and forward, laughing. Stirling never reacted to the pain. He snuggled against Pallas. The look on his face was one of happiness, joy. Eagerness.

Pallas sank fangs into his neck. Stirling spasmed for a second, then relaxed and began making soft noises in his throat.

Pallas moved Stirling's head to one side, sucking on the wound but leaving enough room on the other side for someone else. Bettina sank fangs into the exposed flesh.

The two vampires fed, heads so close together their hair mingled, gold and black. And Raymond Stirling made happy noises while they killed him.

Larry walked away to the edge of the clearing, hugging his arms tight across his chest.

I stayed where I was. I watched. I had wanted Stirling dead. It would be cowardly to look away. Besides, I should have to watch. I needed to remember who the monsters were. Maybe if I forced myself not to look away, not to blink, I wouldn't forget again.

I stared at Stirling's happy, eager face, until his arm dropped away from Pallas's back, and his eyes closed. He passed out from blood loss and shock, and the vampires hugged him tight, and fed.

His eyes flew open wide, and a gurgling sound crawled out of his throat. Fear screamed out of his eyes. Pallas raised a hand and stroked Stirling's hair, a gesture you'd use on a frightened child. The fear died out of his eyes, and I watched the last light die with it. I watched Raymond Stirling die, and knew I would remember that last look of terror in my dreams for weeks to come.

37

THERE WAS A rush of wind that raised a fine cloud of dirt. Jean-Claude appeared as if conjured from the air itself. I had never been so happy to see him. I didn't run to his arms, but I moved to stand near him. Larry followed me.

Jean-Claude wasn't always the safest refuge, but right now he looked pretty damn good.

He was dressed in one of his white shirts. This one had so much lace on the front it looked fluffy. A short white jacket hit him just at the waist. More lace peeked from the sleeves of the jacket. He wore tight white pants with a black belt. The belt matched his velvet black boots.

"I did not expect you here, Jean-Claude," Janos said. I couldn't tell for sure, but he sounded surprised. Goody.

"Serephina delivered her invitation in person, Janos, but it was not enough."

"You surprise me, Jean-Claude," he said.

"I surprised Serephina, as well." He sounded terribly calm. If he was afraid standing outnumbered on the hilltop, it didn't show. I'd have loved to know how he'd surprised Serephina.

Jason walked up the far side of the hill, from the direction of the Jeep. He wore black leather pants that looked like they'd been poured on him, short black boots, and no shirt. There was what looked like a silver-studded dog collar around his neck, and a black glove on either hand, but other than that he was naked from the waist up. I hoped Jason had chosen his own outfit for tonight.

The right side of his face was bruised from chin to forehead as though something large had hit him.

"I see your pet joined the struggle," Janos said.

"He is mine in every way, Janos. They are all mine."

Just this once I let it go. If my choice was belonging to Jean-Claude or to Serephina, I knew what my vote would be.

Larry moved so close to me that I could have taken his hand. Maybe he didn't like being included in Jean-Claude's menagerie.

"You have lost that air of humbleness that I found so appealing, Jean-Claude. Have you refused Serephina's invitation altogether?"

"I will come to Serephina's party, but on my own with my people around me."

I glanced at him. Was he crazy?

He frowned. "Serephina wanted you at the party in chains."

"We can all live with this choice, Janos."

"Are you saying you would challenge us all here and now?" There was an edge of laughter in his voice.

"I will not die alone, Janos. In the end you may have me, but it will cost you dearly."

"If you will truly come of your own free will, then come," Janos said. "Our master calls; let us answer that call." Janos, Bettina, and Pallas were just suddenly airborne. It wasn't flying, or levitation. I had no word for it. Larry whispered, "Dear God." The first time you see a vampire fly is a red-letter night.

The others scattered into the trees in that blurring motion that made them disappear almost as fast as flying. Ellie Quinlan had vanished with the rest of them. Her brother had been carried away by Janos. Until that moment I hadn't known a vampire could carry more than its own body weight while "flying." Learn something new every night.

We found our guns and walked down the mountainside. Our crosses were well and truly lost. Even Jean-Claude walked, and I knew he had other methods of transportation. Was it considered impolite to fly when others couldn't?

The Jeep was still where I'd parked it. The night was still thick. It was hours until dawn, and I just wanted to go home.

"I took the liberty of choosing clothes for you to wear tonight," Jean-Claude said. "They are in the Jeep."

"I locked the Jeep," I said.

He just smiled at me.

I sighed. "Fine." When I tried the handle it was unlocked. Clothes were folded in the passenger seat. They were black leather. I shook my head. "I don't think so."

"Your clothes, *ma petite*, are on the driver's side. Those are Lawrence's clothes."

Larry peered over my shoulder. "You've got to be kidding."

I walked around the Jeep and found a clean pair of black jeans. The tightest pair I owned. A bloodred tank top that I didn't remember buying. It felt like silk. There was a black

duster coat that I had never seen. When I tried it for length
it hit me at mid-calf, and billowed capelike when I moved. I
liked the coat. The silk blouse I could have done without.

"Not bad," I said.

"Mine is bad," Larry said. "I don't even know how to get
into these pants."

"Jason, help him dress." Jason picked up the bundle of
leather and carried them to the back of the Jeep. Larry followed him but didn't look happy.

"No boots?" I said.

Jean-Claude smiled. "I didn't think you would give up
your jogging shoes."

"Damn straight."

"Change quickly, *ma petite;* we must arrive at Serephina's
before she decides to kill the boy just for spite."

"Would Xavier let her kill his new toy?"

"If she is truly his master, he has no choice. Now, dress,
ma petite, quickly." I walked towards the far side of the Jeep
but that brought me within earshot, and nearly eyesight, of
Larry. I stopped and sighed. What the hell.

I turned my back on Jean-Claude and slid out of my
shoulder holster. "How did you guys get away from
Serephina?" I slipped my shirt over my head. I fought the
urge to look back. I knew Jean-Claude was watching; why
check?

"Jason jumped her at a crucial moment. It was distraction
enough for us to flee, but little else. I'm afraid the room is
something of a mess."

His voice was so mild I had to see his face. I slid the red
tank top on and turned. He was standing closer than I'd
thought, nearly within touching distance. He stood there in
his white clothes, spotless and perfect.

"Step a few paces back, please. I'd like a little privacy."

He smiled, but he did what I asked. A first.

"Had she underestimated you that badly?" I asked. I
changed jeans as quickly as I could. I tried not to think of
him watching. It was too embarrassing.

"I was forced to flee, *ma petite.* Janos calls her master,

and he defeated me. I cannot stand against her, not in a fair fight."

I slipped the shoulder holster back on, threading the belt I'd been wearing back through it. The straps chafed a little with no sleeves but it was better than not having it. I got the Firestar from under my seat and tucked the inner pants holster down the front of my jeans. It would show, even with the duster. I finally put it at the small of my back, though it wasn't my first or even second choice of places. I got the silver knives out of the glove compartment and strapped them to my forearms. I also got out a small box. It held two extra crosses. Vampires seemed to always be taking them from me.

Jean-Claude watched it all with interest. His dark eyes followed my hands like he was memorizing the movements.

I put the duster on and walked a few steps to get the feel of everything. I drew both knives just to make sure the coat sleeves weren't too tight. I drew both guns and still didn't like the Firestar. I finally shifted the inner pants holster to one side. It dug into my side hard enough to bruise, but I could draw it in a reasonable time. That was more important than comfort tonight. I slipped an extra clip for both guns in the coat pockets. They were loaded with nonsilver bullets. It made me nervous to only have the silver bullets that were in the guns, but Rawhead and Bloody Bones was going to make his appearance sometime tonight. Magnus might even be there. I wanted ammo for everything I'd meet tonight.

Larry came out from behind the Jeep. I bit my lip to keep from laughing. It wasn't that he looked bad, he just looked so uncomfortable. He seemed to have trouble walking in the black leather pants.

"Just walk naturally," Jason said.

"I can't," Larry said. He had a silk tank top that was the twin of mine except it was blue instead of red. He had short black boots on. The black jacket he'd borrowed from Jason last night completed the outfit.

I looked at the boots.

"Black jogging shoes perhaps, *ma petite,* but white jogging shoes with black leather? I do not think so."

"I feel ridiculous," Larry said. "How can you wear this all the time?"

"I like leather," Jason said.

"We must be off," Jean-Claude said. "Anita, if you would drive?"

"I thought you might want to fly," I said.

"It is important we arrive together," he said.

Larry and I added salt to our pockets. With the extra ammo clips in one pocket and salt in the other, my coat hung a little crooked, but hey, we weren't going to a fashion show. We all slid into the Jeep. There was a lot of protesting from the back seat. "These pants are even more uncomfortable sitting down."

"I will remember your dislike of leather in the future, Lawrence."

"My name is Larry."

I drove the Jeep down the rutted road that led out of the construction site. "Serephina wants to be immortal." I turned onto the main road and headed back towards Branson, though of course we'd be stopping at Serephina's on the way.

Jean-Claude turned in his seat to stare at me. "What are you saying, *ma petite*?"

I told him. I told him about Rawhead and Bloody Bones, and Serephina's plan. "She's mad."

"Not entirely, *ma petite*. It might not give her immortality, but it would give her undreamt-of power. The question remaining is, how did Serephina grow powerful enough to snag Janos before she fed off Magnus and Bloody Bones?"

"What do you mean?"

"Janos was in the old country. He would not have left voluntarily. He followed her. Where did she get the power to subjugate him?"

"Maybe Magnus isn't the first fairie she's fed off," I said.

"Perhaps," he said, "or perhaps she has found other food."

"What other food?"

"That, *ma petite,* is the question that I would very much like answered."

"Thinking of changing diets?" I asked.

"Power is always tempting, *ma petite,* but for tonight I was thinking of more practical matters. If we can discover her source of power, we might be able to undo it."

"How?"

He shook his head. "I do not know, but unless we can find some trick to pull out of our hats tonight, *ma petite,* we are doomed." He sounded remarkably calm about it. I wasn't calm. My pulse was thundering so fast I could feel it in my throat and wrists. Hear it like a rushing in my ears. Doomed: it had a bad ring to it. With Serephina waiting at the other end, it had a very bad ring to it indeed.

38

WE WALKED UP the stone steps to the porch. Moonlight and soft darkness filled the porch. There were no thick, unnatural shadows, no hint of what lay inside. It was just an abandoned house, nothing special. The nervous flutter in my stomach didn't buy it either.

Kissa opened the door. Candlelight spilled behind her from the open door to the far room. No pretense tonight that the empty room was all there was. Sweat beaded on her face, golden drops in the warm light. She was still being punished. I wondered why, but it wasn't my biggest problem.

Kissa led us through that open door without a word. Serephina sat on her throne in the corner of the big room. She was dressed in a white ball gown like Cinderella, her hair piled atop her head. Diamonds like a string of fire glimmered in her hair as she nodded her greeting.

Magnus was curled at her feet in a white tux and tails. Gloves, a white top hat, and a cane were laid next to his knees. His long chestnut hair was the only color in the picture. Every master vamp I'd ever met had been into dramatic presentation. Janos and his two females stood in black behind the throne, like a living curtain of darkness. Ellie lay on her side in the cushions, looking almost alive. Even in her torn and stained black dress she looked content, like a cat that was full of cream. Her eyes sparkled, lips curled with a secret smile. Ellie, alias Angela, was enjoying being undead. So far. Kissa stalked to them, and knelt on the side away from Magnus. Her black leather blended with Janos's cloak. Serephina stroked Kissa's sweating face with a white-gloved hand.

Serephina smiled, and it was lovely until you glimpsed her eyes. They glowed with a pale phosphorescence. You could still get a hint of pupil, but it was sinking fast. Her eyes matched her dress. Now that was color-coordinating.

Jeff and Xavier were missing. I didn't like that. I opened my mouth to ask, and Jean-Claude looked at me. For just this once, the look was enough. He was the master; I was playing servant. Fine, as long as he asked the right questions.

"We have come, Serephina," Jean-Claude said. "Give us the boy, and we will leave you in peace."

She laughed. "But I will not leave you in peace, Jean-Claude." She turned her softly glowing eyes to me. It was like being looked at by twin flashlights, and just as human. "Niña, I am so happy to see you."

I stopped breathing for a second. Niña: it had been my mother's nickname for me. Something flared in her eyes, like a distant glimpse of fire; then the light banked back to a cool wavering light. She wasn't trying to capture me with her eyes. Why? Because she was that sure of me.

My skin suddenly went cold. That was it. I would have said it was arrogance, but I believed it. She offered something better than sex, more fulfilling than power. Home. Lie or not, it was a good offer.

Larry touched my hand. "You're shaking."

I swallowed hard. "Never admit how scared you are out loud, Larry; ruins the effect."

"Sorry."

I stepped away from him; no sense in huddling. I glanced at Jean-Claude, sort of silently asking if I was about to break vampire protocol.

"She has acknowledged you as she would another master. Answer as one." He didn't seem bothered by that; I was.

"What do you want, Serephina?" I asked.

She stood, gliding across the carpeted floor. It looked like whatever was under that full skirt wasn't legs. Feet just didn't move like that. Maybe she was levitating. However she managed it, she kept coming closer. I wanted desperately to back away. I didn't want her close to me.

Larry moved a step behind me. Jason moved a step up to Jean-Claude's other side. I stood my ground. It was the best I could do.

Something flickered in her eyes, like a distant glimpse of movement through a fringe of trees. Eyes didn't do that. I looked away and realized I didn't remember looking at her eyes. So how was I looking away?

I felt her move towards me. Her gloved hand came into view. I jerked back and looked up at the same time. I barely glanced at her face, but it was enough. Her eyes had fire burning down a long dark tunnel, as if the inside of her head fell away into an impossible darkness, and some small creatures had lit a fire against that darkness. I could warm my hands by that flame forever.

I screamed. Screamed and covered my eyes with my hands.

A hand touched my shoulder. I jerked away and screamed again. *"Ma petite,* I am here."

"Then do something," I said.

"I am," he said.

"I will have this one by sunrise." She motioned to me. She took a gliding step towards Jason. She caressed her gloved hand down his bare chest. He stood there and took it. I wouldn't have let her touch me on a dare.

"I will give you to Bettina and Pallas. They will teach you to enjoy rotting flesh."

Jason stared straight ahead, but his eyes widened just a little. Bettina and Pallas had moved from behind the throne to stand a few feet behind Serephina. Dramatic gestures are us.

"Or perhaps I will force you to change into wolf form until it becomes more natural than this human shell." She slid a finger under the collar on his throat. "I will chain you to my wall, and you will be my guard dog."

"Enough of this, Serephina," Jean-Claude said. "The night bleeds away. These petty torments are beneath one of your power."

"I am feeling petty tonight, Jean-Claude, and soon I will have the power to be as petty as I feel." She glanced at Larry. "He will join my flock." She stared up at Jean-Claude. I hadn't realized he was taller. "And you, my lovely catamount, will serve us all for all eternity."

Jean-Claude stared down at her, utterly arrogant. "I am Master of the City now, Serephina. We cannot torture each other. We cannot steal each other's possessions, no matter how attractive they are."

It took me a second to realize the possessions he was referring to were us.

Serephina smiled. "I will have your businesses, your money, your lands, and your people before the night is out. Did the council really think I would be content with the crumbs from your table?"

If she challenged him officially, we were all dead. Jean-Claude couldn't take her, and neither could I. Distraction, we needed a distraction. "You're wearing enough diamonds to buy your own businesses, your own house."

She turned those glowing eyes to me, and I half wished I had kept quiet. "Do you think I live in this house because I cannot afford better?"

"I don't know."

She glided back to her throne and settled onto it, smoothing her skirts. "I do not trust your human laws. I will remain the secret we have always been; let others walk in the spotlight. I will be here when such modern thinkers are no more." She suddenly slashed out with one hand.

Jean-Claude staggered. Blood flew from his face, splattering on his white shirt and jacket in bright crimson flecks. Drops of it clung to my hair and cheek.

She slashed again, and another cut exploded on the other side of his face, splashing Jason with Jean-Claude's blood.

Jean-Claude stayed on his feet. He never cried out. He

didn't touch the wounds. He stood there utterly still; except for the blood there was no movement to him. His eyes were drowning pools of sapphire floating in a mask of blood.

Naked muscle twitched in his cheek. Bone glistened at jaw and cheek. It was a frighteningly deep wound. But I knew he could heal it. Horrible as it looked, it was a scare tactic. I kept telling that to the pounding of my heart. I wanted to go for a gun. To shoot the bitch. But I couldn't shoot them all. I wasn't even sure Janos could be shot.

"I don't have to kill you, Jean-Claude. Hot metal in your wounds, and they'll be permanent. Your beautiful face ravaged for all time. You can still pretend to be Master of the City, but I will rule. You will be my puppet."

"Say the word, Serephina," Jean-Claude said. "Say it and be done with these games." His voice was bland, as normal as it ever was. His voice gave nothing away, not pain, or fear, or terror.

"Challenge: is that the word you want to hear, Jean-Claude?"

"It will do." His power crawled over my skin like cool fire. The power lashed out suddenly; I felt it sweep past me like a giant fist. It slammed into Serephina, scattering the air currents. Kissa caught the edge of it and fell back from the throne, thrown nearly prone among the cushions.

Serephina threw back her head and laughed. The laughter died in mid-motion, gone like it had never been. Her face was a mask with eyes of white fire. Her skin seemed to grow paler, whiter until it was like translucent marble. Veins showed under her skin like lines of blue flame. Her power flowed through the room like rising water, deeper and deeper until when she released it we would all be drowned.

"Where are your ghosts, Serephina?" I asked.

I thought for a second she would ignore me, but that masklike face turned slowly, slowly towards me.

"Where are your ghosts?"

Even though she was looking straight at me, I couldn't tell if she heard. It was like trying to read the face of an animal; no, the face of a statue. There was no one home.

"Can't control Bloody Bones and your ghosts at the same time? Is that it? Did you have to give up one of them?"

Serephina rose to her feet, and I knew she was floating, rising on tiny currents of her own power to hover above the cushions. She floated slowly upward towards the ceiling, and it was impressive. I was babbling, trying to buy time, but time for what? What the hell could we do?

A voice echoed in my head. "Crosses, *ma petite*; do not be bashful on my account." I didn't argue or hesitate.

The cross spilled out of my shirt in a ball of light so bright it was painful. I squinted and looked away, only to find Larry's cross behind me blazing to life.

Jean-Claude cowered beside me, hunched away, arms shielding his face. Serephina shrieked and half-fell to the floor. She could stand before a cross, but she couldn't do tricks in front of one. She landed in a heap of silken skirts. The other vamps shielded their faces, hissing.

Magnus rose from the cushions. He stalked towards us. Jason stepped in front of Jean-Claude, moving to stand in front of me. He glanced at me with amber eyes; his beast stared at me over the glow of the cross, and had no fear. For a heartbeat I was glad I had silver bullets just in case.

Serephina said, "No, Magnus, not you."

Magnus hesitated, staring at Jason. A thin growl crawled out of Jason's throat. "I can take him," Magnus said.

There was a sound from the open door to the basement. Something was coming up the stairs. Something heavy. The stairs creaked in protest. A hand came out of the darkness, large enough to palm my head. The fingernails were long and dirty, almost clawlike. Ragged clothes clung to huge, square shoulders. The thing was at least ten feet tall. It had to bend sideways to come through the door, and when it stood, its head brushed the ceiling, and you couldn't pretend it was human anymore.

Its huge, oversized head had no skin. The flesh was raw and open like a wound. The veins pulsed and throbbed with blood flowing through them, but it didn't bleed. It opened a mouth full of broken yellow teeth and said, "I am here." It was shocking to hear words out of that mouth, that face. Its voice was like the sound at the bottom of a well; deep, and rough, and lost.

The room suddenly seemed small. Rawhead and Bloody Bones could have reached out one long arm and touched me. Not good. Jason had moved back a step to rejoin us. Magnus had moved back to Serephina's side. He was staring at the creature as wide-eyed as the rest of us. Had he never seen it in the flesh before?

"Come to me," Serephina said. She held out her hands to the creature, and it moved towards her, surprisingly graceful. It had a liquidness to its walk that was all wrong. Nothing that big and that ugly should move like quicksilver, but it did. In that movement I saw Magnus and Dorrie. It moved like something beautiful.

Serephina cradled its huge, dirty hand in her white-gloved hands. She pushed back the ragged sleeve, laying the thick, muscled wrist bare.

"Stop her, *ma petite*."

I glanced down at Jean-Claude, who was still cowering before the crosses' fire. "What?"

"If she drinks from it, the crosses may not work against her."

I didn't question him; there was no time. I drew the Browning and felt Larry draw his gun.

Serephina bent over the fairie's wrist, mouth wide, fangs glistening.

I pulled the trigger. The bullet smacked into the side of her head. The force rocked her, and blood dribbled down. She could be shot. Life was good. Janos threw himself in front of her, and it was like trying to hit Superman. I pulled the trigger twice, staring at his dead-eyed face from just over a yard. He smiled at me. Silver bullets just weren't going to do it.

Larry had stepped around Jean-Claude. He was firing at Pallas and Bettina. They kept coming. Kissa stayed on the floor. Ellie seemed frozen in the face of the crosses.

Bloody Bones stood there like it was waiting for orders, or didn't give a damn. It was staring at Magnus like it recognized him. It was not a friendly look.

Serephina's voice came from behind Janos's protective body. "Give me your wrist."

The fairie gave a ragged smile. "Soon I will be free to kill you." It looked at Magnus when it said it.

I didn't really want something the size of a small giant mad at me, but I didn't want Serephina to have its power either. I fired into its raw head, and I might as well have spit at it. The shot did earn me a dirty look. "I have no quarrel with you," the fairie said. "Do not make one."

Staring into its monstrous face, I agreed. But what could I do? "What'll we do?" Larry asked. He'd moved to stand nearly back to back with me. Bettina and Pallas had stopped just out of touching range, held at bay by the crosses, not the guns. Jean-Claude had gone to his knees, face cradled away from the glare of the crosses, but he didn't crawl away. He stayed within the protective touch of that light.

Silver bullets wouldn't hurt the fey, so . . . I hit the button on the Browning and popped the clip out. I fished in my pocket for the extra clip and slid it home. I aimed at the thing's chest, where I hoped the heart was, and pulled.

Bloody Bones bellowed. Blood blossomed on its ragged clothes. I knew when it felt Serephina bite into its flesh. Power whirled through the room, raising every hair on my body. For a heartbeat I couldn't breathe; there was too much magic in the room for something as mundane as breathing.

Serephina rose slowly from behind Janos's dark form. She levitated to the ceiling, bathing in the light of the crosses, smiling. The bullet wound in her head was healed. Her eyes licked white flame around her face, and I knew we were going to die.

Xavier appeared in the door to the basement. He held a sword in his hands, but it was heavier, softer-edged than any blade I'd ever seen. He stared at Serephina and smiled.

"I have fed you," Bloody Bones said. "Free me."

Serephina threw her hands skyward, caressing the ceiling. "No," she breathed, "never. I will drink you dry and bathe in your power."

"You promised," Bloody Bones said.

She stared at him, floating; her eyes of fire were even with his raw face. "I lied," she said.

Xavier cried, "No!" He tried to come closer, but the crosses kept him just out of reach.

I threw a handful of salt on Serephina and Bloody Bones. She laughed at me. "What are you doing, Niña?"

"Never break your word to the fey," I said. "It negates all bargains."

A sword appeared in Bloody Bones' hands, just appeared like the fey had grabbed it out of mid-air. It was the one I'd seen Xavier carrying at the Quinlans' house. How many scimitars as long as my upper body could there be? He stabbed it through Serephina's chest, spitting her in midair like a butterfly. Normal steel shouldn't have touched her, but backed by the fairie's magic, it could. He pinned her to the wall, driving the hilt into her chest. He tore the sword out of her, twisting it, doing as much damage as he could.

She shrieked and slid down, leaving a bloody trail on the naked wall.

Bloody Bones turned back to the rest of us. It touched fingers to its bleeding chest. "I will forgive you this wound, because you freed me. When he is dead, there will be no more wounds." He drove the sword into Magnus. The move was so quick, it looked like stop action. He was as fast as Xavier. Shit.

Magnus fell to his knees, mouth wide with a scream he had no breath to make. Bloody Bones drew the sword upward like he had with Serephina, and it reminded me of the wounds that the boys had had.

If Bloody Bones would help us escape Serephina and company, I had no problem with that, but then what? It drew the sword outward, and Magnus was still alive, staring up at me. He reached out to me, and I could have let him die. Bloody Bones raised the blade back for a final blow.

I pointed the Browning at it. "Don't move. Until you kill him, you're mortal, and bullets can kill you."

The fairie froze, staring at me. "What do you want, mortal?"

"You killed the boys in the woods, didn't you?"

Bloody Bones blinked at me. "They were wicked children."

"If you get out of here, will you kill more wicked children?"

Bloody Bones looked at me, blinked, then said, "It is what I do. What I am."

I fired before I could think. If it moved first, I was dead. The bullet took it between the eyes. It staggered backwards, but didn't go down.

"*Ma petite,* the crosses, or I cannot help you." Jean-Claude's voice was a harsh whisper.

I slipped the cross inside my shirt; a second later Larry followed suit. The room was suddenly darker, colder with just the candlelight. Bloody Bones raced forward, and it was just a blur. I fired into it and didn't know if I hit it or not.

The sword swung out to meet me, and Jean-Claude was suddenly there hanging onto the arm, sending it off balance. Larry moved up beside me, and we both fired into the fey's chest.

It shook Jean-Claude off, sending him skittering into a wall. Larry and I stood our ground, shoulder to shoulder. I saw the sword coming like a blur of silver, and knew I couldn't get out of the way in time.

Xavier was suddenly in front of me, the strange sword blocking Bloody Bones' blade. The steel blade stopped an inch from my face. Xavier's sword was notched where the steel had bit into it. The strange sword shoved upward through Bloody Bones' chest. The fairie bellowed, slicing at Xavier, but he was in too close for the fairie's giant sword.

Bloody Bones collapsed to its knees. Xavier twisted the sword as if hunting for the heart. He jerked the sword out in a wash of gore. The fairie collapsed on its stomach, shrieking. It tried to raise itself. I pressed the barrel of the Browning against its skull and fired as fast as I could. From point-blank range you didn't need to aim. Larry moved up beside me and fired. We emptied the clips into it, and it was still breathing. Xavier drove the sword through its back, pinning it to the floor. Its chest rose and fell, struggling for air.

I switched the Firestar and changed its clip to nonsilver.

Three shots more, and as if a critical mass had been reached, the head exploded in a rush of bone and blood and thicker, wetter things.

Xavier was on its back when it blew. We stood there covered in bloody brains. Xavier drew the sword out of its back. The sword came out notched, dented from contact with bone. We stood there by the dead giant, the two of us isolated in one clear moment of understanding.

"The sword's cold iron, isn't it?" I asked.

"Yes," he said. The pupils of his eyes were scarlet as a cherry, not the blood color of an albino, but truly red. Humans didn't have eyes like that.

"You're fey," I said.

"Don't be silly. The fairie can't become vampires, everyone knows that."

I stared at him, and shook my head. "You tampered with Magnus's spell. You did this to him."

"He did this to himself," Xavier said.

"Did you help Bloody Bones kill the teenagers, the children, or did you just give him the sword?"

"I fed him my victims when I grew tired of them."

I had eight shots left in the Firestar. Maybe he saw the thought move behind my eyes. "Neither lead nor silver bullets will harm me. I am proof against both."

"Where's Jeff Quinlan?"

"He's down in the basement."

"Get him."

"I don't think so." And suddenly there was sound again, movement again, besides us. He'd bespelled me, and had things had been happening while I'd been caught.

Jason was coughing blood on the carpet. If he'd been human, I'd have said he was dying. Being a lycanthrope, he might live to see morning. One of the vampires had hurt him badly. I didn't know which one.

Jean-Claude was lying under a pile of vampires made up of Ellie, Kissa, Bettina, and Pallas. His voice came out in a thundering yell, echoing through the room. It was impressive, but not enough. "Do not do it, *ma petite*."

Janos stood near the throne with Larry. They'd tied his

hands behind his back with one of the cords that held the drapes. A piece of cloth was shoved in his mouth. Janos had one pale spider hand around Larry's neck.

Serephina was propped on her throne, black blood pouring out of her. I'd never seen anyone lose so much blood so quickly. Her chest was torn open so wide I had a glimpse of a frantically beating heart.

"What do you want?" I asked.

"No, *ma petite*." Jean-Claude struggled to move and couldn't. "It is a trap."

"Tell me something I don't know."

"She wants you, necromancer," Janos said.

I let that sink in for a minute. "Why?"

"You have stolen her immortal blood from her. You will take its place."

"It wasn't immortal," I said. "We proved that."

"It was powerful, necromancer, as you are powerful. She will drink you up and live."

"What about me?"

"You will live forever, Anita, forever."

I let the "forever" part go; I knew better.

"She will take you and kill him anyway," Jean-Claude said.

He was probably right, but what could I do? "She let the girls go."

"You do not know that, *ma petite*. Have you seen them alive?" He had a point.

"Necromancer." Janos's voice jerked me back to him. Serephina lay propped on the throne beside him. Blood had drenched the white dress, turning it black, plastering it to her thin body.

"Come, necromancer," Janos said. "Come now, or the human suffers."

I started forward and Jean-Claude yelled, "No!"

Janos slashed outward with one pale spider-hand, just above Larry's body. Larry's white shirt sliced open, and blood soaked it. He couldn't scream with the gag, but if Janos hadn't held him, he'd have fallen.

"Drop all your weapons and come to us, necromancer."

"*Ma petite,* do not do this. I beg you."

"I have to do this, Jean-Claude. You know that."

"*She* knows that," he said.

I looked at him, struggling helplessly under three times his body weight in vampires. It should have been ridiculous, but it wasn't.

"She doesn't just want you for herself. She doesn't want me to have you. She will take you to spite me."

"I invited you to come play this time, remember?" I said. "It's my party."

I walked towards Janos. I tried not to look behind him, not to see what else I was moving towards.

"*Ma petite,* don't do this. You are an acknowledged master. She cannot take you by force. You must consent. Refuse."

I just shook my head and kept going.

"Your weapons first, necromancer," Janos said.

I laid both guns on the floor.

Larry was shaking his head furiously. He made little protesting noises. He struggled, falling to his knees. Janos had to release his grip on his neck to keep from strangling him.

"Now your knives," Janos said.

"I don't . . ."

"Do not try to lie to us here and now."

He had a point. I put the knives on the floor.

My heart was hammering so hard I could barely breathe. I stopped just in front of Larry. I stared into Larry's blue eyes. I pulled out the gag, somebody's silk scarf.

"Don't do it. God, Anita, don't do it. Not for me. Please!"

Fresh slashes cut his shirt; more blood flowed. He gasped, but didn't scream.

I looked up at Serephina. "You said this slashing only works with an aura of power."

"He has his own aura," Janos said.

"Let him go. Let them all go, and I'll do it."

"Do not do this for me, *ma petite.*"

"I'm doing it for Larry; doesn't cost any more to throw everybody in."

Janos glanced at Serephina. She was slumped to one side, eyes half-closed. "Come to me, Anita. Let me touch your arm, and they will release them all, my word, one master to another."

"Anita, no!" Larry struggled not to get away but to come after me.

Janos slashed his hand through the air, and the sleeve of Larry's jacket flew with blood. Larry screamed.

"Stop it," I said. "Stop it." I stalked towards him. "Don't touch him again. Don't ever touch him again."

I spit the last words in his face, staring up into his dead eyes and feeling nothing. A hand brushed my arm, and I jerked, gasping. I'd let anger carry me those last few steps. What I was about to do scared me too much to think about it.

Serephina had lost a glove. It was her bare hand that encircled my wrist, not too tight, not painful in the least. I stared at her hand on my arm and couldn't talk past the beating of my own heart.

"Release him," she said.

The minute Janos let him go, Larry tried to come to me. Janos gave him a casual slap that knocked him to the floor and sent him skidding back a couple of yards.

I stayed frozen with her hand on my arm. For one awful moment I thought they'd killed him, but he moaned and tried to get back up.

I glanced past Larry, and met Jean-Claude's eyes. He'd been after me for years; now here I was letting another master vamp sink her fangs into me.

Serephina jerked me to my knees, squeezing the bones of my arm so hard I thought she'd broken it. The pain brought me up to meet her eyes. They were solid perfect brown, so dark they were nearly black. Those eyes smiled at me gently.

I smelled my mother's perfume, her hair spray, her skin. I shook my head. It was a lie. It was all a lie. I couldn't breathe. She knelt over me, and when her face came forward it was my mother's thick, black hair that fell against my cheek.

"No! It's not real."

"It can be as real as you want it to be, Niña." I stared up into those eyes, and I fell down the long black tunnel of her eyes. I fell towards that tiny flame. I reached towards it. It would warm my flesh, comfort my heart. It would be all things, all people, everything to me.

Distant and dreamlike I heard Jean-Claude scream my name, "Anita!" But it was too late. Her fire warmed me, made me feel whole. The pain was such a small price to pay.

The black tunnel collapsed behind me until there was nothing but the darkness and the flicker of Serephina's eyes.

39

I DREAMED. I was very small. Small enough that I fit all in my mother's lap, only my feet stuck off the edge of her knees. When she wrapped her arms around me I was so safe, so sure that nothing could ever hurt me as long as Mommy was here. I laid my head against her chest. I could hear the beat of her heart against my ear. A strong, sure rhythm that pounded louder and louder against my face.

The sound woke me. But I wasn't awake. The darkness was so complete it was like being blind. I lay in my mother's arms in the dark. I'd fallen asleep in bed with her and Dad. Her heart pounded against my ear, and the rhythm was wrong. Mommy had a heart murmur. The beat of her heart was a fraction of a second slow, a hesitation, then two quick thumps to catch up. The heart beating against my skin was as regular as a clock.

I tried to raise up, off her, and bumped my head against something hard and firm. My hands slid over the body that I was pinned to. I touched a satin dress with smooth jewels sewn into it. I lay there in the absolute dark and tried to roll off her. I slid into the crook of her arm. Her naked flesh slid along my bare shoulders, boneless as the dead, but her heart filled the darkness even with me struggling not to touch her.

Our bodies were molded against each other. It was not a coffin built for two. Sweat broke out on my skin in a rush. The dark was suddenly chokingly close, hot. I couldn't breathe. I tried to roll onto my back. Tried to roll off her, and I couldn't. There wasn't room.

Every small struggle made her boneless body move, jiggling the soft, loose flesh. I couldn't smell my mother's perfume anymore. I smelled old blood, and a stale, neck-ruffling smell that I'd smelled before. Vampires.

I screamed and tried to do a push-up to get some distance, and the lid moved. I stayed on my arms, shoving my back into the satin and wood. The lid slammed backwards, and I was suddenly straddling her body, my upper body raised in a half push-up.

Dim light edged the lines in her face. The careful makeup looked wrong, like a badly made-up corpse. I scrambled out of the coffin, nearly falling to the floor.

Serephina's coffin sat on the stage in the Bloody Bones bar and grill. Ellie lay curled at the base of the stage. I stepped around her, half-expecting her to grab at my ankles, but she did not move. Not even to breathe. She was the newly dead, and with the sun up she was truly dead.

Serephina wasn't breathing either, but her heart was pounding, beating, alive. Why? For my comfort? Because of my touch? Hell, I didn't know. If I got out, I'd ask Jean-Claude. If he was alive. If she had kept her word.

Janos lay in the middle of the floor, on his back, hands folded on his chest. Bettina and Pallas were snuggled up against him, one on either side. A coffin lay on the floor. I had no way of knowing what time of day it was. I would have bet that Serephina didn't have to sleep all day. I was getting out of here.

"I told her you wouldn't sleep all day."

The voice jerked me around. Magnus was behind the bar, leaning his elbows on its smooth surface. He was slicing a lime with a very sharp-looking knife. He looked at me with his green-blue eyes. His long auburn hair spilled around his face. He straightened up suddenly, stretching his back. He was wearing one of those frilly shirts that you rent for wearing with a tux. The shirt was pale green and brought out the green in his eyes.

"You scared me," I said.

He leaped over the bar easily, landing on his feet light as a cat. He smiled, and it wasn't a friendly smile. "I didn't think you scared that easy."

I took a step back. "You recovered damn fast."

"I drank immortal blood; it helps." He stared at me with a heat in his eyes that I didn't like at all.

"What's wrong with you, Magnus?"

He swept his long hair to one side. He pulled the collar of his shirt until the first two buttons popped, spinning to the floor. There was a new bite mark on the smooth skin of his neck.

I took another step back towards the door. "So what?" I ran my hand over my neck and found my own bite marks. "So we've got a matching pair. So what?"

"She forbade me to drink. She said you'd sleep all day. That she'd keep you sleeping all day, but I thought she'd underestimated you."

I took another step towards the door.

"Don't, Anita."

"Why not?" But I was afraid I knew the answer.

"Serephina told me to keep you here until she wakes." He looked at me, and it was a sad, woebegone expression. "Just have a seat. I'll fix you something to eat."

"No, thanks."

"Don't run, Anita. Don't make me hurt you."

"Who's in the other coffin?" I asked.

The question seemed to surprise him. He let his hair fall back over his neck. The shirt gaped open over his chest. I didn't remember noticing his chest this much last time, or the way his hair swept over his shoulders. The ointment must have worn off.

"Stop it, Magnus."

"Stop what?"

"Glamor won't work on me."

"Glamor would be a more pleasant alternative," he said.
"Who's in the coffin?"

"Xavier and the boy."

I ran for the door. He was suddenly behind me, impossibly fast, but I'd seen faster. Most of them just happened to be dead. I didn't try to open the door. I turned into his body, and it surprised him. He fell into a shoulder roll almost textbook perfect. I tried to throw him three feet under the floor, everything I had.

He lay stunned for a second. I flung open the door. The spring sunlight poured in and fell on Janos and his women. Janos's face twisted away from the light. I didn't wait to see more. I ran.

Screams followed me out into the sunlight. I heard the door slam behind me, but didn't look back. I hit the gravel parking lot running with everything I had. I heard him pounding up behind me. I wasn't going to outrun him. I waited until the last second, stopped running, and kicked him. He saw it coming and dived under it, taking my other leg out from under me, sending us both to the ground. I threw a handful of gravel at his face, and he hit me in the jaw with his fist. There is a frozen moment after a really good shot to the face. A moment of shock, of paralysis where all you can do is blink. Magnus's face appeared over me. He didn't ask if I was alright; that had been the point. He picked me up and flung me over his shoulders. I got a nice view of the ground about the time I was able to move again.

I walked my hands up his back, trying to get enough leverage to swing a two-handed grip at his shoulders. I let him brace my lower body, but before I could try it, he kicked the door open and tossed me to the floor, none too gently. He leaned against the door and locked it.

"You just had to do it the hard way, didn't you?"

I got to my feet and backed away from him, which took me closer to the vampires. Not an improvement. I backed towards the bar. There had to be a back door. "I don't know any other way, Magnus."

He took a deep breath and pushed away from the door. "It's going to be a long day, then."

I put a hand on the smooth wood of the bar. "Yeah," I said. The half-sliced lime and the knife lay just a few inches away. I stared at Magnus, trying very hard not to look at the knife again. To not draw attention to it. Which isn't nearly as easy as it sounds.

His eyes flicked to the knife. He smiled and shook his head. "Don't do it, Anita."

I put my hands on the bar and pushed myself up on it. I heard him coming, but I didn't look back. Never look back; something is always gaining on you. I grabbed the knife and rolled over the bar at the same time. Magnus's face appeared above the bar too fast. I wasn't ready. All I could do was look up at him with the knife gripped in my hand. If he'd been just a little slower, I'd have stabbed him in the throat, or that had been the plan.

Magnus crouched on the bar, staring down at me. His aquamarine eyes glittered. Lights and colors placed in them, reflecting things that were not there. He stayed on the bar above me, swaying slightly on the balls of his feet, one hand on the bar for balance. His hair had fallen forward, trailing thick strands across his face. He was going all feral on me, like he had at the mound. But this time he wasn't trying to be one of the good guys. I expected him to leap down on me, but he didn't. Of course, he wasn't fighting me, he was just trying to keep me from leaving.

I glanced at what was under the bar. Liquor in bottles, clean glasses, a tub of ice, some clean towels, napkins. None of it looked helpful. Shit. I got slowly to my feet, back pressed to the wall, as far from Magnus as I could get. I began to inch my way towards the side of the bar towards the door. Magnus paced me, sidling on the bar, making the awkward movement graceful.

He was faster than me, stronger than me, but I was armed. The knife was good quality, made for slicing food, not people, but a good knife is a good knife. It's versatile. I had to force myself not to squeeze too tight on the handle, to relax. I'd get out of this. I would. My eyes flicked to Serephina's open coffin. I thought I saw her breathe.

Magnus jumped me. His body slammed into mine, and I

drove the knife into his stomach. He grunted, and his weight rode me to the floor. I drove the knife in hilt-deep. His fist closed over my hand, and he rolled off me, taking the knife with him.

I scrambled around the edge of the bar on all fours. Magnus was there, yanking me to my feet by one arm. Blood had soaked the front of his shirt. He raised the bloody knife in front of my face. "That hurt," he said. He laid the edge of the blade against the side of my throat. It felt like my pulse was jumping out to meet the blade. He started backing up, pulling me with him.

"Where are we going?" I asked.

"You'll see," he said. I didn't like that he wouldn't tell me.

His feet bumped against Ellie's body. I could glimpse Serephina's coffin behind him, if I rolled my eyes. Hard to move your head when a knife's at your throat. He pulled on my arm, and I didn't go. I leaned back on my heels, just a little, aware of the knife, but I was more afraid of Serephina than any blade.

"Come on, Anita."

"Not until you tell me what we're doing." I spoke very carefully around the knife.

Ellie lay motionless, boneless, dead at our feet. Magnus's blood dropped onto her empty face. If it had been one of the others, they might have licked the blood off even in their slumber, but Ellie was well and truly dead. She was the newly risen, empty, waiting for her "personality" to rebuild, if it ever did. I'd seen vamps that never recovered. Never became close to the human being they'd once been.

"I'm going to put you in the coffin and lock it until Serephina wakes up."

"No," I said.

Magnus squeezed my arm like his fingers were searching for the bone. If he didn't break it, it would be a hell of a bruise. I didn't cry out, but it was an effort. "I can hurt you, Anita, in all sorts of ways. Just get in."

"Nothing you can do to me scares me as much as getting in that coffin again." I meant it. Which meant unless he was really going to kill me, the knife didn't work anymore. I turned my head into the blade. He was forced to move it away from my skin before I drove it into myself.

I stared at him from about a foot away, and saw something in his eyes that I hadn't seen before. He was afraid.

"Bloody Bones died because he shared your mortality. Were you harder to kill before, Magnus? No immortality to draw from, is that it?"

"You are just too damn smart for your own good," he said softly.

I smiled. "Mortal just like the rest of us; poor baby."

He smiled, a quick baring of teeth. "I can still take more damage than you can dish out."

"If you really believed that, you wouldn't be putting me back in the coffin."

His hand moved in a blur of speed that was almost vampire-quick. He hit my arm, and it took a handful of seconds to realize he'd cut me. Blood welled from the cut and dripped down my arm. He switched his grip from my upper arm to my wrist, faster than I could take advantage of it.

I watched the blood drip down my arm towards my elbow. It wasn't much of a cut, might not even leave a scar; of course, on my left arm, who could tell? "Couldn't you have cut the right arm? I haven't got nearly as many scars on that one."

He made one quick slice downward and opened my right arm from my shoulder damn near to my elbow. "Always happy to oblige a lady."

The slice hurt and was deeper than the first one. Me and my big mouth. Blood ran down my arm in a thin crimson line. Blood on my left arm trembled on my elbow and fell with a soft *plop* onto Ellie's cheek. The blood slid down her skin, into her mouth. A tingle of magic went up my spine. I held my breath. I could feel it. I could feel the body at our feet.

It was broad daylight. I shouldn't have been able to raise even a zombie, let alone a vampire. It was impossible; yet I could feel the body feel the magic. I knew it was mine if I wanted it. I wanted it.

"What's wrong?" Magnus jerked my arm, bringing my eyes back to his face. I'd been staring at the vampire. Hadn't meant to, it was just so damn unexpected.

I could feel the magic just out of reach, almost there. But how to push it over the edge? How? I smiled at Magnus. "You planning to just whittle me down until I get in the coffin?"

"I could."

"The only way I'm going in that coffin is dead, Magnus, and Serephina doesn't want me dead." I stepped into him; he started to move back, but forced himself to stand his ground. Our bodies were nearly pressed against each other. Great. I ran my hand under his shirt, along his bare skin.

Magnus's eyes widened. "What are you up to?"

I smiled, and traced the trail of fresh blood upward to the wound. I trailed the edge of the wound, and he made a small sound like it had hurt. I smoothed my one free hand over his skin, smearing his blood across his flesh like finger paints.

"You saw the murder scene when you touched me and still wanted to have sex with me, remember?"

He took a breath, and it trembled when he let it out between his lips.

I drew my blood-coated hand out from under his shirt. I held it up to him, let him see it. His breath came just a little quicker. I knelt, slowly; he didn't let go, he didn't put down the knife, but he didn't stop me. I smeared the blood on Ellie's mouth. The magic flared, sparked down my skin like cool fire. It crawled up my arm and onto Magnus.

"Shit!" Magnus swung the knife at me.

I blocked his wrist with my arm and came up under him, driving up from my knees. He was balanced across my shoulders, but he still had the knife. I flung him on top of Ellie.

I stood over him, breathing hard. "Ellie, rise."

The vampire's eyes flew open wide. Magnus started to push away from her.

"Grab him," I said.

Ellie wrapped her arms around his waist and held on. He stabbed her with the knife, and she screamed. God help me, she screamed. Zombies didn't scream.

I ran for the door.

Magnus came after me, dragging Ellie behind him. He was moving faster than I'd thought he would, but not fast enough. I flung open the door, and a long bar of sunlight spilled in through the door. I was a step out the door when the screaming started. I glanced back; I couldn't help it. Ellie was on fire. Magnus tried to loosen her arms, screaming. But nothing holds on like the dead.

I ran out into the parking lot.

"Niña, don't go."

The voice stopped me at the edge of the parking lot. I looked back. Magnus had dragged himself out the door and onto the gravel. Ellie was burning white hot. Magnus's shirt and hair were burning.

I screamed, "Go back, you son of a bitch!" But the same voice that kept me pinned to the edge of the parking lot kept him coming out into the light.

The voice came again. "Come back to bed, Anita. You're tired. You must rest."

I was suddenly tired, so tired. I felt every cut, every bruise. She would make it all better. She would touch me with her cool hands and make it all better.

Magnus collapsed in the middle of the driveway, shrieking. The vampire was melting into him, burning him alive. Sweet Jesus.

He reached one hand out to me. He screamed, "Help me!" The vampire was melting into his flesh, eating it away.

I ran. I ran with Serephina's voice whispering in my ear: "Niña, Mother misses you."

40

I FLAGGED A car down on the highway. I was covered in dried blood, cut, scraped, bruised, and still an elderly couple picked me up. Who says there are no more good Samaritans? They wanted to take me to the police, and I let them.

The nice policemen took one look at me and asked if I needed an ambulance. I said no, and could they page Special Agent Bradford, and tell him it was Anita Blake.

They tried to get me to go to the hospital, but there was no time. It was mid-afternoon. We had to move before dark. I asked the police to send a two-man car to make sure that no one moved the coffins. I told them there might be a hurt man in the parking lot and if he was still there to call an ambulance, but under no circumstances go inside the place.

Everybody nodded and agreed with me. Most of the cops in the area had been through Serephina's house last night and today. The cops told me Kirkland had brought the cops back to the vampire's lair after they took me. It took me a second to realize that Kirkland was Larry. Which meant Serephina had kept her word and let them go. The relief at knowing for sure that Larry was alive made me weak-kneed, and I was wobbly enough as it was.

The cops had found over a dozen bodies buried in the basement of Serephina's house. She should have buried them in the woods. For all I knew, she'd raised their ghosts. I didn't know. It didn't matter. All that mattered was that we had a warrant of execution, and the cops were listening to me today.

They sat me in an interrogation room with a cup of black coffee, thick enough to walk on, and a blanket to wrap around me. I was shivering and couldn't seem to stop.

Bradford came in and sat down across from me. He stared at me with eyes that were just a little too wide. "The locals say you found the master vampire's lair."

I laughed, and it came out wrong, almost like a sob. "I wouldn't say I found Serephina's lair. More like I woke up in it." I raised the coffee to my mouth and had to stop in mid-motion. My hands were shaking so badly I was about to slosh coffee onto the table. I took a deep breath, blew it out, and concentrated on taking a drink of coffee. Just concentrated on the simple physical movement. It helped. I got coffee, and calmer at the same time.

"You need to go to the hospital," Bradford said.

"I need Serephina dead."

"We've got warrants for all of them. All the vampires involved. How do you want to do it?"

"Burn them out. Block off everything but the front door. If Magnus is inside, he'll come out."

"Magnus Bouvier?" he asked.

"Yeah." There was something about the way he said it that I didn't like.

"The cops found what's left of him in the parking lot. It looks like something melted the lower half of his body. Would you know anything about that?" He looked at me very steadily when he asked it.

I took another careful sip of coffee, and met his eyes without blinking. What was I supposed to say? "The vampires were controlling him. He was supposed to keep me in the bar until nightfall. Maybe they punished him for failing." What I'd done to Magnus and Ellie was enough to earn me a death sentence. I wasn't admitting that to the Feds.

"The vampires punished him?" He made it a question.

"Yeah."

He looked at me for a long time, then nodded and changed the subject. "Won't the vampires try to make a break when the fire starts?"

"Sunlight or fire," I said. "Just a choice of how well done you want your vampires to be." I finished the last of the coffee in my cup.

"Your protege, Mr. Kirkland, said you were kidnapped from the graveyard. Is that your story, too?"

"It happens to be the truth, Agent Bradford." It was the truth as far as it went. Omission is a wonderful thing.

He smiled and shook his head. "You are hiding more shit from me than you're telling me."

I stared at him until the smile wilted around the edges. "Truth is a mixed blessing, Agent Bradford, don't you think?"

He stared at me for a moment, then nodded. "Maybe, Ms. Blake, maybe."

I called the hotel, and no one answered in Larry's room. I tried my room, and got Larry there. There was a moment of stunned silence when he realized it was me.

"Anita, oh my God, oh my God. Are you alright? Where are you? I'll come get you."

"I'm at the police station in town. I'm alright, sort of. I need you to bring me some clothes to change into. The ones I have on smell like vampire. We're going after Serephina."

Another silence. "When?"

"Now, today."

"I'll be right there."

"Larry?"

"I'll bring the guns and the knives, and an extra cross."

"Thanks."

"I've never been so glad to hear anybody's voice in my entire life," he said.

"Yeah," I said. "Get here soon. Wait, Larry."

"You need something else?" he said.

"Are Jean-Claude and Jason alright?"

"Yeah. Jason's in the hospital, but he'll live. Jean-Claude's in the bedroom asleep. After Serephina bit you, she hit Jean-Claude with some kind of power, energy. I felt it, and it was awesome. She knocked him out and left. The others went with her."

Everyone was alive, or as alive as they had started out. It was more than I'd hoped for. "Great; I'll see you soon." I hung up the phone and had a horrible urge to cry, but I fought it off. I was afraid if I started to cry I wouldn't be able to stop. I couldn't have hysterics just yet.

As agent on site, Bradford was in charge. Special Agent Bradley Bradford, yes Bradley Bradford, seemed to think I knew what I was doing. Nothing like getting almost killed to give you credentials. For once, badge or no badge, nobody was arguing with me. A refreshing change, that.

I did not hug Larry when he brought my clothes; he hugged me. I pushed away sooner than I wanted to, because I wanted to collapse into his arms in tears. To just let a pair of friendly arms hold me while I melted down. Later, later.

A huge bruise had blossomed on the side of his face from

jaw to mid-temple. It looked like he'd been hit by a baseball bat. He was lucky Janos hadn't broken his jaw.

Larry had brought me blue jeans, a red polo shirt, jogging socks, my white Nikes, an extra cross from my suitcase, the silver knives, the Firestar complete with inner pants holster, and the Browning and its shoulder holster. He'd forgotten a bra, but hey, except for that it was perfect.

The wrist sheaths stung going over the cuts, but it felt wonderful to be armed again. I didn't try to hide the guns. The cops knew who I was, and I wasn't fooling any of the bad guys.

Barely two hours after I'd crawled out of Serephina's coffin, we pulled up in front of Bloody Bones. There were ambulances, and more cops than you could shake a stick at. Local cops, state cops, federal cops; it was a smorgasbord of policemen. A fire truck plus fire emergency services completed the official list. Oh, Larry and me.

With Magnus dead, Serephina and company were unguarded. Not helpless. Oh, no. Nothing this side of Hell would have gotten me inside that building voluntarily. But there were alternatives.

The gas truck pulled around to the back and busted out a window. I watched them snake the hose into the window of the back door and turn on the juice.

I stood there in the warm sunlight, a cool breeze playing on my skin, and whispered, "May you rot in Hell."

"Did you say something?" Larry asked.

I shook my head. "Nothing important."

The hose shivered to life, and the sharp, sweet smell of gasoline filled the air.

I felt her wake up. I felt her eyes open wide in the dark. I breathed in the sweet smell of gasoline, felt my hands gripping the coffin edges.

I put my hands over my eyes. "Oh, God."

Larry touched my shoulder. "What is it?"

I kept my hands pressed to my face. "Take the guns, now."

"What . . ."

"Do it!" My hands came down and I looked at him. I looked at his familiar face, and Serephina saw him, too.

She whispered, "Kill him."

I ripped the knives out of the sheaths and let them fall to the ground. I started backing up towards the cops. I needed people with guns around me, right now.

The voice in my head said, "Anita, what are you doing to your mother? You don't want to hurt me. Niña, help Mommy."

"Oh, God." I ran and nearly collided with Bradford.

"Help me, Niña. Help me!"

My hand closed on the Browning. I balled my hands into fists at my side. "Bradford, disarm me now. Please."

He stared at me, but he took the guns from their holsters. "What's wrong, Blake?"

"Cuffs, you got cuffs?"

"Yeah."

I held my hands out to him. "Use them." My voice sounded squeezed, my throat so tight I couldn't breathe.

I smelled Hypnotique perfume, tasted my mother's lipstick on my mouth. The cuffs snapped into place. I jerked away from him, stared at the handcuffs. I opened my mouth to say "Take them off," and closed it.

I could feel my mother's hair tickling my face.

"I smell perfume," Larry said.

I looked at him with wide eyes. I couldn't speak, I couldn't move. I didn't trust myself to do anything at that moment.

"Oh, my God," Larry said. "You're going to feel her burn."

I just looked at him.

"What can I do?"

"Help me." My voice was squeezed down to a whisper.

"What's happening to her?" Bradford asked.

"Serephina's trying to get Anita to help save her."

"The vampire's awake in there?" he asked.

"Yes," I said.

Serephina was out of her coffin. The full skirt of her ball gown brushed the edges of the door that led to the kitchen. She couldn't go closer, because there was a spill of daylight from the window. Gasoline was pouring across the floor towards her.

"Anita, help Mommy."

"It's a lie," I said.

"What's a lie?" Bradford said.

I shook my head.

"Anita, help me, you don't want me to die. You don't want me to die, not when you can save me."

I collapsed to my knees, cuffed hands digging into the gravel of the parking lot. "Stop the gasoline."

Larry knelt beside me. "Why?"

It was a good question. Serephina had a good answer. "Jeff Quinlan is in there. He's inside."

"Shit," Larry said. He looked up at Bradford. "We can't torch the place. There's a kid inside."

"Stop the gas," Bradford said. He walked away from us, towards the truck, motioning them off.

And I felt a surge of triumph from Serephina. It was a lie. Xavier had brought Jeff over last night. There was nothing alive in that building.

I gripped Larry's arm with my cuffed hands. "Larry, it's a lie. She's lying to me. Through me. Get me in the back of a squad car, now, and torch the place."

He stared at me. "But if Jeff . . ."

"Don't argue with me, just do it!" I screamed it, burying my face between my arms, trying to ignore the voice in my head.

I could taste Hypnotique on my tongue. It was too much. Serephina was scared.

Larry called Bradford back, and they half-carried me to a marked car. I started to struggle when they tried to shove me in the back, but I did my best not to fight, and they closed the door. I was in a metal and glass cage. I gripped my fingers through the mesh in front of me, digging it into my skin until it hurt. But even pain didn't help.

The gasoline was everywhere, soaking into everything. Serephina was choking on it. "Niña, don't do this. Don't hurt your Mommy. Don't lose me again."

I started rocking back and forth, hands digging into the

wire. Back and forth, back and forth. It'd be over soon. It'd be over soon.

I felt a gentle touch on my face, a memory so real it made me turn and look for someone. "My death will be as real, Anita."

Somebody lit it. The flames roared to life, and I screamed before they hit her. I slammed my cuffed hands against the glass and screamed, "Nooo!"

Heat washed over her, crumbled the cloth of her dress like a melting flower, and ate her flesh.

I pounded my hands against the glass until I couldn't feel them anymore. I had to help her. I had to go to her. I fell to my back and kicked the window. I kicked it and kicked it, feeling the shock all the way up my back. I screamed and kicked the glass, and it cracked. The glass cracked and fell outward.

She was screaming my name. "Anita! Anita!"

I was halfway out the window before somebody tried to grab me. I let them grab my arm, but pushed my legs free of the window. I had to get to her; nothing else mattered. Nothing.

I fell to the ground with someone holding my arm. I got halfway up and threw them in a shoulder roll onto the ground. I ran for the fire. I could feel the heat now, rippling along my skin. I could feel the heat inside eating us alive.

Someone tackled me, and I beat at them with my hands made into one fist. The hands let go, and I scrambled to my feet. Shouting, and someone else holding me. He lifted me off the ground, arms wrapped around my waist, pinning my arms. I kicked backwards, and hit his knees. The arms loosened, but there were more arms. More hands. Someone lay on top of me. A hand the size of my head pressed the side of my face against the rocks. Hands pinned my hands against the rocks, his full body weight on just my wrists. Someone was sitting on my legs.

"Niña! Niña!"

I screamed with her. I screamed while I choked on the smell of burning hair and Hypnotique bath powder. I saw the needle coming in from the side, and started to cry, "No, no! Mommy! Mommy!"

The needle sank home, and darkness swallowed the world. A darkness that smelled like burning flesh, and tasted like lipstick, and blood.

41

I SPENT A few days in the hospital. Bruises, cuts, some stitches, but mainly the second-degree burns on my back and arms. The burns weren't that bad; there wouldn't be any scarring. The doctors just couldn't figure out how I'd gotten burned. I didn't feel like explaining, mainly because I wasn't sure I could.

Jason had broken ribs, a punctured lung, and other internal damage. He healed perfectly and in record time. There are benefits to being a lycanthrope.

Jean-Claude healed. His face was once again that perfection that had attracted Serephina to him so long ago.

Stirling's company rebought the land from Dorcas Bouvier, and made her wealthy. With Bloody Bones dead, she can leave the land. She's free.

The Quinlans are still suing me. Bert has lawyers that promise to keep us out of court, though I'm not sure how. If I'd walked the house personally, checked every inch of it myself, maybe . . . Hell, even I might not have protected the doggie door. Maybe I do deserve to be sued. I told the Quinlans Ellie was dead. They had to take my word for it; there wasn't anything left of Ellie to prove it. When vampires burn, they burn; no dental records, no nothing. Jeff was well and truly dead, too. Both their children were lost to them. It had to be somebody's fault; why not mine?

I'd raised a vampire like a zombie, which wasn't possible. Necromancers were supposed to be able to control all types of undead. But that was legend, not real. Right?

Serephina is dead, but the nightmares live on. The nightmares are tangled with the real memories of my mother's death. They are a bitch. For the first time in my life, I'm having insomnia.

What to do with the two men in my life? How the hell do I know? In Richard's arms, breathing in the warmth of his body, is the closest I've ever found to my mother's arms. It isn't the same, because I know that though Richard would give his life for me, even that might not be enough. When I was a child, I believed it would be. There is no real safety. Innocence lost can never be regained. But sometimes with Richard I want to believe in it again.

There is nothing comforting about Jean-Claude's arms. He doesn't make me feel safe in the least. He's like some forbidden pleasure that you know eventually you'll regret. I've decided not to wait; I'm regretting it now, but I'm still seeing him.

Somehow Jean-Claude has crossed that line that a handful of other vampires have crossed. I don't think of him as a monster anymore.

God have mercy on my soul.

THE LUNATIC CAFE

An Anita Blake, Vampire Hunter Novel

Laurell K. Hamilton

Don't miss the fourth book in the bestselling
Anita Blake, Vampire Hunter Series.

You don't volunteer for slugfests with vampires. It
shortens your life expectancy. And you don't fall in
love with a werewolf. It interferes with your work.
Especially when you're a preternatural expert, like me.
My business brings me up close and personal with all
shapes and sizes of monsters. And not ALL of them
want to kill me.

Take, for instance, the local pack of lycanthropes –
they're werewolves to you. A number of them are
missing, and they've come to me for help. Maybe
because I'm dating the leader of the pack. I've
survived a lot – from jealous vampires to killer
zombies – but this love thing may kill me yet.

THE KILLING DANCE

An Anita Blake, Vampire Hunter Novel

Laurell K. Hamilton

The sixth book in the bestselling Anita Blake,
Vampire Hunter series.

The first hit man came after me at home, which should
be against the rules. Then there was a second, and a
third. Eventually, I found out that the word on the
street was that Anita Blake, preternatural expert and
vampire killer extraordinaire, was worth half a million
dollars. Dead, not alive. So what's a girl to do but turn
to the men in her life for help? Which in my case
means an alpha werewolf and a master vampire. With
professional killers on your trail, it's not a bad idea
to have as much protection as possible,
human or otherwise.

But I'm beginning to wonder if two monsters are
better than one . . .

BURNT OFFERINGS

An Anita Blake, Vampire Hunter Novel

Laurell K. Hamilton

The seventh book in the bestselling Anita Blake,
Vampire Hunter series.

'You can't trust anyone who sleeps with the monsters.'
That's what I've always said. That's what I've always
believed. But now I'm the one sharing a bed with the
Master Vampire of the City. Me, Anita Blake. The
woman the vampires call The Executioner. From part
of the solution, I've become part of the problem. So it
hits close to home when an arsonist begins to target
vampire-owned businesses all over town – an arsonist
who seems to want to destroy more than just property.
It's the monsters who are in danger now. And it's up to
The Executioner to save them from the inferno . . .

NYLON ANGEL

A Parrish Plessis Book

Marianne de Pierres

In a future where the rich live behind the safety of a
giant fortress-wall and everyone else can go to hell,
Parrish Plessis has learnt some useful survival tactics.
Like don't cross Jamon Mondo – unless you want to
be dead by morning.

But what's a girl supposed to do when a very real
chance of escaping his sordid clutches presents itself?
even if it means cutting a deal with the amoral gang-lord
Io Lang, and sheltering two suspects in the murder of
media darling Razz Retribution. Lang is renowned
for being from way beyond the border of
psychoticsville, and the media always get bloody
revenge on anyone foolish enough to mess with
their own – it's good for ratings. But Parrish is
sick of doing what she's told. She's tooled up,
jacked full of stun, and tonight she's going to
take her chance.

NYLON ANGEL is the first Parrish Plessis novel.
She will be back. When you've met her,
you'll understand why.